Julian Hawthorne

Mystery and Detective Stories

Old Time English

Julian Hawthorne

Mystery and Detective Stories

Old Time English

ISBN/EAN: 9783955630348

Auflage: 1

Erscheinungsjahr: 2013

Erscheinungsort: Bremen, Deutschland

@ Leseklassiker in Access Verlag GmbH, Fahrenheitstr. 1, 28359 Bremen. Alle Rechte beim Verlag und bei den jeweiligen Lizenzgebern.

Contents

CHARLES DICKENS

The Haunted House

The Mortals in the House

Under none of the accredited ghostly circumstances, and en-
vironed by none of the conventional ghostly surroundings, did I
first make acquaintance with the house which is the subject of
this Christmas piece. I saw it in the daylight, with the sun upon it.
There was no wind, no rain, no lightning, no thunder, no awful or
unwonted circumstance, of any kind, to heighten its effect. More
than that: I had come to it direct from a railway station: it was not
more than a mile distant from the railway station; and, as I stood
outside the house, looking back upon the way I had come, I could
see the goods train running smoothly along the embankment in
the valley. I will not say that everything was utterly commonplace, because I doubt if anything can be that, except to utterly
commonplace people – and there my vanity steps in; but, I will
take it on myself to say that anybody might see the house as I saw
it, any fine autumn morning.

The manner of my lighting on it was this.

I was travelling towards London out of the North, intending
to stop by the way, to look at the house. My health required a
temporary residence in the country; and a friend of mine who
knew that, and who had happened to drive past the house, had
written to me to suggest it as a likely place. I had got into the
train at midnight, and had fallen asleep, and had woke up and
had sat looking out of window at the brilliant Northern Lights in
the sky, and had fallen asleep again, and had woke up again to
find the night gone, with the usual discontented conviction on me
that I hadn't been to sleep at all; – upon which question, in the
first imbecility of that condition, I am ashamed to believe that I
would have done wager by battle with the man who sat opposite
me. That opposite man had had, through the night – as that opposite man always has – several legs too many, and all of them
too long. In addition to this unreasonable conduct (which was
only to be expected of him), he had had a pencil and a pocket-

1

book, and had been perpetually listening and taking notes. It had appeared to me that these aggravating notes related to the jolts and bumps of the carriage, and I should have resigned myself to his taking them, under a general supposition that he was in the civil-engineering way of life, if he had not sat staring straight over my head whenever he listened. He was a goggle-eyed gentleman of a perplexed aspect, and his demeanor became unbearable.

It was a cold, dead morning (the sun not being up yet), and when I had out-watched the paling light of the fires of the iron country, and the curtain of heavy smoke that hung at once between me and the stars and between me and the day, I turned to my fellow-traveller and said:

"I BEG your pardon, sir, but do you observe anything particular in me?" For, really, he appeared to be taking down, either my travelling-cap or my hair, with a minuteness that was a liberty.

The goggle-eyed gentleman withdrew his eyes from behind me, as if the back of the carriage were a hundred miles off, and said, with a lofty look of compassion for my insignificance:

"In you, sir? – B."

"B, sir?" said I, growing warm.

"I have nothing to do with you, sir," returned the gentleman; "pray let me listen – O."

He enunciated this vowel after a pause, and noted it down.

At first I was alarmed, for an Express lunatic and no communication with the guard, is a serious position. The thought came to my relief that the gentleman might be what is popularly called a Rapper: one of a sect for (some of) whom I have the highest respect, but whom I don't believe in. I was going to ask him the question, when he took the bread out of my mouth.

"You will excuse me," said the gentleman contemptuously, "if I am too much in advance of common humanity to trouble myself at all about it. I have passed the night – as indeed I pass the whole of my time now – in spiritual intercourse."

"O!" said I, somewhat snappishly.

"The conferences of the night began," continued the gentleman, turning several leaves of his note-book, "with this message: 'Evil communications corrupt good manners.'"

"Sound," said I; "but, absolutely new?"

"New from spirits," returned the gentleman.

I could only repeat my rather snappish "O!" and ask if I might be favored with the last communication.

"'A bird in the hand,'" said the gentleman, reading his last entry with great solemnity, "'is worth two in the Bosh.'"

"Truly I am of the same opinion," said I; "but shouldn't it be Bush?"

"It came to me, Bosh," returned the gentleman.

The gentleman then informed me that the spirit of Socrates had delivered this special revelation in the course of the night. "My friend, I hope you are pretty well. There are two in this railway carriage. How do you do? There are seventeen thousand four hundred and seventy-nine spirits here, but you cannot see them. Pythagoras is here. He is not at liberty to mention it, but hopes you like travelling." Galileo likewise had dropped in, with this scientific intelligence. "I am glad to see you, amico. Come sta? Water will freeze when it is cold enough. Addio!" In the course of the night, also, the following phenomena had occurred. Bishop Butler had insisted on spelling his name, "Bubler," for which offence against orthography and good manners he had been dismissed as out of temper. John Milton (suspected of wilful mystification) had repudiated the authorship of Paradise Lost, and had introduced, as joint authors of that poem, two Unknown gentlemen, respectively named Grungers and Scadgingtone. And Prince Arthur, nephew of King John of England, had described himself as tolerably comfortable in the seventh circle, where he was learning to paint on velvet, under the direction of Mrs. Trimmer and Mary Queen of Scots.

If this should meet the eye of the gentleman who favored me

with these disclosures, I trust he will excuse my confessing that the sight of the rising sun, and the contemplation of the magnificent Order of the vast Universe, made me impatient of them. In a word, I was so impatient of them, that I was mightily glad to get out at the next station, and to exchange these clouds and vapors for the free air of Heaven.

By that time it was a beautiful morning. As I walked away among such leaves as had already fallen from the golden, brown, and russet trees; and as I looked around me on the wonders of Creation, and thought of the steady, unchanging, and harmonious laws by which they are sustained; the gentleman's spiritual intercourse seemed to me as poor a piece of journey-work as ever this world saw. In which heathen state of mind, I came within view of the house, and stopped to examine it attentively.

It was a solitary house, standing in a sadly neglected garden: a pretty even square of some two acres. It was a house of about the time of George the Second; as stiff, as cold, as formal, and in as bad taste, as could possibly be desired by the most loyal admirer of the whole quartet of Georges. It was uninhabited, but had, within a year or two, been cheaply repaired to render it habitable; I say cheaply, because the work had been done in a surface manner, and was already decaying as to the paint and plaster, though the colors were fresh. A lop-sided board drooped over the garden wall, announcing that it was "to let on very reasonable terms, well furnished." It was much too closely and heavily shadowed by trees, and, in particular, there were six tall poplars before the front windows, which were excessively melancholy, and the site of which had been extremely ill chosen.

It was easy to see that it was an avoided house – a house that was shunned by the village, to which my eye was guided by a church spire some half a mile off – a house that nobody would take. And the natural inference was, that it had the reputation of being a haunted house.

No period within the four-and-twenty hours of day and night is so solemn to me, as the early morning. In the summertime, I often rise very early, and repair to my room to do a day's

4

work before breakfast, and I am always on those occasions deeply impressed by the stillness and solitude around me. Besides that there is something awful in the being surrounded by familiar faces asleep – in the knowledge that those who are dearest to us and to whom we are dearest, are profoundly unconscious of us, in an impassive state, anticipative of that mysterious condition to which we are all tending – the stopped life, the broken threads of yesterday, the deserted seat, the closed book, the unfinished but abandoned occupation, all are images of Death. The tranquillity of the hour is the tranquillity of Death. The color and the chill have the same association. Even a certain air that familiar household objects take upon them when they first emerge from the shadows of the night into the morning, of being newer, and as they used to be long ago, has its counterpart in the subsidence of the worn face of maturity or age, in death, into the old youthful look. Moreover, I once saw the apparition of my father, at this hour. He was alive and well, and nothing ever came of it, but I saw him in the daylight, sitting with his back towards me, on a seat that stood beside my bed. His head was resting on his hand, and whether he was slumbering or grieving, I could not discern. Amazed to see him there, I sat up, moved my position, leaned out of bed, and watched him. As he did not move, I spoke to him more than once. As he did not move then, I became alarmed and laid my hand upon his shoulder, as I thought – and there was no such thing.

For all these reasons, and for others less easily and briefly statable, I find the early morning to be my most ghostly time. Any house would be more or less haunted, to me, in the early morning; and a haunted house could scarcely address me to greater advantage than then.

I walked on into the village, with the desertion of this house upon my mind, and I found the landlord of the little inn, sanding his door-step. I bespoke breakfast, and broached the subject of the house.

"Is it haunted?" I asked.

The landlord looked at me, shook his head, and answered, "I

say nothing."

"Then it IS haunted?"

"Well!" cried the landlord, in an outburst of frankness that had the appearance of desperation – "I wouldn't sleep in it."

"Why not?"

"If I wanted to have all the bells in a house ring, with nobody to ring 'em; and all the doors in a house bang, with nobody to bang 'em; and all sorts of feet treading about, with no feet there; why, then," said the landlord, "I'd sleep in that house."

"Is anything seen there?"

The landlord looked at me again, and then, with his former appearance of desperation, called down his stable-yard for "Ikey!"

The call produced a high-shouldered young fellow, with a round red face, a short crop of sandy hair, a very broad humorous mouth, a turned-up nose, and a great sleeved waistcoat of purple bars, with mother-of-pearl buttons, that seemed to be growing upon him, and to be in a fair way – if it were not pruned – of covering his head and overrunning his boots.

"This gentleman wants to know," said the landlord, "if anything's seen at the Poplars."

"'Ooded woman with a howl," said Ikey, in a state of great freshness.

"Do you mean a cry?"

"I mean a bird, sir."

"A hooded woman with an owl. Dear me! Did you ever see her?"

"I seen the howl."

"Never the woman?"

"Not so plain as the howl, but they always keeps together."

"Has anybody ever seen the woman as plainly as the owl?"

"Lord bless you, sir! Lots."

"Who?"

"Lord bless you, sir! Lots."

"The general-dealer opposite, for instance, who is opening his shop?"

"Perkins? Bless you, Perkins wouldn't go a-nigh the place. No!" observed the young man, with considerable feeling; "he an't overwise, an't Perkins, but he an't such a fool as THAT."

(Here, the landlord murmured his confidence in Perkins's knowing better.)

"Who is – or who was – the hooded woman with the owl? Do you know?"

"Well!" said Ikey, holding up his cap with one hand while he scratched his head with the other, "they say, in general, that she was murdered, and the howl he 'ooted the while."

This very concise summary of the facts was all I could learn, except that a young man, as hearty and likely a young man as ever I see, had been took with fits and held down in 'em, after seeing the hooded woman. Also, that a personage, dimly described as "a hold chap, a sort of one-eyed tramp, answering to the name of Joby, unless you challenged him as Greenwood, and then he said, 'Why not? and even if so, mind your own business,'" had encountered the hooded woman, a matter of five or six times. But, I was not materially assisted by these witnesses: inasmuch as the first was in California, and the last was, as Ikey said (and he was confirmed by the landlord), Anywheres.

Now, although I regard with a hushed and solemn fear, the mysteries, between which and this state of existence is interposed the barrier of the great trial and change that fall on all the things that live; and although I have not the audacity to pretend that I know anything of them; I can no more reconcile the mere banging of doors, ringing of bells, creaking of boards, and such- like insignificances, with the majestic beauty and pervading analogy of all the Divine rules that I am permitted to understand, than I had been able, a little while before, to yoke the spiritual intercourse of my fellow- traveller to the chariot of the rising sun. Moreover, I had lived in two haunted houses – both abroad. In one of these, an old Italian palace, which bore the reputation of being very badly haunted indeed, and which had recently been twice abandoned on that account, I lived eight months, most tranquilly and pleasantly: notwithstanding that the house had a score of mysterious bedrooms, which were never used, and possessed, in one large room in which I sat reading, times out of number at all hours, and next to which I slept, a haunted chamber of the first pretensions. I gently hinted these considerations to the landlord. And as to this particular house having a bad name, I reasoned with him, Why, how many things had bad names undeservedly, and how easy it was to give bad names, and did he not think that if he and I were persistently to whisper in the village that any weird-looking old drunken tinker of the neighborhood had sold himself to the Devil, he would come in time to be suspected of that commercial venture! All this wise talk was perfectly ineffective with the landlord, I am bound to confess, and was as dead a failure as ever I made in my life.

To cut this part of the story short, I was piqued about the haunted house, and was already half resolved to take it. So, after breakfast, I got the keys from Perkins's brother-in-law (a whip and harness maker, who keeps the Post Office, and is under submission to a most rigorous wife of the Doubly Seceding Little Emmanuel persuasion), and went up to the house, attended by my landlord and by Ikey.

Within, I found it, as I had expected, transcendently dismal. The slowly changing shadows waved on it from the heavy trees, were doleful in the last degree; the house was ill-placed, ill-built, ill-planned, and ill-fitted. It was damp, it was not free from dry rot, there was a flavor of rats in it, and it was the gloomy victim of that indescribable decay which settles on all the work of man's hands whenever it's not turned to man's account. The kitchens and offices were too large, and too remote from each other. Above stairs and below, waste tracts of passage intervened between patches of fertility represented by rooms; and there was a

mouldy old well with a green growth upon it, hiding like a murderous trap, near the bottom of the back-stairs, under the double
row of bells. One of these bells was labelled, on a black ground in
faded white letters, MASTER B. This, they told me, was the bell
that rang the most.

"Who was Master B.?" I asked. "Is it known what he did
while the owl hooted?"

"Rang the bell," said Ikey.

I was rather struck by the prompt dexterity with which this
young man pitched his fur cap at the bell, and rang it himself. It
was a loud, unpleasant bell, and made a very disagreeable sound.
The other bells were inscribed according to the names of the
rooms to which their wires were conducted: as "Picture Room,"
"Double Room," "Clock Room," and the like. Following Master
B.'s bell to its source I found that young gentleman to have had
but indifferent third-class accommodation in a triangular cabin
under the cock- loft, with a corner fireplace which Master B. must
have been exceedingly small if he were ever able to warm himself
at, and a corner chimney-piece like a pyramidal staircase to the
ceiling for Tom Thumb. The papering of one side of the room had
dropped down bodily, with fragments of plaster adhering to it,
and almost blocked up the door. It appeared that Master B., in his
spiritual condition, always made a point of pulling the paper
down. Neither the landlord nor Ikey could suggest why he made
such a fool of himself.

Except that the house had an immensely large rambling loft
at top, I made no other discoveries. It was moderately well furnished, but sparely. Some of the furniture – say, a third – was as
old as the house; the rest was of various periods within the last
half- century. I was referred to a corn-chandler in the market-
place of the county town to treat for the house. I went that day,
and I took it for six months.

It was just the middle of October when I moved in with my
maiden sister (I venture to call her eight-and-thirty, she is so very
handsome, sensible, and engaging). We took with us, a deaf sta-
ble- man, my bloodhound Turk, two women servants, and a

9

young person called an Odd Girl. I have reason to record of the attendant last enumerated, who was one of the Saint Lawrence's Union Female Orphans, that she was a fatal mistake and a disastrous engagement.

The year was dying early, the leaves were falling fast, it was a raw cold day when we took possession, and the gloom of the house was most depressing. The cook (an amiable woman, but of a weak turn of intellect) burst into tears on beholding the kitchen, and requested that her silver watch might be delivered over to her sister (2 Tuppintock's Gardens, Liggs's Walk, Clapham Rise), in the event of anything happening to her from the damp. Streaker, the housemaid, feigned cheerfulness, but was the greater martyr. The Odd Girl, who had never been in the country, alone was pleased, and made arrangements for sowing an acorn in the garden outside the scullery window, and rearing an oak.

We went, before dark, through all the natural – as opposed to supernatural – miseries incidental to our state. Dispiriting reports ascended (like the smoke) from the basement in volumes, and descended from the upper rooms. There was no rolling-pin, there was no salamander (which failed to surprise me, for I don't know what it is), there was nothing in the house; what there was, was broken, the last people must have lived like pigs, what could the meaning of the landlord be? Through these distresses, the Odd Girl was cheerful and exemplary. But within four hours after dark we had got into a supernatural groove, and the Odd Girl had seen "Eyes," and was in hysterics.

My sister and I had agreed to keep the haunting strictly to ourselves, and my impression was, and still is, that I had not left Ikey, when he helped to unload the cart, alone with the women, or any one of them, for one minute. Nevertheless, as I say, the Odd Girl had "seen Eyes" (no other explanation could ever be drawn from her), before nine, and by ten o'clock had had as much vinegar applied to her as would pickle a handsome salmon.

I leave a discerning public to judge of my feelings, when, under these untoward circumstances, at about half-past ten o'clock Master B.'s bell began to ring in a most infuriated manner, and Turk howled until the house resounded with his lamentations!

I hope I may never again be in a state of mind so unchristian as the mental frame in which I lived for some weeks, respecting the memory of Master B. Whether his bell was rung by rats, or mice, or bats, or wind, or what other accidental vibration, or sometimes by one cause, sometimes another, and sometimes by collusion, I don't know; but, certain it is, that it did ring two nights out of three, until I conceived the happy idea of twisting Master B.'s neck – in other words, breaking his bell short off – and silencing that young gentleman, as to my experience and belief, for ever.

But, by that time, the Odd Girl had developed such improving powers of catalepsy, that she had become a shining example of that very inconvenient disorder. She would stiffen, like a Guy Fawkes endowed with unreason, on the most irrelevant occasions. I would address the servants in a lucid manner, pointing out to them that I had painted Master B.'s room and balked the paper, and taken Master B.'s bell away and balked the ringing, and if they could suppose that that confounded boy had lived and died, to clothe himself with no better behavior than would most unquestionably have brought him and the sharpest particles of a birch-broom into close acquaintance in the present imperfect state of existence, could they also suppose a mere poor human being, such as I was, capable by those contemptible means of counteracting and limiting the powers of the disembodied spirits of the dead, or of any spirits? – I say I would become emphatic and cogent, not to say rather complacent, in such an address, when it would all go for nothing by reason of the Odd Girl's suddenly stiffening from the toes upward, and glaring among us like a parochial petrifaction.

Streaker, the housemaid, too, had an attribute of a most discomfiting nature. I am unable to say whether she was of an usually lymphatic temperament, or what else was the matter with her, but this young woman became a mere Distillery for the production of the largest and most transparent tears I ever met with. Combined with these characteristics, was a peculiar tenacity of hold in those specimens, so that they didn't fall, but hung upon her face and nose. In this condition, and mildly and deplorably shaking her head, her silence would throw me more heavily than the Admirable Crichton could have done in a verbal disputation for a purse of money. Cook, likewise, always covered me with confusion as with a garment, by neatly winding up the session with the protest that the Ouse was wearing her out, and by meekly repeating her last wishes regarding her silver watch.

As to our nightly life, the contagion of suspicion and fear was among us, and there is no such contagion under the sky. Hooded woman? According to the accounts, we were in a perfect Convent of hooded women. Noises? With that contagion downstairs, I myself have sat in the dismal parlor, listening, until I have heard so many and such strange noises, that they would have chilled my blood if I had not warmed it by dashing out to make discoveries. Try this in bed, in the dead of the night: try this at your own comfortable fire-side, in the life of the night. You can fill any house with noises, if you will, until you have a noise for every nerve in your nervous system.

I repeat; the contagion of suspicion and fear was among us, and there is no such contagion under the sky. The women (their noses in a chronic state of excoriation from smelling-salts) were always primed and loaded for a swoon, and ready to go off with hair- triggers. The two elder detached the Odd Girl on all expeditions that were considered doubly hazardous, and she always established the reputation of such adventures by coming back cataleptic. If Cook or Streaker went overhead after dark, we knew we should presently hear a bump on the ceiling; and this took place so constantly, that it was as if a fighting man were engaged to go about the house, administering a touch of his art which I believe is called The Auctioneer, to every domestic he met with.

It was in vain to do anything. It was in vain to be frightened, for the moment in one's own person, by a real owl, and then to show the owl. It was in vain to discover, by striking an accidental discord on the piano, that Turk always howled at particular notes and combinations. It was in vain to be a Rhadamanthus with the bells, and if an unfortunate bell rang without leave, to have it

12

down inexorably and silence it. It was in vain to fire up chimneys, let torches down the well, charge furiously into suspected rooms and recesses. We changed servants, and it was no better. The new set ran away, and a third set came, and it was no better. At last, our comfortable housekeeping got to be so disorganised and wretched, that I one night dejectedly said to my sister: "Patty, I begin to despair of our getting people to go on with us here, and I think we must give this up."

My sister, who is a woman of immense spirit, replied, "No, John, don't give it up. Don't be beaten, John. There is another way."

"And what is that?" said I.

"John," returned my sister, "if we are not to be driven out of this house, and that for no reason whatever, that is apparent to you or me, we must help ourselves and take the house wholly and solely into our own hands."

"But, the servants," said I.

"Have no servants," said my sister, boldly.

Like most people in my grade of life, I had never thought of the possibility of going on without those faithful obstructions. The notion was so new to me when suggested, that I looked very doubtful.

"We know they come here to be frightened and infect one another, and we know they are frightened and do infect one another," said my sister.

"With the exception of Bottles," I observed, in a meditative tone.

(The deaf stable-man. I kept him in my service, and still keep him, as a phenomenon of moroseness not to be matched in England.)

"To be sure, John," assented my sister; "except Bottles. And what does that go to prove? Bottles talks to nobody, and hears nobody unless he is absolutely roared at, and what alarm has

Bottles ever given, or taken? None."

This was perfectly true; the individual in question having retired, every night at ten o'clock, to his bed over the coach-house,
with no other company than a pitchfork and a pail of water. That
the pail of water would have been over me, and the pitchfork
through me, if I had put myself without announcement in Bottles's way after that minute, I had deposited in my own mind as a
fact worth remembering. Neither had Bottles ever taken the least
notice of any of our many uproars. An imperturbable and speechless man, he had sat at his supper, with Streaker present in a
swoon, and the Odd Girl marble, and had only put another po-
tato in his cheek, or profited by the general misery to help himself
to beefsteak pie.

"And so," continued my sister, "I exempt Bottles. And considering, John, that the house is too large, and perhaps too lonely,
to be kept well in hand by Bottles, you, and me, I propose that we
cast about among our friends for a certain selected number of the
most reliable and willing – form a Society here for three months –
wait upon ourselves and one another – live cheerfully and socially – and see what happens."

I was so charmed with my sister, that I embraced her on the
spot, and went into her plan with the greatest ardor.

We were then in the third week of November; but, we took
our measures so vigorously, and were so well seconded by the
friends in whom we confided, that there was still a week of the
month unexpired, when our party all came down together merrily, and mustered in the haunted house.

I will mention, in this place, two small changes that I made
while my sister and I were yet alone. It occurring to me as not
improbable that Turk howled in the house at night, partly because he wanted to get out of it, I stationed him in his kennel
outside, but unchained; and I seriously warned the village that
any man who came in his way must not expect to leave him without a rip in his own throat. I then casually asked Ikey if he were a
judge of a gun? On his saying, "Yes, sir, I knows a good gun when
I sees her," I begged the favor of his stepping up to the house and

looking at mine.

"SHE'S a true one, sir," said Ikey, after inspecting a double-barrelled rifle that I bought in New York a few years ago. "No mistake about HER, sir."

"Ikey," said I, "don't mention it; I have seen something in this house."

"No, sir?" he whispered, greedily opening his eyes. "'Ooded lady, sir?"

"Don't be frightened," said I. "It was a figure rather like you."

"Lord, sir?"

"Ikey!" said I, shaking hands with him warmly, I may say affectionately; "if there is any truth in these ghost-stories, the greatest service I can do you, is, to fire at that figure. And I promise you, by Heaven and earth, I will do it with this gun if I see it again!"

The young man thanked me, and took his leave with some little precipitation, after declining a glass of liquor. I imparted my secret to him, because I had never quite forgotten his throwing his cap at the bell; because I had, on another occasion, noticed something very like a fur cap, lying not far from the bell, one night when it had burst out ringing; and because I had remarked that we were at our ghostliest whenever he came up in the evening to comfort the servants. Let me do Ikey no injustice. He was afraid of the house, and believed in its being haunted; and yet he would play false on the haunting side, so surely as he got an opportunity. The Odd Girl's case was exactly similar. She went about the house in a state of real terror, and yet lied monstrously and wilfully, and invented many of the alarms she spread, and made many of the sounds we heard. I had had my eye on the two, and I know it. It is not necessary for me, here, to account for this preposterous state of mind; I content myself with remarking that it is familiarly known to every intelligent man who has had fair medical, legal, or other watchful experience; that it is as well established and as common a state of mind as any with which observers are acquainted; and that it is one of the first elements,

15

above all others, rationally to be suspected in, and strictly looked for, and separated from, any question of this kind.

To return to our party. The first thing we did when we were all assembled, was, to draw lots for bedrooms. That done, and every bedroom, and, indeed, the whole house, having been minutely examined by the whole body, we allotted the various household duties, as if we had been on a gipsy party, or a yachting party, or a hunting party, or were shipwrecked. I then recounted the floating rumors concerning the hooded lady, the owl, and Master B.: with others, still more filmy, which had floated about during our occupation, relative to some ridiculous old ghost of the female gender who went up and down, carrying the ghost of a round table; and also to an impalpable Jackass, whom nobody was ever able to catch. Some of these ideas I really believe our people below had communicated to one another in some diseased way, without conveying them in words. We then gravely called one another to witness, that we were not there to be deceived, or to deceive – which we considered pretty much the same thing – and that, with a serious sense of responsibility, we would be strictly true to one another, and would strictly follow out the truth. The understanding was established, that any one who heard unusual noises in the night, and who wished to trace them, should knock at my door; lastly, that on Twelfth Night, the last night of holy Christmas, all our individual experiences since that then present hour of our coming together in the haunted house, should be brought to light for the good of all; and that we would hold our peace on the subject till then, unless on some remarkable provocation to break silence.

We were, in number and in character, as follows:

First – to get my sister and myself out of the way – there were we two. In the drawing of lots, my sister drew her own room, and I drew Master B.'s. Next, there was our first cousin John Herschel, so called after the great astronomer: than whom I suppose a better man at a telescope does not breathe. With him, was his wife: a charming creature to whom he had been married in the previous spring. I thought it (under the circumstances) rather imprudent to bring her, because there is no knowing what even a false alarm may do at such a time; but I suppose he knew his own business best, and I must say that if she had been MY wife, I never could have left her endearing and bright face behind. They drew the Clock Room. Alfred Starling, an uncommonly agreeable young fellow of eight-and- twenty for whom I have the greatest liking, was in the Double Room; mine, usually, and designated by that name from having a dressing- room within it, with two large and cumbersome windows, which no wedges I was ever able to make, would keep from shaking, in any weather, wind or no wind. Alfred is a young fellow who pretends to be "fast" (another word for loose, as I understand the term), but who is much too good and sensible for that nonsense, and who would have distinguished himself before now, if his father had not unfortunately left him a small independence of two hundred a year, on the strength of which his only occupation in life has been to spend six. I am in hopes, however, that his Banker may break, or that he may enter into some speculation guaranteed to pay twenty per cent.; for, I am convinced that if he could only be ruined, his fortune is made. Belinda Bates, bosom friend of my sister, and a most intellectual, amiable, and delightful girl, got the Picture Room. She has a fine genius for poetry, combined with real business earnestness, and "goes in" – to use an expression of Alfred's – for Woman's mission, Woman's rights, Woman's wrongs, and everything that is woman's with a capital W, or is not and ought to be, or is and ought not to be. "Most praiseworthy, my dear, and Heaven prosper you!" I whispered to her on the first night of my taking leave of her at the Picture-Room door, "but don't overdo it. And in respect of the great necessity there is, my darling, for more employments being within the reach of Woman than our civilisation has as yet assigned to her, don't fly at the unfortunate men, even those men who are at first sight in your way, as if they were the natural oppressors of your sex; for, trust me, Belinda, they do sometimes spend their wages among wives and daughters, sisters, mothers, aunts, and grandmothers; and the play is, really, not ALL Wolf and Red Riding-Hood, but has other parts in it." However, I digress.

Belinda, as I have mentioned, occupied the Picture Room. We had but three other chambers: the Corner Room, the Cupboard Room, and the Garden Room. My old friend, Jack Governor, "slung his hammock," as he called it, in the Corner Room. I have always regarded Jack as the finest-looking sailor that ever sailed. He is gray now, but as handsome as he was a quarter of a century ago – nay, handsomer. A portly, cheery, well-built figure of a broad- shouldered man, with a frank smile, a brilliant dark eye, and a rich dark eyebrow. I remember those under darker hair, and they look all the better for their silver setting. He has been wherever his Union namesake flies, has Jack, and I have met old shipmates of his, away in the Mediterranean and on the other side of the Atlantic, who have beamed and brightened at the casual mention of his name, and have cried, "You know Jack Governor? Then you know a prince of men!" That he is! And so unmistakably a naval officer, that if you were to meet him coming out of an Esquimaux snow-hut in seal's skin, you would be vaguely persuaded he was in full naval uniform.

Jack once had that bright clear eye of his on my sister; but, it fell out that he married another lady and took her to South America, where she died. This was a dozen years ago or more. He brought down with him to our haunted house a little cask of salt beef; for, he is always convinced that all salt beef not of his own pickling, is mere carrion, and invariably, when he goes to London, packs a piece in his portmanteau. He had also volunteered to bring with him one "Nat Beaver," an old comrade of his, captain of a merchantman. Mr. Beaver, with a thick-set wooden face and figure, and apparently as hard as a block all over, proved to be an intelligent man, with a world of watery experiences in him, and great practical knowledge. At times, there was a curious nervousness about him, apparently the lingering result of some old illness; but, it seldom lasted many minutes. He got the Cupboard Room, and lay there next to Mr. Undery, my friend and solicitor: who came down, in an amateur capacity, "to go through with it," as he said, and who plays whist better than the whole Law List, from the red cover at the beginning to the red cover at the end.

I never was happier in my life, and I believe it was the universal feeling among us. Jack Governor, always a man of wonderful resources, was Chief Cook, and made some of the best dishes I ever ate, including unapproachable curries. My sister was pastry cook and confectioner. Starling and I were Cook's Mate, turn and turn about, and on special occasions the chief cook "pressed" Mr. Beaver. We had a great deal of outdoor sport and exercise, but nothing was neglected within, and there was no ill-humor or misunderstanding among us, and our evenings were so delightful that we had at least one good reason for being reluctant to go to bed.

We had a few night alarms in the beginning. On the first night, I was knocked up by Jack with a most wonderful ship's lantern in his hand, like the gills of some monster of the deep, who informed me that he "was going aloft to the main truck," to have the weathercock down. It was a stormy night and I remonstrated; but Jack called my attention to its making a sound like a cry of despair, and said somebody would be "hailing a ghost" presently, if it wasn't done. So, up to the top of the house, where I could hardly stand for the wind, we went, accompanied by Mr. Beaver; and there Jack, lantern and all, with Mr. Beaver after him, swarmed up to the top of a cupola, some two dozen feet above the chimneys, and stood upon nothing particular, coolly knocking the weathercock off, until they both got into such good spirits with the wind and the height, that I thought they would never come down. Another night, they turned out again, and had a chimney-cowl off. Another night, they cut a sobbing and gulping water-pipe away. Another night, they found out something else. On several occasions, they both, in the coolest manner, simultaneously dropped out of their respective bedroom windows, hand over hand by their counterpanes, to "overhaul" something mysterious in the garden.

The engagement among us was faithfully kept, and nobody revealed anything. All we knew was, if any one's room were haunted, no one looked the worse for it.

The foregoing story is particularly interesting as illustrating the leaning of Dickens's mind toward the spiritualistic and mystical fancies current in his time, and the counterbalance of his common sense and fun.

"He probably never made up his own mind," Mr. Andrew Lang declares in a discussion of this Haunted House story. Mr. Lang says he once took part in a similar quest, and "can recognize the accuracy of most of Dickens's remarks. Indeed, even to persons not on the level of the Odd Girl in education, the temptation to produce 'phenomena' for fun is all but overwhelming. That people communicate hallucinations to each other 'in some diseased way without words,' is a modern theory perhaps first formulated here by Dickens."

"The Signal Man's Story," which follows, is likewise, Mr. Lang believes, "probably based on some real story of the kind, some anecdote of premonitions. There are scores in the records of the Society for Psychical Research." – The Editor.

No. 1 Branch Line: The Signal-Man

"Halloa! Below there!"

When he heard a voice thus calling to him, he was standing at the door of his box, with a flag in his hand, furled round its short pole. One would have thought, considering the nature of the ground, that he could not have doubted from what quarter the voice came; but instead of looking up to where I stood on the top of the steep cutting nearly over his head, he turned himself about, and looked down the Line. There was something remarkable in his manner of doing so, though I could not have said for my life what. But I know it was remarkable enough to attract my notice, even though his figure was foreshortened and shadowed, down in the deep trench, and mine was high above him, so steeped in the glow of an angry sunset, that I had shaded my eyes with my hand before I saw him at all.

"Halloa! Below!"

From looking down the Line, he turned himself about again, and, raising his eyes, saw my figure high above him.

"Is there any path by which I can come down and speak to you?"

He looked up at me without replying, and I looked down at him without pressing him too soon with a repetition of my idle question. Just then there came a vague vibration in the earth and air, quickly changing into a violent pulsation, and an oncoming rush that caused me to start back, as though it had a force to draw me down. When such vapor as rose to my height from this rapid train had passed me, and was skimming away over the landscape, I looked down again, and saw him refurling the flag he had shown while the train went by.

I repeated my inquiry. After a pause, during which he seemed to regard me with fixed attention, he motioned with his rolled-up flag towards a point on my level, some two or three hundred yards distant. I called down to him, "All right!" and made for that point. There, by dint of looking closely about me, I found a rough zigzag descending path notched out, which I followed.

The cutting was extremely deep, and unusually precipitate. It was made through a clammy stone, that became oozier and wetter as I went down. For these reasons, I found the way long enough to give me time to recall a singular air of reluctance or compulsion with which he had pointed out the path.

When I came down low enough upon the zigzag descent to see him again, I saw that he was standing between the rails on the way by which the train had lately passed, in an attitude as if he were waiting for me to appear. He had his left hand at his chin, and that left elbow rested on his right hand, crossed over his breast. His attitude was one of such expectation and watchfulness that I stopped a moment, wondering at it.

I resumed my downward way, and stepping out upon the level of the railroad, and drawing nearer to him, saw that he was a dark, sallow man, with a dark beard and rather heavy eyebrows. His post was in as solitary and dismal a place as ever I saw. On either side, a dripping-wet wall of jagged stone, excluding all view but a strip of sky; the perspective one way only a crooked prolongation of this great dungeon; the shorter perspective in the other direction terminating in a gloomy red light, and the gloomier entrance to a black tunnel, in whose massive architecture there was a barbarous, depressing, and forbidding air. So little sunlight ever found its way to this spot, that it had an earthy, deadly smell; and so much cold wind rushed through it, that it struck chill to me, as if I had left the natural world.

Before he stirred, I was near enough to him to have touched him. Not even then removing his eyes from mine, he stepped back one step, and lifted his hand.

This was a lonesome post to occupy (I said), and it had riveted my attention when I looked down from up yonder. A visitor was a rarity, I should suppose; not an unwelcome rarity, I hoped? In me, he merely saw a man who had been shut up within narrow limits all his life, and who, being at last set free, had a newly-awakened interest in these great works. To such purpose I spoke to him; but I am far from sure of the terms I used; for, besides that I am not happy in opening any conversation, there was something in the man that daunted me.

He directed a most curious look towards the red light near the tunnel's mouth, and looked all about it, as if something were missing from it, and then looked it me.

That light was part of his charge? Was it not?

He answered in a low voice, – "Don't you know it is?"

The monstrous thought came into my mind, as I perused the fixed eyes and the saturnine face, that this was a spirit, not a man. I have speculated since, whether there may have been infection in his mind.

In my turn, I stepped back. But in making the action, I detected in his eyes some latent fear of me. This put the monstrous thought to flight.

"You look at me," I said, forcing a smile, "as if you had a dread of me."

"I was doubtful," he returned, "whether I had seen you before."

"Where?"

He pointed to the red light he had looked at.

"There?" I said.

Intently watchful of me, he replied (but without sound), "Yes."

"My good fellow, what should I do there? However, be that as it may, I never was there, you may swear."

"I think I may," he rejoined. "Yes; I am sure I may."

His manner cleared, like my own. He replied to my remarks with readiness, and in well-chosen words. Had he much to do there? Yes; that was to say, he had enough responsibility to bear; but exactness and watchfulness were what was required of him, and of actual work – manual labor – he had next to none. To change that signal, to trim those lights, and to turn this iron handle now and then, was all he had to do under that head. Regarding those many long and lonely hours of which I seemed to make so much, he could only say that the routine of his life had shaped itself into that form, and he had grown used to it. He had taught himself a language down here, – if only to know it by sight, and to have formed his own crude ideas of its pronunciation, could be called learning it. He had also worked at fractions and decimals, and tried a little algebra; but he was, and had been as a boy, a poor hand at figures. Was it necessary for him when on duty always to remain in that channel of damp air, and could he never rise into the sunshine from between those high stone walls? Why, that depended upon times and circumstances. Under some conditions there would be less upon the Line than under others, and the same held good as to certain hours of the day and night. In bright weather, he did choose occasions for getting a little above these lower shadows; but, being at all times liable to be called by his electric bell, and at such times listening for it with redoubled anxiety, the relief was less than I would suppose.

He took me into his box, where there was a fire, a desk for an official book in which he had to make certain entries, a telegraphic instrument with its dial, face, and needles, and the little bell of which he had spoken. On my trusting that he would excuse the remark that he had been well educated, and (I hoped I might say without offence) perhaps educated above that station, he observed that instances of slight incongruity in such wise would rarely be found wanting among large bodies of men; that he had heard it was so in workhouses, in the police force, even in that last desperate resource, the army; and that he knew it was so, more or less, in any great railway staff. He had been, when young (if I could believe it, sitting in that hut, – he scarcely could), a student of natural philosophy, and had attended lectures; but he had run wild, misused his opportunities, gone down, and never risen again. He had no complaint to offer about that. He had made his bed, and he lay upon it. It was far too late to make another.

All that I have here condensed he said in a quiet manner, with his grave dark regards divided between me and the fire. He threw in the word, "Sir," from time to time, and especially when he referred to his youth, – as though to request me to understand that he claimed to be nothing but what I found him. He was several times interrupted by the little bell, and had to read off messages, and send replies. Once he had to stand without the door, and display a flag as a train passed, and make some verbal communication to the driver. In the discharge of his duties, I observed him to be remarkably exact and vigilant, breaking off his discourse at a syllable, and remaining silent until what he had to do was done.

In a word, I should have set this man down as one of the safest of men to be employed in that capacity, but for the circumstance that while he was speaking to me he twice broke off with a fallen color, turned his face towards the little bell when it did NOT ring, opened the door of the hut (which was kept shut to exclude the unhealthy damp), and looked out towards the red light near the mouth of the tunnel. On both of those occasions, he came back to the fire with the inexplicable air upon him which I had remarked, without being able to define, when we were so far asunder.

Said I, when I rose to leave him, "You almost make me think that I have met with a contented man."

(I am afraid I must acknowledge that I said it to lead him on.)

"I believe I used to be so," he rejoined, in the low voice in which he had first spoken; "but I am troubled, sir, I am troubled."

He would have recalled the words if he could. He had said them, however, and I took them up quickly.

"With what? What is your trouble?"

"It is very difficult to impart, sir. It is very, very difficult to speak of. If ever you make me another visit, I will try to tell you."

"But I expressly intend to make you another visit. Say, when shall it be?"

"I go off early in the morning, and I shall be on again at ten to- morrow night, sir."

"I will come at eleven."

He thanked me, and went out at the door with me. "I'll show my white light, sir," he said, in his peculiar low voice, "till you have found the way up. When you have found it, don't call out! And when you are at the top, don't call out!"

His manner seemed to make the place strike colder to me, but I said no more than, "Very well."

"And when you come down to-morrow night, don't call out! Let me ask you a parting question. What made you cry, 'Halloa! Below there!' to-night?"

"Heaven knows," said I. "I cried something to that effect – "

"Not to that effect, sir. Those were the very words. I know them well."

"Admit those were the very words. I said them, no doubt, because I saw you below."

"For no other reason?"

"What other reason could I possibly have?"

"You had no feeling that they were conveyed to you in any supernatural way?"

"No."

He wished me good-night, and held up his light. I walked by the side of the down Line of rails (with a very disagreeable sensation of a train coming behind me) until I found the path. It was easier to mount than to descend, and I got back to my inn without any adventure.

Punctual to my appointment, I placed my foot on the first notch of the zigzag next night, as the distant clocks were striking eleven. He was waiting for me at the bottom, with his white light on. "I have not called out," I said, when we came close together; "may I speak now?" "By all means, sir." "Good-night, then, and here's my hand." "Good-night, sir, and here's mine." With that we walked side by side to his box, entered it, closed the door, and sat down by the fire.

"I have made up my mind, sir," he began, bending forward as soon as we were seated, and speaking in a tone but a little above a whisper, "that you shall not have to ask me twice what troubles me. I took you for some one else yesterday evening. That troubles me."

"That mistake?"

"No. That some one else."

"Who is it?"

"I don't know."

"Like me?"

"I don't know. I never saw the face. The left arm is across the face, and the right arm is waved, – violently waved. This way."

I followed his action with my eyes, and it was the action of an arm gesticulating, with the utmost passion and vehemence,

"For God's sake, clear the way!"

"One moonlight night," said the man, "I was sitting here, when I heard a voice cry, 'Halloa! Below there!' I started up, looked from that door, and saw this Someone else standing by the red light near the tunnel, waving as I just now showed you. The voice seemed hoarse with shouting, and it cried, 'Look out! Look out!' And then attain, 'Halloa! Below there! Look out!' I caught up my lamp, turned it on red, and ran towards the figure, calling, 'What's wrong? What has happened? Where?' It stood just out-side the blackness of the tunnel. I advanced so close upon it that I wondered at its keeping the sleeve across its eyes. I ran right up at it, and had my hand stretched out to pull the sleeve away, when it was gone."

"Into the tunnel?" said I.

"No. I ran on into the tunnel, five hundred yards. I stopped, and held my lamp above my head, and saw the figures of the measured distance, and saw the wet stains stealing down the walls and trickling through the arch. I ran out again faster than I had run in (for I had a mortal abhorrence of the place upon me), and I looked all round the red light with my own red light, and I went up the iron ladder to the gallery atop of it, and I came down again, and ran back here. I telegraphed both ways, 'An alarm has been given. Is anything wrong?' The answer came back, both ways, 'All well.'"

Resisting the slow touch of a frozen finger tracing out my spine, I showed him how that this figure must be a deception of his sense of sight; and how that figures, originating in disease of the delicate nerves that minister to the functions of the eye, were known to have often troubled patients, some of whom had be-come conscious of the nature of their affliction, and had even proved it by experiments upon themselves. "As to an imaginary cry," said I, "do but listen for a moment to the wind in this un-natural valley while we speak so low, and to the wild harp it makes of the telegraph wires."

That was all very well, he returned, after we had sat listening for a while, and he ought to know something of the wind and the wires, – he who so often passed long winter nights there, alone and watching. But he would beg to remark that he had not finished.

I asked his pardon, and he slowly added these words, touching my arm –

"Within six hours after the Appearance, the memorable accident on this Line happened, and within ten hours the dead and wounded were brought along through the tunnel over the spot where the figure had stood."

A disagreeable shudder crept over me, but I did my best against it. It was not to be denied, I rejoined, that this was a remarkable coincidence, calculated deeply to impress his mind. But it was unquestionable that remarkable coincidences did continually occur, and they must be taken into account in dealing with such a subject. Though to be sure I must admit, I added (for I thought I saw that he was going to bring the objection to bear upon me), men of common sense did not allow much for coincidences in making the ordinary calculations of life.

He again begged to remark that he had not finished.

I again begged his pardon for being betrayed into interruptions.

"This," he said, again laying his hand upon my arm, and glancing over his shoulder with hollow eyes, "was just a year ago. Six or seven months passed, and I had recovered from the surprise and shock, when one morning, as the day was breaking, I, standing at the door, looked towards the red light, and saw the spectre again." He stopped, with a fixed look at me.

"Did it cry out?"

"No. It was silent."

"Did it wave its arm?"

"No. It leaned against the shaft of the light, with both hands before the face. Like this."

Once more I followed his action with my eyes. It was an action of mourning. I have seen such an attitude in stone figures on tombs.

"Did you go up to it?"

"I came in and sat down, partly to collect my thoughts, partly because it had turned me faint. When I went to the door again, daylight was above me, and the ghost was gone."

"But nothing followed? Nothing came of this?"

He touched me on the arm with his forefinger twice or thrice giving a ghastly nod each time:-

"That very day, as a train came out of the tunnel, I noticed, at a carriage window on my side, what looked like a confusion of hands and heads, and something waved. I saw it just in time to signal the driver, Stop! He shut off, and put his brake on, but the train drifted past here a hundred and fifty yards or more. I ran after it, and, as I went along, heard terrible screams and cries. A beautiful young lady had died instantaneously in one of the compartments, and was brought in here, and laid down on this floor between us."

Involuntarily I pushed my chair back, as I looked from the boards at which he pointed to himself.

"True, sir. True. Precisely as it happened, so I tell it you."

I could think of nothing to say, to any purpose, and my mouth was very dry. The wind and the wires took up the story with a long lamenting wail.

He resumed. "Now, sir, mark this, and judge how my mind is troubled. The spectre came back a week ago. Ever since, it has been there, now and again, by fits and starts."

"At the light?"

"At the Danger-light."

"What does it seem to do?"

He repeated, if possible with increased passion and vehemence, that former gesticulation of, "For God's sake, clear the way!"

Then he went on. "I have no peace or rest for it. It calls to me, for many minutes together, in an agonised manner, 'Below there! Look out! Look out!' It stands waving to me. It rings my little bell – "

I caught at that. "Did it ring your bell yesterday evening when I was here, and you went to the door?"

"Twice."

"Why, see," said I, "how your imagination misleads you. My eyes were on the bell, and my ears were open to the bell, and if I am a living man, it did NOT ring at those times. No, nor at any other time, except when it was rung in the natural course of physical things by the station communicating with you."

He shook his head. "I have never made a mistake as to that yet, sir. I have never confused the spectre's ring with the man's. The ghost's ring is a strange vibration in the bell that it derives from nothing else, and I have not asserted that the bell stirs to the eye. I don't wonder that you failed to hear it. But I heard it."

"And did the spectre seem to be there, when you looked out?"

"It WAS there."

"Both times?"

He repeated firmly: "Both times."

"Will you come to the door with me, and look for it now?"

He bit his under lip as though he were somewhat unwilling, but arose. I opened the door, and stood on the step, while he stood in the doorway. There was the Danger-light. There was the dismal mouth of the tunnel. There were the high, wet stone walls of the cutting. There were the stars above them.

"Do you see it?" I asked him, taking particular note of his face. His eyes were prominent and strained, but not very much more so, perhaps, than my own had been when I had directed them earnestly towards the same spot.

"No," he answered. "It is not there."

"Agreed," said I.

We went in again, shut the door, and resumed our seats. I was thinking how best to improve this advantage, if it might be called one, when he took up the conversation in such a matter-of-course way, so assuming that there could be no serious question of fact between us, that I felt myself placed in the weakest of positions.

"By this time you will fully understand, sir," he said, "that what troubles me so dreadfully is the question, What does the spectre mean?"

I was not sure, I told him, that I did fully understand.

"What is its warning against?" he said, ruminating, with his eyes on the fire, and only by times turning them on me. "What is the danger? Where is the danger? There is danger overhanging somewhere on the Line. Some dreadful calamity will happen. It is not to be doubted this third time, after what has gone before. But surely this is a cruel haunting of ME. What can I do?"

He pulled out his handkerchief, and wiped the drops from his heated forehead.

"If I telegraph Danger, on either side of me, or on both, I can give no reason for it," he went on, wiping the palms of his hands. "I should get into trouble, and do no good. They would think I was mad. This is the way it would work, – Message: 'Danger! Take care!' Answer: 'What Danger? Where?' Message: 'Don't know. But, for God's sake, take care!' They would displace me. What else could they do?"

His pain of mind was most pitiable to see. It was the mental torture of a conscientious man, oppressed beyond endurance by an unintelligible responsibility involving life.

"When it first stood under the Danger-light," he went on, putting his dark hair back from his head, and drawing his hands outward across and across his temples in an extremity of feverish distress, "why not tell me where that accident was to happen, – if it must happen? Why not tell me how it could be averted, – if it could have been averted? When on its second coming it hid its face, why not tell me, instead, 'She is going to die. Let them keep her at home'? If it came, on those two occasions, only to show me that its warnings were true, and so to prepare me for the third, why not warn me plainly now? And I, Lord help me! A mere poor signal-man on this solitary station! Why not go to somebody with credit to be believed, and power to act?"

When I saw him in this state, I saw that for the poor man's sake, as well as for the public safety, what I had to do for the time was to compose his mind. Therefore, setting aside all question of reality or unreality between us, I represented to him that whoever thoroughly discharged his duty must do well, and that at least it was his comfort that he understood his duty, though he did not understand these confounding Appearances. In this effort I succeeded far better than in the attempt to reason him out of his conviction. He became calm; the occupations incidental to his post as the night advanced began to make larger demands on his attention: and I left him at two in the morning. I had offered to stay through the night, but he would not hear of it.

That I more than once looked back at the red light as I ascended the pathway, that I did not like the red light, and that I should have slept but poorly if my bed had been under it, I see no reason to conceal. Nor did I like the two sequences of the accident and the dead girl. I see no reason to conceal that either.

But what ran most in my thoughts was the consideration how ought I to act, having become the recipient of this disclosure? I had proved the man to be intelligent, vigilant, painstaking, and exact; but how long might he remain so, in his state of mind? Though in a subordinate position, still he held a most important trust, and would I (for instance) like to stake my own life on the chances of his continuing to execute it with precision?

Unable to overcome a feeling that there would be something treacherous in my communicating what he had told me to his superiors in the Company, without first being plain with himself and proposing a middle course to him, I ultimately resolved to offer to accompany him (otherwise keeping his secret for the present) to the wisest medical practitioner we could hear of in those parts, and to take his opinion. A change in his time of duty would come round next night, he had apprised me, and he would be off an hour or two after sunrise, and on again soon after sunset. I had appointed to return accordingly.

Next evening was a lovely evening, and I walked out early to enjoy it. The sun was not yet quite down when I traversed the field-path near the top of the deep cutting. I would extend my walk for an hour, I said to myself, half an hour on and half an hour back, and it would then be time to go to my signal-man's box.

Before pursuing my stroll, I stepped to the brink, and mechanically looked down, from the point from which I had first seen him. I cannot describe the thrill that seized upon me, when, close at the mouth of the tunnel, I saw the appearance of a man, with his left sleeve across his eyes, passionately waving his right arm.

The nameless horror that oppressed me passed in a moment, for in a moment I saw that this appearance of a man was a man indeed, and that there was a little group of other men, standing at a short distance, to whom he seemed to be rehearsing the gesture he made. The Danger-light was not yet lighted. Against its shaft, a little low hut, entirely new to me, had been made of some wooden supports and tarpaulin. It looked no bigger than a bed.

With an irresistible sense that something was wrong, – with a flashing self-reproachful fear that fatal mischief had come of my leaving the man there, and causing no one to be sent to overlook or correct what he did, – I descended the notched path with all the speed I could make.

"What is the matter?" I asked the men.

"Signal-man killed this morning, sir."

"Not the man belonging to that box?"

"Yes, sir."

"Not the man I know?"

"You will recognise him, sir, if you knew him," said the man who spoke for the others, solemnly uncovering his own head, and raising an end of the tarpaulin, "for his face is quite composed."

"Oh, how did this happen, how did this happen?" I asked, turning from one to another as the hut closed in again.

"He was cut down by an engine, sir. No man in England knew his work better. But somehow he was not clear of the outer rail. It was just at broad day. He had struck the light, and had the lamp in his hand. As the engine came out of the tunnel, his back was towards her, and she cut him down. That man drove her, and was showing how it happened. Show the gentleman, Tom."

The man, who wore a rough dark dress, stepped back to his former place at the mouth of the tunnel.

"Coming round the curve in the tunnel, sir," he said, "I saw him at the end, like as if I saw him down a perspective-glass. There was no time to check speed, and I knew him to be very careful. As he didn't seem to take heed of the whistle, I shut it off when we were running down upon him, and called to him as loud as I could call."

"What did you say?"

"I said, 'Below there! Look out! Look out! For God's sake, clear the way!'"

I started.

"Ah! it was a dreadful time, sir. I never left off calling to him. I put this arm before my eyes not to see, and I waved this arm to the last; but it was no use."

Without prolonging the narrative to dwell on any one of its curious circumstances more than on any other, I may, in closing it, point out the coincidence that the warning of the Engine-Driver included, not only the words which the unfortunate Signal-man had repeated to me as haunting him, but also the words which I myself – not he – had attached, and that only in my own mind, to the gesticulation he had imitated.

BULWER LYTTON

The Haunted and the Haunters;
Or, The House and the Brain

A friend of mine, who is a man of letters and a philosopher, said to me one day, as if between jest and earnest, "Fancy! since we last met I have discovered a haunted house in the midst of London."

"Really haunted, – and by what? – ghosts?"

"Well, I can't answer that question; all I know is this: six weeks ago my wife and I were in search of a furnished apartment. Passing a quiet street, we saw on the window of one of the houses a bill, 'Apartments, Furnished.' The situation suited us; we entered the house, liked the rooms, engaged them by the week, – and left them the third day. No power on earth could have reconciled my wife to stay longer; and I don't wonder at it."

"What did you see?"

"Excuse me; I have no desire to be ridiculed as a superstitious dreamer, – nor, on the other hand, could I ask you to accept on my affirmation what you would hold to be incredible without the evidence of your own senses. Let me only say this, it was not so much what we saw or heard (in which you might fairly suppose that we were the dupes of our own excited fancy, or the victims of imposture in others) that drove us away, as it was an indefinable terror which seized both of us whenever we passed by the door of a certain unfurnished room, in which we neither saw nor heard anything. And the strangest marvel of all was, that for once in my life I agreed with my wife, silly woman though she be, – and allowed, after the third night, that it was impossible to stay a fourth in that house. Accordingly, on the fourth morning I summoned the woman who kept the house and attended on us, and told her that the rooms did not quite suit us, and we would not stay out our week. She said dryly, 'I know why; you have stayed longer than any other lodger. Few ever stayed a second night; none before you a third. But I take it they have been very kind to you.'

"'They, – who?' I asked, affecting to smile.

"'Why, they who haunt the house, whoever they are. I don't mind them. I remember them many years ago, when I lived in this house, not as a servant; but I know they will be the death of me some day. I don't care, – I'm old, and must die soon anyhow; and then I shall be with them, and in this house still.' The woman spoke with so dreary a calmness that really it was a sort of awe that prevented my conversing with her further. I paid for my week, and too happy were my wife and I to get off so cheaply."

"You excite my curiosity," said I; "nothing I should like better than to sleep in a haunted house. Pray give me the address of the one which you left so ignominiously."

My friend gave me the address; and when we parted, I walked straight toward the house thus indicated.

It is situated on the north side of Oxford Street, in a dull but respectable thoroughfare. I found the house shut up, – no bill at the window, and no response to my knock. As I was turning away, a beer-boy, collecting pewter pots at the neighboring areas, said to me, "Do you want any one at that house, sir?"

"Yes, I heard it was to be let."

"Let! – why, the woman who kept it is dead, – has been dead these three weeks, and no one can be found to stay there, though Mr. J – – offered ever so much. He offered mother, who chars for him, one pound a week just to open and shut the windows, and she would not."

"Would not! – and why?"

"The house is haunted; and the old woman who kept it was found dead in her bed, with her eyes wide open. They say the devil strangled her."

"Pooh! You speak of Mr. J – – . Is he the owner of the house?"

"Yes."

"Where does he live?"

"In G – – Street, No. – ."

"What is he? In any business?"

"No, sir, – nothing particular; a single gentleman."

I gave the potboy the gratuity earned by his liberal information, and proceeded to Mr. J – – , in G – – Street, which was close
by the street that boasted the haunted house. I was lucky enough
to find Mr. J – – at home, – an elderly man with intelligent countenance and prepossessing manners.

I communicated my name and my business frankly. I said I
heard the house was considered to be haunted, that I had a strong
desire to examine a house with so equivocal a reputation; that I
should be greatly obliged if he would allow me to hire it, though
only for a night. I was willing to pay for that privilege whatever
he might be inclined to ask. "Sir," said Mr. J – – , with great courtesy, "the house is at your service, for as short or as long a time as
you please. Rent is out of the question, – the obligation will be on
my side should you be able to discover the cause of the strange
phenomena which at present deprive it of all value. I cannot let it,
for I cannot even get a servant to keep it in order or answer the
door. Unluckily the house is haunted, if I may use that expression, not only by night, but by day; though at night the distur-
bances are of a more unpleasant and sometimes of a more alarming character. The poor old woman who died in it three weeks
ago was a pauper whom I took out of a workhouse; for in her
childhood she had been known to some of my family, and had
once been in such good circumstances that she had rented that
house of my uncle. She was a woman of superior education and
strong mind, and was the only person I could ever induce to remain in the house. Indeed, since her death, which was sudden,
and the coroner's inquest, which gave it a notoriety in the
neighborhood, I have so despaired of finding any person to take
charge of the house, much more a tenant, that I would willingly
let it rent free for a year to anyone who would pay its rates and
taxes."

"How long is it since the house acquired this sinister character?"

"That I can scarcely tell you, but very many years since. The old woman I spoke of, said it was haunted when she rented it between thirty and forty years ago. The fact is, that my life has been spent in the East Indies, and in the civil service of the Company. I returned to England last year, on inheriting the fortune of an uncle, among whose possessions was the house in question. I found it shut up and uninhabited. I was told that it was haunted, that no one would inhabit it. I smiled at what seemed to me so idle a story. I spent some money in repairing it, added to its old-fashioned furniture a few modern articles, – advertised it, and obtained a lodger for a year. He was a colonel on half pay. He came in with his family, a son and a daughter, and four or five servants: they all left the house the next day; and, although each of them declared that he had seen something different from that which had scared the others, a something still was equally terrible to all. I really could not in conscience sue, nor even blame, the colonel for breach of agreement. Then I put in the old woman I have spoken of, and she was empowered to let the house in apartments. I never had one lodger who stayed more than three days. I do not tell you their stories, – to no two lodgers have there been exactly the same phenomena repeated. It is better that you should judge for yourself, than enter the house with an imagination influenced by previous narratives; only be prepared to see and to hear something or other, and take whatever precautions you yourself please."

"Have you never had a curiosity yourself to pass a night in that house?"

"Yes. I passed not a night, but three hours in broad daylight alone in that house. My curiosity is not satisfied, but it is quenched. I have no desire to renew the experiment. You cannot complain, you see, sir, that I am not sufficiently candid; and unless your interest be exceedingly eager and your nerves unusually strong, I honestly add, that I advise you NOT to pass a night in that house."

"My interest IS exceedingly keen," said I; "and though only a coward will boast of his nerves in situations wholly unfamiliar to him, yet my nerves have been seasoned in such variety of danger that I have the right to rely on them, – even in a haunted house."

Mr. J – – said very little more; he took the keys of the house out of his bureau, gave them to me, – and, thanking him cordially for his frankness, and his urbane concession to my wish, I carried off my prize.

Impatient for the experiment, as soon as I reached home, I summoned my confidential servant, – a young man of gay spirits, fearless temper, and as free from superstitious prejudice as any-one I could think of.

F – – ," said I, "you remember in Germany how disappointed we were at not finding a ghost in that old castle, which was said to be haunted by a headless apparition? Well, I have heard of a house in London which, I have reason to hope, is decidedly haunted. I mean to sleep there to-night. From what I hear, there is no doubt that something will allow itself to be seen or to be heard, – something, perhaps, excessively horrible. Do you think if I take you with me, I may rely on your presence of mind, what-ever may happen?"

"Oh, sir, pray trust me," answered F – – , grinning with de-light.

"Very well; then here are the keys of the house, – this is the address. Go now, – select for me any bedroom you please; and since the house has not been inhabited for weeks, make up a good fire, air the bed well, – see, of course, that there are candles as well as fuel. Take with you my revolver and my dagger, – so much for my weapons; arm yourself equally well; and if we are not a match for a dozen ghosts, we shall be but a sorry couple of Englishmen.

I was engaged for the rest of the day on business so urgent that I had not leisure to think much on the nocturnal adventure to which I had plighted my honor. I dined alone, and very late, and while dining, read, as is my habit. I selected one of the volumes of Macaulay's Essays. I thought to myself that I would take the book with me; there was so much of healthfulness in the style, and practical life in the subjects, that it would serve as an antidote against the influences of superstitious fancy.

Accordingly, about half-past nine, I put the book into my pocket, and strolled leisurely toward the haunted house. I took with me a favorite dog: an exceedingly sharp, bold, and vigilant bull terrier, – a dog fond of prowling about strange, ghostly corners and passages at night in search of rats; a dog of dogs for a ghost.

I reached the house, knocked, and my servant opened with a cheerful smile.

We did not stay long in the drawing-rooms, – in fact, they felt so damp and so chilly that I was glad to get to the fire upstairs. We locked the doors of the drawing-rooms, – a precaution which, I should observe, we had taken with all the rooms we had searched below. The bedroom my servant had selected for me was the best on the floor, – a large one, with two windows fronting the street. The four-posted bed, which took up no inconsiderable space, was opposite to the fire, which burned clear and bright; a door in the wall to the left, between the bed and the window, communicated with the room which my servant appropriated to himself. This last was a small room with a sofa bed, and had no communication with the landing place, – no other door but that which conducted to the bedroom I was to occupy. On either side of my fireplace was a cupboard without locks, flush with the wall, and covered with the same dull-brown paper. We examined these cupboards, – only hooks to suspend female dresses, nothing else; we sounded the walls, – evidently solid, the outer walls of the building. Having finished the survey of these apartments, warmed myself a few moments, and lighted my cigar, I then, still accompanied by F – – , went forth to complete my reconnoiter. In the landing place there was another door; it was closed firmly. "Sir," said my servant, in surprise, "I unlocked this door with all the others when I first came; it cannot have got locked from the inside, for – "

Before he had finished his sentence, the door, which neither of us then was touching, opened quietly of itself. We looked at each other a single instant. The same thought seized both, – some

41

human agency might be detected here. I rushed in first, my servant followed. A small, blank, dreary room without furniture; a few empty boxes and hampers in a corner; a small window; the shutters closed; not even a fireplace; no other door but that by which we had entered; no carpet on the floor, and the floor seemed very old, uneven, worm-eaten, mended here and there, as was shown by the whiter patches on the wood; but no living being, and no visible place in which a living being could have hidden. As we stood gazing round, the door by which we had entered closed as quietly as it had before opened; we were imprisoned.

For the first time I felt a creep of indefinable horror. Not so my servant. "Why, they don't think to trap us, sir; I could break that trumpery door with a kick of my foot."

"Try first if it will open to your hand," said I, shaking off the vague apprehension that had seized me, "while I unclose the shutters and see what is without."

I unbarred the shutters, – the window looked on the little back yard I have before described; there was no ledge without, – nothing to break the sheer descent of the wall. No man getting out of that window would have found any footing till he had fallen on the stones below.

F – – , meanwhile, was vainly attempting to open the door. He now turned round to me and asked my permission to use force. And I should here state, in justice to the servant, that, far from evincing any superstitious terrors, his nerve, composure, and even gayety amidst circumstances so extraordinary, compelled my admiration, and made me congratulate myself on having secured a companion in every way fitted to the occasion. I willingly gave him the permission he required. But though he was a remarkably strong man, his force was as idle as his milder efforts; the door did not even shake to his stoutest kick. Breathless and panting, he desisted. I then tried the door myself, equally in vain. As I ceased from the effort, again that creep of horror came over me; but this time it was more cold and stubborn. I felt as if some strange and ghastly exhalation were rising up from the chinks of that rugged floor, and filling the atmosphere with a venomous influence hostile to human life. The door now very slowly and quietly opened as of its own accord. We precipitated ourselves into the landing place. We both saw a large, pale light – as large as the human figure, but shapeless and unsubstantial – move before us, and ascend the stairs that led from the landing into the attics. I followed the light, and my servant followed me. It entered, to the right of the landing, a small garret, of which the door stood open. I entered in the same instant. The light then collapsed into a small globule, exceedingly brilliant and vivid, rested a moment on a bed in the corner, quivered, and vanished. We approached the bed and examined it, – a half-tester, such as is commonly found in attics devoted to servants. On the drawers that stood near it we perceived an old faded silk kerchief, with the needle still left in a rent half repaired. The kerchief was covered with dust; probably it had belonged to the old woman who had last died in that house, and this might have been her sleeping room. I had sufficient curiosity to open the drawers: there were a few odds and ends of female dress, and two letters tied round with a narrow ribbon of faded yellow. I took the liberty to possess myself of the letters. We found nothing else in the room worth noticing, – nor did the light reappear; but we distinctly heard, as we turned to go, a pattering footfall on the floor, just before us. We went through the other attics (in all four), the footfall still preceding us. Nothing to be seen, – nothing but the footfall heard. I had the letters in my hand; just as I was descending the stairs I distinctly felt my wrist seized, and a faint, soft effort made to draw the letters from my clasp. I only held them the more tightly, and the effort ceased.

We regained the bedchamber appropriated to myself, and I then remarked that my dog had not followed us when we had left it. He was thrusting himself close to the fire, and trembling. I was impatient to examine the letters; and while I read them, my servant opened a little box in which he had deposited the weapons I had ordered him to bring, took them out, placed them on a table close at my bed head, and then occupied himself in soothing the dog, who, however, seemed to heed him very little.

The letters were short, - they were dated; the dates exactly thirty- five years ago. They were evidently from a lover to his mistress, or a husband to some young wife. Not only the terms of expression, but a distinct reference to a former voyage, indicated the writer to have been a seafarer. The spelling and handwriting were those of a man imperfectly educated, but still the language itself was forcible. In the expressions of endearment there was a kind of rough, wild love; but here and there were dark unintelligible hints at some secret not of love, - some secret that seemed of crime. "We ought to love each other," was one of the sentences I remember, "for how everyone else would execrate us if all was known." Again: "Don't let anyone be in the same room with you at night, - you talk in your sleep." And again: "What's done can't be undone; and I tell you there's nothing against us unless the dead could come to life." Here there was underlined in a better handwriting (a female's), "They do!" At the end of the letter latest in date the same female hand had written these words: "Lost at sea the 4th of June, the same day as - "

I put down the letters, and began to muse over their contents.

Fearing, however, that the train of thought into which I fell might unsteady my nerves, I fully determined to keep my mind in a fit state to cope with whatever of marvelous the advancing night might bring forth. I roused myself; laid the letters on the table; stirred up the fire, which was still bright and cheering; and opened my volume of Macaulay. I read quietly enough till about half past eleven. I then threw myself dressed upon the bed, and told my servant he might retire to his own room, but must keep himself awake. I bade him leave open the door between the two rooms. Thus alone, I kept two candles burning on the table by my bed head. I placed my watch beside the weapons, and calmly resumed my Macaulay. Opposite to me the fire burned clear; and on the hearth rug, seemingly asleep, lay the dog. In about twenty minutes I felt an exceedingly cold air pass by my cheek, like a sudden draught. I fancied the door to my right, communicating with the landing place, must have got open; but no, - it was closed. I then turned my glance to my left, and saw the flame of the candles violently swayed as by a wind. At the same moment the watch beside the revolver softly slid from the table, – softly, softly; no visible hand, – it was gone. I sprang up, seizing the revolver with the one hand, the dagger with the other; I was not willing that my weapons should share the fate of the watch. Thus armed, I looked round the floor, – no sign of the watch. Three slow, loud, distinct knocks were now heard at the bed head; my servant called out, "Is that you, sir?"

"No; be on your guard."

The dog now roused himself and sat on his haunches, his ears moving quickly backward and forward. He kept his eyes fixed on me with a look so strange that he concentered all my attention on himself. Slowly he rose up, all his hair bristling, and stood perfectly rigid, and with the same wild stare. I had no time, however, to examine the dog. Presently my servant emerged from his room; and if ever I saw horror in the human face, it was then. I should not have recognized him had we met in the street, so altered was every lineament. He passed by me quickly, saying, in a whisper that seemed scarcely to come from his lips, "Run, run! it is after me!" He gained the door to the landing, pulled it open, and rushed forth. I followed him into the landing involuntarily, calling him to stop; but, without heeding me, he bounded down the stairs, clinging to the balusters, and taking several steps at a time. I heard, where I stood, the street door open, – heard it again clap to. I was left alone in the haunted house.

It was but for a moment that I remained undecided whether or not to follow my servant; pride and curiosity alike forbade so dastardly a flight. I re-entered my room, closing the door after me, and proceeded cautiously into the interior chamber. I encountered nothing to justify my servant's terror. I again carefully examined the walls, to see if there were any concealed door. I could find no trace of one, – not even a seam in the dull-brown paper with which the room was hung. How, then, had the THING, whatever it was, which had so scared him, obtained ingress except though my own chamber?

I returned to my room, shut and locked the door that opened

upon the interior one, and stood on the hearth, expectant and prepared. I now perceived that the dog had slunk into an angle of the wall, and was pressing himself close against it, as if literally striving to force his way into it. I approached the animal and spoke to it; the poor brute was evidently beside itself with terror. It showed all its teeth, the slaver dropping from its jaws, and would certainly have bitten me if I had touched it. It did not seem to recognize me. Whoever has seen at the Zoological Gardens a rabbit, fascinated by a serpent, cowering in a corner, may form some idea of the anguish which the dog exhibited. Finding all efforts to soothe the animal in vain, and fearing that his bite might be as venomous in that state as in the madness of hydrophobia, I left him alone, placed my weapons on the table beside the fire, seated myself, and recommenced my Macaulay.

Perhaps, in order not to appear seeking credit for a courage, or rather a coolness, which the reader may conceive I exaggerate, I may be pardoned if I pause to indulge in one or two egotistical remarks.

As I hold presence of mind, or what is called courage, to be precisely proportioned to familiarity with the circumstances that lead to it, so I should say that I had been long sufficiently familiar with all experiments that appertain to the marvelous. I had witnessed many very extraordinary phenomena in various parts of the world, – phenomena that would be either totally disbelieved if I stated them, or ascribed to supernatural agencies. Now, my theory is that the supernatural is the impossible, and that what is called supernatural is only a something in the laws of Nature of which we have been hitherto ignorant. Therefore, if a ghost rise before me, I have not the right to say, "So, then, the supernatural is possible;" but rather, "So, then, the apparition of a ghost is, contrary to received opinion, within the laws of Nature, – that is, not supernatural."

Now, in all that I had hitherto witnessed, and indeed in all the wonders which the amateurs of mystery in our age record as facts, a material living agency is always required. On the Continent you will find still magicians who assert that they can raise spirits. Assume for the moment that they assert truly, still the living material form of the magician is present; and he is the material agency by which, from some constitutional peculiarities, certain strange phenomena are represented to your natural senses.

Accept, again, as truthful, the tales of spirit manifestation in America, – musical or other sounds; writings on paper, produced by no discernible hand; articles of furniture moved without apparent human agency; or the actual sight and touch of hands, to which no bodies seem to belong, – still there must be found the MEDIUM, or living being, with constitutional peculiarities capable of obtaining these signs. In fine, in all such marvels, supposing even that there is no imposture, there must be a human being like ourselves by whom, or through whom, the effects presented to human beings are produced. It is so with the now familiar phenomena of mesmerism or electro-biology; the mind of the person operated on is affected through a material living agent. Nor, supposing it true that a mesmerized patient can respond to the will or passes of a mesmerizer a hundred miles distant, is the response less occasioned by a material being; it may be through a material fluid – call it Electric, call it Odic, call it what you will – which has the power of traversing space and passing obstacles, that the material effect is communicated from one to the other. Hence, all that I had hitherto witnessed, or expected to witness, in this strange house, I believed to be occasioned through some agency or medium as mortal as myself; and this idea necessarily prevented the awe with which those who regard as supernatural things that are not within the ordinary operations of Nature, might have been impressed by the adventures of that memorable night.

As, then, it was my conjecture that all that was presented, or would be presented to my senses, must originate in some human being gifted by constitution with the power so to present them, and having some motive so to do, I felt an interest in my theory which, in its way, was rather philosophical than superstitious. And I can sincerely say that I was in as tranquil a temper for observation as any practical experimentalist could be in awaiting the effects of some rare, though perhaps perilous, chemical combination. Of course, the more I kept my mind detached from fancy, the more the temper fitted for observation would be obtained; and I therefore riveted eye and thought on the strong daylight sense in the page of my Macaulay.

I now became aware that something interposed between the page and the light, – the page was overshadowed. I looked up, and I saw what I shall find it very difficult, perhaps impossible, to describe.

It was a Darkness shaping itself forth from the air in very undefined outline. I cannot say it was of a human form, and yet it had more resemblance to a human form, or rather shadow, than to anything else. As it stood, wholly apart and distinct from the air and the light around it, its dimensions seemed gigantic, the summit nearly touching the ceiling. While I gazed, a feeling of intense cold seized me. An iceberg before me could not more have chilled me; nor could the cold of an iceberg have been more purely physical. I feel convinced that it was not the cold caused by fear. As I continued to gaze, I thought – but this I cannot say with precision – that I distinguished two eyes looking down on me from the height. One moment I fancied that I distinguished them clearly, the next they seemed gone; but still two rays of a pale- blue light frequently shot through the darkness, as from the height on which I half believed, half doubted, that I had encountered the eyes.

I strove to speak, – my voice utterly failed me; I could only think to myself, "Is this fear? It is NOT fear!" I strove to rise, – in vain; I felt as if weighed down by an irresistible force. Indeed, my impression was that of an immense and overwhelming Power opposed to my volition, – that sense of utter inadequacy to cope with a force beyond man's, which one may feel PHYSICALLY in a storm at sea, in a conflagration, or when confronting some terrible wild beast, or rather, perhaps, the shark of the ocean, I felt MORALLY. Opposed to my will was another will, as far superior to its strength as storm, fire, and shark are superior in material force to the force of man.

And now, as this impression grew on me, – now came, at

last, horror, horror to a degree that no words can convey. Still I retained pride, if not courage; and in my own mind I said, "This is horror; but it is not fear; unless I fear I cannot be harmed; my reason rejects this thing; it is an illusion, – I do not fear." With a violent effort I succeeded at last in stretching out my hand toward the weapon on the table; as I did so, on the arm and shoulder I received a strange shock, and my arm fell to my side powerless. And now, to add to my horror, the light began slowly to wane from the candles, – they were not, as it were, extinguished, but their flame seemed very gradually withdrawn; it was the same with the fire, – the light was extracted from the fuel; in a few minutes the room was in utter darkness. The dread that came over me, to be thus in the dark with that dark Thing, whose power was so intensely felt, brought a reaction of nerve. In fact, terror had reached that climax, that either my senses must have deserted me, or I must have burst through the spell. I did burst through it. I found voice, though the voice was a shriek. I remember that I broke forth with words like these, "I do not fear, my soul does not fear"; and at the same time I found strength to rise. Still in that profound gloom I rushed to one of the windows; tore aside the curtain; flung open the shutters; my first thought was – LIGHT. And when I saw the moon high, clear, and calm, I felt a joy that almost compensated for the previous terror. There was the moon, there was also the light from the gas lamps in the deserted slumberous street. I turned to look back into the room; the moon penetrated its shadow very palely and partially – but still there was light. The dark Thing, whatever it might be, was gone, – except that I could yet see a dim shadow, which seemed the shadow of that shade, against the opposite wall.

My eye now rested on the table, and from under the table (which was without cloth or cover, – an old mahogany round table) there rose a hand, visible as far as the wrist. It was a hand, seemingly, as much of flesh and blood as my own, but the hand of an aged person, lean, wrinkled, small too, – a woman's hand. That hand very softly closed on the two letters that lay on the table; hand and letters both vanished. There then came the same three loud, measured knocks I had heard at the bed head before this extraordinary drama had commenced.

As those sounds slowly ceased, I felt the whole room vibrate sensibly; and at the far end there rose, as from the floor, sparks or globules like bubbles of light, many colored, – green, yellow, fire-red, azure. Up and down, to and fro, hither, thither as tiny Will-o'-the-Wisps, the sparks moved, slow or swift, each at its own caprice. A chair (as in the drawing-room below) was now advanced from the wall without apparent agency, and placed at the opposite side of the table. Suddenly, as forth from the chair, there grew a shape, – a woman's shape. It was distinct as a shape of life, – ghastly as a shape of death. The face was that of youth, with a strange, mournful beauty; the throat and shoulders were bare, the rest of the form in a loose robe of cloudy white. It began sleeking its long, yellow hair, which fell over its shoulders; its eyes were not turned toward me, but to the door; it seemed listening, watching, waiting. The shadow of the shade in the background grew darker; and again I thought I beheld the eyes gleaming out from the summit of the shadow, – eyes fixed upon that shape.

As if from the door, though it did not open, there grew out another shape, equally distinct, equally ghastly, – a man's shape, a young man's. It was in the dress of the last century, or rather in a likeness of such dress (for both the male shape and the female, though defined, were evidently unsubstantial, impalpable, – simulacra, phantasms); and there was something incongruous, grotesque, yet fearful, in the contrast between the elaborate finery, the courtly precision of that old-fashioned garb, with its ruffles and lace and buckles, and the corpselike aspect and ghostlike stillness of the flitting wearer. Just as the male shape approached the female, the dark Shadow started from the wall, all three for a moment wrapped in darkness. When the pale light returned, the two phantoms were as if in the grasp of the Shadow that towered between them; and there was a blood stain on the breast of the female; and the phantom male was leaning on its phantom sword, and blood seemed trickling fast from the ruffles from the lace; and the darkness of the intermediate Shadow swallowed them up, – they were gone. And again the bubbles of light shot, and sailed, and undulated, growing thicker and thicker and more wildly confused in their movements.

The closet door to the right of the fireplace now opened, and from the aperture there came the form of an aged woman. In her hand she held letters, – the very letters over which I had seen THE Hand close; and behind her I heard a footstep. She turned round as if to listen, and then she opened the letters and seemed to read; and over her shoulder I saw a livid face, the face as of a man long drowned, – bloated, bleached, seaweed tangled in its dripping hair; and at her feet lay a form as of a corpse; and beside the corpse there cowered a child, a miserable, squalid child, with famine in its cheeks and fear in its eyes. And as I looked in the old woman's face, the wrinkles and lines vanished, and it became a face of youth, – hard-eyed, stony, but still youth; and the Shadow darted forth, and darkened over these phantoms as it had darkened over the last.

Nothing now was left but the Shadow, and on that my eyes were intently fixed, till again eyes grew out of the Shadow, – malignant, serpent eyes. And the bubbles of light again rose and fell, and in their disordered, irregular, turbulent maze, mingled with the wan moonlight. And now from these globules themselves, as from the shell of an egg, monstrous things burst out; the air grew filled with them: larvae so bloodless and so hideous that I can in no way describe them except to remind the reader of the swarming life which the solar microscope brings before his eyes in a drop of water, – things transparent, supple, agile, chasing each other, devouring each other; forms like naught ever beheld by the naked eye. As the shapes were without symmetry, so their movements were without order. In their very vagrancies there was no sport; they came round me and round, thicker and faster and swifter, swarming over my head, crawling over my right arm, which was outstretched in involuntary command against all evil beings. Sometimes I felt myself touched, but not by them; invisible hands touched me. Once I felt the clutch as of cold, soft fingers at my throat. I was still equally conscious that if I gave way to fear I should be in bodily peril; and I concentered all my faculties in the single focus of resisting stubborn will. And I turned my sight from the Shadow; above all, from those strange serpent eyes, – eyes that had now become distinctly visible. For there, though in naught else around me, I was aware that there was a WILL, and will of intense, creative, working evil, which might crush down my own.

The pale atmosphere in the room began now to redden as if in the air of some near conflagration. The larvae grew lurid as things that live in fire. Again the room vibrated; again were heard the three measured knocks; and again all things were swallowed up in the darkness of the dark Shadow, as if out of that darkness all had come, into that darkness all returned.

As the gloom receded, the Shadow was wholly gone. Slowly, as it had been withdrawn, the flame grew again into the candles on the table, again into the fuel in the grate. The whole room came once more calmly, healthfully into sight.

The two doors were still closed, the door communicating with the servant's room still locked. In the corner of the wall, into which he had so convulsively niched himself, lay the dog. I called to him, - no movement; I approached, - the animal was dead: his eyes protruded; his tongue out of his mouth; the froth gathered round his jaws. I took him in my arms; I brought him to the fire. I felt acute grief for the loss of my poor favorite, - acute self- reproach; I accused myself of his death; I imagined he had died of fright. But what was my surprise on finding that his neck was actually broken. Had this been done in the dark? Must it not have been by a hand human as mine; must there not have been a human agency all the while in that room? Good cause to suspect it. I cannot tell. I cannot do more than state the fact fairly; the reader may draw his own inference.

Another surprising circumstance, - my watch was restored to the table from which it had been so mysteriously withdrawn; but it had stopped at the very moment it was so withdrawn, nor, despite all the skill of the watchmaker, has it ever gone since, - that is, it will go in a strange, erratic way for a few hours, and then come to a dead stop; it is worthless.

Nothing more chanced for the rest of the night. Nor, indeed, had I long to wait before the dawn broke. Not till it was broad daylight did I quit the haunted house. Before I did so, I revisited the little blind room in which my servant and myself had been for a time imprisoned. I had a strong impression – for which I could not account – that from that room had originated the mechanism of the phenomena, if I may use the term, which had been experienced in my chamber. And though I entered it now in the clear day, with the sun peering through the filmy window, I still felt, as I stood on its floors, the creep of the horror which I had first there experienced the night before, and which had been so aggravated by what had passed in my own chamber. I could not, indeed, bear to stay more than half a minute within those walls. I descended the stairs, and again I heard the footfall before me; and when I opened the street door, I thought I could distinguish a very low laugh. I gained my own home, expecting to find my runaway servant there; but he had not presented himself, nor did I hear more of him for three days, when I received a letter from him, dated from Liverpool to this effect: –

"HONORED SIR, – I humbly entreat your pardon, though I can scarcely hope that you will think that I deserve it, unless – which Heaven forbid! – you saw what I did. I feel that it will be years before I can recover myself; and as to being fit for service, it is out of the question. I am therefore going to my brother-in-law at Melbourne. The ship sails to-morrow. Perhaps the long voyage may set me up. I do nothing now but start and tremble, and fancy it is behind me. I humbly beg you, honored sir, to order my clothes, and whatever wages are due to me, to be sent to my mother's, at Walworth, – John knows her address."

The letter ended with additional apologies, somewhat incoherent, and explanatory details as to effects that had been under the writer's charge.

This flight may perhaps warrant a suspicion that the man wished to go to Australia, and had been somehow or other fraudulently mixed up with the events of the night. I say nothing in refutation of that conjecture; rather, I suggest it as one that would seem to many persons the most probable solution of improbable occurrences. My belief in my own theory remained unshaken. I returned in the evening to the house, to bring away in a hack cab the things I had left there, with my poor dog's body. In this task I was not disturbed, nor did any incident worth note befall me, except that still, on ascending and descending the stairs, I heard the same footfall in advance. On leaving the house, I went to Mr. J – – 's. He was at home. I returned him the keys, told him that my curiosity was sufficiently gratified, and was about to relate quickly what had passed, when he stopped me, and said, though with much politeness, that he had no longer any interest in a mystery which none had ever solved.

I determined at least to tell him of the two letters I had read, as well as of the extraordinary manner in which they had disappeared; and I then inquired if he thought they had been addressed to the woman who had died in the house, and if there were anything in her early history which could possibly confirm the dark suspicions to which the letters gave rise. Mr. J – – seemed startled, and, after musing a few moments, answered, "I am but little acquainted with the woman's earlier history, except as I before told you, that her family were known to mine. But you revive some vague reminiscences to her prejudice. I will make inquiries, and inform you of their result. Still, even if we could admit the popular superstition that a person who had been either the perpetrator or the victim of dark crimes in life could revisit, as a restless spirit, the scene in which those crimes had been committed, I should observe that the house was infested by strange sights and sounds before the old woman died – you smile – what would you say?"

"I would say this, that I am convinced, if we could get to the bottom of these mysteries, we should find a living human agency."

"What! you believe it is all an imposture? For what object?"

"Not an imposture in the ordinary sense of the word. If suddenly I were to sink into a deep sleep, from which you could not awake me, but in that sleep could answer questions with an accuracy which I could not pretend to when awake, – tell you what money you had in your pocket, nay, describe your very thoughts, – it is not necessarily an imposture, any more than it is necessarily supernatural. I should be, unconsciously to myself, under a mesmeric influence, conveyed to me from a distance by a human being who had acquired power over me by previous rapport."

"But if a mesmerizer could so affect another living being, can you suppose that a mesmerizer could also affect inanimate objects: move chairs, - open and shut doors?"

"Or impress our senses with the belief in such effects, - we never having been en rapport with the person acting on us? No. What is commonly called mesmerism could not do this; but there may be a power akin to mesmerism, and superior to it, - the power that in the old days was called Magic. That such a power may extend to all inanimate objects of matter, I do not say; but if so, it would not be against Nature, - it would be only a rare power in Nature which might be given to constitutions with certain peculiarities, and cultivated by practice to an extraordinary degree. That such a power might extend over the dead, - that is, over certain thoughts and memories that the dead may still retain, - and compel, not that which ought properly to be called the SOUL, and which is far beyond human reach, but rather a phantom of what has been most earth- stained on earth, to make itself apparent to our senses, is a very ancient though obsolete theory upon which I will hazard no opinion. But I do not conceive the power would be supernatural. Let me illustrate what I mean from an experiment which Paracelsus describes as not difficult, and which the author of the 'Curiosities of Literature' cites as credible: A flower perishes; you burn it. Whatever were the elements of that flower while it lived are gone, dispersed, you know not whither; you can never discover nor re-collect them. But you can, by chemistry, out of the burned dust of that flower, raise a spectrum of the flower, just as it seemed in life. It may be the same with the human being. The soul has as much escaped you as the essence or elements of the flower. Still you may make a spectrum of it. And this phantom, though in the popular superstition it is held to be the soul of the departed, must not be confounded with the true soul; it is but the eidolon of the dead form. Hence, like the best-attested stories of ghosts or spirits, the thing that most strikes us is the absence of what we hold to be soul, - that is, of superior emancipated intelligence. These apparitions come for little or no object, - they seldom speak when they do come; if they speak, they utter no ideas above those of an ordinary person on earth. American spirit seers have published volumes of communications, in prose and verse, which they assert to be given in the names of the most illustrious dead: Shakespeare, Bacon, – Heaven knows whom. Those communications, taking the best, are certainly not a whit of higher order than would be communications from living persons of fair talent and education; they are wondrously inferior to what Bacon, Shakespeare, and Plato said and wrote when on earth. Nor, what is more noticeable, do they ever contain an idea that was not on the earth before. Wonderful, therefore, as such phenomena may be (granting them to be truthful), I see much that philosophy may question, nothing that it is incumbent on philosophy to deny, – namely, nothing supernatural. They are but ideas conveyed somehow or other (we have not yet discovered the means) from one mortal brain to another. Whether, in so doing, tables walk of their own accord, or fiendlike shapes appear in a magic circle, or bodiless hands rise and remove material objects, or a Thing of Darkness, such as presented itself to me, freeze our blood, – still am I persuaded that these are but agencies conveyed, as by electric wires, to my own brain from the brain of another. In some constitutions there is a natural chemistry, and those constitutions may produce chemic wonders, – in others a natural fluid, call it electricity, and these may produce electric wonders. But the wonders differ from Normal Science in this, – they are alike objectless, purposeless, puerile, frivolous. They lead on to no grand results; and therefore the world does not heed, and true sages have not cultivated them. But sure I am, that of all I saw or heard, a man, human as myself, was the remote originator; and I believe unconsciously to himself as to the exact effects produced, for this reason: no two persons, you say, have ever told you that they experienced exactly the same thing. Well, observe, no two persons ever experience exactly the same dream. If this were an ordinary imposture, the machinery would be arranged for results that would but little vary; if it were a supernatural agency permitted by the Almighty, it would surely be for some definite end. These phenomena belong to neither class; my persuasion is, that they originate in some brain now far distant; that that brain had no distinct volition in anything that occurred; that what does occur reflects but its devious, motley, ever-shifting, half-formed thoughts; in short, that it has been but the dreams of such a brain put into action and invested with a semisubstance. That this brain is of immense power, that it can set matter into movement, that it is malignant and destructive, I believe; some material force must have killed my dog; the same force might, for aught I know, have sufficed to kill myself, had I been as subjugated by terror as the dog, – had my intellect or my spirit given me no countervailing resistance in my will."

"It killed your dog, – that is fearful! Indeed it is strange that no animal can be induced to stay in that house; not even a cat. Rats and mice are never found in it."

"The instincts of the brute creation detect influences deadly to their existence. Man's reason has a sense less subtle, because it has a resisting power more supreme. But enough; do you comprehend my theory?"

"Yes, though imperfectly, – and I accept any crotchet (pardon the word), however odd, rather than embrace at once the notion of ghosts and hobgoblins we imbibed in our nurseries. Still, to my unfortunate house, the evil is the same. What on earth can I do with the house?"

"I will tell you what I would do. I am convinced from my own internal feelings that the small, unfurnished room at right angles to the door of the bedroom which I occupied, forms a starting point or receptacle for the influences which haunt the house; and I strongly advise you to have the walls opened, the floor removed, – nay, the whole room pulled down. I observe that it is detached from the body of the house, built over the small backyard, and could be removed without injury to the rest of the building."

"And you think, if I did that – "

"You would cut off the telegraph wires. Try it. I am so persuaded that I am right, that I will pay half the expense if you will allow me to direct the operations."

"Nay, I am well able to afford the cost; for the rest allow me to write to you."

About ten days after I received a letter from Mr. J – – telling me that he had visited the house since I had seen him; that he had found the two letters I had described, replaced in the drawer from which I had taken them; that he had read them with misgivings like my own; that he had instituted a cautious inquiry about the woman to whom I rightly conjectured they had been written. It seemed that thirty-six years ago (a year before the date of the letters) she had married, against the wish of her relations, an American of very suspicions character; in fact, he was generally believed to have been a pirate. She herself was the daughter of very respectable tradespeople, and had served in the capacity of a nursery governess before her marriage. She had a brother, a widower, who was considered wealthy, and who had one child of about six years old. A month after the marriage the body of this brother was found in the Thames, near London Bridge; there seemed some marks of violence about his throat, but they were not deemed sufficient to warrant the inquest in any other verdict that that of "found drowned."

The American and his wife took charge of the little boy, the deceased brother having by his will left his sister the guardian of his only child, – and in event of the child's death the sister inherited. The child died about six months afterwards, – it was supposed to have been neglected and ill-treated. The neighbors deposed to have heard it shriek at night. The surgeon who had examined it after death said that it was emaciated as if from want of nourishment, and the body was covered with livid bruises. It seemed that one winter night the child had sought to escape; crept out into the back yard; tried to scale the wall; fallen back exhausted; and been found at morning on the stones in a dying state. But though there was some evidence of cruelty, there was none of murder; and the aunt and her husband had sought to palliate cruelty by alleging the exceeding stubbornness and perversity of the child, who was declared to be half-witted. Be that as it may, at the orphan's death the aunt inherited her brother's fortune. Before the first wedded year was out, the American quitted England abruptly, and never returned to it. He obtained a cruising vessel, which was lost in the Atlantic two years afterwards. The widow was left in affluence, but reverses of various kinds had befallen her: a bank broke; an investment failed; she went into a small business and became insolvent; then she entered into service, sinking lower and lower, from housekeeper down to maid-of-all-work, – never long retaining a place, though nothing decided against her character was ever alleged. She was considered sober, honest, and peculiarly quiet in her ways; still nothing prospered with her. And so she had dropped into the workhouse, from which Mr. J – – had taken her, to be placed in charge of the very house which she had rented as mistress in the first year of her wedded life.

Mr. J – – added that he had passed an hour alone in the unfurnished room which I had urged him to destroy, and that his impressions of dread while there were so great, though he had neither heard nor seen anything, that he was eager to have the walls bared and the floors removed as I had suggested. He had engaged persons for the work, and would commence any day I would name.

The day was accordingly fixed. I repaired to the haunted house, – we went into the blind, dreary room, took up the skirting, and then the floors. Under the rafters, covered with rubbish, was found a trapdoor, quite large enough to admit a man. It was closely nailed down, with clamps and rivets of iron. On removing these we descended into a room below, the existence of which had never been suspected. In this room there had been a window and a flue, but they had been bricked over, evidently for many years. By the help of candles we examined this place; it still retained some moldering furniture, – three chairs, an oak settle, a table, – all of the fashion of about eighty years ago. There was a chest of drawers against the wall, in which we found, half rotted away, old-fashioned articles of a man's dress, such as might have been worn eighty or a hundred years ago by a gentleman of some rank; costly steel buckles and buttons, like those yet worn in court dresses, a handsome court sword; in a waistcoat which had once been rich with gold lace, but which was now blackened and foul with damp, we found five guineas, a few silver coins, and an ivory ticket, probably for some place of entertainment long since passed away. But our main discovery was in a kind of iron safe fixed to the wall, the lock of which it cost us much trouble to get picked.

In this safe were three shelves and two small drawers. Ranged on the shelves were several small bottles of crystal, hermetically stopped. They contained colorless, volatile essences, of the nature of which I shall only say that they were not poisons, – phosphor and ammonia entered into some of them. There were also some very curious glass tubes, and a small pointed rod of iron, with a large lump of rock crystal, and another of amber, – also a loadstone of great power.

In one of the drawers we found a miniature portrait set in gold, and retaining the freshness of its colors most remarkably, considering the length of time it had probably been there. The portrait was that of a man who might be somewhat advanced in middle life, perhaps forty-seven or forty-eight. It was a remarkable face, – a most impressive face. If you could fancy some mighty serpent transformed into man, preserving in the human lineaments the old serpent type, you would have a better idea of that countenance than long descriptions can convey: the width and flatness of frontal; the tapering elegance of contour disguising the strength of the deadly jaw; the long, large, terrible eye, glittering and green as the emerald, – and withal a certain ruthless calm, as if from the consciousness of an immense power.

Mechanically I turned round the miniature to examine the back of it, and on the back was engraved a pentacle; in the middle of the pentacle a ladder, and the third step of the ladder was formed by the date 1765. Examining still more minutely, I detected a spring; this, on being pressed, opened the back of the miniature as a lid. Within-side the lid were engraved, "Marianna to thee. Be faithful in life and in death to – – ." Here follows a name that I will not mention, but it was not unfamiliar to me. I had heard it spoken of by old men in my childhood as the name borne by a dazzling charlatan who had made a great sensation in London for a year or so, and had fled the country on the charge of a double murder within his own house, – that of his mistress and his rival. I said nothing of this to Mr. J - - , to whom reluctantly I resigned the miniature.

We had found no difficulty in opening the first drawer within the iron safe; we found great difficulty in opening the second: it was not locked, but it resisted all efforts, till we inserted in the chinks the edge of a chisel. When we had thus drawn it forth, we found a very singular apparatus in the nicest order. Upon a small, thin book, or rather tablet, was placed a saucer of crystal; this saucer was filled with a clear liquid, – on that liquid floated a kind of compass, with a needle shifting rapidly round; but instead of the usual points of a compass were seven strange characters, not very unlike those used by astrologers to denote the planets. A peculiar but not strong nor displeasing odor came from this drawer, which was lined with a wood that we afterwards discovered to be hazel. Whatever the cause of this odor, it produced a material effect on the nerves. We all felt it, even the two workmen who were in the room, – a creeping, tingling sensation from the tips of the fingers to the roots of the hair. Impatient to examine the tablet, I removed the saucer. As I did so the needle of the compass went round and round with exceeding swiftness, and I felt a shock that ran through my whole frame, so that I dropped the saucer on the floor. The liquid was spilled; the saucer was broken; the compass rolled to the end of the room, and at that instant the walls shook to and fro, as if a giant had swayed and rocked them.

The two workmen were so frightened that they ran up the ladder by which we had descended from the trapdoor; but seeing that nothing more happened, they were easily induced to return.

Meanwhile I had opened the tablet: it was bound in plain red leather, with a silver clasp; it contained but one sheet of thick vellum, and on that sheet were inscribed, within a double pentacle, words in old monkish Latin, which are literally to be translated thus: "On all that it can reach within these walls, sentient or inanimate, living or dead, as moves the needle, so works my will! Accursed be the house, and restless be the dwellers therein."

We found no more. Mr. J - - burned the tablet and its anathema. He razed to the foundations the part of the building containing the secret room with the chamber over it. He had then the courage to inhabit the house himself for a month, and a quieter, better- conditioned house could not be found in all London. Subsequently he let it to advantage, and his tenant has made no complaints.

A drowning man clutching at a straw – such is Dr. Fenwick, hero of Bulwer-Lytton's "Strange Story" when he determines to lend himself to alleged "magic" in the hope of saving his suffering wife from the physical dangers which have succeeded her mental disease. The proposition has been made to him by Margrave, a wanderer in many countries, who has followed the Fenwicks from England to Australia. Margrave declares that he needs an accomplice to secure an "elixir of life" which his own failing strength demands. His mysterious mesmeric or hypnotic influence over Mrs. Fenwick had in former days been marked; and on the basis of this undeniable fact, he has endeavored to show that his own welfare and Mrs. Fenwick's are, in some occult fashion, knit together, and that only by aiding him in some extraordinary experiment can the physician snatch his beloved Lilian from her impending doom.

As the first chapter opens, Fenwick is learning his wife's condition from his friend, Dr. Faber.

The Incantation

I

"I believe that for at least twelve hours there will be no change in her state. I believe also that if she recover from it, calm and refreshed, as from a sleep, the danger of death will have passed away."

"And for twelve hours my presence would be hurtful?"

"Rather say fatal, if my diagnosis be right."

I wrung my friend's hand, and we parted.

Oh, to lose her now; now that her love and her reason had

both
returned, each more vivid than before! Futile, indeed, might be
Margrave's boasted secret; but at least in that secret was hope.
In recognized science I saw only despair.

And at that thought all dread of this mysterious visitor vanished – all anxiety to question more of his attributes or his history. His life itself became to me dear and precious. What if it
should fail me in the steps of the process, whatever that was, by
which the life of my Lilian might be saved!

The shades of evening were now closing in. I remembered
that I had left Margrave without even food for many hours. I stole
round to the back of the house, filled a basket with elements more
generous than those of the former day; extracted fresh drugs from
my stores, and, thus laden, hurried back to the hut. I found Margrave in the room below, seated on his mysterious coffer, leaning
his face on his hand. When I entered, he looked up, and said:

"You have neglected me. My strength is waning. Give me
more of the cordial, for we have work before us tonight, and I
need support."

He took for granted my assent to his wild experiment; and
he was right.

I administered the cordial. I placed food before him, and this
time he did not eat with repugnance. I poured out wine, and he
drank it sparingly, but with ready compliance, saying, "In perfect
health, I looked upon wine as poison; now it is like a foretaste of
the glorious elixir."

After he had thus recruited himself, he seemed to acquire an
energy that startlingly contrasted with his languor the day before;
the effort of breathing was scarcely perceptible; the color came
back to his cheeks; his bended frame rose elastic and erect.

"If I understood you rightly," said I, "the experiment you ask
me to aid can be accomplished in a single night?"

"In a single night – this night."

"Command me. Why not begin at once? What apparatus or

chemical agencies do you need?"

"Ah!" said Margrave. "Formerly, how I was misled! Formerly, how my conjectures blundered! I thought, when I asked you to give a month to the experiment I wish to make, that I should need the subtlest skill of the chemist. I then believed, with Van Helmont, that the principle of life is a gas, and that the secret was but in the mode by which the gas might be rightly administered. But now, all that I need is contained in this coffer, save one very simple material – fuel sufficient for a steady fire for six hours. I see even that is at hand, piled up in your outhouse. And now for the substance itself – to that you must guide me."

"Explain."

"Near this very spot is there not gold – in mines yet undiscovered – and gold of the purest metal?"

"There is. What then? Do you, with the alchemists, blend in one discovery, gold and life?"

"No. But it is only where the chemistry of earth or of man produces gold, that the substance from which the great pabulum of life is extracted by ferment can be found. Possibly, in the attempts at that transmutation of metals, which I think your own great chemist, Sir Humphry Davy, allowed might be possible, but held not to be worth the cost of the process – possibly, in those attempts, some scanty grains of this substance were found by the alchemists, in the crucible, with grains of the metal as niggardly yielded by pitiful mimicry of Nature's stupendous laboratory; and from such grains enough of the essence might, perhaps, have been drawn forth, to add a few years of existence to some feeble graybeard – granting, what rests on no proofs, that some of the alchemists reached an age rarely given to man. But it is not in the miserly crucible, it is in the matrix of Nature herself, that we must seek in prolific abundance Nature's grand principle – life. As the loadstone is rife with the magnetic virtue, as amber contains the electric, so in this substance, to which we yet want a name, is found the bright life-giving fluid. In the old gold mines of Asia and Europe the substance exists, but can rarely be met with. The soil for its nutriment may there be well nigh exhausted. It is here, where Nature herself is all vital with youth, that the nutriment of youth must be sought. Near this spot is gold; guide me to it."

"You cannot come with me. The place which I know as auriferous is some miles distant, the way rugged. You cannot walk to it. It is true I have horses, but – "

"Do you think I have come this distance and not foreseen and forestalled all that I want for my object? Trouble yourself not with conjectures how I can arrive at the place. I have provided the means to arrive at and leave it. My litter and its bearers are in reach of my call. Give me your arm to the rising ground, fifty yards from your door."

I obeyed mechanically, stifling all surprise. I had made my resolve, and admitted no thought that could shake it.

When we reached the summit of the grassy hillock, which sloped from the road that led to the seaport, Margrave, after pausing to recover breath, lifted up his voice, in a key, not loud, but shrill and slow and prolonged, half cry and half chant, like the nighthawk's. Through the air – so limpid and still, bringing near far objects, far sounds – the voice pierced its way, artfully pausing, till wave after wave of the atmosphere bore and transmitted it on.

In a few minutes the call seemed re-echoed, so exactly, so cheerily, that for the moment I thought that the note was the mimicry of the shy mocking lyre bird, which mimics so merrily all that it hears in its coverts, from the whir of the locust to the howl of the wild dog.

"What king," said the mystical charmer, and as he spoke he carelessly rested his hand on my shoulder, so that I trembled to feel that this dread son of Nature, Godless and soulless, who had been – and, my heart whispered, who still could be – my bane and mind darkener, leaned upon me for support, as the spoiled younger-born on his brother – "what king," said this cynical mocker, with his beautiful boyish face – "what king in your civilized Europe has the sway of a chief of the East? What link is so strong between mortal and mortal as that between lord and slave? I transport you poor fools from the land of their birth; they preserve here their old habits – obedience and awe. They would wait till they starved in the solitude – wait to hearken and answer my call. And I, who thus rule them, or charm them – I use and despise them. They know that, and yet serve me! Between you and me, my philosopher, there is but one thing worth living for – life for oneself."

Is it age, is it youth, that thus shocks all my sense, in my solemn completeness of man? Perhaps, in great capitals, young men of pleasure will answer, "It is youth; and we think what he says!" Young friends, I do not believe you.

II

Along the grass track I saw now, under the moon, just risen, a strange procession – never seen before in Australian pastures. It moved on, noiselessly but quickly. We descended the hillock, and met it on the way; a sable litter, borne by four men, in unfamiliar Eastern garments; two other servitors, more bravely dressed, with yataghans and silver-hilted pistols in their belts, preceded this somber equipage. Perhaps Margrave divined the disdainful thought that passed through my mind, vaguely and half-unconsciously; for he said with a hollow, bitter laugh that had replaced the lively peal of his once melodious mirth:

"A little leisure and a little gold, and your raw colonist, too, will have the tastes of a pasha."

I made no answer. I had ceased to care who and what was my tempter. To me his whole being was resolved into one problem: had he a secret by which death could be turned from Lilian?

But now, as the litter halted, from the long, dark shadow which it cast upon the turf, the figure of a woman emerged and stood before us. The outlines of her shape were lost in the loose folds of a black mantle, and the features of her face were hidden by a black veil, except only the dark-bright, solemn eyes. Her stature was lofty, her bearing majestic, whether in movement or repose.

Margrave accosted her in some language unknown to me. She replied in what seemed to me the same tongue. The tones of her voice were sweet, but inexpressibly mournful. The words that they uttered appeared intended to warn, or deprecate, or dissuade; but they called to Margrave's brow a lowering frown, and drew from his lips a burst of unmistakable anger. The woman rejoined, in the same melancholy music of voice. And Margrave then, leaning his arm upon her shoulder, as he had leaned it on mine, drew her away from the group into a neighboring copse of the flowering eucalypti – mystic trees, never changing the hues of their pale-green leaves, ever shifting the tints of their ash-gray, shedding bark. For some moments I gazed on the two human forms, dimly seen by the glinting moonlight through the gaps in the foliage. Then turning away my eyes, I saw, standing close at my side, a man whom I had not noticed before. His footstep, as it stole to me, had fallen on the sward without sound. His dress, though Oriental, differed from that of his companions, both in shape and color – fitting close to the breast, leaving the arms bare to the elbow, and of a uniform ghastly white, as are the cerements of the grave. His visage was even darker than those of the Syrians or Arabs behind him, and his features were those of a bird of prey: the beak of the eagle, but the eye of the vulture. His cheeks were hollow; the arms, crossed on his breast, were long and fleshless. Yet in that skeleton form there was a something which conveyed the idea of a serpent's suppleness and strength; and as the hungry, watchful eyes met my own startled gaze, I recoiled impulsively with that inward warning of danger which is conveyed to man, as to inferior animals, in the very aspect of the creatures that sting or devour. At my movement the man inclined his head in the submissive Eastern salutation, and spoke in his foreign tongue, softly, humbly, fawningly, to judge by his tone and his gesture.

I moved yet farther away from him with loathing, and now the human thought flashed upon me: was I, in truth, exposed to no danger in trusting myself to the mercy of the weird and remorseless master of those hirelings from the East – seven men in number, two at least of them formidably armed, and docile as bloodhounds to the hunter, who has only to show them their prey? But fear of man like myself is not my weakness; where fear found its way to my heart, it was through the doubts or the fancies in which man like myself disappeared in the attributes, dark and unknown, which we give to a fiend or a specter. And, perhaps, if I could have paused to analyze my own sensations, the very presence of this escort – creatures of flesh and blood – lessened the dread of my incomprehensible tempter. Rather, a hundred times, front and defy those seven Eastern slaves – I, haughty son of the Anglo-Saxon who conquers all races because he fears no odds – than have seen again on the walls of my threshold the luminous, bodiless shadow! Besides: Lilian – Lilian! for one chance of saving her life, however wild and chimerical that chance might be, I would have shrunk not a foot from the march of an army.

Thus reassured and thus resolved, I advanced, with a smile of disdain, to meet Margrave and his veiled companion, as they now came from the moonlit copse.

"Well," I said to him, with an irony that unconsciously mimicked his own, "have you taken advice with your nurse? I assume that the dark form by your side is that of Ayesha!"*

* Margrave's former nurse and attendant.

The woman looked at me from her sable veil, with her steadfast, solemn eyes, and said, in English, though with a foreign accent: "The nurse born in Asia is but wise through her love; the pale son of Europe is wise through his art. The nurse says, 'Forbear!' Do you say, 'Adventure'?"

"Peace!" exclaimed Margrave, stamping his foot on the ground. "I take no counsel from either; it is for me to resolve, for you to obey, and for him to aid. Night is come, and we waste it; move on."

The woman made no reply, nor did I. He took my arm and walked back to the hut. The barbaric escort followed. When we reached the door of the building, Margrave said a few words to the woman and to the litter bearers. They entered the hut with us. Margrave pointed out to the woman his coffer, to the men the fuel stowed in the outhouse. Both were borne away and placed within the litter. Meanwhile I took from the table, on which it was carelessly thrown, the light hatchet that I habitually carried with me in my rambles.

"Do you think that you need that idle weapon?" said Margrave. "Do you fear the good faith of my swarthy attendants?"

"Nay, take the hatchet yourself; its use is to sever the gold from the quartz in which we may find it imbedded, or to clear, as this shovel, which will also be needed, from the slight soil above it, the ore that the mine in the mountain flings forth, as the sea casts its waifs on the sands."

"Give me your hand, fellow laborer!" said Margrave, joyfully. "Ah, there is no faltering terror in this pulse! I was not mistaken in the man. What rests, but the place and the hour? – I shall live, I shall live!"

III

Margrave now entered the litter, and the Veiled Woman drew the black curtains round him. I walked on, as the guide, some yards in advance. The air was still, heavy, and parched with the breath of the Australasian sirocco.

We passed through the meadow lands, studded with slumbering flocks; we followed the branch of the creek, which was linked to its source in the mountains by many a trickling waterfall; we threaded the gloom of stunted, misshapen trees, gnarled with the stringy bark which makes one of the signs of the strata that nourish gold; and at length the moon, now in all her pomp of light, mid-heaven among her subject stars, gleamed through the fissures of the cave, on whose floor lay the relics of antediluvian races, and rested in one flood of silvery splendor upon the hollows of the extinct volcano, with tufts of dank herbage, and wide spaces of paler sward, covering the gold below – gold, the dumb symbol of organized Matter's great mystery, storing in itself, according as Mind, the informer of Matter, can distinguish its uses, evil and good, bane and blessing.

Hitherto the Veiled Woman had remained in the rear, with the white- robed, skeletonlike image that had crept to my side unawares with its noiseless step. Thus, in each winding turn of the difficult path at which the convoy following behind me came into sight, I had seen, first, the two gayly dressed, armed men, next the black, bierlike litter, and last the Black-veiled Woman and the White- robed Skeleton.

But now, as I halted on the tableland, backed by the mountain and fronting the valley, the woman left her companion, passed by the litter and the armed men, and paused by my side, at the mouth of the moonlit cavern.

There for a moment she stood, silent, the procession below mounting upward laboriously and slow; then she turned to me, and her veil was withdrawn.

The face on which I gazed was wondrously beautiful, and severely awful. There was neither youth nor age, but beauty, mature and majestic as that of a marble Demeter.

"Do you believe in that which you seek?" she asked in her foreign, melodious, melancholy accents.

"I have no belief," was my answer. "True science has none. True science questions all things, takes nothing upon credit. It knows but three states of the mind – denial, conviction, and that vast interval between the two which is not belief but suspense of judgment."

The woman let fall her veil, moved from me, and seated herself on a crag above that cleft between mountain and creek, to which, when I had first discovered the gold that the land nourished, the rain from the clouds had given the rushing life of the cataract; but which now, in the drought and the hush of the skies, was but a dead pile of stones.

The litter now ascended the height: its bearers halted; a lean hand tore the curtains aside, and Margrave descended leaning, this time, not on the Black-veiled Woman, but on the White-robed Skeleton.

There, as he stood, the moon shone full on his wasted form; on his face, resolute, cheerful, and proud, despite its hollowed outlines and sicklied hues. He raised his head, spoke in the language unknown to me, and the armed men and the litter bearers grouped round him, bending low, their eyes fixed on the ground. The Veiled Woman rose slowly and came to his side, motioning away, with a mute sign, the ghastly form on which he leaned, and passing round him silently, instead, her own sustaining arm. Margrave spoke again a few sentences, of which I could not even guess the meaning. When he had concluded, the armed men and the litter bearers came nearer to his feet, knelt down, and kissed his hand. They then rose, and took from the bierlike vehicle the coffer and the fuel. This done, they lifted again the litter, and again, preceded by the armed men, the procession descended down the sloping hillside, down into the valley below.

Margrave now whispered, for some moments, into the ear of the hideous creature who had made way for the Veiled Woman. The grim skeleton bowed his head submissively, and strode noiselessly away through the long grasses – the slender stems, trampled under his stealthy feet, relifting themselves as after a passing wind. And thus he, too, sank out of sight down into the valley below. On the tableland of the hill remained only we three – Margrave, myself, and the Veiled Woman.

She had reseated herself apart, on the gray crag above the dried torrent. He stood at the entrance of the cavern, round the sides of which clustered parasital plants, with flowers of all colors, some among them opening their petals and exhaling their fragrance only in the hours of night; so that, as his form filled up the jaws of the dull arch, obscuring the moonbeam that strove to pierce the shadows that slept within, it stood now – wan and blighted – as I had seen it first, radiant and joyous, literally "framed in blooms."

IV

"So," said Margrave, turning to me, "under the soil that spreads around us lies the gold which to you and to me is at this moment of no value, except as a guide to its twin-born – the regenerator of life!"

"You have not yet described to me the nature of the substance which we are to explore, nor the process by which the virtues you impute to it are to be extracted."

"Let us first find the gold, and instead of describing the life-amber, so let me call it, I will point it out to your own eyes. As to the process, your share in it is so simple that you will ask me why I seek aid from a chemist. The life-amber, when found, has but to be subjected to heat and fermentation for six hours; it will be placed in a small caldron which that coffer contains, over the fire which that fuel will feed. To give effect to the process, certain alkalies and other ingredients are required; but these are prepared, and mine is the task to commingle them. From your science as chemist I need and ask naught. In you I have sought only the aid of a man."

"If that be so, why, indeed, seek me at all? Why not confide in those swarthy attendants, who doubtless are slaves to your orders?"

"Confide in slaves, when the first task enjoined to them would be to discover, and refrain from purloining gold! Seven such unscrupulous knaves, or even one such, and I, thus defenseless and feeble! Such is not the work that wise masters confide to fierce slaves. But that is the least of the reasons which exclude them from my choice, and fix my choice of assistant on you. Do you forget what I told you of the danger which the Dervish declared no bribe I could offer could tempt him a second time to brave?"

"I remember now; those words had passed away from my mind."

"And because they had passed away from your mind, I chose you for my comrade. I need a man by whom danger is scorned."

"But in the process of which you tell me I see no possible danger unless the ingredients you mix in your caldron have poisonous fumes."

"It is not that. The ingredients I use are not poisons."

"What other danger, except you dread your own Eastern slaves? But, if so, why lead them to these solitudes; and, if so, why not bid me be armed?"

"The Eastern slaves, fulfilling my commands, wait for my summons, where their eyes cannot see what we do. The danger is of a kind in which the boldest son of the East would be more craven, perhaps, that the daintiest Sybarite of Europe, who would shrink from a panther and laugh at a ghost. In the creed of the Dervish, and of all who adventure into that realm of Nature which is closed to philosophy and open to magic, there are races in the magnitude of space unseen as animalcules in the world of a drop. For the tribes of the drop science has its microscope. Of the host of yon azure Infinite magic gains sight, and through them gains command over fluid conductors that link all the parts of creation. Of these races, some are wholly indifferent to man, some benign to him, and some deadly hostile. In all the regular and prescribed conditions of mortal being, this magic realm seems as blank and tenantless as yon vacant air. But when a seeker of powers beyond the rude functions by which man plies the clock-work that measures his hours, and stops when its chain reaches the end of its coil, strives to pass over those boundaries at which philosophy says, 'Knowledge ends' – then, he is like all other travelers in regions unknown; he must propitiate or brave the tribes that are hostile – must depend for his life on the tribes that are friendly. Though your science discredits the alchemist's dogmas, your learning informs you that all alchemists were not ignorant impostors; yet those whose discoveries prove them to have been the nearest allies to your practical knowledge, ever hint in their mystical works at the reality of that realm which is open to magic – ever hint that some means less familiar than furnace and bellows are essential to him who explores the elixir of life. He who once quaffs that elixir, obtains in his very veins the bright fluid by which he transmits the force of his will to agencies dormant in Nature, to giants unseen in the space. And here, as he passes the boundary which divides his allotted and normal mortality from the regions and races that magic alone can explore, so, here, he breaks down the safeguard between himself and the tribes that are hostile. Is it not ever thus between man and man? Let a race the most gentle and timid and civilized dwell on one side a river or mountain, and another have home in the region beyond, each, if it pass not the intervening barrier, may with each live in peace. But if ambitious adventurers scale the mountain, or cross the river, with design to subdue and enslave the population they boldly invade, then all the invaded arise in wrath and defiance – the neighbors are changed into foes. And therefore this process – by which a simple though rare material of Nature is made to yield to a mortal the boon of a life which brings, with its glorious resistance to Time, desires and faculties to subject to its service beings that dwell in the earth and the air and the deep – has ever been one of the same peril which an invader must brave when he crosses the bounds of his nation. By this key alone you unlock all the cells of the alchemist's lore; by this alone understand how a labor, which a chemist's crudest apprentice could perform, has baffled the giant fathers of all your dwarfed children of science. Nature, that stores this priceless boon, seems to shrink from conceding it to man – the invisible tribes that abhor him oppose themselves to the gain that might give them a master. The duller of those who were the life-seekers of old would have told you how some chance, trivial, unlooked-for, foiled their grand hope at the very point of fruition; some doltish mistake, some improvident oversight, a defect in the sulphur, a wild overflow in the quicksilver, or a flaw in the bellows, or a pupil who failed to replenish the fuel, by falling asleep by the furnace. The invisible foes seldom vouchsafe to make themselves visible where they can frustrate the bungler as they mock at his toils from their ambush. But the mightier adventurers, equally foiled in despite of their patience and skill, would have said, 'Not with us rests the fault; we neglected no caution, we failed from no oversight. But out from the caldron dread faces arose, and the specters or demons dismayed and baffled us.' Such, then, is the danger which seems so appalling to a son of the East, as it seemed to a seer in the dark age of Europe. But we can deride all its threats, you and I. For myself, I own frankly I take all the safety that the charms and resources of magic bestow. You, for your safety, have the cultured and disciplined reason which reduces all fantasies to nervous impressions; and I rely on the courage of one who has questioned, unquailing, the Luminous Shadow, and wrested from the hand of the magician himself the wand which concentered the wonders of will!"

To this strange and long discourse I listened without interruption, and now quietly answered:

"I do not merit the trust you affect in my courage; but I am now on my guard against the cheats of the fancy, and the fumes of a vapor can scarcely bewilder the brain in the open air of this mountain land. I believe in no races like those which you tell me lie viewless in space, as do gases. I believe not in magic; I ask not its aids, and I dread not its terrors. For the rest, I am confident of one mournful courage – the courage that comes from despair. I submit to your guidance, whatever it be, as a sufferer whom colleges doom to the grave submits to the quack who says, 'Take my specific and live!' My life is naught in itself; my life lives in another. You and I are both brave from despair; you would turn death from yourself – I would turn death from one I love more than myself. Both know how little aid we can win from the colleges, and both, therefore, turn to the promises most audaciously cheering. Dervish or magician, alchemist or phantom, what care you and I? And if they fail us, what then? They cannot fail us more than the colleges do!"

V

The gold has been gained with an easy labor. I knew where to seek for it, whether under the turf or in the bed of the creek. But Margrave's eyes, hungrily gazing round every spot from which the ore was disburied, could not detect the substance of which he alone knew the outward appearance. I had begun to believe that, even in the description given to him of this material, he had been credulously duped, and that no such material existed, when, coming back from the bed of the watercourse, I saw a faint, yellow gleam amidst the roots of a giant parasite plant, the leaves and blossoms of which climbed up the sides of the cave with its antediluvian relics. The gleam was the gleam of gold, and on removing the loose earth round the roots of the plant, we came on – No, I will not, I dare not, describe it. The gold digger would cast it aside; the naturalist would pause not to heed it; and did I describe it, and chemistry deign to subject it to analysis, could chemistry alone detach or discover its boasted virtues?

Its particles, indeed, are very minute, not seeming readily to crystallize with each other; each in itself of uniform shape and size, spherical as the egg which contains the germ of life, and small as the egg from which the life of an insect may quicken.

But Margrave's keen eye caught sight of the atoms upcast by the light of the moon. He exclaimed to me, "Found! I shall live!" And then, as he gathered up the grains with tremulous hands, he called out to the Veiled Woman, hitherto still seated motionless on the crag. At his word she rose and went to the place hard by, where the fuel was piled, busying herself there. I had no leisure to heed her. I continued my search in the soft and yielding soil that time and the decay of vegetable life had accumulated over the pre-Adamite strata on which the arch of the cave rested its mighty keystone.

When we had collected of these particles about thrice as much as a man might hold in his hand, we seemed to have exhausted their bed. We continued still to find gold, but no more of the delicate substance to which, in our sight, gold was as dross.

"Enough," then said Margrave, reluctantly desisting. "What we have gained already will suffice for a life thrice as long as legend attributes to Haroun. I shall live – I shall live through the centuries."

"Forget not that I claim my share."

"Your share – yours! True – your half of my life! It is true." He paused with a low, ironical, malignant laugh, and then added, as he rose and turned away, "But the work is yet to be done."

VI

While we had thus labored and found, Ayesha had placed the fuel where the moonlight fell fullest on the sward of the table-land – a part of it already piled as for a fire, the rest of it heaped confusedly close at hand; and by the pile she had placed the coffer. And, there she stood, her arms folded under her mantle, her dark image seeming darker still as the moonlight whitened all the ground from which the image rose motionless. Margrave opened his coffer, the Veiled Woman did not aid him, and I watched in silence, while he as silently made his weird and wizard-like preparations.

VII

On the ground a wide circle was traced by a small rod, tipped apparently with sponge saturated with some combustible naphtha-like fluid, so that a pale, lambent flame followed the course of the rod as Margrave guided it, burning up the herbage over which it played, and leaving a distinct ring, like that which, in our lovely native fable talk, we call the "Fairy's ring," but yet more visible because marked in phosphorescent light. On the ring thus formed were placed twelve small lamps, fed with the fluid from the same vessel, and lighted by the same rod. The light emitted by the lamps was more vivid and brilliant than that which circled round the ring.

Within the circumference, and immediately round the wood-pile, Margrave traced certain geometrical figures, in which – not without a shudder, that I overcame at once by a strong effort of will in murmuring to myself the name of "Lilian" – I recognized the interlaced triangles which my own hand, in the spell enforced on a sleepwalker, had described on the floor of the wizard's pavilion. The figures were traced like the circle, in flame, and at the point of each triangle (four in number) was placed a lamp, brilliant as those on the ring. This task performed, the caldron, based on an iron tripod, was placed on the woodpile. And then the woman, before inactive and unheeding, slowly advanced, knelt by the pile and lighted it. The dry wood crackled and the flame burst forth, licking the rims of the caldron with tongues of fire.

Margrave flung into the caldron the particles we had collected, poured over them first a liquid, colorless as water, from the largest of the vessels drawn from his coffer, and then, more sparingly, drops from small crystal phials, like the phials I had seen in the hand of Philip Derval.

Having surmounted my first impulse of awe, I watched these proceedings, curious yet disdainful, as one who watches the mummeries of an enchanter on the stage.

"If," thought I, "these are but artful devices to inebriate and fool my own imagination, my imagination is on its guard, and reason shall not, this time, sleep at her post!"

"And now," said Margrave, "I consign to you the easy task by which you are to merit your share of the elixir. It is my task to feed and replenish the caldron; it is Ayesha's to feed the fire, which must not for a moment relax in its measured and steady heat. Your task is the lightest of all: it is but to renew from this vessel the fluid that burns in the lamps, and on the ring. Observe, the contents of the vessel must be thriftily husbanded; there is enough, but not more than enough, to sustain the light in the lamps, on the lines traced round the caldron, and on the farther ring, for six hours. The compounds dissolved in this fluid are scarce – only obtainable in the East, and even in the East months might have passed before I could have increased my supply. I had no months to waste. Replenish, then, the light only when it begins to flicker or fade. Take heed, above all, that no part of the outer ring – no, not an inch – and no lamp of the twelve, that are to its zodiac like stars, fade for one moment in darkness."

I took the crystal vessel from his hand.

"The vessel is small," said I, "and what is yet left of its contents is but scanty; whether its drops suffice to replenish the lights I cannot guess – I can but obey your instructions. But, more important by far than the light to the lamps and the circle, which in Asia or Africa might scare away the wild beasts unknown to this land – more important than light to a lamp is the strength to your frame, weak magician! What will support you through six weary hours of night watch?"

"Hope," answered Margrave, with a ray of his old dazzling style. "Hope! I shall live – I shall live through the centuries!"

VIII

One hour passed away; the fagots under the caldron burned clear in the sullen, sultry air. The materials within began to seethe, and their color, at first dull and turbid, changed into a pale-rose hue; from time to time the Veiled Woman replenished the fire, after she had done so reseating herself close by the pyre, with her head bowed over her knees, and her face hid under her veil.

The lights in the lamps and along the ring and the triangles now began to pale. I resupplied their nutriment from the crystal vessel. As yet nothing strange startled my eye or my ear beyond the rim of the circle – nothing audible, save, at a distance, the musical wheel-like click of the locusts, and, farther still, in the forest, the howl of the wild dogs that never bark; nothing visible, but the trees and the mountain range girding the plains silvered by the moon, and the arch of the cavern, the flush of wild blooms on its sides, and the gleam of dry bones on its floor, where the moonlight shot into the gloom.

The second hour passed like the first. I had taken my stand by the side of Margrave, watching with him the process at work in the caldron, when I felt the ground slightly vibrate beneath my feet, and looking up, it seemed as if all the plains beyond the circle were heaving like the swell of the sea, and as if in the air itself there was a perceptible tremor.

I placed my hand on Margrave's shoulder and whispered, "To me earth and air seem to vibrate. Do they seem to vibrate to you?"

"I know not, I care not," he answered impetuously. "The essence is bursting the shell that confined it. Here are my air and my earth! Trouble me not. Look to the circle – feed the lamps if they fail!"

I passed by the Veiled Woman as I walked toward a place in the ring in which the flame was waning dim; and I whispered to her the same question which I had whispered to Margrave. She looked slowly around and answered, "So is it before the Invisible make themselves visible! Did I not bid him forbear?" Her head again drooped on her breast, and her watch was again fixed on the fire.

I advanced to the circle and stooped to replenish the light where it waned. As I did so, on my arm, which stretched somewhat beyond the line of the ring, I felt a shock like that of electricity. The arm fell to my side numbed and nerveless, and from my hand dropped, but within the ring, the vessel that contained the fluid. Recovering my surprise or my stun, hastily with the other hand I caught up the vessel, but some of the scanty liquid was already spilled on the sward; and I saw with a thrill of dismay, that contrasted indeed the tranquil indifference with which I had first undertaken my charge, how small a supply was now left.

I went back to Margrave, and told him of the shock, and of its consequence in the waste of the liquid.

"Beware," said he, that not a motion of the arm, not an inch of the foot, pass the verge of the ring; and if the fluid be thus unhappily stinted, reserve all that is left for the protecting circle and the twelve outer lamps! See how the Grand Work advances, how the hues in the caldron are glowing blood-red through the film on the surface!

And now four hours of the six were gone; my arm had gradually recovered its strength. Neither the ring nor the lamps had again required replenishing; perhaps their light was exhausted less quickly, as it was no longer to be exposed to the rays of the intense Australian moon. Clouds had gathered over the sky, and though the moon gleamed at times in the gaps that they left in blue air, her beam was more hazy and dulled. The locusts no longer were heard in the grass, nor the howl of the dogs in the forest. Out of the circle, the stillness was profound.

And about this time I saw distinctly in the distance a vast Eye. It drew nearer and nearer, seeming to move from the ground at the height of some lofty giant. Its gaze riveted mine; my blood curdled in the blaze from its angry ball; and now as it advanced larger and larger, other Eyes, as if of giants in its train, grew out from the space in its rear – numbers on numbers, like the spear-heads of some Eastern army, seen afar by pale warders of battle-ments doomed to the dust. My voice long refused an utterance to my awe; at length it burst forth shrill and loud:

"Look, look! Those terrible Eyes! Legions on legions. And hark! that tramp of numberless feet; THEY are not seen, but the hollows of earth echo the sound of their march!"

Margrave, more than ever intent on the caldron, in which, from time to time, he kept dropping powders or essences drawn forth from his coffer, looked up, defyingly, fiercely:

"Ye come," he said in a low mutter, his once mighty voice sounding hollow and laboring, but fearless and firm – "ye come – not to conquer, vain rebels! – ye whose dark chief I struck down at my feet in the tomb where my spell had raised up the ghost of your first human master, the Chaldee! Earth and air have their armies still faithful to me, and still I remember the war song that summons them up to confront you! Ayesha, Ayesha! recall the wild troth that we pledged among the roses; recall the dread bond by which we united our sway over hosts that yet own thee as queen, though my scepter is broken, my diadem reft from my brows!"

The Veiled Woman rose at this adjuration. Her veil now was withdrawn, and the blaze of the fire between Margrave and her-self flushed, as with the rosy bloom of youth, the grand beauty of her softened face. It was seen, detached, as it were, from her dark-mantled form; seen through the mist of the vapors which rose from the caldron, framing it round like the clouds that are yield-ingly pierced by the light of the evening star.

Through the haze of the vapor came her voice, more musical, more plaintive than I had heard it before, but far softer, more tender: still in her foreign tongue; the words unknown to me, and yet their sense, perhaps, made intelligible by the love, which has one common language and one common look to all who have loved – the love unmistakably heard in the loving tone, unmistakably seen in the loving face.

A moment or so more and she had come round from the opposite side of the fire pile, and bending over Margrave's upturned brow, kissed it quietly, solemnly; and then her countenance grew fierce, her crest rose erect: it was the lioness protecting her young. She stretched forth her arm from the black mantle, athwart the pale front that now again bent over the caldron – stretched it toward the haunted and hollow-sounding space beyond, in the gesture of one whose right hand has the sway of the scepter. And then her voice stole on the air in the music of a chant, not loud yet far- reaching; so thrilling, so sweet and yet so solemn that I could at once comprehend how legend united of old the spell of enchantment with the power of song. All that I recalled of the effects which, in the former time, Margrave's strange chants had produced on the ear that they ravished and the thoughts they confused, was but as the wild bird's imitative carol, compared to the depth and the art and the soul of the singer, whose voice seemed endowed with a charm to inthrall all the tribes of creation, though the language it used for that charm might to them, as to me, be unknown. As the song ceased, I heard from behind sounds like those I had heard in the spaces before me – the tramp of invisible feet, the whir of invisible wings, as if armies were marching to aid against armies in march to destroy.

"Look not in front nor around," said Ayesha. "Look, like him, on the caldron below. The circle and the lamps are yet bright; I will tell you when the light again fails."

I dropped my eyes on the caldron.

"See," whispered Margrave, "the sparkles at last begin to arise, and the rose hues to deepen – signs that we near the last process."

IX

The fifth hour had passed away, when Ayesha said to me, "Lo! the circle is fading; the lamps grow dim. Look now without fear on the space beyond; the eyes that appalled thee are again lost in air, as lightnings that fleet back into cloud."

I looked up, and the specters had vanished. The sky was tinged with sulphurous hues, the red and the black intermixed. I replenished the lamps and the ring in front, thriftily, heedfully; but when I came to the sixth lamp, not a drop in the vessel that fed them was left. In a vague dismay, I now looked round the half of the wide circle in rear of the two bended figures intent on the caldron. All along that disk the light was already broken, here and there flickering up, here and there dying down; the six lamps in that half of the circle still twinkled, but faintly, as stars shrinking fast from the dawn of day. But it was not the fading shine in that half of the magical ring which daunted my eye and quickened with terror the pulse of my heart; the Bush-land beyond was on fire. From the background of the forest rose the flame and the smoke – the smoke, there, still half smothering the flame. But along the width of the grasses and herbage, between the verge of the forest and the bed of the water creek just below the raised platform from which I beheld the dread conflagration, the fire was advancing – wave upon wave, clear and red against the columns of rock behind; as the rush of a flood through the mists of some Alp crowned with lightnings.

Roused from my stun at the first sight of a danger not foreseen by the mind I had steeled against far rarer portents of Nature, I cared no more for the lamps and the circle. Hurrying hack to Ayesha I exclaimed: "The phantoms have gone from the spaces in front; but what incantation or spell can arrest the red march of the foe speeding on in the rear! While we gazed on the caldron of life, behind us, unheeded, behold the Destroyer!"

Ayesha looked and made no reply, but, as by involuntary instinct, bowed her majestic head, then rearing it erect, placed herself yet more immediately before the wasted form of the young magician (he still, bending over the caldron, and hearing me not in the absorption and hope of his watch) – placed herself before him, as the bird whose first care is her fledgling.

As we two there stood, fronting the deluge of fire, we heard Margrave behind us, murmuring low, "See the bubbles of light, how they sparkle and dance – I shall live, I shall live!" And his words scarcely died in our ears before, crash upon crash, came the fall of the age-long trees in the forest, and nearer, all near us, through the blazing grasses, the hiss of the serpents, the scream of the birds, and the bellow and tramp of the herds plunging wild through the billowy red of their pastures.

Ayesha now wound her arms around Margrave, and wrenched him, reluctant and struggling, from his watch over the seething caldron. In rebuke of his angry exclamations, she pointed to the march of the fire, spoke in sorrowful tones a few words in her own language, and then, appealing to me in English, said:

"I tell him that, here, the Spirits who oppose us have summoned a foe that is deaf to my voice, and – "

"And," exclaimed Margrave, no longer with gasp and effort, but with the swell of a voice which drowned all the discords of terror and of agony sent forth from the Phlegethon burning below – "and this witch, whom I trusted, is a vile slave and impostor, more desiring my death than my life. She thinks that in life I should scorn and forsake her, that in death I should die in her arms! Sorceress, avaunt! Art thou useless and powerless now when I need thee most? Go! Let the world be one funeral pyre! What to ME is the world? My world is my life! Thou knowest that my last hope is here – that all the strength left me this night will die down, like the lamps in the circle, unless the elixir restore it. Bold friend, spurn that sorceress away. Hours yet ere those flames can assail us! A few minutes more, and life to your Lilian and me!"

Thus having said, Margrave turned from us, and cast into the caldron the last essence yet left in his empty coffer.

Ayesha silently drew her black veil over her face, and

turned, with the being she loved, from the terror he scorned, to share in the hope that he cherished.

Thus left alone, with my reason disinthralled, disenchanted, I surveyed more calmly the extent of the actual peril with which we were threatened, and the peril seemed less, so surveyed.

It is true all the Bush-land behind, almost up to the bed of the creek, was on fire; but the grasses, through which the flame spread so rapidly, ceased at the opposite marge of the creek. Watery pools were still, at intervals, left in the bed of the creek, shining tremulous, like waves of fire, in the glare reflected from the burning land; and even where the water failed, the stony course of the exhausted rivulet was a barrier against the march of the conflagration. Thus, unless the wind, now still, should rise, and waft some sparks to the parched combustible herbage immediately around us, we were saved from the fire, and our work might yet be achieved.

I whispered to Ayesha the conclusion to which I came.

"Thinkest thou," she answered without raising her mournful head, "that the Agencies of Nature are the movements of chance? The Spirits I invoked to his aid are leagued with the hosts that assail. A mightier than I am has doomed him!"

Scarcely had she uttered these words before Margrave exclaimed, "Behold how the Rose of the alchemist's dream enlarges its blooms from the folds of its petals! I shall live, I shall live!"

I looked, and the liquid which glowed in the caldron had now taken a splendor that mocked all comparisons borrowed from the luster of gems. In its prevalent color it had, indeed, the dazzle and flash of the ruby; but out from the mass of the molten red, broke coruscations of all prismal hues, shooting, shifting, in a play that made the wavelets themselves seem living things, sensible of their joy. No longer was there scum or film upon the surface; only ever and anon a light, rosy vapor floating up, and quick lost in the haggard, heavy, sulphurous air, hot with the conflagration rushing toward us from behind. And these coruscations formed, on the surface of the molten ruby, literally the shape of a rose, its leaves made distinct in their outlines by sparks of emerald and diamond and sapphire.

Even while gazing on this animated liquid luster, a buoyant delight seemed infused into my senses; all terrors conceived before were annulled; the phantoms, whose armies had filled the wide spaces in front, were forgotten; the crash of the forest behind was unheard. In the reflection of that glory, Margrave's wan cheek seemed already restored to the radiance it wore when I saw it first in the framework of blooms.

As I gazed, thus enchanted, a cold hand touched my own.

"Hush!" whispered Ayesha, from the black veil, against which the rays of the caldron fell blunt, and absorbed into Dark. "Behind us, the light of the circle is extinct; but there, we are guarded from all save the brutal and soulless destroyers. But, before! – but, before! – see, two of the lamps have died out! – see the blank of the gap in the ring! Guard that breach – there the demons will enter."

"Not a drop is there left in this vessel by which to replenish the lamps on the ring."

"Advance, then; thou hast still the light of the soul, and the demons may recoil before a soul that is dauntless and guiltless. If not, Three are lost! – as it is, One is doomed."

Thus adjured, silently, involuntarily, I passed from the Veiled Woman's side, over the sear lines on the turf which had been traced by the triangles of light long since extinguished, and toward the verge of the circle. As I advanced, overhead rushed a dark cloud of wings – birds dislodged from the forest on fire, and screaming, in dissonant terror, as they flew toward the farthermost mountains; close by my feet hissed and glided the snakes, driven forth from their blazing coverts, and glancing through the ring, unscared by its waning lamps; all undulating by me, bright-eyed, and hissing, all made innocuous by fear – even the terrible Death-adder, which I trampled on as I halted at the verge of the circle, did not turn to bite, but crept harmless away. I halted at the gap between the two dead lamps, and bowed my head to look again into the crystal vessel. Were there, indeed, no lingering drops yet left, if but to recruit the lamps for some priceless minutes more? As I thus stood, right into the gap between the two dead lamps strode a gigantic Foot. All the rest of the form was unseen; only, as volume after volume of smoke poured on from the burning land behind, it seemed as if one great column of vapor, eddying round, settled itself aloft from the circle, and that out from that column strode the giant Foot. And, as strode the Foot, so with it came, like the sound of its tread, a roll of muttered thunder.

I recoiled, with a cry that rang loud through the lurid air.

"Courage!" said the voice of Ayesha. "Trembling soul, yield not an inch to the demon!"

At the charm, the wonderful charm, in the tone of the Veiled Woman's voice, my will seemed to take a force more sublime than its own. I folded my arms on my breast, and stood as if rooted to the spot, confronting the column of smoke and the stride of the giant Foot. And the Foot halted, mute.

Again, in the momentary hush of that suspense, I heard a voice – it was Margrave's.

"The last hour expires – the work is accomplished! Come! come! Aid me to take the caldron from the fire; and, quick! – or a drop may be wasted in vapor – the Elixir of Life from the caldron!"

At that cry I receded, and the Foot advanced.

And at that moment, suddenly, unawares, from behind, I was stricken down. Over me, as I lay, swept a whirlwind of trampling hoofs and glancing horns. The herds, in their flight from the burning pastures, had rushed over the bed of the water course, scaled the slopes of the banks. Snorting and bellowing, they plunged their blind way to the mountains. One cry alone, more wild than their own savage blare, pierced the reek through which the Brute Hurricane swept. At that cry of wrath and despair I struggled to rise, again dashed to earth by the hoofs and the horns. But was it the dreamlike deceit of my reeling senses, or did I see that giant Foot stride past through the close-serried ranks of the maddening herds? Did I hear, distinct through all the huge uproar of animal terror, the roll of low thunder which followed the stride of that Foot?

X

When my sense had recovered its shock, and my eyes looked dizzily round, the charge of the beasts had swept by; and of all the wild tribes which had invaded the magical circle, the only lingerer was the brown Death-adder, coiled close by the spot where my head had rested. Beside the extinguished lamps which the hoofs had confusedly scattered, the fire, arrested by the water course, had consumed the grasses that fed it, and there the plains stretched black and desert as the Phlegraean Field of the Poet's Hell. But the fire still raged in the forest beyond – white flames, soaring up from the trunks of the tallest trees, and forming, through the sullen dark of the smoke reck, innumerable pillars of fire, like the halls in the city of fiends.

Gathering myself up, I turned my eyes from the terrible pomp of the lurid forest, and looked fearfully down on the hoof-trampled sward for my two companions.

I saw the dark image of Ayesha still seated, still bending, as I had seen it last. I saw a pale hand feebly grasping the rim of the magical caldron, which lay, hurled down from its tripod by the rush of the beasts, yards away from the dim, fading embers of the scattered wood pyre. I saw the faint writhings of a frail, wasted frame, over which the Veiled Woman was bending. I saw, as I moved with bruised limbs to the place, close by the lips of the dying magician, the flash of the rubylike essence spilled on the sward, and, meteor-like, sparkling up from the torn tufts of herbage.

I now reached Margrave's side. Bending over him as the Veiled Woman bent, and as I sought gently to raise him, he turned his face, fiercely faltering out, "Touch me not, rob me not! YOU share with me! Never, never! These glorious drops are all mine! Die all else! I will live, I will live!" Writhing himself from my pitying arms, he plunged his face amidst the beautiful, play-ful flame of the essence, as if to lap the elixir with lips scorched away from its intolerable burning. Suddenly, with a low shriek, he fell back, his face upturned to mine, and on that face unmis-takably reigned Death.

Then Ayesha tenderly, silently, drew the young head to her lap, and it vanished from my sight behind her black veil.

I knelt beside her, murmuring some trite words of comfort; but she heeded me not, rocking herself to and fro as the mother who cradles a child to sleep. Soon the fast-flickering sparkles of the lost elixir died out on the grass; and with their last sportive diamond- like tremble of light, up, in all the suddenness of Aus-tralian day, rose the sun, lifting himself royally above the moun-tain tops, and fronting the meaner blaze of the forest as a young king fronts his rebels. And as there, where the bush fires had ravaged, all was a desert, so there, where their fury had not spread, all was a garden. Afar, at the foot of the mountains, the fugitive herds were grazing; the cranes, flocking back to the pools, renewed the strange grace of their gambols; and the great kingfisher, whose laugh, half in mirth, half in mockery, leads the choir that welcome the morn – which in Europe is night – alighted bold on the roof of the cavern, whose floors were still white with the bones of races, extinct before – so helpless through instincts, so royal through Soul – rose MAN!

But there, on the ground where the dazzling elixir had wasted its virtues – there the herbage already had a freshness of verdure which, amid the duller sward round it, was like an oasis of green in a desert. And, there, wild flowers, whose chill hues the eye would have scarcely distinguished the day before, now glittered forth in blooms of unfamiliar beauty. Toward that spot were attracted myriads of happy insects, whose hum of intense joy was musically loud. But the form of the life-seeking sorcerer lay rigid and stark; blind to the bloom of the wild flowers, deaf to the glee of the insects – one hand still resting heavily on the rim of the emptied caldron, and the face still hid behind the Black Veil. What! the wondrous elixir, sought with such hope and well-nigh achieved through such dread, fleeting back to the earth from which its material was drawn to give bloom, indeed – but to herbs; joy indeed – but to insects!

And now, in the flash of the sun, slowly wound up the slopes that led to the circle, the same barbaric procession which had sunk into the valley under the ray of the moon. The armed men came first, stalwart and tall, their vests brave with crimson and golden lace, their weapons gayly gleaming with holiday silver. After them, the Black Litter. As they came to the place, Ayesha, not raising her head, spoke to them in her own Eastern tongue. A wail was her answer. The armed men bounded forward, and the bearers left the litter.

All gathered round the dead form with the face concealed under the Black Veil; all knelt, and all wept. Far in the distance, at the foot of the blue mountains, a crowd of the savage natives had risen up as if from the earth; they stood motionless leaning on their clubs and spears, and looking toward the spot on which we were – strangely thus brought into the landscape, as if they too, the wild dwellers on the verge which Humanity guards from the Brute, were among the mourners for the mysterious Child of mysterious Nature! And still, in the herbage, hummed the small insects, and still, from the cavern, laughed the great kingfisher. I said to Ayesha, "Farewell! your love mourns the dead, mine calls me to the living. You are now with your own people, they may console you – say if I can assist."

"There is no consolation for me! What mourner can be consoled if the dead die forever? Nothing for him is left but a grave; that grave shall be in the land where the song of Ayesha first lulled him to sleep. Thou assist ME – thou, the wise man of Europe! From me ask assistance. What road wilt thou take to thy home?"

"There is but one road known to me through the maze of the solitude – that which we took to this upland."

"On that road Death lurks, and awaits thee! Blind dupe, couldst thou think that if the grand secret of life had been won, he whose head rests on my lap would have yielded thee one petty drop of the essence which had filched from his store of life but a

90

moment? Me, who so loved and so cherished him – me he would have doomed to the pitiless cord of my servant, the Strangler, if my death could have lengthened a hairbreadth the span of his being. But what matters to me his crime or his madness? I loved him, I loved him!"

She bowed her veiled head lower and lower; perhaps under the veil her lips kissed the lips of the dead. Then she said whisperingly:

"Juma the Strangler, whose word never failed to his master, whose prey never slipped from his snare, waits thy step on the road to thy home! But thy death cannot now profit the dead, the beloved. And thou hast had pity for him who took but thine aid to design thy destruction. His life is lost, thine is saved!"

She spoke no more in the tongue that I could interpret. She spoke, in the language unknown, a few murmured words to her swarthy attendants; then the armed men, still weeping, rose, and made a dumb sign to me to go with them. I understood by the sign that Ayesha had told them to guard me on my way; but she gave no reply to my parting thanks.

XI

I descended into the valley; the armed men followed. The path, on that side of the water course not reached by the flames, wound through meadows still green, or amidst groves still unscathed. As a turning in the way brought in front of my sight the place I had left behind, I beheld the black litter creeping down the descent, with its curtains closed, and the Veiled Woman walking by its side. But soon the funeral procession was lost to my eyes, and the thoughts that it roused were erased. The waves in man's brain are like those of the sea, rushing on, rushing over the wrecks of the vessels that rode on their surface, to sink, after storm, in their deeps. One thought cast forth into the future now mastered all in the past: "Was Lilian living still?" Absorbed in the gloom of that thought, hurried on by the goad that my heart, in its tortured impatience, gave to my footstep, I outstripped the slow stride of the armed men, and, midway between the place I had left and the home which I sped to, came, far in advance of my guards, into the thicket in which the Bushmen had started up in my path on the night that Lilian had watched for my coming. The earth at my feet was rife with creeping plants and many-colored flowers, the sky overhead was half hid by motionless pines. Suddenly, whether crawling out from the herbage or dropping down from the trees, by my side stood the white-robed and skeleton form – Ayesha's attendant the Strangler.

I sprang from him shuddering, then halted and faced him. The hideous creature crept toward me, cringing and fawning, making signs of humble goodwill and servile obeisance. Again I recoiled – wrathfully, loathingly, turned my face homeward, and fled on. I thought I had baffled his chase, when, just at the mouth of the thicket, he dropped from a bough in my path close behind me. Before I could turn, some dark muffling substance fell between my sight and the sun, and I felt a fierce strain at my throat. But the words of Ayesha had warned me; with one rapid hand I seized the noose before it could tighten too closely, with the other I tore the bandage away from my eyes, and, wheeling round on the dastardly foe, struck him down with one spurn of my foot. His hand, as he fell, relaxed its hold on the noose; I freed my throat from the knot, and sprang from the copse into the broad sunlit plain. I saw no more of the armed men or the Strangler. Panting and breathless, I paused at last before the fence, fragrant with blossoms, that divided my home from the solitude.

The windows of Lilian's room were darkened; all within the house seemed still.

Darkened and silenced home, with the light and sounds of the jocund day all around it. Was there yet hope in the Universe for me? All to which I had trusted Hope had broken down; the anchors I had forged for her hold in the beds of the ocean, her stay from the drifts of the storm, had snapped like the reeds which pierce the side that leans on the barb of their points, and confides in the strength of their stems. No hope in the baffled resources of recognized knowledge! No hope in the daring adventures of Mind into regions unknown; vain alike the calm lore of the practiced physician, and the magical arts of the fated Enchanter! I had fled from the commonplace teachings of Nature, to explore in her Shadowland marvels at variance with reason. Made brave by the grandeur of love, I had opposed without quailing the stride of the Demon, and my hope, when fruition seemed nearest, had been trodden into dust by the hoofs of the beast! And yet, all the while, I had scorned, as a dream, more wild than the word of a sorcerer, the hope that the old man and the child, the wise and the ignorant, took from their souls as in-born. Man and fiend had alike failed a mind, not ignoble, not skill-less, not abjectly craven; alike failed a heart not feeble and selfish, not dead to the hero's devotion, willing to shed every drop of its blood for a something more dear than an animal's life for itself! What remained – what remained for man's hope? – man's mind and man's heart thus exhausting their all with no other result but despair! What remained but the mystery of mysteries, so clear to the sunrise of childhood, the sunset of age, only dimmed by the clouds which collect round the noon of our manhood? Where yet was Hope found? In the soul; in its every-day impulse to supplicate comfort and light, from the Giver of soul, wherever the heart is afflicted, the mind is obscured.

Then the words of Ayesha rushed over me: "What mourner can be consoled, if the dead die forever?" Through every pulse of my frame throbbed that dread question; all Nature around seemed to murmur it. And suddenly, as by a flash from heaven, the grand truth in Faber's grand reasoning shone on me, and lighted up all, within and without. Man alone, of all earthly creatures, asks, "Can the dead die forever?" and the instinct that urges the question is God's answer to man. No instinct is given in vain.

And born with the instinct of soul is the instinct that leads the soul from the seen to the unseen, from time to eternity, from the torrent that foams toward the Ocean of Death, to the source of its stream, far aloft from the Ocean.

"Know thyself," said the Pythian of old. "That precept descended from Heaven." Know thyself! Is that maxim wise? If so, know thy soul. But never yet did man come to the thorough conviction of soul but what he acknowledged the sovereign necessity of prayer. In my awe, in my rapture, all my thoughts seemed enlarged and illumed and exalted. I prayed – all my soul seemed one prayer. All my past, with its pride and presumption and folly, grew distinct as the form of a penitent, kneeling for pardon before setting forth on the pilgrimage vowed to a shrine. And, sure now, in the deeps of a soul first revealed to myself, that the Dead do not die forever, my human love soared beyond its brief trial of terror and sorrow. Daring not to ask from Heaven's wisdom that Lilian, for my sake, might not yet pass away from the earth, I prayed that my soul might be fitted to bear with submission whatever my Maker might ordain. And if surviving her – without whom no beam from yon material sun could ever warm into joy a morrow in human life – so to guide my steps that they might rejoin her at last, and in rejoining, regain forever!

How trivial now became the weird riddle, that, a little while before, had been clothed in so solemn an awe! What mattered it to the vast interests involved in the clear recognition of Soul and Hereafter, whether or not my bodily sense, for a moment, obscured the face of the Nature I should one day behold as a spirit? Doubtless the sights and the sounds which had haunted the last gloomy night, the calm reason of Faber would strip of their magical seemings; the Eyes in the space and the Foot in the circle might be those of no terrible Demons, but of the wild's savage children whom I had seen, halting, curious and mute, in the light of the morning. The tremor of the ground (if not, as heretofore, explicable by the illusory impression of my own treacherous senses) might be but the natural effect of elements struggling yet under a soil unmistakably charred by volcanoes. The luminous atoms dissolved in the caldron might as little be fraught with a vital elixir as are the splendors of naphtha or phosphor. As it was, the weird rite had no magic result. The magician was not rent limb from limb by the fiends. By causes as natural as ever extinguished life's spark in the frail lamp of clay, he had died out of sight – under the black veil.

What mattered henceforth to Faith, in its far grander questions and answers, whether Reason, in Faber, or Fancy, in me, supplied the more probable guess at a hieroglyph which, if construed aright, was but a word of small mark in the mystical language of Nature? If all the arts of enchantment recorded by Fable were attested by facts which Sages were forced to acknowledge, Sages would sooner or later find some cause for such portents – not supernatural. But what Sage, without cause supernatural, both without and within him, can guess at the wonders he views in the growth of a blade of grass, or the tints on an insect's wing? Whatever art Man can achieve in his progress through time, Man's reason, in time, can suffice to explain. But the wonders of God? These belong to the Infinite; and these, O Immortal! will but develop new wonder on wonder, though thy sight be a spirit's, and thy leisure to track and to solve an eternity.

As I raised my face from my clasped hands, my eyes fell full upon a form standing in the open doorway. There, where on the night in which Lilian's long struggle for reason and life had begun, the Luminous Shadow had been beheld in the doubtful light of a dying moon and a yet hazy dawn; there, on the threshold, gathering round her bright locks the aureole of the glorious sun, stood Amy, the blessed child! And as I gazed, drawing nearer and nearer to the silenced house, and that Image of Peace on its threshold, I felt that Hope met me at the door – Hope in the child's steadfast eyes, Hope in the child's welcoming smile!

"I was at watch for you," whispered Amy. "All is well."

"She lives still – she lives! Thank God, thank God!"

"She lives – she will recover!" said another voice, as my head sunk on Faber's shoulder. "For some hours in the night her sleep was disturbed, convulsed. I feared, then, the worst. Suddenly, just before the dawn, she called out aloud, still in sleep:

"'The cold and dark shadow has passed away from me and from Allen – passed away from us both forever!'

"And from that moment the fever left her; the breathing became soft, the pulse steady, and the color stole gradually back to her cheek. The crisis is past. Nature's benign Disposer has permitted Nature to restore your life's gentle partner, heart to heart, mind to mind – "

"And soul to soul," I cried in my solemn joy. "Above as below, soul to soul!" Then, at a sign from Faber, the child took me by the hand and led me up the stairs into Lilian's room.

Again those dear arms closed around me in wifelike and holy love, and those true lips kissed away my tears – even as now, at the distance of years from that happy morn, while I write the last words of this Strange Story, the same faithful arms close around me, the same tender lips kiss away my tears.

THOMAS DE QUINCEY

The Avenger

"Why callest thou me murderer, and not rather the wrath of God burning after the steps of the oppressor, and cleansing the earth when it is wet with blood?"

That series of terrific events by which our quiet city and university in the northeastern quarter of Germany were convulsed during the year 1816, has in itself, and considered merely as a blind movement of human tiger-passion ranging unchained among men, something too memorable to be forgotten or left without its own separate record; but the moral lesson impressed by these events is yet more memorable, and deserves the deep attention of coming generations in their struggle after human improvement, not merely in its own limited field of interest directly awakened, but in all analogous fields of interest; as in fact already, and more than once, in connection with these very events, this lesson has obtained the effectual attention of Christian kings and princes assembled in congress. No tragedy, indeed, among all the sad ones by which the charities of the human heart or of the fireside have ever been outraged, can better merit a separate chapter in the private history of German manners or social life than this unparalleled case. And, on the other hand, no one can put in a better claim to be the historian than myself.

I was at the time, and still am, a professor in that city and university which had the melancholy distinction of being its theater. I knew familiarly all the parties who were concerned in it, either as sufferers or as agents. I was present from first to last, and watched the whole course of the mysterious storm which fell upon our devoted city in a strength like that of a West Indian hurricane, and which did seriously threaten at one time to depopulate our university, through the dark suspicions which settled upon its members, and the natural reaction of generous indignation in repelling them; while the city in its more stationary and native classes would very soon have manifested THEIR awful sense of things, of the hideous insecurity for life, and of the unfathomable dangers which had undermined their hearths below their very feet, by sacrificing, whenever circumstances allowed them, their houses and beautiful gardens in exchange for days uncursed by panic, and nights unpolluted by blood. Nothing, I can take upon myself to assert, was left undone of all that human foresight could suggest, or human ingenuity could accomplish. But observe the melancholy result: the more certain did these arrangements strike people as remedies for the evil, so much the more effectually did they aid the terror, but, above all, the awe, the sense of mystery, when ten cases of total extermination, applied to separate households, had occurred, in every one of which these precautionary aids had failed to yield the slightest assistance. The horror, the perfect frenzy of fear, which seized upon the town after that experience, baffles all attempt at description. Had these various contrivances failed merely in some human and intelligible way, as by bringing the aid too tardily – still, in such cases, though the danger would no less have been evidently deepened, nobody would have felt any further mystery than what, from the very first, rested upon the persons and the motives of the murderers. But, as it was, when, in ten separate cases of exterminating carnage, the astounded police, after an examination the most searching, pursued from day to day, and almost exhausting the patience by the minuteness of the investigation, had finally pronounced that no attempt apparently had been made to benefit by any of the signals preconcerted, that no footstep apparently had moved in that direction – then, and after that result, a blind misery of fear fell upon the population, so much the worse than any anguish of a beleaguered city that is awaiting the storming fury of a victorious enemy, by how much the shadowy, the uncertain, the infinite, is at all times more potent in mastering the mind than a danger that is known, measurable, palpable, and human. The very police, instead of offering protection or encouragement, were seized with terror for themselves. And the general feeling, as it was described to me by a grave citizen whom I met in a morning walk (for the overmastering sense of a public calamity broke down every barrier of reserve, and all men talked freely to all men in the streets, as they would have done during the rockings of an earthquake), was,

even among the boldest, like that which sometimes takes possession of the mind in dreams – when one feels oneself sleeping
alone, utterly divided from all call or hearing of friends, doors
open that should be shut, or unlocked that should be triply secured, the very walls gone, barriers swallowed up by unknown
abysses, nothing around one but frail curtains, and a world of
illimitable night, whisperings at a distance, correspondence going
on between darkness and darkness, like one deep calling to another, and the dreamer's own heart the center from which the
whole network of this unimaginable chaos radiates, by means of
which the blank PRIVATIONS of silence and darkness become
powers the most POSITIVE and awful.

Agencies of fear, as of any other passion, and, above all, of
passion felt in communion with thousands, and in which the
heart beats in conscious sympathy with an entire city, through all
its regions of high and low, young and old, strong and weak;
such agencies avail to raise and transfigure the natures of men;
mean minds become elevated; dull men become eloquent; and
when matters came to this crisis, the public feeling, as made
known by voice, gesture, manner, or words, was such that no
stranger could represent it to his fancy. In that respect, therefore, I
had an advantage, being upon the spot through the whole course
of the affair, for giving a faithful narrative; as I had still more
eminently, from the sort of central station which I occupied, with
respect to all the movements of the case. I may add that I had
another advantage, not possessed, or not in the same degree, by
any other inhabitant of the town. I was personally acquainted
with every family of the slightest account belonging to the resi-
dent population; whether among the old local gentry, or the new
settlers whom the late wars had driven to take refuge within our
walls.

It was in September, 1815, that I received a letter from the
chief secretary to the Prince of M – – , a nobleman connected with
the diplomacy of Russia, from which I quote an extract: "I wish, in
short, to recommend to your attentions, and in terms stronger
than I know how to devise, a young man on whose behalf the
czar himself is privately known to have expressed the very stron-

gest interest. He was at the battle of Waterloo as an aide-de-camp to a Dutch general officer, and is decorated with distinctions won upon that awful day. However, though serving in that instance under English orders, and although an Englishman of rank, he does not belong to the English military service. He has served, young as he is, under VARIOUS banners, and under ours, in particular, in the cavalry of our imperial guard. He is English by birth, nephew to the Earl of E., and heir presumptive to his immense estates. There is a wild story current, that his mother was a gypsy of transcendent beauty, which may account for his somewhat Moorish complexion, though, after all, THAT is not of a deeper tinge than I have seen among many an Englishman. He is himself one of the noblest looking of God's creatures. Both father and mother, however, are now dead. Since then he has become the favorite of his uncle, who detained him in England after the emperor had departed – and, as this uncle is now in the last stage of infirmity, Mr. Wyndham's succession to the vast family estates is inevitable, and probably near at hand. Meantime, he is anxious for some assistance in his studies. Intellectually he stands in the very first rank of men, as I am sure you will not be slow to discover; but his long military service, and the unparalleled tumult of our European history since 1805, have interfered (as you may suppose) with the cultivation of his mind; for he entered the cavalry service of a German power when a mere boy, and shifted about from service to service as the hurricane of war blew from this point or from that. During the French anabasis to Moscow he entered our service, made himself a prodigious favorite with the whole imperial family, and even now is only in his twenty-second year. As to his accomplishments, they will speak for themselves; they are infinite, and applicable to every situation of life. Greek is what he wants from you; – never ask about terms. He will acknowledge any trouble he may give you, as he acknowledges all trouble, en prince. And ten years hence you will look back with pride upon having contributed your part to the formation of one whom all here at St. Petersburg, not soldiers only, but we diplomates, look upon as certain to prove a great man, and a leader among the intellects of Christendom."

Two or three other letters followed; and at length it was arranged that Mr. Maximilian Wyndham should take up his residence at my monastic abode for one year. He was to keep a table, and an establishment of servants, at his own cost; was to have an apartment of some dozen or so of rooms; the unrestricted use of the library; with some other public privileges willingly conceded by the magistracy of the town; in return for all which he was to pay me a thousand guineas; and already beforehand, by way of acknowledgment for the public civilities of the town, he sent, through my hands, a contribution of three hundred guineas to the various local institutions for education of the poor, or for charity.

The Russian secretary had latterly corresponded with me from a little German town, not more than ninety miles distant; and, as he had special couriers at his service, the negotiations advanced so rapidly that all was closed before the end of September. And, when once that consummation was attained, I, that previously had breathed no syllable of what was stirring, now gave loose to the interesting tidings, and suffered them to spread through the whole compass of the town. It will be easily imagined that such a story, already romantic enough in its first outline, would lose nothing in the telling. An Englishman to begin with, which name of itself, and at all times, is a passport into German favor, but much more since the late memorable wars that but for Englishmen would have drooped into disconnected efforts – next, an Englishman of rank and of the haute noblesse – then a soldier covered with brilliant distinctions, and in the most brilliant arm of the service; young, moreover, and yet a veteran by his experience – fresh from the most awful battle of this planet since the day of Pharsalia, – radiant with the favor of courts and of imperial ladies; finally (which alone would have given him an interest in all female hearts), an Antinous of faultless beauty, a Grecian statue, as it were, into which the breath of life had been breathed by some modern Pygmalion; – such a pomp of gifts and endowments settling upon one man's head, should not have required for its effect the vulgar consummation (and yet to many it WAS the consummation and crest of the whole) that he was reputed to be rich beyond the dreams of romance or the necessities of a fairy tale. Unparalleled was the impression made upon our stagnant society; every tongue was busy in discussing the marvelous young Englishman from morning to night; every female fancy was busy in depicting the personal appearance of this gay apparition.

On his arrival at my house, I became sensible of a truth which I had observed some years before. The commonplace maxim is, that it is dangerous to raise expectations too high. This, which is thus generally expressed, and without limitation, is true only conditionally; it is true then and there only where there is but little merit to sustain and justify the expectation. But in any case where the merit is transcendent of its kind, it is always useful to rack the expectation up to the highest point. In anything which partakes of the infinite, the most unlimited expectations will find ample room for gratification; while it is certain that ordinary observers, possessing little sensibility, unless where they have been warned to expect, will often fail to see what exists in the most conspicuous splendor. In this instance it certainly did no harm to the subject of expectation that I had been warned to look for so much. The warning, at any rate, put me on the lookout for whatever eminence there might be of grandeur in his personal appearance; while, on the other hand, this existed in such excess, so far transcending anything I had ever met with in my experience, that no expectation which it is in words to raise could have been disappointed.

These thoughts traveled with the rapidity of light through my brain, as at one glance my eye took in the supremacy of beauty and power which seemed to have alighted from the clouds before me. Power, and the contemplation of power, in any absolute incarnation of grandeur or excess, necessarily have the instantaneous effect of quelling all perturbation. My composure was restored in a moment. I looked steadily at him. We both bowed. And, at the moment when he raised his head from that inclination, I caught the glance of his eye; an eye such as might have been looked for in a face of such noble lineaments –

"Blending the nature of the star
With that of summer skies;"

and, therefore, meant by nature for the residence and organ

of serene and gentle emotions; but it surprised, and at the same time filled me more almost with consternation than with pity, to observe that in those eyes a light of sadness had settled more profound than seemed possible for youth, or almost commensurate to a human sorrow; a sadness that might have become a Jewish prophet, when laden with inspirations of woe.

Two months had now passed away since the arrival of Mr. Wyndham. He had been universally introduced to the superior society of the place; and, as I need hardly say, universally received with favor and distinction. In reality, his wealth and importance, his military honors, and the dignity of his character, as expressed in his manners and deportment, were too eminent to allow of his being treated with less than the highest attention in any society whatever. But the effect of these various advantages, enforced and recommended as they were by a personal beauty so rare, was somewhat too potent for the comfort and self-possession of ordinary people; and really exceeded in a painful degree the standard of pretensions under which such people could feel themselves at their ease. He was not naturally of a reserved turn; far from it. His disposition had been open, frank, and confiding, originally; and his roving, adventurous life, of which considerably more than one half had been passed in camps, had communicated to his manners a more than military frankness. But the profound melancholy which possessed him, from whatever cause it arose, necessarily chilled the native freedom of his demeanor, unless when it was revived by strength of friendship or of love. The effect was awkward and embarrassing to all parties. Every voice paused or faltered when he entered a room – dead silence ensued – not an eye but was directed upon him, or else, sunk in timidity, settled upon the floor; and young ladies seriously lost the power, for a time, of doing more than murmuring a few confused, half-inarticulate syllables, or half-inarticulate sounds. The solemnity, in fact, of a first presentation, and the utter impossibility of soon recovering a free, unembarrassed movement of conversation, made such scenes really distressing to all who participated in them, either as actors or spectators. Certainly this result was not a pure effect of manly beauty, however heroic, and in whatever excess; it arose in part from the many and extraordinary endowments which had centered in his person, not less from fortune than from nature; in part also, as I have said, from the profound sadness and freezing gravity of Mr. Wyndham's manner; but still more from the perplexing mystery which surrounded that sadness.

Were there, then, no exceptions to this condition of awe-struck admiration? Yes; one at least there was in whose bosom the spell of all-conquering passion soon thawed every trace of icy reserve. While the rest of the world retained a dim sentiment of awe toward Mr. Wyndham, Margaret Liebenheim only heard of such a feeling to wonder that it could exist toward HIM. Never was there so victorious a conquest interchanged between two youthful hearts – never before such a rapture of instantaneous sympathy. I did not witness the first meeting of this mysterious Maximilian and this magnificent Margaret, and do not know whether Margaret manifested that trepidation and embarrassment which distressed so many of her youthful co-rivals; but, if she did, it must have fled before the first glance of the young man's eye, which would interpret, past all misunderstanding, the homage of his soul and the surrender of his heart. Their third meeting I DID see; and there all shadow of embarrassment had vanished, except, indeed, of that delicate embarrassment which clings to impassioned admiration. On the part of Margaret, it seemed as if a new world had dawned upon her that she had not so much as suspected among the capacities of human experience. Like some bird she seemed, with powers unexercised for soaring and flying, not understood even as yet, and that never until now had found an element of air capable of sustaining her wings, or tempting her to put forth her buoyant instincts. He, on the other hand, now first found the realization of his dreams, and for a mere possibility which he had long too deeply contemplated, fearing, however, that in his own case it might prove a chimera, or that he might never meet a woman answering the demands of his heart, he now found a corresponding reality that left nothing to seek.

Here, then, and thus far, nothing but happiness had resulted from the new arrangement. But, if this had been little anticipated by many, far less had I, for my part, anticipated the unhappy revolution which was wrought in the whole nature of Ferdinand von Harrelstein. He was the son of a German baron; a man of good family, but of small estate who had been pretty nearly a soldier of fortune in the Prussian service, and had, late in life, won sufficient favor with the king and other military superiors, to have an early prospect of obtaining a commission, under flattering auspices, for this only son – a son endeared to him as the companion of unprosperous years, and as a dutifully affectionate child. Ferdinand had yet another hold upon his father's affections: his features preserved to the baron's unclouded remembrance a most faithful and living memorial of that angelic wife who had died in giving birth to this third child – the only one who had long survived her. Anxious that his son should go through a regular course of mathematical instruction, now becoming annually more important in all the artillery services throughout Europe, and that he should receive a tincture of other liberal studies which he had painfully missed in his own military career, the baron chose to keep his son for the last seven years at our college, until he was now entering upon his twenty-third year. For the four last he had lived with me as the sole pupil whom I had, or meant to have, had not the brilliant proposals of the young Russian guardsman persuaded me to break my resolution. Ferdinand von Harrelstein had good talents, not dazzling but respectable; and so amiable were his temper and manners that I had introduced him everywhere, and everywhere he was a favorite; and everywhere, indeed, except exactly there where only in this world he cared for favor. Margaret Liebenheim, she it was whom he loved, and had loved for years, with the whole ardor of his ardent soul; she it was for whom, or at whose command, he would willingly have died. Early he had felt that in her hands lay his destiny; that she it was who must be his good or his evil genius.

At first, and perhaps to the last, I pitied him exceedingly. But my pity soon ceased to be mingled with respect. Before the arrival of Mr. Wyndham he had shown himself generous, indeed magnanimous. But never was there so painful an overthrow of a noble nature as manifested itself in him. I believe that he had not himself suspected the strength of his passion; and the sole re-source for him, as I said often, was to quit the city – to engage in active pursuits of enterprise, of ambition, or of science. But he heard me as a somnambulist might have heard me – dreaming with his eyes open. Sometimes he had fits of reverie, starting, fearful, agitated; sometimes he broke out into maniacal move-ments of wrath, invoking some absent person, praying, beseech-ing, menacing some air-wove phantom; sometimes he slunk into solitary corners, muttering to himself, and with gestures sorrow-fully significant, or with tones and fragments of expostulation that moved the most callous to compassion. Still he turned a deaf ear to the only practical counsel that had a chance for reaching his ears. Like a bird under the fascination of a rattlesnake, he would not summon up the energies of his nature to make an effort at flying away. "Begone, while it is time!" said others, as well as myself; for more than I saw enough to fear some fearful catastro-phe. "Lead us not into temptation!" said his confessor to him in my hearing (for, though Prussians, the Von Harrelsteins were Roman Catholics), "lead us not into temptation! – that is our daily prayer to God. Then, my son, being led into temptation, do not you persist in courting, nay, almost tempting temptation. Try the effects of absence, though but for a month." The good father even made an overture toward imposing a penance upon him, that would have involved an absence of some duration. But he was obliged to desist; for he saw that, without effecting any good, he would merely add spiritual disobedience to the other offenses of the young man. Ferdinand himself drew his attention to THIS; for he said: "Reverend father! do not you, with the purpose of remov-ing me from temptation, be yourself the instrument for tempting me into a rebellion against the church. Do not you weave snares about my steps; snares there are already, and but too many." The old man sighed, and desisted.

Then came – But enough! From pity, from sympathy, from counsel, and from consolation, and from scorn – from each of these alike the poor stricken deer "recoiled into the wilderness;" he fled for days together into solitary parts of the forest; fled, as I still hoped and prayed, in good earnest and for a long farewell; but, alas! no: still he returned to the haunts of his ruined happiness and his buried hopes, at each return looking more like the wreck of his former self; and once I heard a penetrating monk observe, whose convent stood near the city gates: "There goes one ready equally for doing or suffering, and of whom we shall soon hear that he is involved in some great catastrophe – it may be of deep calamity – it may be of memorable guilt."

So stood matters among us. January was drawing to its close; the weather was growing more and more winterly; high winds, piercingly cold, were raving through our narrow streets; and still the spirit of social festivity bade defiance to the storms which sang through our ancient forests. From the accident of our magistracy being selected from the tradesmen of the city, the hospitalities of the place were far more extensive than would otherwise have happened; for every member of the corporation gave two annual entertainments in his official character. And such was the rivalship which prevailed, that often one quarter of the year's income was spent upon these galas. Nor was any ridicule thus incurred; for the costliness of the entertainment was understood to be an expression of OFFICIAL pride, done in honor of the city, not as an effort of personal display. It followed, from the spirit in which these half-yearly dances originated, that, being given on the part of the city, every stranger of rank was marked out as a privileged guest, and the hospitality of the community would have been equally affronted by failing to offer or by failing to accept the invitation.

Hence it had happened that the Russian guardsman had been introduced into many a family which otherwise could not have hoped for such a distinction. Upon the evening at which I am now arrived, the twenty-second of January, 1816, the whole city, in its wealthier classes, was assembled beneath the roof of a tradesman who had the heart of a prince. In every point our entertainment was superb; and I remarked that the music was the finest I had heard for years. Our host was in joyous spirits; proud to survey the splendid company he had gathered under his roof; happy to witness their happiness; elated in their elation. Joyous was the dance – joyous were all faces that I saw – up to midnight, very soon after which time supper was announced; and that also,

I think, was the most joyous of all the banquets I ever witnessed. The accomplished guardsman outshone himself in brilliancy; even his melancholy relaxed. In fact, how could it be otherwise? near to him sat Margaret Liebenheim – hanging upon his words – more lustrous and bewitching than ever I had beheld her. There she had been placed by the host; and everybody knew why. That is one of the luxuries attached to love; all men cede their places with pleasure; women make way. Even she herself knew, though not obliged to know, why she was seated in that neighborhood; and took her place, if with a rosy suffusion upon her cheeks, yet with fullness of happiness at her heart.

The guardsman pressed forward to claim Miss Liebenheim's hand for the next dance; a movement which she was quick to favor, by retreating behind one or two parties from a person who seemed coming toward her. The music again began to pour its voluptuous tides through the bounding pulses of the youthful company; again the flying feet of the dancers began to respond to the measures; again the mounting spirit of delight began to fill the sails of the hurrying night with steady inspiration. All went happily. Already had one dance finished; some were pacing up and down, leaning on the arms of their partners; some were re-posing from their exertions; when – O heavens! what a shriek! what a gathering tumult!

Every eye was bent toward the doors – every eye strained forward to discover what was passing. But there, every moment, less and less could be seen, for the gathering crowd more and more intercepted the view; – so much the more was the ear at leisure for the shrieks redoubled upon shrieks. Miss Liebenheim had moved downward to the crowd. From her superior height she overlooked all the ladies at the point where she stood. In the center stood a rustic girl, whose features had been familiar to her for some months. She had recently come into the city, and had lived with her uncle, a tradesman, not ten doors from Margaret's own residence, partly on the terms of a kinswoman, partly as a servant on trial. At this moment she was exhausted with excite-ment, and the nature of the shock she had sustained. Mere panic seemed to have mastered her; and she was leaning, unconscious and weeping, upon the shoulder of some gentleman, who was endeavoring to soothe her. A silence of horror seemed to possess the company, most of whom were still unacquainted with the cause of the alarming interruption. A few, however, who had heard her first agitated words, finding that they waited in vain for a fuller explanation, now rushed tumultuously out of the ball-room to satisfy themselves on the spot. The distance was not great; and within five minutes several persons returned hastily, and cried out to the crowd of ladies that all was true which the young girl had said. "What was true?" That her uncle Mr. Weishaupt's family had been murdered; that not one member of the family had been spared – namely, Mr. Weishaupt himself and his wife, neither of them much above sixty, but both infirm beyond their years; two maiden sisters of Mr. Weishaupt, from forty to forty-six years of age, and an elderly female domestic.

An incident happened during the recital of these horrors, and of the details which followed, that furnished matter for conversation even in these hours when so thrilling an interest had possession of all minds. Many ladies fainted; among them Miss Liebenheim – and she would have fallen to the ground but for Maximilian, who sprang forward and caught her in his arms. She was long of returning to herself; and, during the agony of his suspense, he stooped and kissed her pallid lips. That sight was more than could be borne by one who stood a little behind the group. He rushed forward, with eyes glaring like a tiger's, and leveled a blow at Maximilian. It was poor, maniacal Von Harrelstein, who had been absent in the forest for a week. Many people stepped forward and checked his arm, uplifted for a repetition of this outrage. One or two had some influence with him, and led him away from the spot; while as to Maximilian, so absorbed was he that he had not so much as perceived the affront offered to himself. Margaret, on reviving, was confounded at finding herself so situated amid a great crowd; and yet the prudes complained that there was a look of love exchanged between herself and Maximilian, that ought not to have escaped her in such a situation. If they meant by such a situation, one so public, it must be also recollected that it was a situation of excessive agitation; but, if they alluded to the horrors of the moment, no situation more naturally opens the heart to affection and confiding love than the recoil from scenes of exquisite terror.

An examination went on that night before the magistrates, but all was dark; although suspicion attached to a negro named Aaron, who had occasionally been employed in menial services by the family, and had been in the house immediately before the murder. The circumstances were such as to leave every man in utter perplexity as to the presumption for and against him. His mode of defending himself, and his general deportment, were marked by the coolest, nay, the most sneering indifference. The first thing he did, on being acquainted with the suspicions against himself, was to laugh ferociously, and to all appearance most cordially and unaffectedly. He demanded whether a poor man like himself would have left so much wealth as lay scattered abroad in that house – gold repeaters, massy plate, gold snuff boxes – untouched? That argument certainly weighed much in his favor. And yet again it was turned against him; for a magistrate asked him how HE happened to know already that nothing had been touched. True it was, and a fact which had puzzled no less than it had awed the magistrates, that, upon their examination of the premises, many rich articles of bijouterie, jewelry, and personal ornaments, had been found lying underanged, and apparently in their usual situations; articles so portable that in the very hastiest flight some might have been carried off. In particular, there was a crucifix of gold, enriched with jewels so large and rare, that of itself it would have constituted a prize of great magnitude. Yet this was left untouched, though suspended in a little oratory that had been magnificently adorned by the elder of the maiden sisters. There was an altar, in itself a splendid object, furnished with every article of the most costly material and workmanship, for the private celebration of mass. This crucifix, as well as everything else in the little closet, must have been seen by one at least of the murderous party; for hither had one of the ladies fled; hither had one of the murderers pursued. She had clasped the golden pillars which supported the altar – had turned perhaps her dying looks upon the crucifix; for there, with one arm still wreathed about the altar foot, though in her agony she had turned round upon her face, did the elder sister lie when the magistrates first broke open the street door. And upon the beautiful parquet, or inlaid floor which ran round the room, were still impressed the footsteps of the murderer. These, it was hoped, might furnish a clew to the discovery of one at least among the murderous band. They were rather difficult to trace accurately; those parts of the traces which lay upon the black tessellae being less distinct in the outline than the others upon the white or colored. Most unquestionably, so far as this went, it furnished a negative circumstance in favor of the negro, for the footsteps were very different in outline from his, and smaller, for Aaron was a man of colossal build. And as to his knowledge of the state in which the premises had been found, and his having so familiarly relied upon the fact of no robbery having taken place as an argument on his own behalf, he contended that he had himself been among the crowd that pushed into the house along with the magistrates; that, from his previous acquaintance with the rooms and their ordinary condition, a glance of the eye had been sufficient for him to ascertain the undisturbed condition of all the valuable property most obvious to the grasp of a robber that, in fact, he had seen enough for his argument before he and the rest of the mob had been ejected by the magistrates; but, finally, that independently of all this, he had heard both the officers, as they conducted him, and all the tumultuous gatherings of people in the street, arguing for the mysteriousness of the bloody transaction upon that very circumstance of so much gold, silver, and jewels, being left behind untouched.

In six weeks or less from the date of this terrific event, the negro was set at liberty by a majority of voices among the magistrates. In that short interval other events had occurred no less terrific and mysterious. In this first murder, though the motive was dark and unintelligible, yet the agency was not so; ordinary assassins apparently, and with ordinary means, had assailed a helpless and unprepared family; had separated them; attacked them singly in flight (for in this first case all but one of the murdered persons appeared to have been making for the street door); and in all this there was no subject for wonder, except the original one as to the motive. But now came a series of cases destined to fling this earliest murder into the shade. Nobody could now be unprepared; and yet the tragedies, henceforward, which passed before us, one by one, in sad, leisurely, or in terrific groups, seemed to argue a lethargy like that of apoplexy in the victims, one and all. The very midnight of mysterious awe fell upon all minds.

Three weeks had passed since the murder at Mr. Weishaupt's – three weeks the most agitated that had been known in this sequestered city. We felt ourselves solitary, and thrown upon our own resources; all combination with other towns being unavailing from their great distance. Our situation was no ordinary one. Had there been some mysterious robbers among us, the chances of a visit, divided among so many, would have been too small to distress the most timid; while to young and high-spirited people, with courage to spare for ordinary trials, such a state of expectation would have sent pulses of pleasurable anxiety among the nerves. But murderers! exterminating murderers! – clothed in mystery and utter darkness – these were objects too terrific for any family to contemplate with fortitude. Had these very murderers added to their functions those of robbery, they would have become less terrific; nine out of every ten would have found themselves discharged, as it were, from the roll of those who were liable to a visit; while such as knew themselves liable would have had warning of their danger in the fact of being rich; and would, from the very riches which constituted that danger, have derived the means of repelling it. But, as things were, no man could guess what it was that must make him obnoxious to the murderers. Imagination exhausted itself in vain guesses at the causes which could by possibility have made the poor Weishaupts objects of such hatred to any man. True, they were bigoted in a degree which indicated feebleness of intellect; but THAT wounded no man in particular, while to many it recommended them. True, their charity was narrow and exclusive, but to those of their own religious body it expanded munificently; and, being rich beyond their wants, or any means of employing wealth which their gloomy asceticism allowed, they had the power of doing a great deal of good among the indigent papists of the suburbs. As to the old gentleman and his wife, their infirmities confined them to the house. Nobody remembered to have seen them abroad for years. How, therefore, or when could they have made an enemy? And, with respect to the maiden sisters of Mr. Weishaupt, they were simply weak-minded persons, now and then too censorious, but not placed in a situation to incur serious anger from any quarter, and too little heard of in society to occupy much of anybody's attention.

Conceive, then, that three weeks have passed away, that the poor Weishaupts have been laid in that narrow sanctuary which no murderer's voice will ever violate. Quiet has not returned to us, but the first flutterings of panic have subsided. People are beginning to respire freely again; and such another space of time would have cicatrized our wounds – when, hark! a church bell rings out a loud alarm; – the night is starlight and frosty – the iron notes are heard clear, solemn, but agitated. What could this mean? I hurried to a room over the porter's lodge, and, opening the window, I cried out to a man passing hastily below, "What, in God's name, is the meaning of this?" It was a watchman belonging to our district. I knew his voice, he knew mine, and he replied in great agitation:

"It is another murder, sir, at the old town councilor's, Albernass; and this time they have made a clear house of it."

"God preserve us! Has a curse been pronounced upon this city? What can be done? What are the magistrates going to do?"

"I don't know, sir. I have orders to run to the Black Friars, where another meeting is gathering. Shall I say you will attend, sir?"

"Yes – no – stop a little. No matter, you may go on; I'll follow immediately."

I went instantly to Maximilian's room. He was lying asleep on a sofa, at which I was not surprised, for there had been a severe stag chase in the morning. Even at this moment I found myself arrested by two objects, and I paused to survey them. One was Maximilian himself. A person so mysterious took precedency of other interests even at a time like this; and especially by his features, which, composed in profound sleep, as sometimes happens, assumed a new expression, which arrested me chiefly by awaking some confused remembrance of the same features seen under other circumstances and in times long past; but where? This was what I could not recollect, though once before a thought of the same sort had crossed my mind. The other object of my interest was a miniature, which Maximilian was holding in his hand. He had gone to sleep apparently looking at this picture; and the hand which held it had slipped down upon the sofa, so that it was in danger of falling. I released the miniature from his hand, and surveyed it attentively. It represented a lady of sunny, oriental complexion, and features the most noble that it is possible to conceive. One might have imagined such a lady, with her raven locks and imperial eyes, to be the favorite sultana of some Amurath or Mohammed. What was she to Maximilian, or what HAD she been? For, by the tear which I had once seen him drop upon this miniature when he believed himself unobserved, I conjectured that her dark tresses were already laid low, and her name among the list of vanished things. Probably she was his mother, for the dress was rich with pearls, and evidently that of a person in the highest rank of court beauties. I sighed as I thought of the stern melancholy of her son, if Maximilian were he, as connected, probably, with the fate and fortunes of this majestic beauty; somewhat haughty, perhaps, in the expression of her fine features, but still noble – generous – confiding. Laying the picture on the table, I awoke Maximilian, and told him of the dreadful news. He listened attentively, made no remark, but proposed that we should go together to the meeting of our quarter at the Black Friars. He colored upon observing the miniature on the table; and, therefore, I frankly told him in what situation I had found it, and that I had taken the liberty of admiring it for a few moments. He pressed it tenderly to his lips, sighed heavily, and we walked away together.

I pass over the frenzied state of feeling in which we found the meeting. Fear, or rather horror, did not promote harmony; many quarreled with each other in discussing the suggestions brought forward, and Maximilian was the only person attended to. He proposed a nightly mounted patrol for every district. And in particular he offered, as being himself a member of the university, that the students should form themselves into a guard, and go out by rotation to keep watch and ward from sunset to sunrise. Arrangements were made toward that object by the few people who retained possession of their senses, and for the present we separated.

Never, in fact, did any events so keenly try the difference between man and man. Some started up into heroes under the excitement. Some, alas for the dignity of man! drooped into helpless imbecility. Women, in some cases, rose superior to men, but yet not so often as might have happened under a less mysterious danger. A woman is not unwomanly because she confronts danger boldly. But I have remarked, with respect to female courage, that it requires, more than that of men, to be sustained by hope; and that it droops more certainly in the presence of a MYSTERIOUS danger. The fancy of women is more active, if not stronger, and it influences more directly the physical nature. In this case few were the women who made even a show of defying the danger. On the contrary, with THEM fear took the form of sadness, while with many of the men it took that of wrath.

And how did the Russian guardsman conduct himself amidst this panic? Many were surprised at his behavior; some complained of it; I did neither. He took a reasonable interest in each separate case, listened to the details with attention, and, in the examination of persons able to furnish evidence, never failed to suggest judicious questions. But still he manifested a coolness almost amounting to carelessness, which to many appeared revolting. But these people I desired to notice that all the other military students, who had been long in the army, felt exactly in the same way. In fact, the military service of Christendom, for the last ten years, had been anything but a parade service; and to those, therefore, who were familiar with every form of horrid butchery, the mere outside horrors of death had lost much of their terror. In the recent murder there had not been much to call forth sympathy. The family consisted of two old bachelors, two sisters, and one grandniece. The niece was absent on a visit, and the two old men were cynical misers, to whom little personal interest attached. Still, in this case as in that of the Weishaupts, the same

115

twofold mystery confounded the public mind – the mystery of the HOW, and the profounder mystery of the WHY. Here, again, no atom of property was taken, though both the misers had hordes of ducats and English guineas in the very room where they died. Their bias, again, though of an unpopular character, had rather availed to make them unknown than to make them hateful. In one point this case differed memorably from the other – that, instead of falling helpless, or flying victims (as the Weishaupts had done), these old men, strong, resolute, and not so much taken by surprise, left proofs that they had made a desperate defense. The furniture was partly smashed to pieces, and the other details furnished evidence still more revolting of the acharnement with which the struggle had been maintained. In fact, with THEM a surprise must have been impracticable, as they admitted nobody into their house on visiting terms. It was thought singular that from each of these domestic tragedies a benefit of the same sort should result to young persons standing in nearly the same relation. The girl who gave the alarm at the ball, with two little sisters, and a little orphan nephew, their cousin, divided the very large inheritance of the Weishaupts; and in this latter case the accumulated savings of two long lives all vested in the person of the amiable grandniece.

But now, as if in mockery of all our anxious consultations and elaborate devices, three fresh murders took place on the two consecutive nights succeeding these new arrangements. And in one case, as nearly as time could be noted, the mounted patrol must have been within call at the very moment when the awful work was going on. I shall not dwell much upon them; but a few circumstances are too interesting to be passed over. The earliest case on the first of the two nights was that of a currier. He was fifty years old; not rich, but well off. His first wife was dead, and his daughters by her were married away from their father's house. He had married a second wife, but, having no children by her, and keeping no servants, it is probable that, but for an accident, no third person would have been in the house at the time when the murderers got admittance. About seven o'clock, a wayfaring man, a journeyman currier, who, according to our German system, was now in his wanderjahre, entered the city from the

116

forest. At the gate he made some inquiries about the curriers and tanners of our town; and, agreeably to the information he received, made his way to this Mr. Heinberg. Mr. Heinberg refused to admit him, until he mentioned his errand, and pushed below the door a letter of recommendation from a Silesian correspondent, describing him as an excellent and steady workman. Wanting such a man, and satisfied by the answers returned that he was what he represented himself, Mr. Heinberg unbolted his door and admitted him. Then, after slipping the bolt into its place, he bade him sit to the fire, brought him a glass of beer, conversed with him for ten minutes, and said: "You had better stay here to-night; I'll tell you why afterwards; but now I'll step upstairs, and ask my wife whether she can make up a bed for you; and do you mind the door while I'm away." So saying, he went out of the room. Not one minute had he been gone when there came a gentle knock at the door. It was raining heavily, and, being a stranger to the city, not dreaming that in any crowded town such a state of things could exist as really did in this, the young man, without hesitation, admitted the person knocking. He has declared since – but, perhaps, confounding the feelings gained from better knowledge with the feelings of the moment – that from the moment he drew the bolt he had a misgiving that he had done wrong. A man entered in a horseman's cloak, and so muffled up that the journeyman could discover none of his features. In a low tone the stranger said, "Where's Heinberg?" – "Upstairs." – "Call him down, then." The journeyman went to the door by which Mr. Heinberg had left him, and called, "Mr. Heinberg, here's one wanting you!" Mr. Heinberg heard him, for the man could distinctly catch these words: "God bless me! has the man opened the door? O, the traitor! I see it." Upon this he felt more and more consternation, though not knowing why. Just then he heard a sound of feet behind him. On turning round, he beheld three more men in the room; one was fastening the outer door; one was drawing some arms from a cupboard, and two others were whispering together. He himself was disturbed and perplexed, and felt that all was not right. Such was his confusion, that either all the men's faces must have been muffled up, or at least he remembered nothing distinctly but one fierce pair of eyes glaring upon him. Then, before he could look round, came a man from behind and threw a sack over his head, which was drawn tight about his waist, so as to confine his arms, as well as to impede his hearing in part, and his voice altogether. He was then pushed into a room; but previously he had heard a rush upstairs, and words like those of a person exulting, and then a door closed. Once it opened, and he could distinguish the words, in one voice, "And for THAT!" to which another voice replied, in tones that made his heart quake, "Aye, for THAT, sir." And then the same voice went on rapidly to say, "O dog! could you hope" – at which word the door closed again. Once he thought that he heard a scuffle, and he was sure that he heard the sound of feet, as if rushing from one corner of a room to another. But then all was hushed and still for about six or seven minutes, until a voice close to his ear said, "Now, wait quietly till some persons come in to release you. This will happen within half an hour." Accordingly, in less than that time, he again heard the sound of feet within the house, his own bandages were liberated, and he was brought to tell his story at the police office. Mr. Heinberg was found in his bedroom. He had died by strangulation, and the cord was still tightened about his neck. During the whole dreadful scene his youthful wife had been locked into a closet, where she heard or saw nothing.

In the second case, the object of vengeance was again an elderly man. Of the ordinary family, all were absent at a country house, except the master and a female servant. She was a woman of courage, and blessed with the firmest nerves; so that she might have been relied on for reporting accurately everything seen or heard. But things took another course. The first warning that she had of the murderers' presence was from their steps and voices already in the hall. She heard her master run hastily into the hall, crying out, "Lord Jesus! – Mary, Mary, save me!" The servant resolved to give what aid she could, seized a large poker, and was hurrying to his assistance, when she found that they had nailed up the door of communication at the head of the stairs. What passed after this she could not tell; for, when the impulse of intrepid fidelity had been balked, and she found that her own safety was provided for by means which made it impossible to aid a poor fellow creature who had just invoked her name, the generous-hearted creature was overcome by anguish of mind, and sank down on the stair, where she lay, unconscious of all that succeeded, until she found herself raised in the arms of a mob who had entered the house. And how came they to have entered? In a way characteristically dreadful. The night was starlit; the patrols had perambulated the street without noticing anything suspicious, when two foot passengers, who were following in their rear, observed a dark-colored stream traversing the causeway. One of them, at the same instant tracing the stream backward with his eyes, observed that it flowed from under the door of Mr. Munzer, and, dipping his finger in the trickling fluid, he held it up to the lamplight, yelling out at the moment, "Why, this is blood!" It was so, indeed, and it was yet warm. The other saw, heard, and like an arrow flew after the horse patrol, then in the act of turning the corner. One cry, full of meaning, was sufficient for ears full of expectation. The horsemen pulled up, wheeled, and in another moment reined up at Mr. Munzer's door. The crowd, gathering like the drifting of snow, supplied implements which soon forced the chains of the door and all other obstacles. But the murderous party had escaped, and all traces of their persons had vanished, as usual.

Rarely did any case occur without some peculiarity more or less interesting. In that which happened on the following night, making the fifth in the series, an impressive incident varied the monotony of horrors. In this case the parties aimed at were two elderly ladies, who conducted a female boarding school. None of the pupils had as yet returned to school from their vacation; but two sisters, young girls of thirteen and sixteen, coming from a distance, had stayed at school throughout the Christmas holidays. It was the youngest of these who gave the only evidence of any value, and one which added a new feature of alarm to the existing panic. Thus it was that her testimony was given: On the day before the murder, she and her sister were sitting with the old ladies in a room fronting to the street; the elder ladies were reading, the younger ones drawing. Louisa, the youngest, never had her ear inattentive to the slightest sound, and once it struck her that she heard the creaking of a foot upon the stairs. She said nothing, but, slipping out of the room, she ascertained that the two female servants were in the kitchen, and could not have been absent; that all the doors and windows, by which ingress was possible, were not only locked, but bolted and barred – a fact which excluded all possibility of invasion by means of false keys. Still she felt persuaded that she had heard the sound of a heavy foot upon the stairs. It was, however, daylight, and this gave her confidence; so that, without communicating her alarm to anybody, she found courage to traverse the house in every direction; and, as nothing was either seen or heard, she concluded that her ears had been too sensitively awake. Yet that night, as she lay in bed, dim terrors assailed her, especially because she considered that, in so large a house, some closet or other might have been overlooked, and, in particular, she did not remember to have examined one or two chests, in which a man could have lain concealed. Through the greater part of the night she lay awake; but as one of the town clocks struck four, she dismissed her anxieties, and fell asleep. The next day, wearied with this unusual watching, she proposed to her sister that they should go to bed earlier than usual. This they did; and, on their way upstairs, Louisa happened to think suddenly of a heavy cloak, which would improve the coverings of her bed against the severity of the night. The cloak was hanging up in a closet within a closet, both leading off from a large room used as the young ladies' dancing school. These closets she had examined on the previous day, and therefore she felt no particular alarm at this moment. The cloak was the first article which met her sight; it was suspended from a hook in the wall, and close to the door. She took it down, but, in doing so, exposed part of the wall and of the floor, which its folds had previously concealed. Turning away hastily, the chances were that she had gone without making any discovery. In the act of turning, however, her light fell brightly on a man's foot and leg. Matchless was her presence of mind; having previously been humming an air, she continued to do so. But now came the trial; her sister was bending her steps to the same closet. If she suffered her to do so, Lottchen would stumble on the same discovery, and expire of fright. On the other hand, if she gave her a hint, Lottchen would either fail to understand her, or, gaining but a glimpse of her meaning, would shriek aloud, or by some equally decisive expression convey the fatal news to the assassin that he had been discovered. In this torturing dilemma fear prompted an expedient, which to Lottchen appeared madness, and to Louisa herself the act of a sibyl instinct with blind inspiration. "Here," said she, "is our dancing room. When shall we all meet and dance again together?" Saying which, she commenced a wild dance, whirling her candle round her head until the motion extinguished it; then, eddying round her sister in narrowing circles, she seized Lottchen's candle also, blew it out, and then interrupted her own singing to attempt a laugh. But the laugh was hysterical. The darkness, however, favored her; and, seizing her sister's arm, she forced her along, whispering, "Come, come, come!" Lottchen could not be so dull as entirely to misunderstand her. She suffered herself to be led up the first flight of stairs, at the head of which was a room looking into the street. In this they would have gained an asylum, for the door had a strong bolt. But, as they were on the last steps of the landing, they could hear the hard breathing and long strides of the murderer ascending behind them. He had watched them through a crevice, and had been satisfied by the hysterical laugh of Louisa that she had seen him. In the darkness he could not follow fast, from ignorance of the localities, until he found himself upon the stairs. Louisa, dragging her sister along, felt strong as with the strength of lunacy, but Lottchen hung like a weight of lead upon her. She rushed into the room, but at the very entrance Lottchen fell. At that moment the assassin exchanged his stealthy pace for a loud clattering ascent. Already he was on the topmost stair; already he was throwing himself at a bound against the door, when Louisa, having dragged her sister into the room, closed the door and sent the bolt home in the very instant that the murderer's hand came into contact with the handle. Then, from the violence of her emotions, she fell down in a fit, with her arm around the sister whom she had saved.

How long they lay in this state neither ever knew. The two old ladies had rushed upstairs on hearing the tumult. Other persons had been concealed in other parts of the house. The servants found themselves suddenly locked in, and were not sorry to be saved from a collision which involved so awful a danger. The old ladies had rushed, side by side, into the very center of those who were seeking them. Retreat was impossible; two persons at least were heard following them upstairs. Something like a shrieking expostulation and counter-expostulation went on between the ladies and the murderers; then came louder voices – then one heart-piercing shriek, and then another – and then a slow moaning and a dead silence. Shortly afterwards was heard the first crashing of the door inward by the mob; but the murderers had fled upon the first alarm, and, to the astonishment of the servants, had fled upward. Examination, however, explained this: from a window in the roof they had passed to an adjoining house recently left empty; and here, as in other cases, we had proof how apt people are, in the midst of elaborate provisions against remote dangers, to neglect those which are obvious.

The reign of terror, it may be supposed, had now reached its acme. The two old ladies were both lying dead at different points on the staircase, and, as usual, no conjecture could be made as to the nature of the offense which they had given; but that the murder WAS a vindictive one, the usual evidence remained behind, in the proofs that no robbery had been attempted. Two new features, however, were now brought forward in this system of horrors, one of which riveted the sense of their insecurity to all families occupying extensive houses, and the other raised ill blood between the city and the university, such as required years to allay. The first arose out of the experience, now first obtained, that these assassins pursued the plan of secreting themselves within the house where they meditated a murder. All the care, therefore, previously directed to the securing of doors and windows after nightfall appeared nugatory. The other feature brought to light on this occasion was vouched for by one of the servants, who declared that, the moment before the door of the kitchen was fastened upon herself and fellow servant, she saw two men in the hall, one on the point of ascending the stairs, the other making toward the kitchen; that she could not distinguish the faces of either, but that both were dressed in the academic costume belonging to the students of the university. The consequences of such a declaration need scarcely be mentioned. Suspicion settled upon the students, who were more numerous since the general peace, in a much larger proportion military, and less select or respectable than heretofore. Still, no part of the mystery was cleared up by this discovery. Many of the students were poor enough to feel the temptation that might be offered by any LU-CRATIVE system of outrage. Jealous and painful collusions were, in the meantime, produced; and, during the latter two months of this winter, it may be said that our city exhibited the very anarchy of evil passions. This condition of things lasted until the dawning of another spring.

It will be supposed that communications were made to the supreme government of the land as soon as the murders in our city were understood to be no casual occurrences, but links in a systematic series. Perhaps it might happen from some other business, of a higher kind, just then engaging the attention of our governors, that our representations did not make the impression we had expected. We could not, indeed, complain of absolute neglect from the government. They sent down one or two of their most accomplished police officers, and they suggested some counsels, especially that we should examine more strictly into the quality of the miscellaneous population who occupied our large suburb. But they more than hinted that no necessity was seen either for quartering troops upon us, or for arming our local magistracy with ampler powers.

This correspondence with the central government occupied the month of March, and, before that time, the bloody system had ceased as abruptly as it began. The new police officer flattered himself that the terror of his name had wrought this effect; but judicious people thought otherwise. All, however, was quiet until the depth of summer, when, by way of hinting to us, perhaps, that the dreadful power which clothed itself with darkness had not expired, but was only reposing from its labors, all at once the chief jailer of the city was missing. He had been in the habit of taking long rides in the forest, his present situation being much of a sinecure. It was on the first of July that he was missed. In riding through the city gates that morning, he had mentioned the direction which he meant to pursue; and the last time he was seen alive was in one of the forest avenues, about eight miles from the city, leading toward the point he had indicated. This jailer was not a man to be regretted on his own account; his life had been a tissue of cruelty and brutal abuse of his powers, in which he had been too much supported by the magistrates, partly on the plea that it was their duty to back their own officers against all complainers, partly also from the necessities created by the turbulent times for a more summary exercise of their magisterial authority. No man, therefore, on his own separate account, could more willingly have been spared than this brutal jailer; and it was a general remark that, had the murderous band within our walls swept away this man only, they would have merited the public gratitude as purifiers from a public nuisance. But was it certain that the jailer had died by the same hands as had so deeply afflicted the peace of our city during the winter – or, indeed, that he had been murdered at all? The forest was too extensive to be searched; and it was possible that he might have met with some fatal accident. His horse had returned to the city gates in the night, and was found there in the morning. Nobody, however, for months could give information about his rider; and it seemed probable that he would not be discovered until the autumn and the winter should again carry the sportsman into every thicket and dingle of this sylvan tract. One person only seemed to have more knowledge on this subject than others, and that was poor Ferdinand von Harrelstein. He was now a mere ruin of what he had once been, both as to intellect and moral feeling; and I observed him frequently smile when the jailer was mentioned. "Wait," he would say, "till the leaves begin to drop; then you will see what fine fruit our forest bears." I did not repeat these expressions to anybody except one friend, who agreed with me that the jailer had probably been hanged in some recess of the forest, which summer veiled with its luxuriant umbrage; and that Ferdinand, constantly wandering in the forest, had discovered the body; but we both acquitted him of having been an accomplice in the murder.

Meantime the marriage between Margaret Liebenheim and Maximilian was understood to be drawing near. Yet one thing struck everybody with astonishment. As far as the young people were concerned, nobody could doubt that all was arranged; for never was happiness more perfect than that which seemed to unite them. Margaret was the impersonation of May-time and youthful rapture; even Maximilian in her presence seemed to forget his gloom, and the worm which gnawed at his heart was charmed asleep by the music of her voice, and the paradise of her smiles. But, until the autumn came, Margaret's grandfather had never ceased to frown upon this connection, and to support the pretensions of Ferdinand. The dislike, indeed, seemed reciprocal between him and Maximilian. Each avoided the other's company and as to the old man, he went so far as to speak sneeringly of Maximilian. Maximilian despised him too heartily to speak of him at all. When he could not avoid meeting him, he treated him with a stern courtesy, which distressed Margaret as often as she witnessed it. She felt that her grandfather had been the aggressor; and she felt also that he did injustice to the merits of her lover. But she had a filial tenderness for the old man, as the father of her sainted mother, and on his own account, continually making more claims on her pity, as the decay of his memory, and a childish fretfulness growing upon him from day to day, marked his increasing imbecility.

Equally mysterious it seemed, that about this time Miss Liebenheim began to receive anonymous letters, written in the darkest and most menacing terms. Some of them she showed to me. I could not guess at their drift. Evidently they glanced at Maximilian, and bade her beware of connection with him; and dreadful things were insinuated about him. Could these letters be written by Ferdinand? Written they were not, but could they be dictated by him? Much I feared that they were; and the more so for one reason.

All at once, and most inexplicably, Margaret's grandfather showed a total change of opinion in his views as to her marriage. Instead of favoring Harrelstein's pretensions, as he had hitherto done, he now threw the feeble weight of his encouragement into Maximilian's scale; though, from the situation of all the parties, nobody attached any PRACTICAL importance to the change in Mr. Liebenheim's way of thinking. Nobody? Is that true? No; one person DID attach the greatest weight to the change – poor, ruined Ferdinand. He, so long as there was one person to take his part, so long as the grandfather of Margaret showed countenance to himself, had still felt his situation not utterly desperate.

Thus were things situated, when in November, all the leaves daily blowing off from the woods, and leaving bare the most secret haunts of the thickets, the body of the jailer was left exposed in the forest; but not, as I and my friend had conjectured, hanged. No; he had died apparently by a more horrid death – by that of crucifixion. The tree, a remarkable one, bore upon a part of its trunk this brief but savage inscription: – "T. H., jailer at – – –; Crucified July 1, 1816."

A great deal of talk went on throughout the city upon this discovery; nobody uttered one word of regret on account of the wretched jailer; on the contrary, the voice of vengeance, rising up in many a cottage, reached my ears in every direction as I walked abroad. The hatred in itself seemed horrid and unchristian, and still more so after the man's death; but, though horrid and fiendish for itself, it was much more impressive, considered as the measure and exponent of the damnable oppression which must have existed to produce it.

At first, when the absence of the jailer was a recent occurrence, and the presence of the murderers among us was, in consequence, revived to our anxious thoughts, it was an event which few alluded to without fear. But matters were changed now; the jailer had been dead for months, and this interval, during which the murderer's hand had slept, encouraged everybody to hope that the storm had passed over our city; that peace had returned to our hearths; and that henceforth weakness might sleep in safety, and innocence without anxiety. Once more we had peace within our walls, and tranquillity by our firesides. Again the child went to bed in cheerfulness, and the old man said his prayers in serenity. Confidence was restored; peace was re-established; and once again the sanctity of human life became the rule and the principle for all human hands among us. Great was the joy; the happiness was universal.

O heavens! by what a thunderbolt were we awakened from

our security! On the night of the twenty-seventh of December, half an hour, it might be, after twelve o'clock, an alarm was given that all was not right in the house of Mr. Liebenheim. Vast was the crowd which soon collected in breathless agitation. In two minutes a man who had gone round by the back of the house was heard unbarring Mr. Liebenheim's door: he was incapable of uttering a word; but his gestures, as he threw the door open and beckoned to the crowd, were quite enough. In the hall, at the further extremity, and as if arrested in the act of making for the back door, lay the bodies of old Mr. Liebenheim and one of his sisters, an aged widow; on the stair lay another sister, younger and unmarried, but upward of sixty. The hall and lower flight of stairs were floating with blood. Where, then, was Miss Liebenheim, the granddaughter? That was the universal cry; for she was beloved as generally as she was admired. Had the infernal murderers been devilish enough to break into that temple of innocent and happy life? Everyone asked the question, and everyone held his breath to listen; but for a few moments no one dared to advance; for the silence of the house was ominous. At length some one cried out that Miss Liebenheim had that day gone upon a visit to a friend, whose house was forty miles distant in the forest. "Aye," replied another," she had settled to go; but I heard that something had stopped her." The suspense was now at its height, and the crowd passed from room to room, but found no traces of Miss Liebenheim. At length they ascended the stair, and in the very first room, a small closet, or boudoir, lay Margaret, with her dress soiled hideously with blood. The first impression was that she also had been murdered; but, on a nearer approach, she appeared to be unwounded, and was manifestly alive. Life had not departed, for her breath sent a haze over a mirror, but it was suspended, and she was laboring in some kind of fit. The first act of the crowd was to carry her into the house of a friend on the opposite side of the street, by which time medical assistance had crowded to the spot. Their attentions to Miss Liebenheim had naturally deranged the condition of things in the little room, but not before many people found time to remark that one of the murderers must have carried her with his bloody hands to the sofa on which she lay, for water had been sprinkled profusely over her face and throat, and water was even placed ready to her hand, when she might happen to recover, upon a low foot-stool by the side of the sofa.

On the following morning, Maximilian, who had been upon a hunting party in the forest, returned to the city, and immediately learned the news. I did not see him for some hours after, but he then appeared to me thoroughly agitated, for the first time I had known him to be so. In the evening another perplexing piece of intelligence transpired with regard to Miss Liebenheim, which at first afflicted every friend of that young lady. It was that she had been seized with the pains of childbirth, and delivered of a son, who, however, being born prematurely, did not live many hours. Scandal, however, was not allowed long to batten upon this imaginary triumph, for within two hours after the circulation of this first rumor, followed a second, authenticated, announcing that Maximilian had appeared with the confessor of the Liebenheim family, at the residence of the chief magistrate, and there produced satisfactory proofs of his marriage with Miss Liebenheim, which had been duly celebrated, though with great secrecy, nearly eight months before. In our city, as in all the cities of our country, clandestine marriages, witnessed, perhaps, by two friends only of the parties, besides the officiating priest, are exceedingly common. In the mere fact, therefore, taken separately, there was nothing to surprise us, but, taken in connection with the general position of the parties, it DID surprise us all; nor could we conjecture the reason for a step apparently so needless. For, that Maximilian could have thought it any point of prudence or necessity to secure the hand of Margaret Liebenheim by a private marriage, against the final opposition of her grandfather, nobody who knew the parties, who knew the perfect love which possessed Miss Liebenheim, the growing imbecility of her grandfather, or the utter contempt with which Maximilian regarded him, could for a moment believe. Altogether, the matter was one of profound mystery.

Meantime, it rejoiced me that poor Margaret's name had been thus rescued from the fangs of the scandalmongers. These harpies had their prey torn from them at the very moment when they were sitting down to the unhallowed banquet. For this I rejoiced, but else there was little subject for rejoicing in anything which concerned poor Margaret. Long she lay in deep insensibility, taking no notice of anything, rarely opening her eyes, and apparently unconscious of the revolutions, as they succeeded, of morning or evening, light or darkness, yesterday or to-day. Great was the agitation which convulsed the heart of Maximilian during this period; he walked up and down in the cathedral nearly all day long, and the ravages which anxiety was working in his physical system might be read in his face. People felt it an intrusion upon the sanctity of his grief to look at him too narrowly, and the whole town sympathized with his situation.

At length a change took place in Margaret, but one which the medical men announced to Maximilian as boding ill for her recovery. The wanderings of her mind did not depart, but they altered their character. She became more agitated; she would start up suddenly, and strain her eye-sight after some figure which she seemed to see; then she would apostrophize some person in the most piteous terms, beseeching him, with streaming eyes, to spare her old grandfather. "Look, look," she would cry out, "look at his gray hairs! O, sir! he is but a child; he does not know what he says; and he will soon be out of the way and in his grave; and very soon, sir, he will give you no more trouble." Then, again, she would mutter indistinctly for hours together; sometimes she would cry out frantically, and say things which terrified the bystanders, and which the physicians would solemnly caution them how they repeated; then she would weep, and invoke Maximilian to come and aid her. But seldom, indeed, did that name pass her lips that she did not again begin to strain her eyeballs, and start up in bed to watch some phantom of her poor, fevered heart, as if it seemed vanishing into some mighty distance.

After nearly seven weeks passed in this agitating state, suddenly, on one morning, the earliest and the loveliest of dawning spring, a change was announced to us all as having taken place in Margaret; but it was a change, alas! that ushered in the last great change of all. The conflict, which had for so long a period raged within her, and overthrown her reason, was at an end; the strife was over, and nature was settling into an everlasting rest. In the course of the night she had recovered her senses. When the morning light penetrated through her curtain, she recognized her attendants, made inquiries as to the month and the day of the month, and then, sensible that she could not outlive the day, she requested that her confessor might be summoned.

About an hour and a half the confessor remained alone with her. At the end of that time he came out, and hastily summoned the attendants, for Margaret, he said, was sinking into a fainting fit. The confessor himself might have passed through many a fit, so much was he changed by the results of this interview. I crossed him coming out of the house. I spoke to him – I called to him; but he heard me not – he saw me not. He saw nobody. Onward he strode to the cathedral, where Maximilian was sure to be found, pacing about upon the graves. Him he seized by the arm, whispered something into his ear, and then both retired into one of the many sequestered chapels in which lights are continually burning. There they had some conversation, but not very long, for within five minutes Maximilian strode away to the house in which his young wife was dying. One step seemed to carry him upstairs. The attendants, according to the directions they had received from the physicians, mustered at the head of the stairs to oppose him. But that was idle: before the rights which he held as a lover and a husband – before the still more sacred rights of grief, which he carried in his countenance, all opposition fled like a dream. There was, besides, a fury in his eye. A motion of his hand waved them off like summer flies; he entered the room, and once again, for the last time, he was in company with his beloved.

What passed who could pretend to guess? Something more than two hours had elapsed, during which Margaret had been able to talk occasionally, which was known, because at times the attendants heard the sound of Maximilian's voice evidently in tones of reply to something which she had said. At the end of that time, a little bell, placed near the bedside, was rung hastily. A fainting fit had seized Margaret; but she recovered almost before her women applied the usual remedies. They lingered, however, a little, looking at the youthful couple with an interest which no restraints availed to check. Their hands were locked together, and in Margaret's eyes there gleamed a farewell light of love, which settled upon Maximilian, and seemed to indicate that she was becoming speechless. Just at this moment she made a feeble effort to draw Maximilian toward her; he bent forward and kissed her with an anguish that made the most callous weep, and then he whispered something into her ear, upon which the attendants retired, taking this as a proof that their presence was a hindrance to a free communication. But they heard no more talking, and in less than ten minutes they returned. Maximilian and Margaret still retained their former position. Their hands were fast locked together; the same parting ray of affection, the same farewell light of love, was in the eye of Margaret, and still it settled upon Maximilian. But her eyes were beginning to grow dim; mists were rapidly stealing over them. Maximilian, who sat stupefied and like one not in his right mind, now, at the gentle request of the women, resigned his seat, for the hand which had clasped his had already relaxed its hold; the farewell gleam of love had departed. One of the women closed her eyelids; and there fell asleep forever the loveliest flower that our city had reared for generations.

The funeral took place on the fourth day after her death. In the morning of that day, from strong affection – having known her from an infant – I begged permission to see the corpse. She was in her coffin; snowdrops and crocuses were laid upon her innocent bosom, and roses, of that sort which the season allowed, over her person. These and other lovely symbols of youth, of springtime, and of resurrection, caught my eye for the first moment; but in the next it fell upon her face. Mighty God! what a change! what a transfiguration! Still, indeed, there was the same innocent sweetness; still there was something of the same loveliness; the expression still remained; but for the features – all trace of flesh seemed to have vanished; mere outline of bony structure remained; mere pencilings and shadowings of what she once had been. This is, indeed, I exclaimed, "dust to dust – ashes to ashes!"

Maximilian, to the astonishment of everybody, attended the funeral. It was celebrated in the cathedral. All made way for him, and at times he seemed collected; at times he reeled like one who was drunk. He heard as one who hears not; he saw as one in a dream. The whole ceremony went on by torchlight, and toward the close he stood like a pillar, motionless, torpid, frozen. But the great burst of the choir, and the mighty blare ascending from our vast organ at the closing of the grave, recalled him to himself, and he strode rapidly homeward. Half an hour after I returned, I was summoned to his bedroom. He was in bed, calm and collected. What he said to me I remember as if it had been yesterday, and the very tone with which he said it, although more than twenty years have passed since then. He began thus: "I have not long to live"; and when he saw me start, suddenly awakened into a consciousness that perhaps he had taken poison, and meant to intimate as much, he continued: "You fancy I have taken poison; – no matter whether I have or not; if I have, the poison is such that no antidote will now avail; or, if they would, you well know that some griefs are of a kind which leave no opening to any hope. What difference, therefore, can it make whether I leave this earth to-day, to- morrow, or the next day? Be assured of this – that whatever I have determined to do is past all power of being affected by a human opposition. Occupy yourself not with any fruitless attempts, but calmly listen to me, else I know what to do." Seeing a suppressed fury in his eye, notwithstanding I saw also some change stealing over his features as if from some subtle poison beginning to work upon his frame, awestruck I consented to listen, and sat still. "It is well that you do so, for my time is short. Here is my will, legally drawn up, and you will see that I have committed an immense property to your discretion. Here, again, is a paper still more important in my eyes; it is also testamentary, and binds you to duties which may not be so easy to execute as the disposal of my property. But now listen to something else, which concerns neither of these papers. Promise me, in the first place, solemnly, that whenever I die you will see me buried in the same grave as my wife, from whose funeral we are just returned. Promise." – I promised. – "Swear." – I swore. – "Finally, promise me that, when you read this second paper which I have put into your hands, whatsoever you may think of it, you will say nothing – publish nothing to the world until three years shall have passed." – I promised. – "And now farewell for three hours.

Come to me again about ten o'clock, and take a glass of wine in memory of old times." This he said laughingly; but even then a dark spasm crossed his face. Yet, thinking that this might be the mere working of mental anguish within him, I complied with his desire, and retired. Feeling, however, but little at ease, I devised an excuse for looking in upon him about one hour and a half after I had left him. I knocked gently at his door; there was no answer. I knocked louder; still no answer. I went in. The light of day was gone, and I could see nothing. But I was alarmed by the utter stillness of the room. I listened earnestly, but not a breath could be heard. I rushed back hastily into the hall for a lamp; I returned; I looked in upon this marvel of manly beauty, and the first glance informed me that he and all his splendid endowments had departed forever. He had died, probably, soon after I left him, and had dismissed me from some growing instinct which informed him that his last agonies were at hand.

I took up his two testamentary documents; both were addressed in the shape of letters to myself. The first was a rapid though distinct appropriation of his enormous property. General rules were laid down, upon which the property was to be distributed, but the details were left to my discretion, and to the guidance of circumstances as they should happen to emerge from the various inquiries which it would become necessary to set on foot. This first document I soon laid aside, both because I found that its provisions were dependent for their meaning upon the second, and because to this second document I looked with confidence for a solution of many mysteries; – of the profound sadness which had, from the first of my acquaintance with him, possessed a man so gorgeously endowed as the favorite of nature and fortune; of his motives for huddling up, in a clandestine manner, that connection which formed the glory of his life; and possibly (but then I hesitated) of the late unintelligible murders, which still lay under as profound a cloud as ever. Much of this WOULD be unveiled – all might be: and there and then, with the corpse lying beside me of the gifted and mysterious writer, I seated myself, and read the following statement:

"My trial is finished; my conscience, my duty, my honor, are liberated; my 'warfare is accomplished.' Margaret, my innocent young wife, I have seen for the last time. Her, the crown that might have been of my earthly felicity – her, the one temptation to put aside the bitter cup which awaited me – her, sole seductress (O innocent seductress!) from the stern duties which my fate had imposed upon me – her, even her, I have sacrificed.

"Before I go, partly lest the innocent should be brought into question for acts almost exclusively mine, but still more lest the lesson and the warning which God, by my hand, has written in blood upon your guilty walls, should perish for want of its authentic exposition, hear my last dying avowal, that the murders which have desolated so many families within your walls, and made the household hearth no sanctuary, age no charter of protection, are all due originally to my head, if not always to my hand, as the minister of a dreadful retribution.

"That account of my history, and my prospects, which you received from the Russian diplomatist, among some errors of little importance, is essentially correct. My father was not so immediately connected with English blood as is there represented. However, it is true that he claimed descent from an English family of even higher distinction than that which is assigned in the Russian statement. He was proud of this English descent, and the more so as the war with revolutionary France brought out more prominently than ever the moral and civil grandeur of England. This pride was generous, but it was imprudent in his situation. His immediate progenitors had been settled in Italy – at Rome first, but latterly at Milan; and his whole property, large and scattered, came, by the progress of the revolution, to stand under French domination. Many spoliations he suffered; but still he was too rich to be seriously injured. But he foresaw, in the progress of events, still greater perils menacing his most capital resources. Many of the states or princes in Italy were deeply in his debt; and, in the great convulsions which threatened his country, he saw that both the contending parties would find a colorable excuse for absolving themselves from engagements which pressed unpleasantly upon their finances. In this embarrassment he formed an intimacy with a French officer of high rank and high principle. My father's friend saw his danger, and advised him to enter the French service. In his younger days, my father had served extensively under many princes, and had found in every other military service a spirit of honor governing the conduct of the officers. Here only, and for the first time, he found ruffian manners and universal rapacity. He could not draw his sword in company with such men, nor in such a cause. But at length, under the pressure of necessity, he accepted (or rather bought with an immense bribe) the place of a commissary to the French forces in Italy. With this one resource, eventually he succeeded in making good the whole of his public claims upon the Italian states. These vast sums he remitted, through various channels, to England, where he became proprietor in the funds to an immense amount. Incautiously, however, something of this transpired, and the result was doubly unfortunate; for, while his intentions were thus made known as finally pointing to England, which of itself made him an object of hatred and suspicion, it also diminished his means of bribery. These considerations, along with another, made some French officers of high rank and influence the bitter enemies of my father. My mother, whom he had married when holding a brigadier-general's commission in the Austrian service, was, by birth and by religion, a Jewess. She was of exquisite beauty, and had been sought in Morganatic marriage by an archduke of the Austrian family; but she had relied upon this plea, that hers was the purest and noblest blood among all Jewish families – that her family traced themselves, by tradition and a vast series of attestations under the hands of the Jewish high priests, to the Maccabees, and to the royal houses of Judea; and that for her it would be a degradation to accept even of a sovereign prince on the terms of such marriage. This was no vain pretension of ostentatious vanity. It was one which had been admitted as valid for time immemorial in Transylvania and adjacent countries, where my mother's family were rich and honored, and took their seat among the dignitaries of the land. The French officers I have alluded to, without capacity for anything so dignified as a deep passion, but merely in pursuit of a vagrant fancy that would, on the next day, have given place to another equally fleeting, had dared to insult my mother with proposals the most licentious – proposals as much below her rank and birth, as, at any rate, they would have been below her dignity of mind and her purity. These she had communicated to my father, who bitterly resented the chains of subordination which tied up his hands from avenging his injuries. Still his eye told a tale which his superiors could brook as little as they could the disdainful neglect of his wife. More than one had been concerned in the injuries to my father and mother; more than one were interested in obtaining revenge. Things could be done in German towns, and by favor of old German laws or usages, which even in France could not have been tolerated. This my father's enemies well knew, but this my father also knew; and he endeavored to lay down his office of commissary. That, however, was a favor which he could not obtain. He was compelled to serve on the German campaign then commencing, and on the subsequent one of Friedland and Eylau. Here he was caught in some one of the snares laid for him; first trepanned into an act which violated some rule of the service; and then provoked into a breach of discipline against the general officer who had thus trepanned him. Now was the long-sought opportunity gained, and in that very quarter of Germany best fitted for improving it. My father was thrown into prison in your city, subjected to the atrocious oppression of your jailer, and the more detestable oppression of your local laws. The charges against him were thought even to affect his life, and he was humbled into suing for permission to send for his wife and children. Already, to his proud spirit, it was punishment enough that he should be reduced to sue for favor to one of his bitterest foes. But it was no part of their plan to refuse THAT. By way of expediting my mother's arrival, a military courier, with every facility for the journey, was forwarded to her without delay. My mother, her two daughters, and myself, were then residing in Venice. I had, through the aid of my father's connections in Austria, been appointed in the imperial service, and held a high commission for my age. But, on my father's marching northward with the French army, I had been recalled as an indispensable support to my mother. Not that my years could have made me such, for I had barely accomplished my twelfth year; but my premature growth, and my military station, had given me considerable knowledge of the world and presence of mind.

"Our journey I pass over; but as I approach your city, that sepulcher of honor and happiness to my poor family, my heart beats with frantic emotions. Never do I see that venerable dome of your minster from the forest, but I curse its form, which reminds me of what we then surveyed for many a mile as we traversed the forest. For leagues before we approached the city, this object lay before us in relief upon the frosty blue sky; and still it seemed never to increase. Such was the complaint of my little sister Mariamne. Most innocent child! would that it never had increased for thy eyes, but remained forever at a distance! That same hour began the series of monstrous indignities which terminated the career of my ill-fated family. As we drew up to the city gates, the officer who inspected the passports, finding my mother and sisters described as Jewesses, which in my mother's ears (reared in a region where Jews are not dishonored) always sounded a title of distinction, summoned a subordinate agent, who in coarse terms demanded his toll. We presumed this to be a road tax for the carriage and horses, but we were quickly undeceived; a small sum was demanded for each of my sisters and my mother, as for so many head of cattle. I, fancying some mistake, spoke to the man temperately, and, to do him justice, he did not seem desirous of insulting us; but he produced a printed board, on which, along with the vilest animals, Jews and Jewesses were rated at so much a head. While we were debating the point, the officers of the gate wore a sneering smile upon their faces – the postilions were laughing together; and this, too, in the presence of three creatures whose exquisite beauty, in different styles, agreeably to their different ages, would have caused noblemen to have fallen down and worshiped. My mother, who had never yet met with any flagrant insult on account of her national distinctions, was too much shocked to be capable of speaking. I whispered to her a few words, recalling her to her native dignity of mind, paid the money, and we drove to the prison. But the hour was past at which we could be admitted, and, as Jewesses, my mother and sisters could not be allowed to stay in the city; they were to go into the Jewish quarter, a part of the suburb set apart for Jews, in which it was scarcely possible to obtain a lodging tolerably clean. My father, on the next day, we found, to our horror, at the point of death. To my mother he did not tell the worst of what he had endured. To me he told that, driven to madness by the insults offered to him, he had upbraided the court- martial with their corrupt propensities, and had even mentioned that overtures had been made to him for quashing the proceedings in return for a sum of two millions of francs; and that his sole reason for not entertaining the proposal was his distrust of those who made it. 'They would have taken my money,' said he, 'and then found a pretext for putting me to death, that I might tell no secrets.' This was too near the truth to be tolerated; in concert with the local authorities, the military enemies of my father conspired against him – witnesses were suborned; and, finally, under some antiquated law of the place, he was subjected, in secret, to a mode of torture which still lingers in the east of Europe.

"He sank under the torture and the degradation. I, too, thoughtlessly, but by a natural movement of filial indignation, suffered the truth to escape me in conversing with my mother. And she – ;but I will preserve the regular succession of things. My father died; but he had taken such measures, in concert with me, that his enemies should never benefit by his property. Meantime my mother and sisters had closed my father's eyes; had attended his remains to the grave; and in every act connected with this last sad rite had met with insults and degradations too mighty for human patience. My mother, now become incapable of self-command, in the fury of her righteous grief, publicly and in court denounced the conduct of the magistracy – taxed some of them with the vilest proposals to herself – taxed them as a body with having used instruments of torture upon my father; and, finally, accused them of collusion with the French military oppressors of the district. This last was a charge under which they quailed; for by that time the French had made themselves odious to all who retained a spark of patriotic feeling. My heart sank within me when I looked up at the bench, this tribunal of tyrants, all purple or livid with rage; when I looked at them alternately and at my noble mother with her weeping daughters – these so powerless, those so basely vindictive, and locally so omnipotent. Willingly I would have sacrificed all my wealth for a simple permission to quit this infernal city with my poor female relations safe and undishonored. But far other were the intentions of that incensed magistracy. My mother was arrested, charged with some offense equal to petty treason, or scandalum magnatum, or the sowing of sedition; and, though what she said was true, where, alas! was she to look for evidence? Here was seen the want of gentlemen. Gentlemen, had they been even equally tyrannical, would have recoiled with shame from taking vengeance on a woman. And what a vengeance! O heavenly powers! that I should live to mention such a thing! Man that is born of woman, to inflict upon woman personal scourging on the bare back, and through the streets at noonday! Even for Christian women the punishment was severe which the laws assigned to the offense in question. But for Jewesses, by one of the ancient laws against that persecuted people, far heavier and more degrading punishments were annexed to almost every offense. What else could be looked for in a city which welcomed its Jewish guests by valuing them at its gates as brute beasts? Sentence was passed, and the punishment was to be inflicted on two separate days, with an interval between each – doubtless to prolong the tortures of mind, but under a vile pretense of alleviating the physical torture. Three days after would come the first day of punishment. My mother spent the time in reading her native Scriptures; she spent it in prayer and in musing; while her daughters clung and wept around her day and night – groveling on the ground at the feet of any people in authority that entered their mother's cell. That same interval – how was it passed by me? Now mark, my friend. Every man in office, or that could be presumed to bear the slightest influence, every wife, mother, sister, daughter of such men, I besieged morning, noon, and night. I wearied them with my supplications. I humbled myself to the dust; I, the haughtiest of God's creatures, knelt and prayed to them for the sake of my mother. I besought them that I might undergo the punishment ten times over in her stead. And once or twice I DID obtain the encouragement of a few natural tears – given more, however, as I was told, to my piety than to my mother's deserts. But rarely was I heard out with patience; and from some houses repelled with personal indignities. The day came: I saw my mother half undressed by the base officials; I heard the prison gates expand; I heard the trumpets of the magistracy sound. She had warned me what to do; I had warned myself. Would I sacrifice a retribution sacred and comprehensive, for the momentary triumph over an individual? If not, let me forbear to look out of doors; for I felt that in the self-same moment in which I saw the dog of an executioner raise his accursed hand against my mother, swifter than the lightning would my dagger search his heart. When I heard the roar of the cruel mob, I paused – endured – forbore. I stole out by by-lanes of the city from my poor exhausted sisters, whom I left sleeping in each other's innocent arms, into the forest. There I listened to the shouting populace; there even I fancied that I could trace my poor mother's route by the course of the triumphant cries. There, even then, even then, I made – O silent forest! thou heardst me when I made – a vow that I have kept too faithfully. Mother, thou art avenged: sleep, daughter of Jerusalem! for at length the oppressor sleeps with thee. And thy poor son has paid, in discharge of his vow, the forfeit of his own happiness, of a paradise opening upon earth, of a heart as innocent as thine, and a face as fair.

"I returned, and found my mother returned. She slept by starts, but she was feverish and agitated; and when she awoke and first saw me, she blushed, as if I could think that real degradation had settled upon her. Then it was that I told her of my vow. Her eyes were lambent with fierce light for a moment; but, when I went on more eagerly to speak of my hopes and projects, she called me to her – kissed me, and whispered: 'Oh, not so, my son! think not of me – think not of vengeance – think only of poor Berenice and Mariamne.' Aye, that thought WAS startling. Yet this magnanimous and forbearing mother, as I knew by the report of our one faithful female servant, had, in the morning, during her bitter trial, behaved as might have become a daughter of Judas Maccabaeus: she had looked serenely upon the vile mob, and awed even them by her serenity; she had disdained to utter a shriek when the cruel lash fell upon her fair skin. There is a point that makes the triumph over natural feelings of pain easy or not easy – the degree in which we count upon the sympathy of the bystanders. My mother had it not in the beginning; but, long before the end, her celestial beauty, the divinity of injured innocence, the pleading of common womanhood in the minds of the lowest class, and the reaction of manly feeling in the men, had worked a great change in the mob. Some began now to threaten those who had been active in insulting her. The silence of awe and respect succeeded to noise and uproar; and feelings which they scarcely understood, mastered the rude rabble as they witnessed more and more the patient fortitude of the sufferer. Menaces began to rise toward the executioner. Things wore such an aspect that the magistrates put a sudden end to the scene.

"That day we received permission to go home to our poor house in the Jewish quarter. I know not whether you are learned enough in Jewish usages to be aware that in every Jewish house, where old traditions are kept up, there is one room consecrated to confusion; a room always locked up and sequestered from vulgar use, except on occasions of memorable affliction, where everything is purposely in disorder – broken – shattered – mutilated: to typify, by symbols appalling to the eye, that desolation which has so long trampled on Jerusalem, and the ravages of the boar within the vineyards of Judea. My mother, as a Hebrew princess, maintained all traditional customs. Even in this wretched suburb she had her 'chamber of desolation.' There it was that I and my sisters heard her last words. The rest of her sentence was to be carried into effect within a week. She, meantime, had disdained to utter any word of fear; but that energy of self-control had made the suffering but the more bitter. Fever and dreadful agitation had succeeded. Her dreams showed sufficiently to us, who watched her couch, that terror for the future mingled with the sense of degradation for the past. Nature asserted her rights. But the more she shrank from the suffering, the more did she proclaim how severe it had been, and consequently how noble the self-conquest. Yet, as her weakness increased, so did her terror; until I besought her to take comfort, assuring her that, in case any attempt should be made to force her out again to public exposure, I would kill the man who came to execute the order – that we would all die together – and there would be a common end to her injuries and her fears. She was reassured by what I told her of my belief that no future attempt would be made upon her. She slept more tranquilly – but her fever increased; and slowly she slept away into the everlasting sleep which knows of no to-morrow.

"Here came a crisis in my fate. Should I stay and attempt to protect my sisters? But, alas! what power had I to do so among our enemies? Rachael and I consulted; and many a scheme we planned. Even while we consulted, and the very night after my mother had been committed to the Jewish burying ground, came an officer, bearing an order for me to repair to Vienna. Some officer in the French army, having watched the transaction respecting my parents, was filled with shame and grief. He wrote a statement of the whole to an Austrian officer of rank, my father's friend, who obtained from the emperor an order, claiming me as a page of his own, and an officer in the household service. O heavens! what a neglect that it did not include my sisters! However, the next best thing was that I should use my influence at the imperial court to get them passed to Vienna. This I did, to the utmost of my power. But seven months elapsed before I saw the emperor. If my applications ever met his eye he might readily suppose that your city, my friend, was as safe a place as another for my sisters. Nor did I myself know all its dangers. At length, with the emperor's leave of absence, I returned. And what did I find? Eight months had passed, and the faithful Rachael had died. The poor sisters, clinging together, but now utterly bereft of friends, knew not which way to turn. In this abandonment they fell into the insidious hands of the ruffian jailer. My eldest sister, Berenice, the stateliest and noblest of beauties, had attracted this ruffian's admiration while she was in the prison with her mother. And when I returned to your city, armed with the imperial passports for all, I found that Berenice had died in the villain's custody; nor could I obtain anything beyond a legal certificate of her death. And, finally, the blooming, laughing Mariamne, she also had died – and of affliction for the loss of her sister. You, my friend, had been absent upon your travels during the calamitous history I have recited. You had seen neither my father nor my mother. But you came in time to take under your protection, from the abhorred wretch the jailer, my little broken-hearted Mariamne. And when sometimes you fancied that you had seen me under other circumstances, in her it was, my dear friend, and in her features that you saw mine.

"Now was the world a desert to me. I cared little, in the way of love, which way I turned. But in the way of hatred I cared everything. I transferred myself to the Russian service, with the view of gaining some appointment on the Polish frontier, which might put it in my power to execute my vow of destroying all the magistrates of your city. War, however, raged, and carried me into far other regions. It ceased, and there was little prospect that another generation would see it relighted; for the disturber of peace was a prisoner forever, and all nations were exhausted. Now, then, it became necessary that I should adopt some new mode for executing my vengeance; and the more so, because annually some were dying of those whom it was my mission to punish. A voice ascended to me, day and night, from the graves of my father and mother, calling for vengeance before it should be too late.

I took my measures thus: Many Jews were present at Waterloo. From among these, all irritated against Napoleon for the expectations he had raised, only to disappoint, by his great assembly of Jews at Paris, I selected eight, whom I knew familiarly as men hardened by military experience against the movements of pity. With these as my beagles, I hunted for some time in your forest before opening my regular campaign; and I am surprised that you did not hear of the death which met the executioner – him I mean who dared to lift his hand against my mother. This man I met by accident in the forest; and I slew him. I talked with the wretch, as a stranger at first, upon the memorable case of the Jewish lady. Had he relented, had he expressed compunction, I might have relented. But far otherwise: the dog, not dreaming to whom he spoke, exulted; he – But why repeat the villain's words? I cut him to pieces. Next I did this: My agents I caused to matriculate separately at the college. They assumed the college dress. And now mark the solution of that mystery which caused such perplexity. Simply as students we all had an unsuspected admission at any house. Just then there was a common practice, as you will remember, among the younger students, of going out a masking – that is, of entering houses in the academic dress, and with the face masked. This practice subsisted even during the most intense alarm from the murderers; for the dress of the students was supposed to bring protection along with it. But, even after suspicion had connected itself with this dress, it was sufficient that I should appear unmasked at the head of the maskers, to insure them a friendly reception. Hence the facility with which death was inflicted, and that unaccountable absence of any motion toward an alarm. I took hold of my victim, and he looked at me with smiling security. Our weapons were hid under our academic robes; and even when we drew them out, and at the moment of applying them to the threat, they still supposed our gestures to be part of the pantomime we were performing. Did I relish this abuse of personal confidence in myself? No – I loathed it, and I grieved for its necessity; but my mother, a phantom not seen with bodily eyes, but ever present to my mind, continually ascended before me; and still I shouted aloud to my astounded victim, 'This comes from the Jewess! Hound of hounds! Do you remember the Jewess whom you dishonored, and the oaths which you broke in order that you might dishonor her, and the righteous law which you violated, and the cry of anguish from her son which you scoffed at?' Who I was, what I avenged, and whom, I made every man aware, and every woman, before I punished them. The details of the cases I need not repeat. One or two I was obliged, at the beginning, to commit to my Jews. The suspicion was thus, from the first, turned aside by the notoriety of my presence elsewhere; but I took care that none suffered who had not either been upon the guilty list of magistrates who condemned the mother, or of those who turned away with mockery from the supplication of the son.

"It pleased God, however, to place a mighty temptation in my path, which might have persuaded me to forego all thoughts of vengeance, to forget my vow, to forget the voices which invoked me from the grave. This was Margaret Liebenheim. Ah! how terrific appeared my duty of bloody retribution, after her angel's face and angel's voice had calmed me. With respect to her grandfather, strange it is to mention, that never did my innocent wife appear so lovely as precisely in the relation of granddaughter. So beautiful was her goodness to the old man, and so divine was the childlike innocence on her part, contrasted with the guilty recollections associated with him – for he was among the guiltiest toward my mother – still I delayed HIS punishment to the last; and, for his child's sake, I would have pardoned him – nay, I had resolved to do so, when a fierce Jew, who had a deep malignity toward this man, swore that he would accomplish HIS vengeance at all events, and perhaps might be obliged to include Margaret in the ruin, unless I adhered to the original scheme. Then I yielded; for circumstances armed this man with momentary power. But the night fixed on was one in which I had reason to know that my wife would be absent; for so I had myself arranged with her, and the unhappy counter-arrangement I do not yet understand. Let me add, that the sole purpose of my clandestine marriage was to sting her grandfather's mind with the belief that HIS family had been dishonored, even as he had dishonored mine. He learned, as I took care that he should, that his granddaughter carried about with her the promises of a mother, and did not know that she had the sanction of a wife. This discovery made him, in one day, become eager for the marriage he had previously opposed; and this discovery also embittered the misery of his death. At that moment I attempted to think only of my mother's wrongs; but, in spite of all I could do, this old man appeared to me in the light of Margaret's grandfather – and, had I been left to myself, he would have been saved. As it was, never was horror equal to mine when I met her flying to his succor. I had relied upon her absence; and the misery of that moment, when her eye fell upon me in the very act of seizing her grandfather, far transcended all else that I have suffered in these terrific scenes. She fainted in my arms, and I and another carried her upstairs and procured water. Meantime her grandfather had been murdered, even while Margaret fainted. I had, however, under the fear of discovery, though never anticipating a reencounter with herself, forestalled the explanation requisite in such a case to make my conduct intelligible. I had told her, under feigned names, the story of my mother and my sisters. She knew their wrongs: she had heard me contend for the right of vengeance. Consequently, in our parting interview, one word only was required to place myself in a new position to her thoughts. I needed only to say I was that son; that unhappy mother, so miserably degraded and outraged, was mine.

"As to the jailer, he was met by a party of us. Not suspecting that any of us could be connected with the family, he was led to talk of the most hideous details with regard to my poor Berenice. The child had not, as had been insinuated, aided her own degradation, but had nobly sustained the dignity of her sex and her family. Such advantages as the monster pretended to have gained over her – sick, desolate, and latterly delirious – were, by his own confession, not obtained without violence. This was too much. Forty thousand lives, had he possessed them, could not have gratified my thirst for revenge. Yet, had he but showed courage, he should have died the death of a soldier. But the wretch showed cowardice the most abject, and – ,but you know his fate.

"Now, then, all is finished, and human nature is avenged. Yet, if you complain of the bloodshed and the terror, think of the wrongs which created my rights; think of the sacrifice by which I gave a tenfold strength to those rights; think of the necessity for a dreadful concussion and shock to society, in order to carry my lesson into the councils of princes.

"This will now have been effected. And ye, victims of dishonor, will be glorified in your deaths; ye will not have suffered in vain, nor died without a monument. Sleep, therefore, sister Berenice – sleep, gentle Mariamne, in peace. And thou, noble mother, let the outrages sown in thy dishonor, rise again and blossom in wide harvests of honor for the women of thy afflicted race. Sleep, daughters of Jerusalem, in the sanctity of your sufferings. And thou, if it be possible, even more beloved daughter of a Christian fold, whose company was too soon denied to him in life, open thy grave to receive HIM, who, in the hour of death, wishes to remember no title which he wore on earth but that of thy chosen and adoring lover,

"MAXIMILIAN."

146

Introduction to "A Mystery with a Moral"

The next Mystery Story is like no other in these volumes. The editor's defense lies in the plea that Laurence Sterne is not like other writers of English. He is certainly one of the very greatest. Yet nowadays he is generally unknown. His rollicking frankness, his audacious unconventionality, are enough to account for the neglect. Even the easy mannered England of 1760 opened its eyes in horror when "Tristram Shandy" appeared. "A most unclerical clergyman," the public pronounced the rector of Sutton and prebendary of York.

Besides, his style was rambling to the last degree. Plot concerned him least of all authors of fiction.

For instance, it is more than doubtful that the whimsical parson really INTENDED a moral to be read into the adventures of his "Sentimental Journey" that follow in these pages. He used to declare that he never intended anything – he never knew whither his pen was leading – the rash implement, once in hand, was likely to fly with him from Yorkshire to Italy – or to Paris – or across the road to Uncle Toby's; and what could the helpless author do but improve each occasion?

So here is one such "occasion" thus "improved" by disjointed sequels – heedless, one would say, and yet glittering with the unreturnable thrust of subtle wit, or softening with simple emotion, like a thousand immortal passages of this random philosopher.

Even the slightest turns of Sterne's pen bear inspiration. No less a critic than the severe Hazlitt was satisfied that "his works consist only of brilliant passages."

And because the editors of the present volumes found added to "The Mystery" not only a "Solution" but an "Application" of worldly wisdom, and a "Contrast" in Sterne's best vein of quiet happiness – they have felt emboldened to ascribe the passage "A Mystery with a Moral."

As regards the "Application": Sterne knew whereof he wrote. He sought the South of France for health in 1762, and was run after and feted by the most brilliant circles of Parisian litterateurs. This foreign sojourn failed to cure his lung complaint, but suggested the idea to him of the rambling and charming "Sentimental Journey." Only three weeks after its publication, on March 18, 1768, Sterne died alone in his London lodgings.

Spite of all that marred his genius, his work has lived and will live, if only for the exquisite literary art which ever made great things out of little. – The EDITOR.

LAURENCE STERNE

A Mystery with a Moral

Parisian Experience of Parson Yorick, on his "Sentimental Journey"

A Riddle

I remained at the gate of the hotel for some time, looking at everyone who passed by, and forming conjectures upon them, till my attention got fixed upon a single object, which confounded all kind of reasoning upon him.

It was a tall figure of a philosophic, serious adult look, which passed and repassed sedately along the street, making a turn of about sixty paces on each side of the gate of the hotel. The man was about fifty-two, had a small cane under his arm, was dressed in a dark drab-colored coat, waistcoat, and breeches, which seemed to have seen some years' service. They were still clean, and there was a little air of frugal propriete throughout him. By his pulling off his hat, and his attitude of accosting a good many in his way, I saw he was asking charity; so I got a sous or two out of my pocket, ready to give him as he took me in his turn. He passed by me without asking anything, and yet he did not go five steps farther before he asked charity of a little woman. I was much more likely to have given of the two. He had scarce done with the woman, when he pulled his hat off to another who was coming the same way. An ancient gentleman came slowly, and after him a young smart one. He let them both pass and asked nothing. I stood observing him half an hour, in which time he had made a dozen turns backward and forward, and found that he invariably pursued the same plan.

There were two things very singular in this which set my brain to work, and to no purpose; the first was, why the man should only tell his story to the sex; and secondly, what kind of a story it was and what species of eloquence it could be which softened the hearts of the women which he knew it was to no purpose to practice upon the men.

There were two other circumstances which entangled this mystery. The one was, he told every woman what he had to say in her ear, and in a way which had much more the air of a secret than a petition; the other was, it was always successful – he never stopped a woman but she pulled out her purse and immediately gave him something.

I could form no system to explain the phenomenon.

I had got a riddle to amuse me for the rest of the evening, so I walked upstairs to my chamber.

Overheard

The man who either disdains or fears to walk up a dark entry may be an excellent, good man, and fit for a hundred things, but he will not do to make a sentimental traveler. I count little of the many things I see pass at broad noonday, in large and open streets; Nature is shy, and hates to act before spectators; but in such an unobservable corner you sometimes see a single short scene of hers worth all the sentiments of a dozen French plays compounded together; and yet they are ABSOLUTELY fine, and whenever I have a more brilliant affair upon my hands than common, as they suit a preacher just as well as a hero, I generally make my sermon out of them, and for the text, "Cappadocia, Pontus and Asia, Phrygia and Pamphilia," is as good as anyone in the Bible.

There is a long, dark passage issuing out from the Opera Comique into a narrow street. It is trod by a few who humbly wait for a fiacre* or wish to get off quietly o' foot when the opera is done. At the end of it, toward the theater, 'tis lighted by a small candle, the light of which is almost lost before you get halfway down, but near the door – it is more for ornament than use – you see it as a fixed star of the least magnitude; it burns, but does little good to the world that we know of.

*Hackney coach.

In returning [from the opera] along this passage, I discerned, as I approached within five or six paces of the door, two ladies standing arm in arm with their backs against the wall, waiting, as

150

I imagined, for a fiacre. As they were next the door, I thought they had a prior right, so I edged myself up within a yard or little more of them, and quietly took my stand. I was in black and scarce seen.

The lady next me was a tall, lean figure of a woman of about thirty-six; the other, of the same size and make of about forty. There was no mark of wife or widow in any one part of either of them. They seemed to be two upright vestal sisters, unsapped by caresses, unbroke in upon by tender salutations. I could have wished to have made them happy. Their happiness was destined, that night, to come from another quarter.

A low voice with a good turn of expression and sweet cadence at the end of it, begged for a twelve-sous piece between them for the love of heaven. I thought it singular that a beggar should fix the quota of an alms, and that the sum should be twelve times as much as what is usually given in the dark. They both seemed astonished at it as much as myself. "Twelve sous," said one. "A twelve-sous piece," said the other, and made no reply.

The poor man said he knew not how to ask less of ladies of their rank, and bowed down his head to the ground.

"Pooh!" said they, "we have no money."

The beggar remained silent for a moment or two, and renewed his supplication.

"Do not, my fair young ladies," said he, "stop your good ears against me."

"Upon my word, honest man," said the younger, "we have no change."

"Then God bless you," said the poor man, "and multiply those joys which you can give to others without change."

I observed the older sister put her hand into her pocket. "I will see," said she, "if I have a sous."

"A sous! Give twelve," said the suppliant. "Nature has been bountiful to you; be bountiful to a poor man."

"I would, friend, with all my heart," said the younger, "if I had it."

"My fair charitable," said he, addressing himself to the elder, "what is it but your goodness and humanity which make your bright eyes so sweet that they outshine the morning even in this dark passage? And what was it which made the Marquis de Santerre and his brother say so much of you both, as they just passed by?"

The two ladies seemed much affected, and impulsively at the same time they put their hands into their pockets and each took out a twelve-sous piece.

The contest between them and the poor suppliant was no more. It was continued between themselves which of the two should give the twelve-sous piece in charity, and, to end the dispute, they both gave it together, and the man went away.

Solution

I stepped hastily after him; it was the very man whose success in asking charity of the woman before the door of the hotel had so puzzled me, and I found at once his secret, or at least the basis of it: it was flattery.

Delicious essence! how refreshing art thou to Nature! How strongly are all its powers and all its weaknesses on thy side! How sweetly dost thou mix with the blood, and help it through the most difficult and tortuous passages to the heart!

The poor man, as he was not straitened for time, had given it here in a larger dose. It is certain he had a way of bringing it into less form for the many sudden causes he had to do with in the streets; but how he contrived to correct, sweeten, concenter, and qualify it – I vex not my spirit with the inquiry. It is enough, the beggar gained two twelve-sous pieces, and they can best tell the rest who have gained much greater matters by it.

Application

We get forward in the world not so much by doing services as receiving them. You take a withering twig and put it in the ground, and then you water it because you have planted it.

Monsieur le Comte de B - - , merely because he had done me one kindness in the affair of my passport, would go on and do me another the few days he was at Paris, in making me known to a few people of rank; and they were to present me to others, and so on.

I had got master of my SECRET just in time to turn these honors to some little account; otherwise, as is commonly the case, I should have dined or supped a single time or two round, and then by TRANSLATING French looks and attitudes into plain English, I should presently have seen that I had got hold of the couvert* of some more entertaining guest; and in course of time should have resigned all my places one after another, merely upon the principle that I could not keep them. As it was, things did not go much amiss.

* Plate, napkin, knife, fork, and spoon.

I had the honor of being introduced to the old Marquis de B - - . In days of yore he had signalized himself by some small feats of chivalry in the Cour d'Amour, and had dressed himself out to the idea of tilts and tournaments ever since. The Marquis de B - - wished to have it thought the affair was somewhere else than in his brain. "He could like to take a trip to England," and asked much of the English ladies. "Stay where you are, I beseech you, Monsieur le Marquis," said I. "Les Messieurs Anglais can scarce get a kind look from them as it is." The marquis invited me to supper.

M. P - - , the farmer-general, was just as inquisitive about our taxes. They were very considerable, he heard. "If we knew but how to collect them," said I, making him a low bow.

I could never have been invited to M. P - - 's concerts upon any other terms.

I had been misrepresented to Mme. de Q – – as an esprit –
Mme. de Q – – was an esprit herself; she burned with impatience
to see me and hear me talk. I had not taken my seat before I saw
she did not care a sou whether I had any wit or no. I was let in to
be convinced she had. I call Heaven to witness I never once
opened the door of my lips.

Mme. de V – – vowed to every creature she met, "She had
never had a more improving conversation with a man in her life."

There are three epochs in the empire of a Frenchwoman –
she is coquette, then deist, then devote. The empire during these
is never lost – she only changes her subjects. When thirty-five
years and more have unpeopled her dominion of the slaves of
love she repeoples it with slaves of infidelity, and, then with the
slaves of the church.

Mme. de V – – was vibrating between the first of these epochs; the color of the rose was fading fast away; she ought to have
been a deist five years before the time I had the honor to pay my
first visit.

She placed me upon the same sofa with her for the sake of
disputing the point of religion more closely. In short, Mme. de
V – – told me she believed nothing.

I told Mme. de V – – it might be her principle, but I was sure
it could not be her interest, to level the outworks, without which I
could not conceive how such a citadel as hers could be defended;
that there was not a more dangerous thing in the world than for a
beauty to be a deist; that it was a debt I owed my creed not to
conceal it from her; that I had not been five minutes upon the sofa
beside her before I had begun to form designs; and what is it but
the sentiments of religion, and the persuasion they had existed in
her breast, which could have checked them as they rose up?

"We are not adamant," said I, taking hold of her hand, "and
there is need of all restraints till age in her own time steals in and
lays them on us; but, my dear lady," said I, kissing her hand, "it is
too – too soon."

I declare I had the credit all over Paris of unperverting Mme.

de V – – . She affirmed to M. D – – and the Abbe M – – that in one half hour I had said more for revealed religion than all their encyclopaedia had said against it. I was listed directly into Mme. de V – – o's coterie, and she put off the epoch of deism for two years.

I remember it was in this coterie, in the middle of a discourse, in which I was showing the necessity of a first cause, that the young Count de Faineant took me by the hand to the farthest corner of the room, to tell me that my solitaire was pinned too strait about my neck. "It should be plus badinant," said the count, looking down upon his own; "but a word, M. Yorick, to the wise – "

"And from the wise, M. le Comte," replied I, making him a bow, "is enough."

The Count de Faineant embraced me with more ardor than ever I was embraced by mortal man.

For three weeks together I was of every man's opinion I met. "Pardi! ce M. Yorick a autant d'esprit que nous autres."

"Il raisonne bien," said another.

"C'est un bon enfant," said a third.

And at this price I could have eaten and drunk and been merry all the days of my life at Paris; but it was a dishonest reckoning. I grew ashamed of it; it was the gain of a slave; every sentiment of honor revolted against it; the higher I got, the more was I forced upon my beggarly system; the better the coterie, the more children of Art, I languished for those of Nature. And one night, after a most vile prostitution of myself to half a dozen different people, I grew sick, went to bed, and ordered horses in the morning to set out for Italy.

Contrast

A shoe coming loose from the forefoot of the thill horse at the beginning of the ascent of Mount Taurira, the postilion dismounted, twisted the shoe off, and put it in his pocket; as the ascent was of five or six miles, and that horse our main dependence I made a point of having the shoe fastened on again as well as we could, but the postilion had thrown away the nails, and the hammer in the chaise box being of no great use without them, I submitted to go on.

He had not mounted half a mile higher when, coming to a flinty piece of road, the poor devil lost a second shoe, and from off his other forefoot. I then got out of the chaise in good earnest, and seeing a house about a quarter of a mile to the left hand, with a great deal to do I prevailed upon the postilion to turn up to it. The look of the house, and of everything about it, as we drew nearer, soon reconciled me to the disaster. It was a little farm-house surrounded with about twenty acres of vineyard, about as much corn, and close to the house on one side was a potagerie of an acre and a half, full of everything which could make plenty in a French peasant's house, and on the other side was a little wood which furnished wherewithal to dress it. It was about eight in the evening when I got to the house, so I left the postilion to manage his point as he could, and for mine I walked directly into the house.

The family consisted of an old gray-headed man and his wife, with five or six sons and sons-in-laws, and their several wives, and a joyous genealogy out of them.

They were all sitting down together to their lentil soup. A large wheaten loaf was in the middle of the table, and a flagon of wine at each end of it promised joy through the stages of the re-past – 'twas a feast of love.

The old man rose up to meet me, and with a respectful cor-diality would have me sit down at the table. My heart was sat down the moment I entered the room, so I sat down at once like a son of the family, and to invest myself in the character as speedily as I could, I instantly borrowed the old man's knife, and taking up the loaf cut myself a hearty luncheon; and, as I did it, I saw a testimony in every eye, not only of an honest welcome, but of a welcome mixed with thanks that I had not seemed to doubt it.

Was it this, or tell me, Nature, what else it was that made this morsel so sweet, and to what magic I owe it that the draught

I took of their flagon was so delicious with it that they remain upon my palate to this hour?

If the supper was to my taste, the grace which followed it was much more so.

When supper was over, the old man gave a knock upon the table with the haft of his knife to bid them prepare for the dance. The moment the signal was given, the women and girls ran all together into a back apartment to tie up their hair, and the young men to the door to wash their faces and change their sabots, and in three minutes every soul was ready upon a little esplanade before the house to begin. The old man and his wife came out last, and, placing me betwixt them, sat down upon a sofa of turf by the door.

The old man had some fifty years ago been no mean performer upon the vielle,* and at the age he was then of, touched well enough for the purpose. His wife sung now and then a little to the tune, then intermitted, and joined her old man again, as their children and grandchildren danced before them.

* A small violin, such as was used by the wandering jongleurs of the Middle Ages. - EDITOR.

It was not till the middle of the second dance when, from some pauses in the movement wherein they all seemed to look up, I fancied I could distinguish an elevation of spirit different from that which is the cause or the effect of simple jollity. In a word, I thought I beheld RELIGION mixing in the dance; but, as I had never seen her so engaged, I should have looked upon it now as one of the illusions of an imagination, which is eternally misleading me, had not the old man, as soon as the dance ended, said that this was their constant way, and that all his life long he had made it a rule, after supper was over, to call out his family to dance and rejoice, believing, he said, that a cheerful and contented mind was the best sort of thanks to heaven that an illiterate peasant could pay –

"Or a learned prelate either," said I.

When you have gained the top of Mount Taurira, you run

presently down to Lyons. Adieu then to all rapid movements! It is a journey of caution, and it fares better with sentiments not to be in a hurry with them, so I contracted with a volturin to take his time with a couple of mules and convey me in my own chaise safe to Turin through Savoy.

Poor, patient, quiet, honest people, fear not! Your poverty, the treasury of your simple virtues, will not be envied you by the world, nor will your values be invaded by it. Nature, in the midst of thy disorders, thou art still friendly to the scantiness thou hast created; with all thy great works about thee little hast thou left to give, either to the scythe or to the sickle, but to that little thou grantest safety and protection, and sweet are the dwellings which stand so sheltered!

WILLIAM MAKEPEACE THACKERAY

On Being Found Out

At the close (let us say) of Queen Anne's reign, when I was a boy at a private and preparatory school for young gentlemen, I remember the wiseacre of a master ordering us all, one night, to march into a little garden at the back of the house, and thence to proceed one by one into a tool or hen house (I was but a tender little thing just put into short clothes, and can't exactly say whether the house was for tools or hens), and in that house to put our hands into a sack which stood on a bench, a candle burning beside it. I put my hand into the sack. My hand came out quite black. I went and joined the other boys in the schoolroom; and all their hands were black too.

By reason of my tender age (and there are some critics who, I hope, will be satisfied by my acknowledging that I am a hundred and fifty-six next birthday) I could not understand what was the meaning of this night excursion – this candle, this tool house, this bag of soot. I think we little boys were taken out of our sleep to be brought to the ordeal. We came, then, and showed our little hands to the master; washed them or not – most probably, I should say, not – and so went bewildered back to bed.

Something had been stolen in the school that day; and Mr. Wiseacre having read in a book of an ingenious method of finding out a thief by making him put his hand into a sack (which, if guilty, the rogue would shirk from doing), all we boys were subjected to the trial. Goodness knows what the lost object was, or who stole it. We all had black hands to show the master. And the thief, whoever he was, was not Found Out that time.

I wonder if the rascal is alive – an elderly scoundrel he must be by this time; and a hoary old hypocrite, to whom an old schoolfellow presents his kindest regards – parenthetically remarking what a dreadful place that private school was; cold, chilblains, bad dinners, not enough victuals, and caning awful! – Are you alive still, I say, you nameless villain, who escaped discovery on that day of crime? I hope you have escaped often since, old sinner. Ah, what a lucky thing it is, for you and me, my man, that we are NOT found out in all our peccadilloes; and that our backs can slip away from the master and the cane!

Just consider what life would be, if every rogue was found out, and flogged coram populo! What a butchery, what an indecency, what an endless swishing of the rod! Don't cry out about my misanthropy. My good friend Mealymouth, I will trouble you to tell me, do you go to church? When there, do you say, or do you not, that you are a miserable sinner, and saying so do you believe or disbelieve it? If you are a M. S., don't you deserve correction, and aren't you grateful if you are to be let off? I say again what a blessed thing it is that we are not all found out!

Just picture to yourself everybody who does wrong being found out, and punished accordingly. Fancy all the boys in all the school being whipped; and then the assistants, and then the headmaster (Dr. Badford let us call him). Fancy the provost marshal being tied up, having previously superintended the correction of the whole army. After the young gentlemen have had their turn for the faulty exercises, fancy Dr. Lincolnsinn being taken up for certain faults in HIS Essay and Review. After the clergyman has cried his peccavi, suppose we hoist up a bishop, and give him a couple of dozen! (I see my Lord Bishop of Double-Gloucester sitting in a very uneasy posture on his right reverend bench.) After we have cast off the bishop, what are we to say to the Minister who appointed him? My Lord Cinqwarden, it is painful to have to use personal correction to a boy of your age; but really... Siste tandem carnifex! The butchery is too horrible. The hand drops powerless, appalled at the quantity of birch which it must cut and brandish. I am glad we are not all found out, I say again; and protest, my dear brethren, against our having our deserts.

To fancy all men found out and punished is bad enough; but imagine all the women found out in the distinguished social circle in which you and I have the honor to move. Is it not a mercy that a many of these fair criminals remain unpunished and undiscovered! There is Mrs. Longbow, who is forever practicing, and who shoots poisoned arrows, too; when you meet her you don't call her liar, and charge her with the wickedness she has done and is

160

doing. There is Mrs. Painter, who passes for a most respectable woman, and a model in society. There is no use in saying what you really know regarding her and her goings on. There is Diana Hunter – what a little haughty prude it is; and yet WE know stories about her which are not altogether edifying. I say it is best for the sake of the good, that the bad should not all be found out. You don't want your children to know the history of that lady in the next box, who is so handsome, and whom they admire so. Ah me, what would life be if we were all found out and punished for all our faults? Jack Ketch would be in permanence; and then who would hang Jack Ketch?

They talk of murderers being pretty certainly found out. Psha! I have heard an authority awfully competent vow and declare that scores and hundreds of murders are committed, and nobody is the wiser. That terrible man mentioned one or two ways of committing murder, which he maintained were quite common, and were scarcely ever found out. A man, for instance, comes home to his wife, and... but I pause – I know that this Magazine has a very large circulation.* Hundreds and hundreds of thousands – why not say a million of people at once? – well, say a million, read it. And among these countless readers, I might be teaching some monster how to make away with his wife without being found out, some fiend of a woman how to destroy her dear husband. I will NOT then tell this easy and simple way of murder, as communicated to me by a most respectable party in the confidence of private intercourse. Suppose some gentle reader were to try this most simple and easy receipt – it seems to me almost infallible – and come to grief in consequence, and be found out and hanged? Should I ever pardon myself for having been the means of doing injury to a single one of our esteemed subscribers? The prescription whereof I speak – that is to say, whereof I DON'T speak – shall be buried in this bosom. No, I am a humane man. I am not one of your Bluebeards to go and say to my wife, "My dear! I am going away for a few days to Brighton. Here are all the keys of the house. You may open every door and closet, except the one at the end of the oak room opposite the fireplace, with the little bronze Shakespeare on the mantelpiece (or what not)." I don't say this to a woman – unless, to be sure, I want to get rid of her – because, after such a caution, I know she'll peep into the closet. I say nothing about the closet at all. I keep the key in my pocket, and a being whom I love, but who, as I know, has many weaknesses, out of harm's way. You toss up your head, dear angel, drub on the ground with your lovely little feet, on the table with your sweet rosy fingers, and cry, "Oh, sneerer! You don't know the depth of woman's feeling, the lofty scorn of all deceit, the entire absence of mean curiosity in the sex, or never, never would you libel us so!" Ah, Delia! dear, dear Delia! It is because I fancy I DO know something about you (not all, mind – no, no; no man knows that). – Ah, my bride, my ring-dove, my rose, my poppet – choose, in fact, whatever name you like – bulbul of my grove, fountain of my desert, sunshine of my darkling life, and joy of my dungeoned existence, it is because I DO know a little about you that I conclude to say nothing of that private closet, and keep my key in my pocket. You take away that closet key then, and the house key. You lock Delia in. You keep her out of harm's way and gadding, and so she never CAN be found out.

* The Cornhill. – editor.

And yet by little strange accidents and coincidents how we are being found out every day. You remember that old story of the Abbe Kakatoes, who told the company at supper one night how the first confession he ever received was – from a murderer, let us say. Presently enters to supper the Marquis de Croque-mitaine. "Palsambleu, abbe!" says the brilliant marquis, taking a pinch of snuff, "are you here? Gentlemen and ladies! I was the abbe's first penitent, and I made him a confession, which I prom-ise you astonished him."

To be sure how queerly things are found out! Here is an in-stance. Only the other day I was writing in these Roundabout Papers about a certain man, whom I facetiously called Baggs, and who had abused me to my friends, who of course told me. Shortly after that paper was published another friend – Sacks let us call him – scowls fiercely at me as I am sitting in perfect good humor at the club, and passes on without speaking. A cut. A quarrel. Sacks thinks it is about him that I was writing: whereas, upon my honor and conscience, I never had him once in my mind, and was pointing my moral from quite another man. But don't you see, by this wrath of the guilty- conscienced Sacks, that he had been abusing me too? He has owned himself guilty, never having been accused. He has winced when nobody thought of hitting him. I did but put the cap out, and madly butting and chafing, behold my friend rushes out to put his head into it! Never mind, Sacks, you are found out; but I bear you no malice, my man.

And yet to be found out, I know from my own experience, must be painful and odious, and cruelly mortifying to the inward vanity. Suppose I am a poltroon, let us say. With fierce mustache, loud talk, plentiful oaths, and an immense stick, I keep up nevertheless a character for courage. I swear fearfully at cabmen and women; brandish my bludgeon, and perhaps knock down a little man or two with it: brag of the images which I break at the shooting gallery, and pass among my friends for a whiskery fire-eater, afraid of neither man nor dragon. Ah me! Suppose some brisk little chap steps up and gives me a caning in St. James's Street, with all the heads of my friends looking out of all the club windows. My reputation is gone. I frighten no man more. My nose is pulled by whipper-snappers, who jump up on a chair to reach it. I am found out. And in the days of my triumphs, when people were yet afraid of me, and were taken in by my swagger, I always knew that I was a lily liver, and expected that I should be found out some day.

That certainty of being found out must haunt and depress many a bold braggadocio spirit. Let us say it is a clergyman, who can pump copious floods of tears out of his own eyes and those of his audience. He thinks to himself, "I am but a poor swindling, chattering rogue. My bills are unpaid. I have jilted several women whom I have promised to marry. I don't know whether I believe what I preach, and I know I have stolen the very sermon over which I have been sniveling. Have they found me out?" says he, as his head drops down on the cushion.

Then your writer, poet, historian, novelist, or what not? The Beacon says that "Jones's work is one of the first order." The Lamp declares that Jones's tragedy surpasses every work since the days of Him of Avon." The Comet asserts that "J's 'Life of Goody Twoshoes' is a noble and enduring monument to the fame of that admirable Englishwoman," and so forth. But then Jones knows that he has lent the critic of the Beacon five pounds; that his publisher has a half share in the Lamp; and that the Cornet comes repeatedly to dine with him. It is all very well. Jones is immortal until he is found out; and then down comes the extinguisher, and the immortal is dead and buried. The idea (dies irae!) of discovery must haunt many a man, and make him uneasy, as the trumpets are puffing in his triumph. Brown, who has a higher place than he deserves, cowers before Smith, who has found him out. What is the chorus of critics shouting "Bravo"? – a public clapping hands and flinging garlands? Brown knows that Smith has found him out. Puff, trumpets! Wave, banners! Huzza, boys, for the immortal Brown! This is all very well," B. thinks (bowing the while, smiling, laying his hand to his heart); "but there stands Smith at the window: HE has measured me; and some day the others will find me out too." It is a very curious sensation to sit by a man who has found you out, and who, as you know, has found you out; or, vice versa, to sit with a man whom YOU have found out. His talent? Bah! His virtue? We know a little story or two about his virtue, and he knows we know it. We are thinking over friend Robinson's antecedents, as we grin, bow and talk; and we are both humbugs together. Robinson a good fellow, is he? You know how he behaved to Hicks? A good-natured man, is he? Pray do you remember that little story of Mrs. Robinson's black eye? How men have to work, to talk, to smile, to go to bed, and try and sleep, with this dread of being found out on their consciences! Bardolph, who has robbed a church, and Nym, who has taken a purse, go to their usual haunts, and smoke their pipes with their companions. Mr. Detective Bullseye appears, and says, "Oh, Bardolph! I want you about that there pyx business!" Mr. Bardolph knocks the ashes out of his pipe, puts out his hands to the little steel cuffs, and walks away quite meekly. He is found out. He must go. "Good-by, 'Doll Tearsheet! Good-by, Mrs. Quickly, ma'am!" The other gentlemen and ladies de la societe look on and exchange mute adieux with the departing friends.

And an assured time will come when the other gentlemen and ladies will be found out too.

What a wonderful and beautiful provision of nature it has been that, for the most part, our womankind are not endowed with the faculty of finding us out! THEY don't doubt, and probe, and weigh, and take your measure. Lay down this paper, my benevolent friend and reader, go into your drawing-room now, and utter a joke ever so old, and I wager sixpence the ladies there will all begin to laugh. Go to Brown's house, and tell Mrs. Brown and the young ladies what you think of him, and see what a welcome you will get! In like manner, let him come to your house, and tell YOUR good lady his candid opinion of you, and fancy how she will receive him! Would you have your wife and children know you exactly for what you are, and esteem you precisely at your worth? If so, my friend, you will live in a dreary house, and you will have but a chilly fireside. Do you suppose the people round it don't see your homely face as under a glamour, and, as it were, with a halo of love round it? You don't fancy you ARE as you seem to them? No such thing, my man. Put away that monstrous conceit, and be thankful that THEY have not found you out.

The Notch on the Ax

A Story a la Mode*

* (Here Thackeray reduces to an absurdity the literary fashion of the day – the vogue for startling stories and "Tales of Terror," which was high in his time, and which influenced several of the stories which precede in this volume. But while Dickens made fun, with mental reservations; while Bulwer Lytton tried to explain by rising to the heights of natural philosophy, and Maturin did not explain at all, but let his extravagant genius roam between heaven and earth – Thackeray's keen wit saw mainly one chance for exquisite literary satire and parody. At one point or another in this skit, the style of each principal sensational novelist of the day is delightfully imitated. – EDITOR.)

Every one remembers in the Fourth Book of the immortal poem of your
Blind Bard (to whose sightless orbs no doubt Glorious Shapes were apparent, and Visions Celestial), how Adam discourses to Eve of the Bright Visitors who hovered round their Eden –

'Millions of spiritual creatures walk the earth,
Unseen, both when we wake and when we sleep.'

'"How often,' says Father Adam, 'from the steep of echoing hill or thicket, have we heard celestial voices to the midnight air, sole, or responsive to each other's notes, singing!' After the Act of Disobedience, when the erring pair from Eden took their solitary way, and went forth to toil and trouble on common earth – though the Glorious Ones no longer were visible, you cannot say they were gone. It was not that the Bright Ones were absent, but that the dim eyes of rebel man no longer could see them. In your chamber hangs a picture of one whom you never knew, but whom you have long held in tenderest regard, and who was painted for you by a friend of mine, the Knight of Plympton. She communes with you. She smiles on you. When your spirits are low, her bright eyes shine on you and cheer you. Her innocent sweet smile is a caress to you. She never fails to soothe you with her speechless prattle. You love her. She is alive with you. As you extinguish your candle and turn to sleep, though your eyes see her not, is she not there still smiling? As you lie in the night awake, and thinking of your duties, and the morrow's inevitable toil oppressing the busy, weary, wakeful brain as with a remorse, the crackling fire flashes up for a moment in the grate, and she is there, your little Beauteous Maiden, smiling with her sweet eyes! When moon is down, when fire is out, when curtains are drawn, when lids are closed, is she not there, the little Beautiful One, though invisible, present and smiling still? Friend, the Unseen Ones are round about us. Does it not seem as if the time were drawing near when it shall be given to men to behold them?"

The print of which my friend spoke, and which, indeed, hangs in my room, though he has never been there, is that charming little winter piece of Sir Joshua, representing the little Lady Caroline Montague, afterwards Duchess of Buccleuch. She is represented as standing in the midst of a winter landscape, wrapped in muff and cloak; and she looks out of her picture with a smile so exquisite that a Herod could not see her without being charmed.

"I beg your pardon, Mr. PINTO," I said to the person with whom I was conversing. (I wonder, by the way, that I was not surprised at his knowing how fond I am of this print.) "You spoke of the Knight of Plympton. Sir Joshua died 1792: and you say he was your dear friend?"

As I spoke I chanced to look at Mr. Pinto; and then it suddenly struck me: Gracious powers! Perhaps you ARE a hundred years old, now I think of it. You look more than a hundred. Yes, you may be a thousand years old for what I know. Your teeth are false. One eye is evidently false. Can I say that the other is not? If a man's age may be calculated by the rings round his eyes, this man may be as old as Methuselah. He has no beard. He wears a large curly glossy brown wig, and his eyebrows are painted a deep olive- green. It was odd to hear this man, this walking mummy, talking sentiment, in these queer old chambers in Shepherd's Inn.

Pinto passed a yellow bandanna handkerchief over his awful white teeth, and kept his glass eye steadily fixed on me. "Sir Joshua's friend?" said he (you perceive, eluding my direct question). "Is not everyone that knows his pictures Reynolds's friend? Suppose I tell you that I have been in his painting room scores of times, and that his sister The has made me tea, and his sister Toffy has made coffee for me? You will only say I am an old ombog." (Mr. Pinto, I remarked, spoke all languages with an accent equally foreign.) "Suppose I tell you that I knew Mr. Sam Johnson, and did not like him? that I was at that very ball at Madame Cornelis', which you have mentioned in one of your little – what do you call them? – bah! my memory begins to fail me – in one of your little Whirligig Papers? Suppose I tell you that Sir Joshua has been here, in this very room?"

"Have you, then, had these apartments for – more – than –

seventy years?" I asked.

"They look as if they had not been swept for that time – don't they? Hey? I did not say that I had them for seventy years, but that Sir Joshua has visited me here."

"When?" I asked, eying the man sternly, for I began to think he was an impostor.

He answered me with a glance still more stern: "Sir Joshua Reynolds was here this very morning, with Angelica Kaufmann and Mr. Oliver Goldschmidt. He is still very much attached to Angelica, who still does not care for him. Because he is dead (and I was in the fourth mourning coach at his funeral) is that any reason why he should not come back to earth again? My good sir, you are laughing at me. He has sat many a time on that very chair which you are now occupying. There are several spirits in the room now, whom you cannot see. Excuse me." Here he turned round as if he was addressing somebody, and began rapidly speaking a language unknown to me. "It is Arabic," he said; "a bad patois, I own. I learned it in Barbary, when I was a prisoner among the Moors. In anno 1609, bin ick aldus ghekledt gheghaen. Ha! you doubt me: look at me well. At least I am like – "

Perhaps some of my readers remember a paper of which the figure of a man carrying a barrel formed the initial letter, and which I copied from an old spoon now in my possession. As I looked at Mr. Pinto I do declare he looked so like the figure on that old piece of plate that I started and felt very uneasy. "Ha!" said he, laughing through his false teeth (I declare they were false – I could see utterly toothless gums working up and down behind the pink coral), "you see I wore a beard den; I am shafed now; perhaps you tink I am A SPOON. Ha, ha!" And as he laughed he gave a cough which I thought would have coughed his teeth out, his glass eye out, his wig off, his very head off; but he stopped this convulsion by stumping across the room and seizing a little bottle of bright pink medicine, which, being opened, spread a singular acrid aromatic odor through the apartment; and I thought I saw – but of this I cannot take an affirmation – a light green and violet flame flickering round the neck of the vial as he opened it. By the way, from the peculiar stumping noise which he made in crossing the bare-boarded apartment, I knew at once that my strange entertainer had a wooden leg. Over the dust which lay quite thick on the boards, you could see the mark of one foot very neat and pretty, and then a round O, which was naturally the impression made by the wooden stump. I own I had a queer thrill as I saw that mark, and felt a secret comfort that it was not CLOVEN.

In this desolate apartment in which Mr. Pinto had invited me to see him, there were three chairs, one bottomless, a little table on which you might put a breakfast tray, and not a single other article of furniture. In the next room, the door of which was open, I could see a magnificent gilt dressing case, with some splendid diamond and ruby shirt studs lying by it, and a chest of drawers, and a cupboard apparently full of clothes.

Remembering him in Baden-Baden in great magnificence I wondered at his present denuded state. "You have a house elsewhere, Mr. Pinto?" I said.

"Many," says he. "I have apartments in many cities. I lock dem up, and do not carry mosh logish."

I then remembered that his apartment at Baden, where I first met him, was bare, and had no bed in it.

"There is, then, a sleeping room beyond?"

"This is the sleeping room." (He pronounces it DIS. Can this, by the way, give any clew to the nationality of this singular man?)

"If you sleep on these two old chairs you have a rickety couch; if on the floor, a dusty one."

"Suppose I sleep up dere?" said this strange man, and he actually pointed up to the ceiling. I thought him mad or what he himself called "an ombog." "I know. You do not believe me; for why should I deceive you? I came but to propose a matter of business to you. I told you I could give you the clew to the mystery of the Two Children in Black, whom you met at Baden, and you came to see me. If I told you you would not believe me. What for try and convinz you? Ha hey?" And he shook his hand once, twice, thrice, at me, and glared at me out of his eye in a peculiar way.

Of what happened now I protest I cannot give an accurate account. It seemed to me that there shot a flame from his eye into my brain, while behind his GLASS eye there was a green illumination as if a candle had been lit in it. It seemed to me that from his long fingers two quivering flames issued, sputtering, as it were, which penetrated me, and forced me back into one of the chairs – the broken one – out of which I had much difficulty in scrambling, when the strange glamour was ended. It seemed to me that, when I was so fixed, so transfixed in the broken chair, the man floated up to the ceiling, crossed his legs, folded his arms as if he was lying on a sofa, and grinned down at me. When I came to myself he was down from the ceiling, and, taking me out of the broken cane-bottomed chair, kindly enough – "Bah!" said he, "it is the smell of my medicine. It often gives the vertigo. I thought you would have had a little fit. Come into the open air." And we went down the steps, and into Shepherd's Inn, where the setting sun was just shining on the statue of Shepherd; the laundresses were traipsing about; the porters were leaning against the railings; and the clerks were playing at marbles, to my inexpressible consolation.

"You said you were going to dine at the 'Gray's-Inn Coffee-House,'" he said. I was. I often dine there. There is excellent wine at the "Gray's-Inn Coffee-House"; but I declare I NEVER SAID so. I was not astonished at his remark; no more astonished than if I was in a dream. Perhaps I WAS in a dream. Is life a dream? Are dreams facts? Is sleeping being really awake? I don't know. I tell you I am puzzled. I have read "The Woman in White," "The Strange Story" – not to mention that story "Stranger than Fiction" in the Cornhill Magazine – that story for which THREE credible witnesses are ready to vouch. I have had messages from the dead; and not only from the dead, but from people who never existed at all. I own I am in a state of much bewilderment: but, if you please, will proceed with my simple, my artless story.

Well, then. We passed from Shepherd's Inn into Holborn,

and looked for a while at Woodgate's bric-a-brac shop, which I never can pass without delaying at the windows – indeed, if I were going to be hung, I would beg the cart to stop, and let me have one look more at that delightful omnium gatherum. And passing Woodgate's, we come to Gale's little shop, "No. 47," which is also a favorite haunt of mine.

Mr. Gale happened to be at his door, and as we exchanged salutations, "Mr. Pinto," I said, "will you like to see a real curiosity in this curiosity shop? Step into Mr. Gale's little back room."

In that little back parlor there are Chinese gongs; there are old Saxe and Sevres plates; there is Furstenberg, Carl Theodor, Worcester, Amstel, Nankin and other jimcrockery. And in the corner what do you think there is? There is an actual GUILLO-TINE. If you doubt me, go and see – Gale, High Holborn, No. 47. It is a slim instrument, much slighter than those which they make now; – some nine feet high, narrow, a pretty piece of upholstery enough. There is the hook over which the rope used to play which unloosened the dreadful ax above; and look! dropped into the orifice where the head used to go – there is THE AX itself, all rusty, with A GREAT NOTCH IN THE BLADE.

As Pinto looked at it – Mr. Gale was not in the room, I recollect; happening to have been just called out by a customer who offered him three pound fourteen and sixpence for a blue Shepherd in pate tendre, – Mr. Pinto gave a little start, and seemed crispe for a moment. Then he looked steadily toward one of those great porcelain stools which you see in gardens – and – it seemed to me – I tell you I won't take my affidavit – I may have been maddened by the six glasses I took of that pink elixir – I may have been sleep- walking: perhaps am as I write now – I may have been under the influence of that astounding MEDIUM into whose hands I had fallen – but I vow I heard Pinto say, with rather a ghastly grin at the porcelain stool,

"Nay, nefer shague your gory locks at me,
Dou canst not say I did it."

(He pronounced it, by the way, I DIT it, by which I KNOW that Pinto was a German.)

171

I heard Pinto say those very words, and sitting on the porcelain stool I saw, dimly at first, then with an awful distinctness – a ghost – an EIDOLON – a form – A HEADLESS MAN seated with his head in his lap, which wore an expression of piteous surprise.

At this minute, Mr. Gale entered from the front shop to show a customer some Delft plates; and he did not see – but WE DID – the figure rise up from the porcelain stool, shake its head, which it held in its hand, and which kept its eyes fixed sadly on us, and disappear behind the guillotine.

"Come to the 'Gray's-Inn Coffee-House,'" Pinto said, "and I will tell you how the notch came to the ax." And we walked down Holborn at about thirty-seven minutes past six o'clock.

If there is anything in the above statement which astonishes the reader, I promise him that in the next chapter of this little story he will be astonished still more.

II

"You will excuse me," I said to my companion, "for remarking that when you addressed the individual sitting on the porcelain stool, with his head in his lap, your ordinarily benevolent features" – (this I confess was a bouncer, for between ourselves a more sinister and ill-looking rascal than Mons. P. I have seldom set eyes on) – "your ordinarily handsome face wore an expression that was by no means pleasing. You grinned at the individual just as you did at me when you went up to the cei – , pardon me, as I THOUGHT you did, when I fell down in a fit in your chambers"; and I qualified my words in a great flutter and tremble; I did not care to offend the man – I did not DARE to offend the man. I thought once or twice of jumping into a cab, and flying; of taking refuge in Day and Martin's Blacking Warehouse; of speaking to a policeman, but not one would come. I was this man's slave. I followed him like his dog. I COULD not get away from him. So, you see, I went on meanly conversing with him, and affecting a simpering confidence. I remember, when I was a little boy at school, going up fawning and smiling in this way to some great hulking bully of a sixth-form boy. So I said in a word, "Your ordinarily handsome face wore a disagreeable expression," &c.

"It is ordinarily VERY handsome," said he, with such a leer at a couple of passers-by, that one of them cried, "Oh, crickey, here's a precious guy!" and a child, in its nurse's arms, screamed itself into convulsions. "Oh, oui, che suis tres-choli garcon, bien peau, cerdainement," continued Mr. Pinto; "but you were right. That – that person was not very well pleased when he saw me. There was no love lost between us, as you say: and the world never knew a more worthless miscreant. I hate him, voyez-vous? I hated him alife; I hate him dead. I hate him man; I hate him ghost: and he know it, and tremble before me. If I see him twenty tausend years hence – and why not? – I shall hate him still. You remarked how he was dressed?"

"In black satin breeches and striped stockings; a white pique waistcoat, a gray coat, with large metal buttons, and his hair in powder. He must have worn a pigtail – only – "

"Only it was CUT OFF! Ha, ha, ha!" Mr. Pinto cried, yelling a laugh, which I observed made the policeman stare very much. "Yes. It was cut off by the same blow which took off the scoundrel's head – ho, ho, ho!" And he made a circle with his hook-nailed finger round his own yellow neck, and grinned with a horrible triumph. "I promise you that fellow was surprised when he found his head in the pannier. Ha! ha! Do you ever cease to hate those whom you hate?" – fire flashed terrifically from his glass eye as he spoke – "or to love dose whom you once loved? Oh, never, never!" And here his natural eye was bedewed with tears. "But here we are at the 'Gray's-Inn CoffeeHouse.' James, what is the joint?"

That very respectful and efficient waiter brought in the bill of fare, and I, for my part, chose boiled leg of pork, and pease pudding, which my acquaintance said would do as well as any-thing else; though I remarked he only trifled with the pease pud-ding, and left all the pork on the plate. In fact, he scarcely ate anything. But he drank a prodigious quantity of wine; and I must say that my friend Mr. Hart's port wine is so good that I myself took – well, I should think, I took three glasses. Yes, three, certainly. HE – I mean Mr. P. – the old rogue, was insatiable: for we had to call for a second bottle in no time. When that was gone, my companion wanted another. A little red mounted up to his yellow cheeks as he drank the wine, and he winked at it in a strange manner. "I remember," said he, musing, "when port wine was scarcely drunk in this country – though the Queen liked it, and so did Hurley; but Bolingbroke didn't – he drank Florence and Champagne. Dr. Swift put water to his wine. 'Jonathan,' I once said to him – but bah! autres temps, autres moeurs. Another magnum, James."

This was all very well. "My good sir," I said, "it may suit YOU to order bottles of '20 port, at a guinea a bottle; but that kind of price does not suit me. I only happen to have thirty-four and sixpence in my pocket, of which I want a shilling for the waiter, and eighteen pence for my cab. You rich foreigners and SWELLS may spend what you like" (I had him there: for my friend's dress was as shabby as an old-clothes man's); "but a man with a family, Mr. Whatd'you-call'im, cannot afford to spend seven or eight hundred a year on his dinner alone."

"Bah!" he said. "Nunkey pays for all, as you say. I will what you call stant the dinner, if you are SO POOR!" and again he gave that disagreeable grin, and placed an odious crook-nailed and by no means clean finger to his nose. But I was not so afraid of him now, for we were in a public place; and the three glasses of port wine had, you see, given me courage.

"What a pretty snuff-box!" he remarked, as I handed him mine, which I am still old-fashioned enough to carry. It is a pretty old gold box enough, but valuable to me especially as a relic of an old, old relative, whom I can just remember as a child, when she was very kind to me. "Yes; a pretty box. I can remember when many ladies – most ladies, carried a box – nay, two boxes – tabatiere and bonbonniere. What lady carries snuff-box now, hey? Suppose your astonishment if a lady in an assembly were to offer you a prise? I can remember a lady with such a box as this, with a tour, as we used to call it then; with paniers, with a tortoise-shell cane, with the prettiest little high-heeled velvet shoes in the world! – ah! that was a time, that was a time! Ah, Eliza, Eliza, I have thee now in my mind's eye! At Bungay on the Waveney, did I not walk with thee, Eliza? Aha, did I not love thee? Did I not walk with thee then? Do I not see thee still?"

This was passing strange. My ancestress – but there is no need to publish her revered name – did indeed live at Bungay St. Mary's, where she lies buried. She used to walk with a tortoise-shell cane. She used to wear little black velvet shoes, with the prettiest high heels in the world.

"Did you – did you – know, then, my great-gr-nd-m-ther?" I said.

He pulled up his coat sleeve – "Is that her name?" he said.

"Eliza – "

There, I declare, was the very name of the kind old creature written in red on his arm.

"YOU knew her old," he said, divining my thoughts (with his strange knack); "I knew her young and lovely. I danced with her at the Bury ball. Did I not, dear, dear Miss – – ?"

As I live, he here mentioned dear gr-nny's MAIDEN name. Her maiden name was – – . Her honored married name was – – .

"She married your great-gr-ndf-th-r the year Poseidon won the Newmarket Plate," Mr. Pinto dryly remarked.

Merciful powers! I remember, over the old shagreen knife and spoon case on the sideboard in my gr-nny's parlor, a print by Stubbs of that very horse. My grandsire, in a red coat, and his fair hair flowing over his shoulders, was over the mantelpiece, and Poseidon won the Newmarket Cup in the year 1783!

"Yes; you are right. I danced a minuet with her at Bury that very night, before I lost my poor leg. And I quarreled with your grandf – , ha!"

As he said "Ha!" there came three quiet little taps on the table – it is the middle table in the "Gray's-Inn CoffeeHouse," under the bust of the late Duke of W-ll-ngt-n.

"I fired in the air," he continued; "did I not?" (Tap, tap, tap.) "Your grandfather hit me in the leg. He married three months afterwards. 'Captain Brown,' I said 'who could see Miss Sm-th without loving her?' She is there! She is there!" (Tap, tap, tap.) "Yes, my first love – "

But here there came tap, tap, which everybody knows means "No."

"I forgot," he said, with a faint blush stealing over his wan features, "she was not my first love. In Germ – in my own country – there WAS a young woman – "

Tap, tap, tap. There was here quite a lively little treble knock; and when the old man said, "But I loved thee better than all the world, Eliza," the affirmative signal was briskly repeated.

And this I declare UPON MY HONOR. There was, I have said, a bottle of port wine before us – I should say a decanter. That decanter was LIFTED UP, and out of it into our respective glasses two bumpers of wine were poured. I appeal to Mr. Hart, the landlord – I appeal to James, the respectful and intelligent waiter, if this statement is not true? And when we had finished that magnum, and I said – for I did not now in the least doubt her presence – "Dear gr-nny, may we have another magnum?" the table DISTINCTLY rapped "No.".

"Now, my good sir," Mr. Pinto said, who really began to be affected by the wine, "you understand the interest I have taken in you. I loved Eliza – – " (of course I don't mention family names). "I knew you had that box which belonged to her – I will give you what you like for that box. Name your price at once, and I pay you on the spot."

"Why, when you came out, you said you had not six-pence in your pocket."

"Bah! give you anything you like – fifty – a hundred – a tausend pound."

"Come, come," said I, "the gold of the box may be worth nine guineas, and the facon we will put at six more."

"One tausend guineas!" he screeched. "One tausend and fifty pound dere!" and he sank back in his chair – no, by the way, on his bench, for he was sitting with his back to one of the partitions of the boxes, as I dare say James remembers.

"DON'T go on in this way," I continued rather weakly, for I did not know whether I was in a dream. "If you offer me a thousand guineas for this box I MUST take it. Mustn't I, dear gr-nny?"

The table most distinctly said "Yes"; and putting out his claws to seize the box, Mr. Pinto plunged his hooked nose into it, and eagerly inhaled some of my 47 with a dash of Hardman.

"But stay, you old harpy!" I exclaimed, being now in a sort of rage, and quite familiar with him. "Where is the money? Where is the check?"

"James, a piece of note paper and a receipt stamp!"

"This is all mighty well, sir," I said, "but I don't know you; I never saw you before. I will trouble you to hand me that box back again, or give me a check with some known signature."

"Whose? Ha, Ha, HA!"

The room happened to be very dark. Indeed all the waiters were gone to supper, and there were only two gentlemen snoring in their respective boxes. I saw a hand come quivering down from the ceiling – a very pretty hand, on which was a ring with a coronet, with a lion rampant gules for a crest. I saw that hand take a dip of ink and write across the paper. Mr. Pinto, then, taking a gray receipt stamp out of his blue leather pocketbook, fastened it on to the paper by the usual process; and the hand then wrote across the receipt stamp, went across the table and shook hands with Pinto, and then, as if waving him an adieu, vanished in the direction of the ceiling.

There was the paper before me, wet with the ink. There was the pen which THE HAND had used. Does anybody doubt me? I have that pen now, – a cedar stick of a not uncommon sort, and holding one of Gillott's pens. It is in my inkstand now, I tell you. Anybody may see it. The handwriting on the check, for such the document was, was the writing of a female. It ran thus: – "London, midnight, March 31, 1862. Pay the bearer one thousand and fifty pounds. Rachel Sidonia. To Messrs. Sidonia, Pozzosanto and Co., London."

"Noblest and best of women!" said Pinto, kissing the sheet of paper with much reverence. "My good Mr. Roundabout, I suppose you do not question THAT signature?"

Indeed the house of Sidonia, Pozzosanto and Co., is known to be one of the richest in Europe, and as for the Countess Rachel, she was known to be the chief manager of that enormously wealthy establishment. There was only one little difficulty, the Countess Rachel died last October.

I pointed out this circumstance, and tossed over the paper to Pinto with a sneer.

"C'est a brandre ou a laisser," he said with some heat. "You literary men are all imbrudent; but I did not tink you such a fool wie dis. Your box is not worth twenty pound, and I offer you a tausend because I know you want money to pay dat rascal Tom's college bills." (This strange man actually knew that my scapegrace Tom had been a source of great expense and annoyance to me.) "You see money costs me nothing, and you refuse to take it! Once, twice; will you take this check in exchange for your trumpery snuff-box?"

What could I do? My poor granny's legacy was valuable and dear to me, but after all a thousand guineas are not to be had every day. "Be it a bargain," said I. "Shall we have a glass of wine on it?" says Pinto; and to this proposal I also unwillingly acceded, reminding him, by the way, that he had not yet told me the story of the headless man.

"Your poor gr-ndm-ther was right just now, when she said she was not my first love. 'Twas one of those banale expressions" (here Mr. P. blushed once more) "which we use to women. We tell each she is our first passion. They reply with a similar illusory formula. No man is any woman's first love; no woman any man's. We are in love in our nurse's arms, and women coquette with their eyes before their tongue can form a word. How could your lovely relative love me? I was far, far too old for her. I am older than I look. I am so old that you would not believe my age were I to tell you. I have loved many and many a woman before your relative. It has not always been fortunate for them to love me. Ah, Sophronia! Round the dreadful circus where you fell, and whence I was dragged corpselike by the heels, there sat multitudes more savage than the lions which mangled your sweet form! Ah, tenez! when we marched to the terrible stake together at Valladolid – the Protestant and the J – But away with memory! Boy! it was happy for thy grandam that she loved me not.

"During that strange period," he went on, "when the teeming Time was great with the revolution that was speedily to be born, I was on a mission in Paris with my excellent, my maligned friend, Cagliostro. Mesmer was one of our band. I seemed to occupy but an obscure rank in it: though, as you know, in secret societies the humble man may be a chief and director – the ostensible leader but a puppet moved by unseen hands. Never mind who was chief, or who was second. Never mind my age. It boots not to tell it: why shall I expose myself to your scornful incredulity – or reply to your questions in words that are familiar to you, but which you cannot understand? Words are symbols of things which you know, or of things which you don't know. If you don't know them, to speak is idle." (Here I confess Mr. P. spoke for exactly thirty-eight minutes, about physics, metaphysics, language, the origin and destiny of man, during which time I was rather bored, and to relieve my ennui, drank a half glass or so of wine.) "LOVE, friend, is the fountain of youth! It may not happen to me once – once in an age: but when I love then I am young. I loved when I was in Paris. Bathilde, Bathilde, I loved thee – ah, how fondly! Wine, I say, more wine! Love is ever young. I was a boy at the little feet of Bathilde de Bechamel – the fair, the fond, the fickle, ah, the false!" The strange old man's agony was here really terrific, and he showed himself much more agitated than when he had been speaking about my gr-ndm-th-r.

"I thought Blanche might love me. I could speak to her in the language of all countries, and tell her the lore of all ages. I could trace the nursery legends which she loved up to their Sanscrit source, and whisper to her the darkling mysteries of the Egyptian Magi. I could chant for her the wild chorus that rang in the disheveled Eleusinian revel: I could tell her and I would, the watchword never known but to one woman, the Saban Queen, which Hiram breathed in the abysmal ear of Solomon – You don't attend. Psha! you have drunk too much wine!" Perhaps I may as well own that I was NOT attending, for he had been carrying on for about fifty-seven minutes; and I don't like a man to have ALL the talk to himself.

"Blanche de Bechamel was wild, then, about this secret of Masonry. In early, early days I loved, I married a girl fair as Blanche, who, too, was tormented by curiosity, who, too, would peep into my closet, into the only secret guarded from her. A dreadful fate befell poor Fatima. An ACCIDENT shortened her life. Poor thing! she had a foolish sister who urged her on. I always told her to beware of Ann. She died. They said her brothers killed me. A gross falsehood. AM I dead? If I were, could I pledge you in this wine?"

"Was your name," I asked, quite bewildered, "was your name, pray, then, ever Blueb – – ?"

"Hush! the waiter will overhear you. Methought we were speaking of Blanche de Bechamel. I loved her, young man. My pearls, and diamonds, and treasure, my wit, my wisdom, my passion, I flung them all into the child's lap. I was a fool. Was strong Samson not as weak as I? Was Solomon the Wise much better when Balkis wheedled him? I said to the king – But enough of that, I spake of Blanche de Bechamel.

"Curiosity was the poor child's foible. I could see, as I talked to her, that her thoughts were elsewhere (as yours, my friend, have been absent once or twice to-night). To know the secret of Masonry was the wretched child's mad desire. With a thousand wiles, smiles, caresses, she strove to coax it from me – from ME – ha! ha!

"I had an apprentice – the son of a dear friend, who died by my side at Rossbach, when Soubise, with whose army I happened to be, suffered a dreadful defeat for neglecting my advice. The Young Chevalier Goby de Mouchy was glad enough to serve as my clerk, and help in some chemical experiments in which I was engaged with my friend Dr. Mesmer. Bathilde saw this young man. Since women were, has it not been their business to smile and deceive, to fondle and lure? Away! From the very first it has been so!" And as my companion spoke, he looked as wicked as the serpent that coiled round the tree, and hissed a poisoned counsel to the first woman.

"One evening I went, as was my wont, to see Blanche. She was radiant: she was wild with spirits: a saucy triumph blazed in her blue eyes. She talked, she rattled in her childish way. She uttered, in the course of her rhapsody, a hint – an intimation – so terrible that the truth flashed across me in a moment. Did I ask her? She would lie to me. But I knew how to make falsehood impossible. And I ordered her to go to sleep."

At this moment the clock (after its previous convulsions) sounded TWELVE. And as the new Editor* of the Cornhill Magazine – and HE, I promise you, won't stand any nonsense – will only allow seven pages, I am obliged to leave off at THE VERY MOST INTERESTING POINT OF THE STORY.

* Mr. Thackeray retired from the Editorship of the Cornhill Magazine in March, 1862

III

"Are you of our fraternity? I see you are not. The secret which Mademoiselle de Bechamel confided to me in her mad triumph and wild hoyden spirits – she was but a child, poor thing, poor thing, scarce fifteen; – but I love them young – a folly not unusual with the old!" (Here Mr. Pinto thrust his knuckles into his hollow eyes; and, I am sorry to say, so little regardful was he of personal cleanliness, that his tears made streaks of white over his guarled dark hands.) "Ah, at fifteen, poor child, thy fate was terrible! Go to! It is not good to love me, friend. They prosper not who do. I divine you. You need not say what you are think-ing – "

In truth, I was thinking, if girls fall in love with this sallow, hook-nosed, glass-eyed, wooden-legged, dirty, hideous old man, with the sham teeth, they have a queer taste. THAT is what I was thinking.

"Jack Wilkes said the handsomest man in London had but half an hour's start of him. And, without vanity, I am scarcely uglier than Jack Wilkes. We were members of the same club at Medenham Abbey, Jack and I, and had many a merry night together. Well, sir, I – Mary of Scotland knew me but as a little hunchbacked music master; and yet, and yet, I think she was not indifferent to her David Riz – and SHE came to misfortune. They all do – they all do!"

"Sir, you are wandering from your point!" I said, with some severity. For, really, for this old humbug to hint that he had been the baboon who frightened the club at Medenham, that he had been in the Inquisition at Valladolid – that under the name of D. Riz, as he called it, he had known the lovely Queen of Scots – was a LITTLE too much. "Sir," then I said, "you were speaking about a Miss Bechamel. I really have not time to hear all of your biography."

"Faith, the good wine gets into my head." (I should think so, the old toper! Four bottles all but two glasses.) "To return to poor Blanche. As I sat laughing, joking with her, she let slip a word, a little word, which filled me with dismay. Some one had told her a part of the Secret – the secret which has been divulged scarce thrice in three thousand years – the Secret of the Freemasons. Do you know what happens to those uninitiate who learn that secret? to those wretched men, the initiate who reveal it?"

As Pinto spoke to me, he looked through and through me with his horrible piercing glance, so that I sat quite uneasily on my bench. He continued: "Did I question her awake? I knew she would lie to me. Poor child! I loved her no less because I did not believe a word she said. I loved her blue eye, her golden hair, her delicious voice, that was true in song, though when she spoke, false as Eblis! You are aware that I possess in rather a remarkable degree what we have agreed to call the mesmeric power. I set the unhappy girl to sleep. THEN she was obliged to tell me all. It was as I had surmised. Goby de Mouchy, my wretched, besotted miserable secretary, in his visits to the chateau of the Marquis de Bechamel, who was one of our society, had seen Blanche. I suppose it was because she had been warned that he was worthless, and poor, artful and a coward, she loved him. She wormed out of the besotted wretch the secrets of our Order. 'Did he tell you the NUMBER ONE?' I asked.

"She said, 'Yes.'

"'Did he,' I further inquired, 'tell you the – '

"'Oh, don't ask me, don't ask me!' she said, writhing on the sofa, where she lay in the presence of the Marquis de Bechamel, her most unhappy father. Poor Bechamel, poor Bechamel! How pale he looked as I spoke! 'Did he tell you,' I repeated with a dreadful calm, 'the NUMBER TWO?' She said, 'Yes.'

"The poor old marquis rose up, and clasping his hands, fell on his knees before Count Cagl – – Bah! I went by a different name then. Vat's in a name? Dat vich ye call a Rosicrucian by any other name vil smell as sveet. 'Monsieur,' he said, 'I am old – I am rich. I have five hundred thousand livres of rentes in Picardy. I have half as much in Artois. I have two hundred and eighty thousand on the Grand Livre. I am promised by my Sovereign a dukedom and his orders with a reversion to my heir. I am a Grandee of Spain of the First Class, and Duke of Volovento. Take my titles, my ready money, my life, my honor, everything I have in the world, but don't ask the THIRD QUESTION.'

"'Godfroid de Bouillon, Comte de Bechamel, Grandee of Spain and Prince of Volovento, in our Assembly what was the oath you swore?' The old man writhed as he remembered its terrific purport.

"Though my heart was racked with agony, and I would have died, aye, cheerfully" (died, indeed, as if THAT were a penalty!) "to spare yonder lovely child a pang, I said to her calmly, 'Blanche de Bechamel, did Goby de Mouchy tell you secret NUMBER THREE?'

"She whispered a oui that was quite faint, faint and small. But her poor father fell in convulsions at her feet.

"She died suddenly that night. Did I not tell you those I love come to no good? When General Bonaparte crossed the Saint Bernard, he saw in the convent an old monk with a white beard, wandering about the corridors, cheerful and rather stout, but mad – mad as a March hare. 'General,' I said to him, 'did you ever see that face before?' He had not. He had not mingled much with the higher classes of our society before the Revolution. I knew the poor old man well enough; he was the last of a noble race, and I loved his child."

"And did she die by – ?"

"Man! did I say so? Do I whisper the secrets of the Vehmgericht? I say she died that night: and he – he, the heartless, the villain, the betrayer, – you saw him seated in yonder curiosity shop, by yonder guillotine, with his scoundrelly head in his lap.

"You saw how slight that instrument was? It was one of the first which Guillotin made, and which he showed to private friends in a hangar in the Rue Picpus, where he lived. The invention created some little conversation among scientific men at the time, though I remember a machine in Edinburgh of a very similar construction, two hundred – well, many, many years ago – and at a breakfast which Guillotin gave he showed us the instrument, and much talk arose among us as to whether people suffered under it.

"And now I must tell you what befell the traitor who had caused all this suffering. Did he know that the poor child's death was a SENTENCE? He felt a cowardly satisfaction that with her was gone the secret of his treason. Then he began to doubt. I had MEANS to penetrate all his thoughts, as well as to know his acts. Then he became a slave to a horrible fear. He fled in abject terror to a convent. They still existed in Paris; and behind the walls of Jacobins the wretch thought himself secure. Poor fool! I had but to set one of my somnambulists to sleep. Her spirit went forth and spied the shuddering wretch in his cell. She described the street, the gate, the convent, the very dress which he wore, and which you saw to-day.

"And now THIS is what happened. In his chamber in the Rue St. Honore, at Paris, sat a man ALONE – a man who has been maligned, a man who has been called a knave and charlatan, a man who has been persecuted even to the death, it is said, in Roman Inquisitions, forsooth, and elsewhere. Ha! ha! A man who has a mighty will.

"And looking toward the Jacobins Convent (of which, from his chamber, he could see the spires and trees), this man WILLED. And it was not yet dawn. And he willed; and one who was lying in his cell in the convent of Jacobins, awake and shuddering with terror for a crime which he had committed, fell asleep.

"But though he was asleep his eyes were open.

"And after tossing and writhing, and clinging to the pallet, and saying 'No, I will not go,' he rose up and donned his clothes – a gray coat, a vest of white pique, black satin small-clothes, ribbed silk stockings, and a white stock with a steel buckle; and he arranged his hair, and he tied his queue, all the while being in that strange somnolence which walks, which moves, which FLIES sometimes, which sees, which is indifferent to pain, which OBEYS. And he put on his hat, and he went forth from his cell: and though the dawn was not yet, he trod the corridors as seeing them. And he passed into the cloister, and then into the garden where lie the ancient dead. And he came to the wicket, which Brother Jerome was opening just at the dawning. And the crowd was already waiting with their cans and bowls to receive the alms of the good brethren.

"And he passed through the crowd and went on his way, and the few people then abroad who marked him, said, 'Tiens! How very odd he looks! He looks like a man walking in his sleep!' This was said by various persons: –

"By milk women, with their cans and carts, coming into the town.

"By roysterers who had been drinking at the taverns of the

Barrier, for it was Mid-Lent.

"By the sergeants of the watch, who eyed him sternly as he passed near their halberds.

"But he passed on unmoved by their halberds,

"Unmoved by the cries of the roysterers,

"By the market women coming with their milk and eggs.

"He walked through the Rue St. Honore, I say: –

"By the Rue Rambuteau,

"By the Rue St. Antoine,

"By the King's Chateau of the Bastille,

"By the Faubourg St. Antoine.

"And he came to No. 29 in the Rue Picpus – a house which then stood between a court and garden –

"That is, there was a building of one story, with a great coach door.

"Then there was a court, around which were stables, coach-houses, offices.

"Then there was a house – a two-storied house, with a perron in front.

"Behind the house was a garden – a garden of two hundred and fifty
French feet in length.

"And as one hundred feet of France equal one hundred and six feet of England, this garden, my friend, equaled exactly two hundred and sixty-five feet of British measure.

"In the center of the garden was a fountain and a statue – or, to speak more correctly, two statues. One was recumbent, – a man. Over him, saber in hand, stood a Woman.

"The man was Olofernes. The woman was Judith. From the head, from the trunk, the water gushed. It was the taste of the doctor: – was it not a droll of taste?

"At the end of the garden was the doctor's cabinet of study. My faith, a singular cabinet, and singular pictures! –

"Decapitation of Charles Premier at Vitehall.

"Decapitation of Montrose at Edimbourg.

"Decapitation of Cinq Mars. When I tell you that he was a man of taste, charming!

"Through this garden, by these statues, up these stairs, went the pale figure of him who, the porter said, knew the way of the house. He did. Turning neither right nor left, he seemed to walk THROUGH the statues, the obstacles, the flower beds, the stairs, the door, the tables, the chairs.

"In the corner of the room was THAT INSTRUMENT, which Guillotin had just invented and perfected. One day he was to lay his own head under his own ax. Peace be to his name! With him I deal not!

"In a frame of mahogany, neatly worked, was a board with a half circle in it, over which another board fitted. Above was a heavy ax, which fell – you know how. It was held up by a rope, and when this rope was untied, or cut, the steel fell.

"To the story which I now have to relate, you may give credence, or not, as you will. The sleeping man went up to that instrument.

"He laid his head in it, asleep."

"Asleep?"

"He then took a little penknife out of the pocket of his white dimity waistcoat.

"He cut the rope asleep.

"The ax descended on the head of the traitor and villain. The notch in it was made by the steel buckle of his stock, which was cut through.

"A strange legend has got abroad that after the deed was

done, the figure rose, took the head from the basket, walked forth through the garden, and by the screaming porters at the gate, and went and laid itself down at the Morgue. But for this I will not vouch. Only of this be sure. 'There are more things in heaven and earth, Horatio, than are dreamed of in your philosophy.' More and more the light peeps through the chinks. Soon, amidst music ravishing, the curtain will rise, and the glorious scene be displayed. Adieu! Remember me. Ha! 'tis dawn," Pinto said. And he was gone.

I am ashamed to say that my first movement was to clutch the check which he had left with me, and which I was determined to present the very moment the bank opened. I know the importance of these things, and that men change their mind sometimes. I sprang through the streets to the great banking house of Manasseh in Duke Street. It seemed to me as if I actually flew as I walked. As the clock struck ten I was at the counter and laid down my check.

The gentleman who received it, who was one of the Hebrew persuasion, as were the other two hundred clerks of the establishment, having looked at the draft with terror in his countenance, then looked at me, then called to himself two of his fellow clerks, and queer it was to see all their aquiline beaks over the paper.

"Come, come!" said I, "don't keep me here all day. Hand me over the money, short, if you please!" for I was, you see, a little alarmed, and so determined to assume some extra bluster.

"Will you have the kindness to step into the parlor to the partners?" the clerk said, and I followed him.

"What, AGAIN?" shrieked a bald-headed, red-whiskered gentleman, whom I knew to be Mr. Manasseh. "Mr. Salathiel, this is too bad! Leave me with this gentleman, S." And the clerk disappeared.

"Sir," he said, "I know how you came by this: the Count de Pinto gave it you. It is too bad! I honor my parents; I honor THEIR parents; I honor their bills! But this one of grandma's is too bad – it is, upon my word, now! She've been dead these five-and- thirty years. And this last four months she has left her burial place and took to drawing on our 'ouse! It's too bad, grandma; it is too bad!" and he appealed to me, and tears actually trickled down his nose.

"Is it the Countess Sidonia's check or not?" I asked, haughtily.

"But, I tell you, she's dead! It's a shame! – it's a shame! – it is, grandmamma!" and he cried, and wiped his great nose in his yellow pocket handkerchief. "Look year – will you take pounds instead of guineas? She's dead, I tell you! It's no go! Take the pounds – one tausend pound! – ten nice, neat, crisp hundred-pound notes, and go away vid you, do!"

"I will have my bond, sir, or nothing," I said; and I put on an attitude of resolution which I confess surprised even myself.

"Wery veil," he shrieked, with many oaths, "then you shall have noting – ha, ha, ha! – noting but a policeman! Mr. Abed-nego, call a policeman! Take that, you humbug and impostor!" and here with an abundance of frightful language which I dare not repeat, the wealthy banker abused and defied me.

Au bout du compte, what was I to do, if a banker did not choose to honor a check drawn by his dead grandmother? I began to wish I had my snuff-box back. I began to think I was a fool for changing that little old-fashioned gold for this slip of strange paper.

Meanwhile the banker had passed from his fit of anger to a paroxysm of despair. He seemed to be addressing some person invisible, but in the room: "Look here, ma'am, you've really been coming it too strong. A hundred thousand in six months, and now a thousand more! The 'ouse can't stand it; it WON'T stand it, I say! What? Oh! mercy, mercy!

As he uttered these words, A HAND fluttered over the table in the air! It was a female hand: that which I had seen the night before. That female hand took a pen from the green baize table, dipped it in a silver inkstand, and wrote on a quarter of a sheet of

189

foolscap on the blotting book, "How about the diamond robbery? If you do not pay, I will tell him where they are."

What diamonds? what robbery? what was this mystery? That will never be ascertained, for the wretched man's demeanor instantly changed. "Certainly, sir; – oh, certainly," he said, forcing a grin. "How will you have the money, sir? All right, Mr. Abednego. This way out."

"I hope I shall often see you again," I said; on which I own poor Manasseh gave a dreadful grin, and shot back into his parlor.

I ran home, clutching the ten delicious, crisp hundred pounds, and the dear little fifty which made up the account. I flew through the streets again. I got to my chambers. I bolted the outer doors. I sank back in my great chair, and slept...

My first thing on waking was to feel for my money. Perdition! Where was I? Ha! – on the table before me was my grandmother's snuff-box, and by its side one of those awful – those admirable – sensation novels, which I had been reading, and which are full of delicious wonder.

But that the guillotine is still to be seen at Mr. Gale's, No. 47, High Holborn, I give you MY HONOR. I suppose I was dreaming about it. I don't know. What is dreaming? What is life? Why shouldn't I sleep on the ceiling? – and am I sitting on it now, or on the floor? I am puzzled. But enough. If the fashion for sensation novels goes on, I tell you I will write one in fifty volumes. For the present, DIXI. But between ourselves, this Pinto, who fought at the Colosseum, who was nearly being roasted by the Inquisition, and sang duets at Holyrood, I am rather sorry to lose him after three little bits of Roundabout Papers. Et vous?

ANONYMOUS

Bourgonef

I

At a Table d'Hote

At the close of February, 1848, I was in Nuremberg. My
original intention had been to pass a couple of days there on my
way to Munich, that being, I thought, as much time as could rea-
sonably be spared for so small a city, beckoned as my footsteps
were to the Bavarian Athens, of whose glories of ancient art and
German Renaissance I had formed expectations the most exaggerated – expectations fatal to any perfect enjoyment, and certain
to be disappointed, however great the actual merit of Munich
might be. But after two days at Nuremberg I was so deeply interested in its antique sequestered life, the charms of which had not
been deadened by previous anticipations, that I resolved to remain there until I had mastered every detail and knew the place
by heart.

I have a story to tell which will move amidst tragic circumstances of too engrossing a nature to be disturbed by archaeologi-
cal interests, and shall not, therefore, minutely describe here what
I observed in Nuremberg, although no adequate description of
that wonderful city has yet fallen in my way. To readers unacquainted with this antique place, it will be enough to say that in it
the old German life seems still to a great extent rescued from the
all- devouring, all-equalizing tendencies of European civilization.
The houses are either of the fifteenth and sixteenth centuries, or
are constructed after those ancient models. The citizens have preserved much of the simple manners and customs of their ancestors. The hurrying feet of commerce and curiosity pass rapidly
by, leaving it sequestered from the agitations and the turmoils of
metropolitan existence. It is as quiet as a village. During my stay
there rose in its quiet streets the startled echoes of horror at a
crime unparalleled in its annals, which, gathering increased horror from the very peacefulness and serenity of the scene, arrested

the attention and the sympathy in a degree seldom experienced. Before narrating that, it will be necessary to go back a little, that my own connection with it may be intelligible, especially in the fanciful weaving together of remote conjectures which strangely involved me in the story.

The table d'hote at the Bayerischer Hof had about thirty visitors – all, with one exception, of that local commonplace which escapes remark. Indeed this may almost always be said of tables d'hote; though there is a current belief, which I cannot share, of a table d'hote being very delightful – of one being certain to meet pleasant people there." It may be so. For many years I believed it was so. The general verdict received my assent. I had never met those delightful people, but was always expecting to meet them. Hitherto they had been conspicuous by their absence. According to my experience in Spain, France, and Germany, such dinners had been dreary or noisy and vapid. If the guests were English, they were chillingly silent, or surlily monosyllabic: to their neighbors they were frigid; amongst each other they spoke in low undertones. And if the guests were foreigners, they were noisy, clattering, and chattering, foolish for the most part, and vivaciously commonplace. I don't know which made me feel most dreary. The predominance of my countrymen gave the dinner the gayety of a funeral; the predominance of the Mossoo gave it the fatigue of got-up enthusiasm, of trivial expansiveness. To hear strangers imparting the scraps of erudition and connoisseurship which they had that morning gathered from their valets de place and guidebooks, or describing the sights they had just seen, to you, who either saw them yesterday, or would see them to-morrow, could not be permanently attractive. My mind refuses to pasture on such food with gusto. I cannot be made to care what the Herr Baron's sentiments about Albert Durer or Lucas Cranach may be. I can digest my rindfleisch without the aid of the commis voyageur's criticisms on Gothic architecture. This may be my misfortune. In spite of the Italian blood which I inherit, I am a shy man – shy as the purest Briton. But, like other shy men, I make up in obstinacy what may be deficient in expansiveness. I can be frightened into silence, but I won't be dictated to. You might as well attempt the persuasive effect of your eloquence upon a snail who has withdrawn into his shell at your approach, and will not emerge till his confidence is restored. To be told that I MUST see this, and ought to go there, because my casual neighbor was charme, has never presented itself to me as an adequate motive.

From this you readily gather that I am severely taciturn at a table d'hote. I refrain from joining in the "delightful conversation" which flies across the table, and know that my reticence is attributed to "insular pride." It is really and truly nothing but impatience of commonplace. I thoroughly enjoy good talk; but, ask yourself, what are the probabilities of hearing that rare thing in the casual assemblage of forty or fifty people, not brought together by any natural affinities or interests, but thrown together by the accident of being in the same district, and in the same hotel? They are not "forty feeding like one," but like forty. They have no community, except the community of commonplace. No, tables d'hote are not delightful, and do not gather interesting people together.

Such has been my extensive experience. But this at Nuremberg is a conspicuous exception. At that table there was one guest who, on various grounds, personal and incidental, remains the most memorable man I ever met. From the first he riveted my attention in an unusual degree. He had not, as yet, induced me to emerge from my habitual reserve, for in truth, although he riveted my attention, he inspired me with a strange feeling of repulsion. I could scarcely keep my eyes from him; yet, except the formal bow on sitting down and rising from the table, I had interchanged no sign of fellowship with him. He was a young Russian, named Bourgonef, as I at once learned; rather handsome, and peculiarly arresting to the eye, partly from an air of settled melancholy, especially in his smile, the amiability of which seemed breaking from under clouds of grief, and still more so from the mute appeal to sympathy in the empty sleeve of his right arm, which was looped to the breast-button of his coat. His eyes were large and soft. He had no beard or whisker, and only delicate moustaches. The sorrow, quiet but profound, the amiable smile and the lost arm, were appealing details which at once arrested attention and excited sympathy. But to me this sympathy was mingled with a vague repulsion, occasioned by a certain falseness in the amiable smile, and a furtiveness in the eyes, which I saw – or fancied – and which, with an inexplicable reserve, forming as it were the impregnable citadel in the center of his outwardly polite and engaging manner, gave me something of that vague impression which we express by the words "instinctive antipathy."

It was, when calmly considered, eminently absurd. To see one so young, and by his conversation so highly cultured and intelligent, condemned to early helplessness, his food cut up for him by a servant, as if he were a child, naturally engaged pity, and, on the first day, I cudgeled my brains during the greater part of dinner in the effort to account for his lost arm. He was obviously not a military man; the unmistakable look and stoop of a student told that plainly enough. Nor was the loss one dating from early life: he used his left arm too awkwardly for the event not to have had a recent date. Had it anything to do with his melancholy? Here was a topic for my vagabond imagination, and endless were the romances woven by it during my silent dinner. For the reader must be told of one peculiarity in me, because to it much of the strange complications of my story are due; complications into which a mind less active in weaving imaginary hypotheses to interpret casual and trifling facts would never have been drawn. From my childhood I have been the victim of my constructive imagination, which has led me into many mistakes and some scrapes; because, instead of contenting myself with plain, obvious evidence, I have allowed myself to frame hypothetical interpretations, which, to acts simple in themselves, and explicable on ordinary motives, render the simple-seeming acts portentous. With bitter pangs of self-reproach I have at times discovered that a long and plausible history constructed by me, relating to personal friends, has crumpled into a ruin of absurdity, by the disclosure of the primary misconception on which the whole history was based. I have gone, let us say, on the supposition that two people were secretly lovers; on this supposition my imagination has constructed a whole scheme to explain certain acts, and one fine day I have discovered indubitably that the supposed lovers were not lovers, but confidants of their passions in other directions, and, of course, all my conjectures have been utterly false. The secret flush of shame at failure has not, however, prevented my falling into similar mistakes immediately after.

When, therefore, I hereafter speak of my "constructive imagination," the reader will know to what I am alluding. It was already busy with Bourgonef. To it must be added that vague repulsion, previously mentioned. This feeling abated on the second day; but, although lessened, it remained powerful enough to prevent my speaking to him. Whether it would have continued to abate until it disappeared, as such antipathies often disappear, under the familiarities of prolonged intercourse, without any immediate appeal to my amour propre, I know not; but every reflective mind, conscious of being accessible to antipathies, will remember that one certain method of stifling them is for the object to make some appeal to our interest or our vanity: in the engagement of these more powerful feelings, the antipathy is quickly strangled. At any rate it is so in my case, and was so now.

On the third day, the conversation at table happening to turn, as it often turned, upon St. Sebald's Church, a young Frenchman, who was criticising its architecture with fluent dogmatism, drew Bourgonef into the discussion, and thereby elicited such a display of accurate and extensive knowledge, no less than delicacy of appreciation, that we were all listening spellbound. In the midst of this triumphant exposition the irritated vanity of the Frenchman could do nothing to regain his position but oppose a flat denial to a historical statement made by Bourgonef, backing his denial by the confident assertion that "all the competent authorities" held with him. At this point Bourgonef appealed to me, and in that tone of deference so exquisitely flattering from one we already know to be superior he requested my decision; observing that, from the manner in which he had seen me examine the details of the architecture, he could not be mistaken in his confidence that I was a connoisseur. All eyes were turned upon me. As a shy man, this made me blush; as a vain man, the blush was accompanied with delight. It might easily have happened that such an appeal, acting at once upon shyness and ignorance, would

195

have inflamed my wrath; but the appeal happening to be directed on a point which I had recently investigated and thoroughly mastered, I was flattered at the opportunity of a victorious display.

The pleasure of my triumph diffused itself over my feelings towards him who had been the occasion of it. The Frenchman was silenced; the general verdict of the company was too obviously on our side. From this time the conversation continued between Bourgonef and myself; and he not only succeeded in entirely dissipating my absurd antipathy – which I now saw to have been founded on purely imaginary grounds, for neither the falseness nor the furtiveness could now be detected – but he succeeded in captivating all my sympathy. Long after dinner was over, and the salle empty, we sat smoking our cigars, and discussing politics, literature, and art in that suggestive desultory manner which often gives a charm to casual acquaintances.

It was a stirring epoch, that of February, 1848. The Revolution, at first so hopeful, and soon to manifest itself in failure so disastrous, was hurrying to an outburst. France had been for many months agitated by cries of electoral reform, and by indignation at the corruption and scandals in high places. The Praslin murder, and the dishonor of M. Teste, terminated by suicide, had been interpreted as signs of the coming destruction. The political banquets given in various important cities had been occasions for inflaming the public mind, and to the far-seeing, these banquets were interpreted as the sounds of the tocsin. Louis Philippe had become odious to France, and contemptible to Europe. Guizot and Duchatel, the ministers of that day, although backed by a parliamentary majority on which they blindly relied, were unpopular, and were regarded as infatuated even by their admirers in Europe. The Spanish marriages had all but led to a war with England. The Opposition, headed by Thiers and Odillon Barrot, was strengthened by united action with the republican party, headed by Ledru Rollin, Marrast, Flocon, and Louis Blanc.

Bourgonef was an ardent republican. So was I; but my color was of a different shade from his. He belonged to the Reds. My own dominant tendencies being artistic and literary, my dream was of a republic in which intelligence would be the archon or ruler; and, of course, in such a republic, art and literature, as the highest manifestation of mind, would have the supreme direction. Do you smile, reader? I smile now; but it was serious earnest with me then. It is unnecessary to say more on this point. I have said so much to render intelligible the stray link of communion which riveted the charm of my new acquaintance's conversation; there was both agreement enough and difference enough in our views to render our society mutually fascinating.

On retiring to my room that afternoon I could not help laughing at my absurd antipathy against Bourgonef. All his remarks had disclosed a generous, ardent, and refined nature. While my antipathy had specially fastened upon a certain falseness in his smile – a falseness the more poignantly hideous if it were falseness, because hidden amidst the wreaths of amiability – my delight in his conversation had specially justified itself by the truthfulness of his mode of looking at things. He seemed to be sincerity itself. There was, indeed, a certain central reserve; but that might only he an integrity of pride; or it might be connected with painful circumstances in his history, of which the melancholy in his face was the outward sign.

That very evening my constructive imagination was furnished with a detail on which it was soon to be actively set to work. I had been rambling about the old fortifications, and was returning at nightfall through the old archway near Albert Durer's house, when a man passed by me. We looked at each other in that automatic way in which men look when they meet in narrow places, and I felt, so to speak, a start of recognition in the eyes of the man who passed. Nothing else, in features or gestures, betrayed recognition or surprise. But although there was only that, it flashed from his eyes to mine like an electric shock. He passed. I looked back. He continued his way without turning. The face was certainly known to me; but it floated in a mist of confused memories.

I walked on slowly, pestering my memory with fruitless calls upon it, hopelessly trying to recover the place where I could have seen the stranger before. In vain memory traveled over Europe in concert-rooms, theaters, shops, and railway carriages. I could not recall the occasion on which those eyes had previously met mine. That they had met them I had no doubt. I went to bed with the riddle undiscovered.

II

The Echoes of Murder

Next morning Nuremberg was agitated with a horror such as can seldom have disturbed its quiet; a young and lovely girl had been murdered. Her corpse was discovered at daybreak under the archway leading to the old fortifications. She had been stabbed to the heart. No other signs of violence were visible; no robbery had been attempted.

In great cities, necessarily great centers of crime, we daily hear of murders; their frequency and remoteness leave us undisturbed. Our sympathies can only be deeply moved either by some scenic peculiarities investing the crime with unusual romance or unusual atrocity, or else by the more immediate appeal of direct neighborly interest. The murder which is read of in the Times as having occurred in Westminster, has seldom any special horror to the inhabitants of Islington or Oxford Street; but to the inhabitants of Westminster, and especially to the inhabitants of the particular street in which it was perpetrated, the crime assumes heart-shaking proportions. Every detail is asked for, and every surmise listened to, with feverish eagerness is repeated and diffused through the crowd with growing interest. The family of the victim; the antecedents of the assassin, if he is known; or the conjectures pointing to the unknown assassin, – are eagerly discussed. All the trivial details of household care or domestic fortunes, all the items of personal gossip, become invested with a solemn and affecting interest. Pity for the victim and survivors mingle and alternate with fierce cries for vengeance on the guilty. The whole street becomes one family, commingled by an energetic sympathy, united by one common feeling of compassion and wrath.

In villages, and in cities so small as Nuremberg, the same

community of feeling is manifested. The town became as one street. The horror spread like a conflagration, the sympathy surged and swelled like a tide. Everyone felt a personal interest in the event, as if the murder had been committed at his own door. Never shall I forget that wail of passionate pity, and that cry for the vengeance of justice, which rose from all sides of the startled city. Never shall I forget the hurry, the agitation, the feverish restlessness, the universal communicativeness, the volunteered services, the eager suggestion, surging round the house of the unhappy parents. Herr Lehfeldt, the father of the unhappy girl, was a respected burgher known to almost every one. His mercer's shop was the leading one of the city. A worthy, pious man, some-what strict, but of irreproachable character; his virtues, no less than those of his wife, and of his only daughter, Lieschen – now, alas; for ever snatched from their yearning eyes – were canvassed everywhere, and served to intensify the general grief. That such a calamity should have fallen on a household so estimable, seemed to add fuel to the people's wrath. Poor Lieschen! her pretty, play-ful ways – her opening prospects, as the only daughter of parents so well to do and so kind – her youth and abounding life – these were detailed with impassioned fervor by friends, and repeated by strangers who caught the tone of friends, as if they, too, had known and loved her. But amidst the surging uproar of this sea of many voices no one clear voice of direction could be heard; no clue given to the clamorous bloodhounds to run down the assas-sin.

Cries had been heard in the streets that night at various parts of the town, which, although then interpreted as the quarrels of drunken brawlers, and the conflicts of cats, were now confidently asserted to have proceeded from the unhappy girl in her death-struggle. But none of these cries had been heard in the immediate neighborhood of the archway. All the inhabitants of that part of the town agreed that in their waking hours the streets had been perfectly still. Nor were there any traces visible of a struggle hav-ing taken place. Lieschen might have been murdered elsewhere, and her corpse quietly deposited where it was found, as far as any evidence went.

Wild and vague were the conjectures. All were baffled in the attempt to give them a definite direction. The crime was apparently prompted by revenge – certainly not by lust, or desire of money. But she was not known to stand in any one's way. In this utter blank as to the assignable motive, I, perhaps alone among the furious crowd, had a distinct suspicion of the assassin. No sooner had the news reached me, than with the specification of the theater of the crime there at once flashed upon me the intellectual vision of the criminal: the stranger with the dark beard and startled eyes stood confessed before me! I held my breath for a few moments, and then there came a tide of objections rushing over my mind, revealing the inadequacy of the grounds on which rested my suspicions. What were the grounds? I had seen a man in a particular spot, not an unfrequented spot, on the evening of the night when the crime had been committed there; that man had seemed to recognize me, and wished to avoid being recognized. Obviously these grounds were too slender to bear any weight of construction such as I had based on them. Mere presence on the spot could no more inculpate him than it could inculpate me; if I had met him there, equally had he met me there. Nor even if my suspicion were correct that he knew me, and refused to recognize me, could that be any argument tending to criminate him in an affair wholly disconnected with me. Besides, he was walking peaceably, openly, and he looked like a gentleman. All these objections pressed themselves upon me, and kept me silent. But in spite of their force I could not prevent the suspicion from continually arising. Ashamed to mention it, because it may have sounded too absurd, I could not prevent my constructive imagination indulging in its vagaries, and with this secret conviction I resolved to await events, and in case suspicion from other quarters should ever designate the probable assassin, I might then come forward with my bit of corroborative evidence, should the suspected assassin be the stranger of the archway.

By twelve o'clock a new direction was given to rumor. Hitherto the stories, when carefully sifted of all exaggerations of flying conjecture, had settled themselves into something like this: The Lehfeldts had retired to rest at a quarter before ten, as was their custom. They had seen Lieschen go into her bedroom for the night, and had themselves gone to sleep with unclouded minds. From this peaceful security they were startled early in the morning by the appalling news of the calamity which had fallen on them. Incredulous at first, as well they might be, and incapable of believing in a ruin so unexpected and so overwhelming, they imagined some mistake, asserting that Lieschen was in her own room. Into that room they rushed, and there the undisturbed bed, and the open window, but a few feet from the garden, silently and pathetically disclosed the fatal truth. The bereaved parents turned a revealing look upon each other's whitened faces, and then slowly retired from the room, followed in affecting silence by the others. Back into their own room they went. The father knelt beside the bed, and, sobbing, prayed. The mother sat staring with a stupefied stare, her lips faintly moving. In a short while the flood of grief, awakened to a thorough consciousness, burst from their laboring hearts. When the first paroxysms were over they questioned others, and gave incoherent replies to the questions addressed to them. From all which it resulted that Lieschen's absence, though obviously voluntary, was wholly inexplicable to them; and no clew whatever could be given as to the motives of the crime. When these details became known, conjecture naturally interpreted Lieschen's absence at night as an assignation. But with whom? She was not known to have a lover. Her father, on being questioned, passionately affirmed that she had none; she loved no one but her parents, poor child! Her mother, on being questioned, told the same story – adding, however, that about seventeen months before, she had fancied that Lieschen was a little disposed to favor Franz Kerkel, their shopman; but on being spoken to on the subject with some seriousness, and warned of the distance between them, she had laughed heartily at the idea, and since then had treated Franz with so much indifference that only a week ago she had drawn from her mother a reproof on the subject.

"I told her Franz was a good lad, though not good enough for her, and that she ought to treat him kindly. But she said my lecture had given her an alarm, lest Franz should have got the same maggot into his head."

This was the story now passing through the curious crowds in every street. After hearing it I had turned into a tobacconist's in the Adlergrasse, to restock my cigar-case, and found there, as everywhere, a group discussing the one topic of the hour. Herr Fischer, the tobacconist, with a long porcelain pipe pendent from his screwed-up lips, was solemnly listening to the particulars volubly communicated by a stout Bavarian priest; while behind the counter, in a corner, swiftly knitting, sat his wife, her black bead-like eyes also fixed on the orator. Of course I was dragged into the conversation. Instead of attending to commercial interests, they looked upon me as the possible bearer of fresh news. Nor was it without a secret satisfaction that I found I could gratify them in that respect. They had not heard of Franz Kerkel in the matter. No sooner had I told what I had heard than the knitting-needles of the vivacious little woman were at once suspended.

"Ach Je!" she exclaimed, "I see it all. He's the wretch!"

"Who?" we all simultaneously inquired.

"Who? Why, Kerkel, of course. If she changed, and treated him with indifference, it was because she loved him; and he has murdered the poor thing."

"How you run on, wife!" remonstrated Fischer; while the priest shook a dubious head.

"I tell you it is so. I'm positive."

"If she loved him."

"She did, I tell you. Trust a woman for seeing through such things."

"Well, say she did," continued Fischer, "and I won't deny that it may be so; but then that makes against the idea of his having done her any harm."

"Don't tell me," retorted the convinced woman. "She loved him. She went out to meet him in secret, and he murdered her – the villain did. I'm as sure of it as if these eyes had seen him do it."

The husband winked at us, as much as to say, "You hear these women!" and the priest and I endeavored to reason her out of her illogical position. But she was immovable. Kerkel had murdered her; she knew it; she couldn't tell why, but she knew it. Perhaps he was jealous, who knows? At any rate, he ought to be arrested.

And by twelve o'clock, as I said, a new rumor ran through the crowd, which seemed to confirm the little woman in her rash logic. Kerkel had been arrested, and a waistcoat stained with blood had been found in his room! By half-past twelve the rumor ran that he had confessed the crime. This, however, proved on inquiry to be the hasty anticipation of public indignation. He had been arrested; the waistcoat had been found: so much was authentic; and the suspicions gathered ominously over him.

When first Frau Fischer had started the suggestion it flew like wildfire. Then people suddenly noticed, as very surprising, that Kerkel had not that day made his appearance at the shop. His absence had not been noticed in the tumult of grief and inquiry; but it became suddenly invested with a dreadful significance, now that it was rumored that he had been Lieschen's lover. Of all men he would be the most affected by the tragic news; of all men he would have been the first to tender sympathy and aid to the afflicted parents, and the most clamorous in the search for the undiscovered culprit. Yet, while all Nuremberg was crowding round the house of sorrow, which was also his house of business, he alone remained away. This naturally pointed suspicion at him. When the messengers had gone to seek him, his mother refused them admission, declaring in incoherent phrases, betraying great agitation, that her son was gone distracted with grief and could see no one. On this it was determined to order his arrest. The police went, the house was searched, and the waistcoat found.

The testimony of the girl who lived as servant in Kerkel's house was also criminatory. She deposed that on the night in question she awoke about half-past eleven with a violent toothache; she was certain as to the hour, because she heard the clock afterwards strike twelve. She felt some alarm at hearing voices in the rooms at an hour when her mistress and young master must long ago have gone to bed; but as the voices were seemingly in quiet conversation, her alarm subsided, and she concluded that instead of having gone to bed her mistress was still up. In her pain she heard the door gently open, and then she heard footsteps in the garden. This surprised her very much. She couldn't think what the young master could want going out at that hour. She became terrified without knowing exactly at what. Fear quite drove away the toothache, which had not since returned. After lying there quaking for some time, again she heard footsteps in the garden; the door opened and closed gently; voices were heard; and she at last distinctly heard her mistress say, "Be a man, Franz. Good-night – sleep well;" upon which Franz replied in a tone of great agony, "There's no chance of sleep for me." Then all was silent. Next morning her mistress seemed "very queer." Her young master went out very early, but soon came back again; and there were dreadful scenes going on in his room, as she heard, but she didn't know what it was all about. She heard of the murder from a neighbor, but never thought of its having any particular interest for Mr. Franz, though, of course, he would be very sorry for the Lehfeldts.

The facts testified to by the servant, especially the going out at that late hour, and the "dreadful scenes" of the morning, seemed to bear but one interpretation. Moreover, she identified the waistcoat as the one worn by Franz on the day preceding the fatal night.

III

The Accused

Now at last the pent-up wrath found a vent. From the distracting condition of wandering uncertain suspicion, it had been recalled into the glad security of individual hate. Although up to this time Kerkel had borne an exemplary reputation, it was now remembered that he had always been of a morose and violent temper, a hypocrite in religion, a selfish sensualist. Several sagacious critics had long "seen through him"; others had "never liked him"; others had wondered how it was he kept his place so long in Lehfeldt's shop. Poor fellow! his life and actions, like those of every one else when illuminated by a light thrown back upon them, seemed so conspicuously despicable, although when illuminated in their own light they had seemed innocent enough. His mother's frantic protestations of her son's innocence – her assertions that Franz loved Lieschen more than his own soul – only served to envelop her in the silent accusation of being an accomplice, or at least of being an accessory after the fact.

I cannot say why it was, but I did not share the universal belief. The logic seemed to me forced; the evidence trivial. On first hearing of Kerkel's arrest, I eagerly questioned my informant respecting his personal appearance; and on hearing that he was fair, with blue eyes and flaxen hair, my conviction of his innocence was fixed. Looking back on these days, I am often amused at this characteristic of my constructive imagination. While rejecting the disjointed logic of the mob, which interpreted his guilt, I was myself deluded by a logic infinitely less rational. Had Kerkel been dark, with dark eyes and beard, I should probably have sworn to his guilt, simply because the idea of that stranger had firmly fixed itself in my mind.

All that afternoon, and all the next day, the busy hum of voices was raised by the one topic of commanding interest. Kerkel had been examined. He at once admitted that a secret betrothal had for some time existed between him and Lieschen. They had been led to take this improper step by fear of her parents, who, had the attachment been discovered, would, it was thought, have separated them for ever. Herr Lehfeldt's sternness, no less than his superior position, seemed an invincible obstacle, and the good mother, although doting upon her only daughter, was led by the very intensity of her affection to form ambitious hopes of her daughter's future. It was barely possible that some turn in events might one day yield an opening for their consent; but meanwhile prudence dictated secrecy, in order to avert the most pressing danger, that of separation.

And so the pretty Lieschen, with feminine instinct of ruse, had affected to treat her lover with indifference; and to compensate him and herself for this restraint, she had been in the habit of escaping from home once or twice a week, and spending a delicious hour or two at night in the company of her lover and his mother. Kerkel and his mother lived in a cottage a little way outside the town. Lehfeldt's shop stood not many yards from the archway. Now, as in Nuremberg no one was abroad after ten o'clock, except a few loungers at the cafes and beer-houses, and these were only to be met inside the town, not outside it, Lieschen ran extremely little risk of being observed in her rapid transit from her father's to her lover's house. Nor, indeed, had she ever met anyone in the course of these visits.

On the fatal night Lieschen was expected at the cottage. Mother and son waited at first hopefully, then anxiously, at last with some vague uneasiness at her non-appearance. It was now a quarter past eleven – nearly an hour later than her usual time. They occasionally went to the door to look for her; then they walked a few yards down the road, as if to catch an earlier glimpse of her advancing steps. But in vain. The half-hour struck. They came back into the cottage, discussing the various probabilities of delay. Three-quarters struck. Perhaps she had been detected; perhaps she was ill; perhaps – but this was his mother's suggestion, and took little hold of him – there had been visitors who had stayed later than usual, and Lieschen, finding the night so advanced, had postponed her visit to the morrow. Franz, who interpreted Lieschen's feelings by his own, was assured that no postponement of a voluntary kind was credible of her. Twelve o'clock struck. Again Franz went out into the road, and walked nearly up to the archway; he returned with heavy sadness and foreboding at his heart, reluctantly admitting that now all hope of seeing her that night was over. That night? Poor sorrowing heart, the night was to be eternal! The anguish of the desolate "never more" was awaiting him.

There is something intensely pathetic in being thus, as it were, spectators of a tragic drama which is being acted on two separate stages at once – the dreadful link of connection, which is unseen to the separate actors, being only too vividly seen by the spectators. It was with some interest that I, who believed in Kerkel's innocence, heard this story; and in imagination followed its unfolding stage. He went to bed, not, as may be expected, to sleep; tossing restlessly in feverish agitation, conjuring up many imaginary terrors – but all of them trifles compared with the dread reality which he was so soon to face. He pictured her weeping – and she was lying dead on the cold pavement of the dark archway. He saw her in agitated eloquence pleading with offended parents – and she was removed for ever from all agitations, with the peace of death upon her young face.

At an early hour he started, that he might put an end to his suspense. He had not yet reached the archway before the shattering news burst upon him. From that moment he remembered nothing. But his mother described his ghastly agitation, as, throwing himself upon her neck, he told her, through dreadful sobs, the calamity which had fallen. She did her best to comfort him; but he grew wilder and wilder, and rolled upon the ground in the agony of an immeasurable despair. She trembled for his reason and his life. And when the messengers came to seek him, she spoke but the simple truth in saying that he was like one distracted. Yet no sooner had a glimpse of light dawned on him that some vague suspicion rested on him in reference to the murder, than he started up, flung away his agitation, and, with a calmness which was awful, answered every question, and seemed nerved for every trial. From that moment not a sob escaped him until, in the narrative of the night's events, he came to that part which told of the sudden disclosure of his bereavement. And the simple, straightforward manner in which he told this tale, with a face entirely bloodless, and eyes that seemed to have withdrawn all their light inwards, made a great impression on the audience, which was heightened into sympathy when the final sob, breaking through the forced calmness, told of the agony which was eating its fiery way through the heart.

The story was not only plausible in itself, but accurately tallied with what before had seemed like the criminating evidence of the maid; tallied, moreover, precisely as to time, which would hardly have been the case had the story been an invention. As to the waistcoat which had figured so conspicuously in all the rumors, it appeared that suspicion had monstrously exaggerated the facts. Instead of a waistcoat plashed with blood – as popular imagination pictured it – it was a gray waistcoat, with one spot and a slight smear of blood, which admitted of a very simple explanation. Three days before, Franz had cut his left hand in cutting some bread; and to this the maid testified, because she was present when the accident occurred. He had not noticed that his waistcoat was marked by it until the next day, and had forgotten to wash out the stains.

People outside shook skeptical heads at this story of the cut hand. The bloody waistcoat was not to be disposed of in that easy way. It had fixed itself too strongly in their imagination. Indeed, my belief is that even could they have seen the waistcoat, its insignificant marks would have appeared murderous patches to their eyes. I had seen it, and my report was listened to with ill-concealed disbelief, when not with open protestation. And when Kerkel was discharged as free from all suspicion, there was a low growl of disappointed wrath heard from numerous groups.

This may sympathetically be understood by whomsoever remembers the painful uneasiness of the mind under a great stress of excitement with no definite issue. The lust for a vengeance, demanded by the aroused sensibilities of compassion, makes men credulous in their impatience; they easily believe anyone is guilty, because they feel an imperious need for fastening the guilt upon some definite head. Few verdicts of "Not Guilty" are well received, unless another victim is at hand upon whom the verdict of guilty is likely to fall. It was demonstrable to all judicial minds that Kerkel was wholly, pathetically innocent. In a few days this gradually became clear to the majority, but at first it was resisted as an attempt to balk justice; and to the last there were some obstinate doubters, who shook their heads mysteriously, and said, with a certain incisiveness, "Somebody must have done it; I should very much like to know who."

Suspicion once more was drifting aimlessly. None had pointed in any new direction. No mention of anyone whom I could identify with the stranger had yet been made; but, although silent on the subject, I kept firm in my conviction, and I sometimes laughed at the pertinacity with which I scrutinized the face of every man I met, if he happened to have a black beard; and as black beards are excessively common, my curiosity, though never gratified, was never allowed repose.

Meanwhile Lieschen's funeral had been emphatically a public mourning. Nay, so great was the emotion, that it almost deadened the interest which otherwise would have been so powerful, in the news now daily reaching us from Paris. Blood had flowed upon her streets – in consequence of that pistol-shot, which, either by accident or criminal intent, had converted the demonstration before the hotel of the Minister of Foreign Affairs into an insurrection. Paris had risen; barricades were erected. The troops were under arms. This was agitating news.

Such is the solidarity of all European nations, and so quick are all to vibrate in unison with the vibrations of each, that events like those transacted in Paris necessarily stirred every city, no matter how remote, nor politically how secure. And it says much for the intense interest excited by the Lehfeldt tragedy that Nuremberg was capable of sustaining that interest even amid the tremendous pressure of the February Revolution. It is true that Nuremberg is at all times somewhat sequestered from the great movements of the day, following slowly in the rear of great waves; it is true, moreover, that some politicians showed remarkable eagerness in canvassing the characters and hopes of Louis Philippe and Guizot; but although such events would at another period have formed the universal interest, the impenetrable mystery hanging over Lieschen's death threw the Revolution into the background of their thoughts. If when a storm is raging over the dreary moorland, a human cry of suffering is heard at the door, at once the thunders and the tumult sink into insignificance, and are not even heard by the ear which is pierced with the feeble human voice: the grandeurs of storm and tempest, the uproar of surging seas, the clamorous wail of sea-birds amid the volleying artillery of heaven, in vain assail the ear that has once caught even the distant cry of a human agony, or serve only as scenical accompaniments to the tragedy which is foreshadowed by that cry. And so it was amid the uproar of 1848. A kingdom was in convulsions; but here, at our door, a young girl had been murdered, and two hearths made desolate. Rumors continued to fly about. The assassin was always about to be discovered; but he remained shrouded in impenetrable darkness. A remark made by Bourgonef struck me much. Our host, Zum Bayerischen Hof, one day announced with great satisfaction that he had himself heard from the syndic that the police were on the traces of the assassin.

"I am sorry to hear it," said Bourgonef.

The guests paused from eating, and looked at him with astonishment.

"It is a proof," he added, "that even the police now give it up as hopeless. I always notice that whenever the police are said to be on the traces the malefactor is never tracked. When they are on his traces they wisely say nothing about it; they allow it to be believed that they are baffled, in order to lull their victim into a dangerous security. When they know themselves to be baffled, there is no danger in quieting the public mind, and saving their own credit, by announcing that they are about to be successful."

IV

A Discovery

Bourgonef's remark had been but too sagacious. The police were hoplessly baffled. In all such cases possible success depends upon the initial suggestion either of a motive which leads to a suspicion of the person, or of some person which leads to a suspicion of the motive. Once set suspicion on the right track, and evidence is suddenly alight in all quarters. But, unhappily, in the present case there was no assignable motive, no shadow darkening any person.

An episode now came to our knowledge in which Bourgonef manifested an unusual depth of interest. I was led to notice this interest, because it had seemed to me that in the crime itself, and the discussions which arose out of it, he shared but little of the universal excitement. I do not mean that he was indifferent - by no means; but the horror of the crime did not seem to fascinate his imagination as it fascinated ours. He could talk quite as readily of other things, and far more readily of the French affairs. But on the contrary, in this new episode he showed peculiar interest. It appeared that Lehfeldt, moved, perhaps, partly by a sense of the injustice which had been done to Kerkel in even suspecting him of the crime, and in submitting him to an examination more poignantly affecting to him under such circumstances than a public trial would have been under others; and moved partly by the sense that Lieschen's love had practically drawn Kerkel within the family – for her choice of him as a husband had made him morally, if not legally, a son-in-law; and moved partly by the sense of loneliness which had now settled on their childless home, – Lehfeldt had in the most pathetic and considerate terms begged Kerkel to take the place of his adopted son, and become joint partner with him in the business. This, however, Kerkel had gently yet firmly declined. He averred that he felt no injury, though great pain had been inflicted on him by the examination. He himself in such a case would not have shrunk from demanding that his own brother should be tried, under suspicions of similar urgency. It was simple justice that all who were suspected should be examined; justice also to them that they might for ever clear themselves of doubtful appearances. But for the rest, while he felt his old affectionate respect for his master, he could recognize no claim to be removed from his present position. Had she lived, said the heartbroken youth, he would gladly have consented to accept any fortune which her love might bestow, because he felt that his own love and the devotion of a life might repay it. But there was nothing now that he could give in exchange. For his services he was amply paid; his feelings towards Lieschen's parents must continue what they had ever been. In vain Lehfeldt pleaded, in vain many friends argued. Franz remained respectfully firm in his refusal.

This, as I said, interested Bourgonef immensely. He seemed to enter completely into the minds of the sorrowing, pleading parents, and the sorrowing, denying lover. He appreciated and expounded their motives with a subtlety and delicacy of perception which surprised and delighted me. It showed the refinement of his moral nature. But, at the same time, it rendered his minor degree of interest in the other episodes of the story, those which had a more direct and overpowering appeal to the heart, a greater paradox.

Human nature is troubled in the presence of all mystery which has not by long familiarity lost its power of soliciting attention; and for my own part, I have always been uneasy in the presence of moral problems. Puzzled by the contradictions which I noticed in Bourgonef, I tried to discover whether he had any general repugnance to stories of crimes, or any special repugnance to murders, or, finally, any strange repugnance to this particular case now everywhere discussed. And it is not a little remarkable that during three separate interviews, in the course of which I severally, and as I thought artfully, introduced these topics, making them seem to arise naturally out of the suggestion of our talk, I totally failed to arrive at any distinct conclusion. I was afraid to put the direct question: Do you not share the common feeling of interest in criminal stories? This question would doubtless have elicited a categorical reply; but somehow, the consciousness of an arriere-pensee made me shrink from putting such a question.

Reflecting on this indifference on a special point, and on the numerous manifestations I had noticed of his sensibility, I came at last to the conclusion that he must be a man of tender heart, whose delicate sensibilities easily shrank from the horrible under every form; and no more permitted him to dwell unnecessarily upon painful facts, than they permit imaginative minds to dwell on the details of an operation.

I had not long settled this in my mind before an accident suddenly threw a lurid light upon many details noticed previously, and painfully revived that inexplicable repulsion with which I had at first regarded him. A new suspicion filled my mind, or rather, let me say, a distinct shape was impressed upon many fluctuating suspicions. It scarcely admitted of argument, and at times seemed preposterous, nevertheless it persisted. The mind which in broad daylight assents to all that can be alleged against the absurdities of the belief in apparitions, will often acknowledge the dim terrors of darkness and loneliness – terrors at possibilities of supernatural visitations. In like manner, in the clear daylight of reason I could see the absurdity of my suspicion, but the vague stirrings of feeling remained unsilenced. I was haunted by the dim horrors of a possibility.

Thus it arose. We were both going to Munich, and Bourgonef had shortened his contemplated stay at Nuremberg that he might have the pleasure of accompanying me; adding also that he, too, should be glad to reach Munich, not only for its art, but for its greater command of papers and intelligence respecting what was then going on in France. On the night preceding the morning of our departure, I was seated in his room, smoking and discussing as usual, while Ivan, his servant, packed up his things in two large portmanteaus.

Ivan was a serf who spoke no word of any language but his own. Although of a brutal, almost idiotic type, he was loudly eulogized by his master as the model of fidelity and usefulness. Bourgonef treated him with gentleness, though with a certain imperiousness; much as one might treat a savage mastiff which it was necessary to dominate without exasperating. He more than once spoke of Ivan as a living satire on physiognomists and phrenologists; and as I am a phrenologist, I listened with some incredulity.

"Look at him," he would say. "Observe the low, retreating brow, the flat face, the surly mouth, the broad base of the head, and the huge bull-like neck. Would not anyone say Ivan was as destructive as a panther, as tenacious as a bull-dog, as brutal as a bull? Yet he is the gentlest of sluggish creatures, and as tender-hearted as a girl! That thick-set muscular frame shrouds a hare's heart. He is so faithful and so attached that I believe for me he would risk his life; but on no account could you get him to place himself in danger on his own account. Part of his love for me is gratitude for having rescued him from the conscription: the dangers incident to a military life had no charm for him!"

Now, although Bourgonef, who was not a phrenologist, might be convinced of the absence of ferocious instincts in Ivan, to me, as a phrenologist, the statement was eminently incredible. All the appearances of his manner were such as to confirm his master's opinion. He was quiet, even tender in his attentions. But the tyrannous influence of ideas and physical impressions cannot be set aside; and no evidence would permanently have kept down my distrust of this man. When women shriek at the sight of a gun, it is in vain that you solemnly assure them that the gun is not loaded. "I don't know," they reply, – "at any rate, I don't like it." I was much in this attitude with regard to Ivan. He might be harmless. I didn't know that; what I did know was – that I didn't like his looks.

On this night he was moving noiselessly about the room, employed in packing. Bourgonef's talk rambled over the old themes; and I thought I had never before met with one of my own age whose society was so perfectly delightful. He was not so conspicuously my superior on all points that I felt the restraints inevitably imposed by superiority; yet he was in many respects sufficiently above me in knowledge and power to make me eager to have his assent to my views where we differed, and to have him enlighten me where I knew myself to be weak.

In the very moment of my most cordial admiration came a shock. Ivan, on passing from one part of the room to the other, caught his foot in the strap of the portmanteau and fell. The small wooden box, something of a glove-box, which he held in his hand at the time, fell on the floor, and falling over, discharged its contents close to Bourgonef's feet. The objects which caught my eyes were several pairs of gloves, a rouge-pot and hare's foot, and a black beard!

By what caprice of imagination was it that the sight of this false beard lying at Bourgonef's feet thrilled me with horror? In one lightning-flash I beheld the archway – the stranger with the startled eyes – this stranger no longer unknown to me, but too fatally recognized as Bourgonef – and at his feet the murdered girl!

Moved by what subtle springs of suggestion I know not, but there before me stood that dreadful vision, seen in a lurid light, but seen as clearly as if the actual presence of the objects were obtruding itself upon my eyes. In the inexpressible horror of this vision my heart seemed clutched with an icy hand.

Fortunately Bourgonef's attention was called away from me. He spoke angrily some short sentence, which of course was in Russian, and therefore unintelligible to me. He then stooped, and picking up the rouge-pot, held it towards me with his melancholy smile. He was very red in the face; but that may have been either anger or the effect of sudden stooping. "I see you are surprised at these masquerading follies," he said in a tone which, though low, was perfectly calm. "You must not suppose that I beautify my sallow cheeks on ordinary occasions."

He then quietly handed the pot to Ivan, who replaced it with the gloves and the beard in the box; and after making an inquiry which sounded like a growl, to which Bourgonef answered negatively, he continued his packing.

Bourgonef resumed his cigar and his argument as if nothing had happened.

The vision had disappeared, but a confused mass of moving figures took its place. My heart throbbed so violently that it seemed to me as if its tumult must be heard by others. Yet my face must have been tolerably calm, since Bourgonef made no comment on it.

I answered his remarks in vague fragments, for, in truth, my thoughts were flying from conjecture to conjecture. I remembered that the stranger had a florid complexion; was this rouge? It is true that I fancied the stranger carried a walking-stick in his right hand; if so, this was enough to crush all suspicions of his identity with Bourgonef; but then I was rather hazy on this point, and probably did not observe a walking-stick.

After a while my inattention struck him, and looking at me with some concern, he inquired if there was anything the matter. I pleaded a colic, which I attributed to the imprudence of having indulged in sauerkraut at dinner. He advised me to take a little brandy; but, affecting a fresh access of pain, I bade him good-night. He hoped I should be all right on the morrow – if not, he added, we can postpone our journey till the day after.

Once in my own room I bolted the door, and sat down on

the edge of the bed in a tumult of excitement.

V

Fluctuations

Alone with my thoughts, and capable of pursuing conjectures and conclusions without external interruption, I quickly exhausted all the hypothetical possibilities of the case, and, from having started with the idea that Bourgonef was the assassin, I came at last to the more sensible conclusion that I was a constructive blockhead. My suspicions were simply outrageous in their defect of evidence, and could never for one moment have seemed otherwise to any imagination less riotously active than mine.

I bathed my heated head, undressed myself, and got into bed, considering what I should say to the police when I went next morning to communicate my suspicions. And it is worthy of remark, as well as somewhat ludicrously self-betraying, that no sooner did I mentally see myself in the presence of the police, and was thus forced to confront my suspicions with some appearance of evidence, than the whole fabric of my vision rattled to the ground. What had I to say to the police? Simply that, on the evening of the night when Lieschen was murdered, I had passed in a public thoroughfare a man whom I could not identify, but who as I could not help fancying, seemed to recognize me. This man, I had persuaded myself, was the murderer; for which persuasion I was unable to adduce a tittle of evidence. It was uncolored by the remotest possibility. It was truly and simply the suggestion of my vagrant fancy, which had mysteriously settled itself into a conviction; and having thus capriciously identified the stranger with Lieschen's murderer, I now, upon evidence quite as preposterous, identified Bourgonef with the stranger.

The folly became apparent even to myself. If Bourgonef had in his possession a rouge-pot and false beard, I could not but acknowledge that he made no attempt to conceal them, nor had he manifested any confusion on their appearance. He had quietly characterized them as masquerading follies. Moreover, I now began to remember distinctly that the stranger did carry a walking-stick in his right hand; and as Bourgonef had lost his right arm, that settled the point.

Into such complications, would the tricks of imagination lead me! I blushed mentally, and resolved to let it serve as a lesson in future. It is needless, however, to say that the lesson was lost, as such lessons always are lost; a strong tendency in any direction soon disregards all the teachings of experience. I am still not the less the victim of my constructive imagination, because I have frequently had to be ashamed of its vagaries.

The next morning I awoke with a lighter breast, rejoicing in the caution which had delayed me from any rash manifestation of suspicions now seen to be absurd. I smiled as the thought arose: what if this suspected stranger should also be pestered by an active imagination, and should entertain similar suspicions of me? He must have seen in my eyes the look of recognition which I saw in his. On hearing of the murder, our meeting may also have recurred to him; and his suspicions would have this color, wanting to mine, that I happen to inherit with my Italian blood a somewhat truculent appearance, which has gained for me among my friends the playful sobriquet of "the brigand."

Anxious to atone at once for my folly, and to remove from my mind any misgiving – if it existed – at my quitting him so soon after the disclosures of the masquerading details, I went to Bourgonef as soon as I was dressed and proposed a ramble till the diligence started for Munich. He was sympathetic in his inquiries about my colic, which I assured him had quite passed away, and out we went. The sharp morning air of March made us walk briskly, and gave a pleasant animation to our thoughts. As he discussed the acts of the provisional government, so wise, temperate, and energetic, the fervor and generosity of his sentiments stood out in such striking contrast with the deed I had last night recklessly imputed to him that I felt deeply ashamed, and was nearly carried away by mingled admiration and self-reproach to confess the absurd vagrancy of my thoughts and humbly ask his pardon. But you can understand the reluctance at a confession so insulting to him, so degrading to me. It is at all times difficult to tell a man, face to face, eye to eye, the evil you have thought of him, unless the recklessness of anger seizes on it as a weapon with which to strike; and I had now so completely unsaid to myself all that I once had thought of evil, that to put it in words seemed a gratuitous injury to me and insult to him.

A day or two after our arrival in Munich a reaction began steadily to set in. Ashamed as I was of my suspicions, I could not altogether banish from my mind the incident which had awakened them. The image of that false beard would mingle with my thoughts. I was vaguely uncomfortable at the idea of Bourgonef's carrying about with him obvious materials of disguise. In itself this would have had little significance; but coupled with the fact that his devoted servant was – in spite of all Bourgonef's eulogies – repulsively ferocious in aspect, capable, as I could not help believing, of any brutality, – the suggestion was unpleasant. You will understand that having emphatically acquitted Bourgonef in my mind, I did not again distinctly charge him with any complicity in the mysterious murder; on the contrary, I should indignantly have repelled such a thought; but the uneasy sense of some mystery about him, coupled with the accessories of disguise, and the aspect of the servant, gave rise to dim, shadowy forebodings which ever and anon passed across my mind.

Did it ever occur to you, reader, to reflect on the depths of deceit which lie still and dark even in the honestest minds? Society reposes on a thin crust of convention, underneath which lie fathomless possibilities of crime, and consequently suspicions of crime. Friendship, however close and dear, is not free from its reserves, unspoken beliefs, more or less suppressed opinions. The man whom you would indignantly defend against any accusation brought by another, so confident are you in his unshakable integrity, you may yourself momentarily suspect of crimes far exceeding those which you repudiate. Indeed, I have known sagacious men hold that perfect frankness in expressing the thoughts is a sure sign of imperfect friendship; something is always suppressed; and it is not he who loves you that "tells you candidly what he thinks" of your person, your pretensions, your children, or your poems. Perfect candor is dictated by envy, or some other unfriendly feeling, making friendship a stalking-horse, under cover of which it shoots the arrow which will rankle. Friendship is candid only when the candor is urgent – meant to avert impending danger or to rectify an error. The candor which is an impertinence never springs from friendship. Love is sympathetic.

I do not, of course, mean to intimate that my feeling for Bourgonef was of that deep kind which justifies the name of friendship. I only want to say that in our social relations we are constantly hiding from each other, under the smiles and courtesies of friendly interest, thoughts which, if expressed, would destroy all possible communion – and that, nevertheless, we are not insincere in our smiles and courtesies; and therefore there is nothing paradoxical in my having felt great admiration for Bourgonef, and great pleasure in his society, while all the time there was deep down in the recesses of my thoughts an uneasy sense of a dark mystery which possibly connected him with a dreadful crime.

This feeling was roused into greater activity by an incident which now occurred. One morning I went to Bourgonef's room, which was at some distance from mine on the same floor, intending to propose a visit to the sculpture at the Glyptothek. To my surprise I found Ivan the serf standing before the closed door. He looked at me like a mastiff about to spring; and intimated by significant gestures that I was not allowed to enter the room. Concluding that his master was occupied in some way, and desired not to be disturbed, I merely signified by a nod that my visit was of no consequence, and went out. On returning about an hour afterwards I saw Ivan putting three pink letters into the letter-box of the hotel. I attached no significance to this very ordinary fact at the time, but went up to my room and began writing my letters, one of which was to my lawyer, sending him an important receipt. The dinner-bell sounded before I had half finished this letter; but I wrote on, determined to have done with it at once, in case the afternoon should offer any expedition with Bourgonef.

At dinner he quietly intimated that Ivan had informed him of my visit, and apologized for not having been able to see me. I, of course, assured him that no apology was necessary, and that we had plenty of time to visit sculpture together without intruding on his private hours. He informed me that he was that afternoon going to pay a visit to Schwanthaler, the sculptor, and if I desired it, he would ask permission on another occasion to take me with him. I jumped at the proposal, as may be supposed.

Dinner over, I strolled into the Englische Garten, and had my coffee and cigar there. On my return I was vexed to find that in the hurry of finishing my letters I had sealed the one to my lawyer, and had not enclosed the receipt which had been the object of writing. Fortunately it was not too late. Descending to the bureau of the hotel, I explained my mistake to the head-waiter, who unlocked the letter-box to search for my letter. It was found at once, for there were only seven or eight in the box. Among these my eye naturally caught the three pink letters which I had that morning seen Ivan drop into the box; but although they were SEEN by me they were not NOTICED at the time, my mind being solely occupied with rectifying the stupid blunder I had made.

Once more in my own room a sudden revelation startled me. Everyone knows what it is to have details come under the eye which the mind first interprets long after the eye ceases to rest upon them. The impressions are received passively; but they are registered, and can be calmly read whenever the mind is in activity. It was so now. I suddenly, as if now for the first time, saw that the addresses on Bourgonef's letters were written in a fluent, masterly hand, bold in character, and with a certain sweep which might have come from a painter. The thrill which this vision gave will be intelligible when you remember that Bourgonef had lost or pretended to have lost his right arm, and was, as I before intimated, far from dexterous with his left. That no man recently thrown upon the use of a left hand could have written those addresses was too evident. What, then, was the alternative? The empty sleeve was an imposture! At once the old horrible suspicion returned, and this time with tenfold violence, and with damnatory confirmation.

Pressing my temples between my hands, I tried to be calm and to survey the evidence without precipitation; but for some time the conflict of thoughts was too violent. Whatever might be the explanation, clear it was that Bourgonef, for some purposes, was practising a deception, and had, as I knew, other means of disguising his appearance. This, on the most favorable interpretation, branded him with suspicion. This excluded him from the circle of honest men.

But did it connect him with the murder of Lieschen Lehfeldt? In my thought it did so indubitably; but I was aware of the difficulty of making this clear to anyone else.

VI

First Love

If the reader feels that my suspicions were not wholly unwarranted, were indeed inevitable, he will not laugh at me on learning that once more these suspicions were set aside, and the fact – the damnatory fact, as I regarded it – discovered by me so accidentally, and, I thought, providentially, was robbed of all its significance by Bourgonef himself casually and carelessly avowing it in conversation, just as one may avow a secret infirmity, with some bitterness, but without any implication of deceit in its concealment.

I was the more prepared for this revulsion of feeling, by the difficulty I felt in maintaining my suspicions in the presence of one so gentle and so refined. He had come into my room that evening to tell me of his visit to Schwanthaler, and of the sculptor's flattering desire to make my personal acquaintance. He spoke of Schwanthaler, and his earnest efforts in art, with so much enthusiasm, and was altogether so charming, that I felt abashed before him, incapable of ridding myself of the dreadful suspicions, yet incapable of firmly believing him to be what I thought. But more than this, there came the new interest awakened in me by his story; and when, in the course of his story, he accidentally disclosed the fact that he had not lost his arm, all my suspicions vanished at once.

We had got, as usual, upon politics, and were differing more than usual, because he gave greater prominence to his sympathy with the Red Republicans. He accused me of not being "thorough-going," which I admitted. This he attributed to the fact of my giving a divided heart to politics – a condition natural enough at my age, and with my hopes. "Well," said I, laughing, "you don't mean to take a lofty stand upon your few years' seniority. If my age renders it natural, does yours profoundly alter such a conviction?"

"My age, no. But you have the hopes of youth. I have none. I am banished for ever from the joys and sorrows of domestic life; and therefore, to live at all, must consecrate my soul to great abstractions and public affairs."

"But why banished, unless self-banished?"

"Woman's love is impossible. You look incredulous. I do not allude to this," he said, taking up the empty sleeve, and by so doing sending a shiver through me.

"The loss of your arm," I said – and my voice trembled slightly, for I felt that a crisis was at hand – "although a misfortune to you, would really be an advantage in gaining a woman's affections. Women are so romantic, and their imaginations are so easily touched!"

"Yes," he replied bitterly; "but the trouble is that I have not lost my arm."

I started. He spoke bitterly, yet calmly. I awaited his explanation in great suspense.

"To have lost my arm in battle, or even by an accident, would perhaps have lent me a charm in woman's eyes. But, as I said, my arm hangs by my side – withered, unpresentable."

I breathed again. He continued in the same tone, and without noticing my looks.

"But it is not this which banishes me. Woman's love might be hoped for, had I far worse infirmities. The cause lies deeper. It lies in my history. A wall of granite has grown up between me and the sex."

"But, my dear fellow, do you – wounded, as I presume to guess, by some unworthy woman – extend the fault of one to the whole sex? Do you despair of finding another true, because a first was false?"

"They are all false," he exclaimed with energy. "Not, perhaps, all false from inherent viciousness, though many are that, but false because their inherent weakness renders them incapable of truth. Oh! I know the catalogue of their good qualities. They are often pitiful, self-devoting, generous; but they are so by fits and starts, just as they are cruel, remorseless, exacting, by fits and starts. They have no constancy – they are too weak to be constant even in evil; their minds are all impressions; their actions are all the issue of immediate promptings. Swayed by the fleeting impulses of the hour, they have only one persistent, calculable motive on which reliance can always be placed – that motive is vanity; you are always sure of them there. It is from vanity they are good – from vanity they are evil; their devotion and their desertion equally vanity. I know them. To me they have disclosed the shallows of their natures. God! how I have suffered from them!"

A deep, low exclamation, half sob, half curse, closed his tirade. He remained silent for a few minutes, looking on the floor, then, suddenly turning his eyes upon me, said:

"Were you ever in Heidelberg?"

"Never."

"I thought all your countrymen went there? Then you will never have heard anything of my story. Shall I tell you how my youth was blighted? Will you care to listen?"

"It would interest me much."

"I had reached the age of seven-and-twenty," he began, "without having once known even the vague stirrings of the passion of love. I admired many women, and courted the admiration of them all; but I was as yet not only heart-whole, but, to use your Shakespeare's phrase, Cupid had not tapped me on the shoulder.

"This detail is not unimportant in my story. You may possibly have observed that in those passionate natures which reserve their force, and do not fritter away their feelings in scattered flirtations or trivial love-affairs, there is a velocity and momentum, when the movement of passion is once excited, greatly transcending all that is ever felt by expansive and expressive natures. Slow to be moved, when they do move it is with the whole mass of the heart. So it was with me. I purchased my immunity from earlier entanglements by the price of my whole life. I am not what I was. Between my past and present self there is a gulf; that gulf is dark, stormy, and profound. On the far side stands a youth of hope, energy, ambition, and unclouded happiness, with great capacities for loving; on this side a blighted manhood, with no prospects but suffering and storm."

He paused. With an effort he seemed to master the suggestions which crowded upon his memory, and continued his narrative in an equable tone.

"I had been for several weeks at Heidelberg. One of my intimate companions was Kestner, the architect, and he one day proposed to introduce me to his sister-in-law, Ottilie, of whom he had repeatedly spoken to me in terms of great affection and esteem.

"We went, and we were most cordially received. Ottilie justified Kestner's praises. Pretty, but not strikingly so – clever, but not obtrusively so; her soft dark eyes were frank and winning; her manner was gentle and retiring, with that dash of sentimentalism which seems native to all German girls, but without any of the ridiculous extravagance too often seen in them. I liked her all the more because I was perfectly at my ease with her, and this was rarely the case in my relations to young women. I don't enjoy their society.

"You leap at once to the conclusion that we fell in love. Your conclusion is precipitate. Seeing her continually, I grew to admire and respect her; but the significant smiles, winks, and hints of friends, pointing unmistakably at a supposed understanding existing between us, only made me more seriously examine the state of my feelings, and assured me that I was not in love. It is true that I felt a serene pleasure in her society, and that when away from her she occupied much of my thoughts. It is true that I often thought of her as a wife; and in these meditations she appeared as one eminently calculated to make a happy home. But it is no less true that during a temporary absence of hers of a few weeks I felt no sort of uneasiness, no yearning for her presence, no vacancy in my life. I knew, therefore, that it was not love which I felt.

"So much for my feelings. What of hers? They seemed very like my own. That she admired me, and was pleased to be with me, was certain. That she had a particle of fiery love for me I did not, could not believe. And it was probably this very sense of her calmness which kept my feelings quiet. For love is a flame which often can be kindled only by contact with flame. Certainly this is so in proud, reserved natures, which are chilled by any contact with temperature not higher than their own.

"On her return, however, from that absence I have mentioned, I was not a little fluttered by an obvious change in her manner; an impression which subsequent meetings only served to confirm. Although still very quiet, her manner had become more tender, and it had that delicious shyness which is the most exquisite of flatteries, as it is one of the most enchanting of graces. I saw her tremble slightly beneath my voice, and blush beneath my gaze.

"There was no mistaking these signs. It was clear that she loved me; and it was no less clear that I, taking fire at this discovery, was myself rapidly falling in love. I will not keep you from my story by idle reflections. Take another cigar." He rose and paced up and down the room in silence.

VII

Agalma

"At this juncture there arrived from Paris the woman to whom the great sorrow of my life is due. A fatalist might read in her appearance at this particular moment the signs of a prear-

225

ranged doom. A few weeks later, and her arrival would have been harmless; I should have been shielded from all external influence by the absorbing force of love. But, alas! this was not to be. My fate had taken another direction. The woman had arrived whose shadow was to darken the rest of my existence. That woman was Agalma Liebenstein.

"How is it that the head which we can only see surrounded with a halo, or a shadow, when the splendors of achievement or the infamy of shame instruct our eyes, is by the uninstructed eye observed as wholly vulgar? We all profess to be physiognomists; how is it we are so lamentably mistaken in our judgments? Here was a woman in whom my ignorant eyes saw nothing at all remarkable except golden hair of unusual beauty. When I say golden, I am not speaking loosely. I do not mean red or flaxen hair, but hair actually resembling burnished gold more than anything else. Its ripples on her brow caught the light like a coronet. This was her one beauty, and it was superb. For the rest, her features were characterless. Her figure was tall and full; not graceful, but sweepingly imposing. At first I noticed nothing about her except the braided splendor of her glorious hair."

He rose, and went into his bedroom, from which he returned with a small trinket-box in his hand. This he laid open on the table, disclosing a long strand of exquisite fair hair lying on a cushion of dark-blue velvet.

"Look at that," he said. "Might it not have been cut from an angel's head?"

"It is certainly wonderful."

"It must have been hair like this which crowned the infamous head of Lucrezia Borgia," he said, bitterly. "She, too, had golden hair; but hers must have been of paler tint, like her nature."

He resumed his seat, and, fixing his eyes upon the lock, continued:

"She was one of Ottilie's friends – dear friends, they called each other, – which meant that they kissed each other profusely,

226

and told each other all their secrets, or as much as the lying nature of the sex permitted and suggested. It is, of course, impossible for me to disentangle my present knowledge from my past impressions so as to give you a clear description of what I then thought of Agalma. Enough that, as a matter of fact, I distinctly remember not to have admired her, and to have told Ottilie so; and when Ottilie, in surprise at my insensibility, assured me that men were in general wonderfully charmed with her (though, for her part, she had never understood why), I answered, and answered sincerely, that it might be true with the less refined order of men, but men of taste would certainly be rather repelled from her.

"This opinion of mine, or some report of it, reached Agalma.

"It may have been the proximate cause of my sorrows. Without this stimulus to her vanity, she might have left me undisturbed. I don't know. All I know is, that over many men Agalma exercised great influence, and that over me she exercised the spell of fascination. No other word will explain her influence; for it was not based on excellences such as the mind could recognize to be attractions; it was based on a mysterious personal power, something awful in its mysteriousness, as all demoniac powers are. One source of her influence over men I think I can explain: she at once captivated and repelled them. By artful appeals to their vanity, she made them interested in her and in her opinion of them, and yet kept herself inaccessible by a pride which was the more fascinating because it always seemed about to give way. Her instinct fastened upon the weak point in those she approached. This made her seductive to men, because she flattered their weak points; and hateful to women, because she flouted and disclosed their weak points.

"Her influence over me began in the following way. One day, at a picnic, having been led by her into a conversation respecting the relative inferiority of the feminine intellect, I was forced to speak rather more earnestly than usual, when suddenly she turned to me and exclaimed in a lower voice:

"'I am willing to credit anything you say; only pray don't

continue talking to me so earnestly.'

"'Why not?' I asked, surprised.

"She looked at me with peculiar significance, but remained silent.

"'May I ask why not?' I asked.

"'Because, if you do, somebody may be jealous.' There was a laughing defiance in her eye as she spoke.

"'And pray, who has a right to be jealous of me?'

"'Oh! you know well enough.'

"It was true; I did know; and she knew that I knew it. To my shame be it said that I was weak enough to yield to an equivocation which I now see to have been disloyal, but which I then pretended to have been no more than delicacy to Ottilie. As, in point of fact, there had never been a word passed between us respecting our mutual feelings, I considered myself bound in honor to assume that there was nothing tacitly acknowledged.

"Piqued by her tone and look, I disavowed the existence of any claims upon my attention; and to prove the sincerity of my words, I persisted in addressing my attentions to her. Once or twice I fancied I caught flying glances, in which some of the company criticised my conduct, and Ottilie also seemed to me unusually quiet. But her manner, though quiet, was untroubled and unchanged. I talked less to her than usual, partly because I talked so much to Agalma, and partly because I felt that Agalma's eyes were on us. But no shadow of 'temper' or reserve darkened our interchange of speech.

"On our way back, I know not what devil prompted me to ask Agalma whether she had really been in earnest in her former allusion to 'somebody.'

"'Yes,' she said, 'I was in earnest then.'

"'And now?'

"'Now I have doubts. I may have been misinformed. It's no

concern of mine, anyway; but I had been given to understand. However, I admit that my own eyes have not confirmed what my ears heard.'

"This speech was irritating on two separate grounds. It implied that people were talking freely of my attachment, which, until I had formally acknowledged it, I resented as an impertinence; and it implied that, from personal observation, Agalma doubted Ottilie's feelings for me. This alarmed my quick-retreating pride! I, too, began to doubt. Once let loose on that field, imagination soon saw shapes enough to confirm any doubt. Ottilie's manner certainly had seemed less tender – nay, somewhat indifferent – during the last few days. Had the arrival of that heavy lout, her cousin, anything to do with this change?

"Not to weary you by recalling all the unfolding stages of this miserable story with the minuteness of detail which my own memory morbidly lingers on, I will hurry to the catastrophe. I grew more and more doubtful of the existence in Ottilie's mind of any feeling stronger than friendship for me; and as this doubt strengthened, there arose the flattering suspicion that I was becoming an object of greater interest to Agalma, who had quite changed her tone towards me, and had become serious in her speech and manner. Weeks passed. Ottilie had fallen from her pedestal, and had taken her place among agreeable acquaintances. One day I suddenly learned that Ottilie was engaged to her cousin.

"You will not wonder that Agalma, who before this had exercised great fascination over me, now doubly became an object of the most tender interest. I fell madly in love. Hitherto I had never known that passion. My feeling for Ottilie I saw was but the inarticulate stammerings of the mighty voice which now sounded throught the depths of my nature. The phrase, madly in love, is no exaggeration; madness alone knows such a fever of the brain, such a tumult of the heart. It was not that reason was overpowered; on the contrary, reason was intensely active, but active with that logic of flames which lights up the vision of maniacs.

"Although, of course, my passion was but too evident to

every one, I dreaded its premature avowal, lest I should lose her; and almost equally dreaded delay, lest I should suffer from that also. At length the avowal was extorted from me by jealousy of a brilliant Pole – Korinski – who had recently appeared in our circle, and was obviously casting me in the shade by his superior advantages of novelty, of personal attraction, and of a romantic history. She accepted me; and now, for a time, I was the happiest of mortals. The fever of the last few weeks was abating; it gave place to a deep tide of hopeful joy. Could I have died then! Could I have even died shortly afterwards, when I knew the delicious mystery of a jealousy not too absorbing! For you must know that my happiness was brief. Jealousy, to which all passion of a deep and exacting power is inevitably allied, soon began to disturb my content. Agalma had no tenderness. She permitted caresses, never returned them. She was ready enough to listen to all my plans for the future, so long as the recital moved amid details of fortune and her position in society – that is, so long as her vanity was interested; but I began to observe with pain that her thoughts never rested on tender domesticities and poetic anticipations. This vexed me more and more. The very spell which she exercised over me made her want of tenderness more intolerable. I yearned for her love – for some sympathy with the vehement passion which was burning within me; and she was as marble.

"You will not be surprised to hear that I reproached her bitterly for her indifference. That is the invariable and fatal folly of lovers – they seem to imagine that a heart can be scolded into tenderness! To my reproaches she at first answered impatiently that they were unjust; that it was not her fault if her nature was less expansive than mine; and that it was insulting to be told she was indifferent to the man whom she had consented to marry. Later she answered my reproaches with haughty defiance, one day intimating that if I really thought what I said, and repented our engagement, it would be most prudent for us to separate ere it was too late. This quieted me for a while. But it brought no balm to my wounds.

"And now fresh tortures were added. Korinski became quite marked in his attentions to Agalma. These she received with evident delight; so much so, that I saw by the glances of others that they were scandalized at it; and this, of course, increased my pain. My renewed reproaches only made her manner colder to me; to Korinski it became what I would gladly have seen towards myself.

"The stress and agitation of those days were too much for me. I fell ill, and for seven weeks lay utterly prostrate. On recovering, this note was handed to me. It was from Agalma."

Bourgonef here held out to me a crumpled letter, and motioned that I should open it and read. It ran thus:

"I have thought much of what you have so often said, that it would be for the happiness of both if our unfortunate engagement were set aside. That you have a real affection for me I believe, and be assured that I once had a real affection for you; not, perhaps, the passionate love which a nature so exacting as yours demands, and which I earnestly hope it may one day find, but a genuine affection nevertheless, which would have made me proud to share your lot. But it would be uncandid in me to pretend that this now exists. Your incessant jealousy, the angry feelings excited by your reproaches, the fretful irritation in which for some time we have lived together, has completely killed what love I had, and I no longer feel prepared to risk the happiness of both of us by a marriage. What you said the other night convinces me that it is even your desire our engagement should cease. It is certainly mine. Let us try to think kindly of each other and meet again as friends.

AGALMA LIEBENSTEIN."

When I had read this and returned it to him, he said:

"You see that this was written on the day I was taken ill. Whether she knew that I was helpless I know not. At any rate, she never sent to inquire after me. She went off to Paris; Korinski followed her; and – as I quickly learned on going once more into society – they were married! Did you ever, in the whole course of your experience, hear of such heartless conduct?"

Bourgonef asked this with a ferocity which quite startled me.

I did not answer him; for, in truth, I could not see that Agalma had been very much to blame, even as he told the story, and felt sure that could I have heard her version it would have worn a very different aspect. That she was cold, and disappointed him, might be true enough, but there was no crime; and I perfectly understood how thoroughly odious he must have made himself to her by his exactions and reproaches. I understood this, per- haps, all the better, because in the course of his narrative Bour- gonef had revealed to me aspects of his nature which were somewhat repulsive. Especially was I struck with his morbid vanity, and his readiness to impute low motives to others. This unpleasant view of his character – a character in many respects so admirable for its generosity and refinement – was deepened as he went on, instead of awaiting my reply to his question.

"For a wrong so measureless, you will naturally ask what measureless revenge I sought."

The idea had not occurred to me; indeed I could see no wrong, and this notion of revenge was somewhat startling in such a case.

"I debated it long," he continued. "I felt that since I was pre- vented from arresting any of the evil to myself, I could at least mature my plans for an adequate discharge of just retributions on her. It reveals the impotence resulting from the trammels of mod- ern civilization, that while the possibilities of wrong are infinite, the openings for vengeance are few and contemptible. Only when a man is thrown upon the necessities of this 'wild justice' does he discover how difficult vengeance really is. Had Agalma been my wife, I could have wreaked my wrath upon her, with assurance that some of the torture she inflicted on me was to fall on her. Not having this power what was I to do? Kill her? That would have afforded one moment of exquisite satisfaction – but to her it would have been simply death – and I wanted to kill the heart."

He seemed working with an insane passion, so that I re- garded him with disgust, mingled with some doubts as to what horrors he was about to relate.

"My plan was chosen. The only way to reach her heart was

to strike through her husband. For several hours daily I practised with the pistol, until – in spite of only having a left hand – I acquired fatal skill. But this was not enough. Firing at a mark is simple work. Firing at a man – especially one holding a pistol pointed at you – is altogether different. I had too often heard of 'crack shots' missing their men, to rely confidently on my skill in the shooting gallery. It was necessary that my eye and hand should be educated to familiarity with the real object. Part of the cause why duelists miss their man is from the trepidation of fear. I was without fear. At no moment in my life have I been afraid; and the chance of being shot by Korinski I counted as nothing. The other cause is unfamiliarity with the mark. This I secured myself against by getting a lay figure of Korinski's height, dressing it to resemble him, placing a pistol in its hand, and then practising at this mark in the woods. After a short time I could send a bullet through the thorax without taking more than a hasty glance at the figure.

"Thus prepared, I started for Paris. But you will feel for me when you learn that my hungry heart was baffled of its vengeance, and baffled for ever. Agalma had been carried off by scarlet fever. Korinski had left Paris, and I felt no strong promptings to follow him, and wreak on him a futile vengeance. It was on HER my wrath had been concentrated, and I gnashed my teeth at the thought that she had escaped me.

"My story is ended. The months of gloomy depression which succeeded, now that I was no longer sustained by the hope of vengeance, I need not speak of. My existence was desolate, and even now the desolation continues over the whole region of the emotions. I carry a dead heart within me."

VIII

A Second Victim

Bourgonef's story has been narrated with some fullness, though in less detail than he told it, in order that the reader may understand its real bearings on MY story. Without it, the motives which impelled the strange pertinacity of my pursuit would have been unintelligible. I have said that a very disagreeable impression remained on my mind respecting certain aspects of his character, and I felt somewhat ashamed of my imperfect sagacity in having up to this period been entirely blind to those aspects. The truth is, every human being is a mystery, and remains so to the last. We fancy we know a character; we form a distinct conception of it; for years that conception remains unmodified, and suddenly the strain of some emergency, of the incidental stimulus of new circumstances, reveals qualities not simply unexpected, but flatly contradictory of our previous conception. We judge of a man by the angle he subtends to our eye – only thus CAN we judge of him; and this angle depends on the relation his qualities and circumstances bear to our interests and sympathies. Bourgonef had charmed me intellectually; morally I had never come closer to him than in the sympathies of public questions and abstract theories. His story had disclosed hidden depths.

My old suspicions reappeared, and a conversation we had two days afterwards helped to strengthen them.

We had gone on a visit to Schwanthaler, the sculptor, at his tiny little castle of Schwaneck, a few miles from Munich. The artist was out for a walk, but we were invited to come in and await his return, which would be shortly; and meanwhile Bourgonef undertook to show me over the castle, interesting as a bit of modern Gothic, realizing on a diminutive scale a youthful dream of the sculptor's. When our survey was completed – and it did not take long – we sat at one of the windows and enjoyed a magnificent prospect. "It is curious," said Bourgonef, "to be shut up here in this imitation of medieval masonry, where every detail speaks of the dead past, and to think of the events now going on in Paris which must find imitators all over Europe, and which open to the mind such vistas of the future. What a grotesque anachronism is this Gothic castle, built in the same age as that which sees a reforming pope!"

"Yes; but is not the reforming pope himself an anachronism?"

"As a Catholic," here he smiled, intimating that his orthodoxy was not very stringent, "I cannot admit that; as a Protestant, you must admit that if there must be a pope, he must in these days be a reformer, or – give up his temporal power. Not that I look on Pio Nono as more than a precursor; he may break ground, and point the way, but he is not the man to lead Europe out of its present slough of despond, and under the headship of the Church found a new and lasting republic. We want a Hildebrand, one who will be to the nineteenth century as Gregory was to the eleventh."

"Do you believe in such a possibility? Do you think the Roman pontiff can ever again sway the destinies of Europe?"

"I can hardly say I believe it; yet I see the possibility of such an opening if the right man were to arise. But I fear he will not arise; or if he should, the Conclave will stifle him. Yet there is but one alternative: either Europe must once more join in a crusade with a pope at the head, or it must hoist the red flag. There is no other issue."

"Heaven preserve us from both! And I think we shall be preserved from the Pope by the rottenness of the Church; from the drapeau rouge by the indignation and horror of all honest men. You see how the Provisional Government has resisted the insane attempt of the fanatics to make the red flag accepted as the national banner?"

"Yes; and it is the one thing which dashes my pleasure in the new revolution. It is the one act of weakness which the Government has exhibited; a concession which will be fatal unless it be happily set aside by the energetic party of action."

"An act of weakness? say rather an act of strength. A concession? say rather the repudiation of anarchy, the assertion of law and justice."

"Not a bit. It was concession to the fears of the timid, and to the vanity of the French people. The tricolor is a French flag – not the banner of humanity. It is because the tricolor has been identified with the victories of France that it appeals to the vanity of the vainest of people. They forget that it is the flag of a revolution which failed, and of an empire which was one perpetual outrage to humanity. Whereas the red is new; it is the symbol of an energetic, thorough-going creed. If it carries terror with it, so much the better. The tyrants and the timid should be made to tremble."

"I had no idea you were so bloodthirsty," said I, laughing at his vehemence.

"I am not bloodthirsty at all; I am only logical and consistent. There is a mass of sophistry current in the world which sickens me. People talk of Robespierre and St. Just, two of the most virtuous men that ever lived – and of Dominic and Torquemada, two of the most single-minded – as if they were cruel and bloodthirsty, whereas they were only convinced."

"Is it from love of paradox that you defend these tigers?"

"Tigers, again – how those beasts are calumniated!"

He said this with a seriousness which was irresistibly comic. I shouted with laughter; but he continued gravely:

"You think I am joking. But let me ask you why you consider the tiger more bloodthirsty than yourself? He springs upon his food – you buy yours from the butcher. He cannot live without animal food: it is a primal necessity, and he obeys the ordained instinct. You can live on vegetables; yet you slaughter beasts of the field and birds of the air (or buy them when slaughtered), and consider yourself a model of virtue. The tiger only kills his food or his enemies; you not only kill both, but you kill one animal to make gravy for another! The tiger is less bloodthirsty than the Christian!"

"I don't know how much of that tirade is meant to be serious; but to waive the question of the tiger's morality, do you really – I will not say sympathize, – but justify Robespierre, Dominic, St. Just, and the rest of the fanatics who have waded to their ends through blood."

"He who wills the END, wills the MEANS."

"A devil's maxim."

"But a truth. What the foolish world shrinks at as blood-thirstiness and cruelty is very often mere force and constancy of intellect. It is not that fanatics thirst for blood – far from it, – but they thirst for the triumph of their cause. Whatever obstacle lies on their path must be removed; if a torrent of blood is the only thing that will sweep it away – the torrent must sweep."

"And sweep with it all the sentiments of pity, mercy, charity, love?"

"No; these sentiments may give a sadness to the necessity; they make the deed a sacrifice, but they cannot prevent the soul from seeing the aim to which it tends."

"This is detestable doctrine! It is the sophism which has destroyed families, devastated cities, and retarded the moral progress of the world more than anything else. No single act of injustice is ever done on this earth but it tends to perpetuate the reign of iniquity. By the feelings it calls forth it keeps up the native savagery of the heart. It breeds injustice, partly by hardening the minds of those who assent, and partly by exciting the passion of revenge in those who resist."

"You are wrong. The great drag-chain on the car of progress is the faltering inconsistency of man. Weakness is more cruel than sternness. Sentiment is more destructive than logic."

The arrival of Schwanthaler was timely, for my indignation was rising. The sculptor received us with great cordiality, and in the pleasure of the subsequent hour I got over to some extent the irritation Bourgonef's talk had excited.

The next day I left Munich for the Tyrol. My parting with Bourgonef was many degrees less friendly than it would have been a week before. I had no wish to see him again, and therefore gave him no address or invitation in case he should come to England. As I rolled away in the Malleposte, my busy thoughts reviewed all the details of our acquaintance, and the farther I was carried from his presence, the more obtrusive became the suspicions which connected him with the murder of Lieschen Lehfeldt. How, or upon what motive, was indeed an utter mystery. He had not mentioned the name of Lehfeldt. He had not mentioned having before been at Nuremberg. At Heidelberg the tragedy occurred – or was Heidelberg only a mask? It occurred to me that he had first ascertained that I had never been at Heidelberg before he placed the scene of his story there.

Thoughts such as these tormented me. Imagine, then, the horror with which I heard, soon after my arrival at Salzburg, that a murder had been committed at Grosshesslohe – one of the pretty environs of Munich much resorted to by holiday folk – corresponding in all essential features with the murder at Nuremberg! In both cases the victim was young and pretty. In both cases she was found quietly lying on the ground, stabbed to the heart, without any other traces of violence. In both cases she was a betrothed bride, and the motive of the unknown assassin a mystery.

Such a correspondence in the essential features inevitably suggested an appalling mystery of unity in these crimes, – either as the crimes of one man, committed under some impulse of motiveless malignity and thirst for innocent blood – or as the equally appalling effect of IMITATION acting contagiously upon a criminal imagination; of which contagion there have been, unfortunately, too many examples – horrible crimes prompting certain weak and feverish imaginations, by the very horror they inspire, first to dwell on, and finally to realize their imitations.

It was this latter hypothesis which found general acceptance. Indeed it was the only one which rested upon any ground of experience. The disastrous influence of imitation, especially under the fascination of horror, was well known. The idea of any diabolical malice moving one man to pass from city to city, and there quietly single out his victims – both of them, by the very hypothesis, unrelated to him, both of them at the epoch of their lives, when

"The bosom's lord sits lightly on its throne,"

when the peace of the heart is assured, and the future is radiantly beckoning to them, – that any man should choose such victims for such crimes was too preposterous an idea long to be entertained. Unless the man were mad, the idea was inconceivable; and even a monomaniac must betray himself in such a course, because he would necessarily conceive himself to be accomplishing some supreme act of justice.

It was thus I argued; and indeed I should much have preferred to believe that one maniac were involved, rather than the contagion of crime, – since one maniac must inevitably be soon detected; whereas there were no assignable limits to the contagion of imitation. And this it was which so profoundly agitated German society. In every family in which there happened to be a bride, vague tremors could not be allayed; and the absolute powerlessness which resulted from the utter uncertainty as to the quarter in which this dreaded phantom might next appear, justified and intensified those tremors. Against such an apparition there was no conceivable safeguard. From a city stricken with the plague, from a district so stricken, flight is possible, and there are the resources of medical aid. But from a moral plague like this, what escape was possible?

So passionate and profound became the terror, that I began to share the opinion which I heard expressed, regretting the widespread publicity of the modern press, since, with many undeniable benefits, it carried also the fatal curse of distributing through households, and keeping constantly under the excitement of discussion, images of crime and horror which would tend to perpetuate and extend the excesses of individual passion. The mere dwelling long on such a topic as this was fraught with evil.

This and more I heard discussed as I hurried back to Munich. To Munich? Yes; thither I was posting with all speed. Not a shadow of doubt now remained in my mind. I knew the assassin, and was resolved to track and convict him. Do not suppose that THIS time I was led away by the vagrant activity of my constructive imagination. I had something like positive proof. No sooner had I learned that the murder had been committed at Grossesslohe, than my thoughts at once carried me to a now memorable visit I had made there in company with Bourgonef and two young Bavarians. At the hotel where we dined, we were waited on by the niece of the landlord, a girl of remarkable beauty, who naturally excited the attention of four young men, and furnished them with a topic of conversation. One of the Bavarians had told us that she would one day be perhaps one of the wealthiest women in the country, for she was engaged to be married to a young farmer who had recently found himself, by a rapid succession of deaths, sole heir to a great brewer, whose wealth was known to be enormous.

At this moment Sophie entered bringing wine, and I saw Bourgonef slowly turn his eyes upon her with a look which then was mysterious to me, but which now spoke too plainly its dreadful meaning.

What is there in a look, you will say? Perhaps nothing; or it may be everything. To my unsuspecting, unenlightened perception, Bourgonef's gaze was simply the melancholy and half-curious gaze which such a man might be supposed to cast upon a young woman who had been made the topic of an interesting discourse. But to my mind, enlightened as to his character, and instructed as to his peculiar feelings arising from his own story, the gaze was charged with horror. It marked a victim. The whole succession of events rose before me in vivid distinctness; the separate details of suspicion gathered into unity.

Great as was Bourgonef's command over his features, he could not conceal uneasiness as well as surprise at my appearance at the table d'hote in Munich. I shook hands with him, putting on as friendly a mask as I could, and replied to his question about my sudden return by attributing it to unexpected intelligence received at Salzburg.

"Nothing serious, I hope?"

"Well, I'm afraid it will prove very serious," I said. "But we shall see. Meanwhile my visit to the Tyrol must be given up or postponed."

"Do you remain here, then?"

"I don't know what my movements will be."

Thus I had prepared him for any reserve or strangeness in my manner; and I had concealed from him the course of my movements; for at whatever cost, I was resolved to follow him and bring him to justice.

But how? Evidence I had none that could satisfy any one else, however convincing it might be to my own mind. Nor did there seem any evidence forthcoming from Grosshesslohe. Sophie's body had been found in the afternoon lying as if asleep in one of the by- paths of the wood. No marks of a struggle; no traces of the murderer. Her affianced lover, who was at Augsburg, on hearing of her fate, hurried to Grosshesslohe, but could throw no light on the murder, could give no hint as to a possible motive for the deed. But this entire absence of evidence, or even ground of suspicion, only made MY case the stronger. It was the motiveless malignity of the deed which fastened it on Bourgonef; or rather, it was the absence of any known motive elsewhere which assured me that I had detected the motive in him.

Should I communicate my conviction to the police? It was possible that I might impress them with at least sufficient suspicion to warrant his examination – and in that case the truth might be elicited; for among the many barbarities and iniquities of the criminal procedure in Continental States which often press heavily on the innocent, there is this compensating advantage, that the pressure on the guilty is tenfold heavier. If the innocent are often unjustly punished – imprisoned and maltreated before their innocence can be established – the guilty seldom escape. In England we give the criminal not only every chance of escape, but many advantages. The love of fair-play is carried to excess. It seems at times as if the whole arrangements of our procedure were established with a view to giving a criminal not only the benefit of every doubt, but of every loophole through which he can slip. Instead of this, the Continental procedure goes on the principle of closing up every loophole, and of inventing endless traps into which the accused may fall. We warn the accused not to say anything that may be prejudicial to him. They entangle him in contradictions and confessions which disclose his guilt.

Knowing this, I thought it very likely that, however artful

Bourgonef might be, a severe examination might extort from him sufficient confirmation of my suspicion to warrant further procedure. But knowing also that THIS resort was open to me when all others had failed, I resolved to wait and watch.

IX

Finale

Two days passed, and nothing occurred. My watching seemed hopeless, and I resolved to try the effect of a disguised interrogatory. It might help to confirm my already settled conviction, if it did not elicit any new evidence.

Seated in Bourgonef's room, in the old place, each with a cigar, and chatting as of old on public affairs, I gradually approached the subject of the recent murder.

"Is it not strange," I said, "that both these crimes should have happened while we were casually staying in both places?"

"Perhaps we are the criminals," he replied, laughing. I shivered slightly at this audacity. He laughed as he spoke, but there was a hard, metallic, and almost defiant tone in his voice which exasperated me.

"Perhaps we are," I answered, quietly. He looked full at me; but I was prepared, and my face told nothing. I added, as in explanation, "The crime being apparently contagious, we may have brought the infection from Nuremberg."

"Do you believe in that hypothesis of imitation?"

"I don't know what to believe. Do you believe in there being only one murderer? It seems such a preposterous idea. We must suppose him, at any rate, to be a maniac."

"Not necessarily. Indeed there seems to have been too much artful contrivance in both affairs, not only in the selection of the victims, but in the execution of the schemes. Cunning as maniacs often are they are still maniacs, and betray themselves."

"If not a maniac," said I, hoping to pique him, "he must be a man of stupendous and pitiable vanity, – perhaps one of your constant- minded friends, whom you refuse to call bloodthirsty."

"Constant-minded, perhaps; but why pitiably vain?"

"Why? Because only a diseased atrocity of imagination, stimulating a nature essentially base and weak in its desire to make itself conspicuous, would or could suggest such things. The silly youth who 'fired the Ephesian dome,' the vain idiot who set fire to York Minster, the miserable Frenchmen who have committed murder and suicide with a view of making their exit striking from a world in which their appearance had been contemptible, would all sink into insignificance beside the towering infamy of baseness which – for the mere love of producing an effect on the minds of men, and thus drawing their attention upon him, which otherwise would never have marked him at all – could scheme and execute crimes so horrible and inexcusable. In common charity to human nature, let us suppose the wretch is mad; because otherwise his miserable vanity would be too loathsome." I spoke with warmth and bitterness, which increased as I perceived him wincing under the degradation of my contempt.

"If his motive WERE vanity," he said, "no doubt it would be horrible; but may it not have been revenge?"

"Revenge!" I exclaimed; "what! on innocent women?"

"You assume their innocence."

"Good God! do you know anything to the contrary?"

"Not I. But as we are conjecturing, I may as well conjecture it to have been the desire to produce a startling effect."

"How do you justify your conjecture?"

"Simply enough. We have to suppose a motive; let us say it was revenge, and see whether that will furnish a clue."

"But it can't. The two victims were wholly unconnected with each other by any intermediate acquaintances, consequently there can have been no common wrong or common enmity in existence to furnish food for vengeance."

"That may be so; it may also be that the avenger made them vicarious victims."

"How so?"

"It is human nature. Did you ever observe a thwarted child striking in its anger the unoffending nurse, destroying its toys to discharge its wrath? Did you ever see a schoolboy, unable to wreak his anger on the bigger boy who has just struck him, turn against the nearest smaller boy and beat him? Did you ever know a schoolmaster, angered by one of the boy's parents, vent his pent-up spleen upon the unoffending class? Did you ever see a subaltern punished because an officer had been reprimanded? These are familiar examples of vicarious vengeance. When the soul is stung to fury, it must solace itself by the discharge of that fury – it must relieve its pain by the sight of pain in others. We are so constituted. We need sympathy above all things. In joy we cannot bear to see others in distress; in distress we see the joy of others with dismal envy which sharpens our pain. That is human nature."

"And," I exclaimed, carried away by my indignation, "you suppose that the sight of these two happy girls, beaming with the quiet joy of brides, was torture to some miserable wretch who had lost his bride."

I had gone too far. His eyes looked into mine. I read in his that he divined the whole drift of my suspicion – the allusion made to himself. There often passes into a look more than words can venture to express. In that look he read that he was discovered, and I read that he had recognized it. With perfect calmness, but with a metallic ring in his voice which was like the clash of swords, he said:

"I did not say that I supposed this; but as we were on the wide field of conjecture – utterly without evidence one way or the other, having no clue either to the man or his motives – I drew from the general principles of human nature a conclusion which was just as plausible – or absurd if you like – as the conclusion that the motive must have been vanity."

"As you say, we are utterly without evidence, and conjecture drifts aimlessly from one thing to another. After all, the most plausible explanation is that of a contagion of imitation."

I said this in order to cover my previous imprudence. He was not deceived – though for a few moments I fancied he was – but replied:

"I am not persuaded of that either. The whole thing is a mystery, and I shall stay here some time in the hope of seeing it cleared up. Meanwhile, for a subject of conjecture, let me show you something on which your ingenuity may profitably be employed."

He rose and passed into his bedroom. I heard him unlocking and rummaging the drawers, and was silently reproaching myself for my want of caution in having spoken as I had done, though it was now beyond all doubt that he was the murderer, and that his motive had been rightly guessed; but with this self-reproach there was mingled a self-gratulation at the way I had got out of the difficulty, as I fancied.

He returned, and as he sat down I noticed that the lower part of his surtout was open. He always wore a long frogged and braided coat reaching to the knees – as I now know, for the purpose of concealing the arm which hung (as he said, withered) at his side. The two last fastenings were now undone.

He held in his hand a tiny chain made of very delicate wire. This he gave me, saying:

"Now what would you conjecture that to be?"

"Had it come into my hands without any remark, I should have said it was simply a very exquisite bit of ironwork; but your question points to something more out of the way."

"It IS iron-work," he said.

Could I be deceived? A third fastening of his surtout was undone! I had seen but two a moment ago.

"And what am I to conjecture?" I asked.

"Where that iron came from? It was NOT from a mine." I looked at it again, and examined it attentively. On raising my eyes in inquiry – fortunately with an expression of surprise, since what met my eyes would have startled a cooler man – I saw the fourth fastening undone!

"You look surprised," he continued, "and will be more surprised when I tell you that the iron in your hands once floated in the circulation of a man. It is made from human blood."

"Human blood!" I murmured.

He went on expounding the physiological wonders of the blood, – how it carried, dissolved in its currents, a proportion of iron and earths; how this iron was extracted by chemists and exhibited as a curiosity; and how this chain had been manufactured from such extracts. I heard every word, but my thoughts were hurrying to and fro in the agitation of a supreme moment. That there was a dagger underneath that coat – that in a few moments it would flash forth – that a death-struggle was at hand, – I knew well. My safety depended on presence of mind. That incalculable rapidity with which, in critical moments, the mind surveys all the openings and resources of an emergency, had assured me that there was no weapon within reach – that before I could give an alarm the tiger would be at my throat, and that my only chance was to keep my eyes fixed upon him, ready to spring on him the moment the next fastening was undone, and before he could use his arm.

At last the idea occurred to me, that as, with a wild beast, safety lies in attacking him just before he attacks you, so with this beast my best chance was audacity. Looking steadily into his face, I said slowly:

"And you would like to have such a chain made from my blood." I rose as I spoke. He remained sitting, but was evidently taken aback.

"What do you mean?" he said.

"I mean," said I, sternly, "that your coat is unfastened, and that if another fastening is loosened in my presence, I fell you to the earth."

"You're a fool!" he exclaimed.

I moved towards the door, keeping my eye fixed upon him as he sat pale and glaring at me.

"YOU are a fool," I said – " and worse, if you stir."

At this moment, I know not by what sense, as if I had eyes at the back of my head, I was aware of some one moving behind me, yet I dared not look aside. Suddenly two mighty folds of darkness seemed to envelop me like arms. A powerful scent ascended my nostrils. There was a ringing in my ears, a beating at my heart. Darkness came on, deeper and deeper, like huge waves. I seemed growing to gigantic stature. The waves rolled on faster and faster. The ringing became a roaring. The beating became a throbbing. Lights flashed across the darkness. Forms moved before me. On came the waves hurrying like a tide, and I sank deeper and deeper into this mighty sea of darkness. Then all was silent. Consciousness was still.

*****

How long I remained unconscious, I cannot tell. But it must have been some considerable time. When consciousness once more began to dawn within me, I found myself lying on a bed surrounded by a group of eager, watching faces, and became aware of a confused murmur of whispering going on around me. "Er Lebt" (he lives) were the words which greeted my opening eyes – words which I recognized as coming from my landlord.

I had had a very narrow escape. Another moment and I should not have lived to tell the tale. The dagger that had already immolated two of Bourgonef's objects of vengeance would have been in my breast. As it was, at the very moment when the terrible Ivan had thrown his arms around me and was stifling me with chloroform, one of the servants of the hotel, alarmed or attracted by curiosity at the sound of high words within the room, had ventured to open the door to see what was going on. The alarm had been given, and Bourgonef had been arrested and handed over to the police. Ivan, however, had disappeared; nor were the police ever able to find him. This mattered comparatively little. Ivan without his master was no more redoubtable than any other noxious animal. As an accomplice, as an instrument to execute the will of a man like Bourgonef, he was a danger to society. The directing intelligence withdrawn, he sank to the level of the brute. I was not uneasy, therefore, at his having escaped. Sufficient for me that the real criminal, the mind that had conceived and directed those fearful murders, was at last in the hands of justice. I felt that my task had been fully accomplished when Bourgonef's head fell on the scaffold.

The Closed Cabinet

I

It was with a little alarm and a good deal of pleasurable excitement that I looked forward to my first grown-up visit to Mervyn Grange. I had been there several times as a child, but never since I was twelve years old, and now I was over eighteen. We were all of us very proud of our cousins the Mervyns: it is not everybody that can claim kinship with a family who are in full and admitted possession of a secret, a curse, and a mysterious cabinet, in addition to the usual surplusage of horrors supplied in such cases by popular imagination. Some declared that a Mervyn of the days of Henry VIII had been cursed by an injured abbot from the foot of the gallows. Others affirmed that a dissipated Mervyn of the Georgian era was still playing cards for his soul in some remote region of the Grange. There were stories of white ladies and black imps, of bloodstained passages and magic stones. We, proud of our more intimate acquaintance with the family, naturally gave no credence to these wild inventions. The Mervyns, indeed, followed the accepted precedent in such cases, and greatly disliked any reference to the reputed mystery being made in their presence; with the inevitable result that there was no subject so pertinaciously discussed by their friends in their absence. My father's sister had married the late Baronet, Sir Henry Mervyn, and we always felt that she ought to have been the means of imparting to us a very complete knowledge of the family secret. But in this connection she undoubtedly failed of her duty. We knew that there had been a terrible tragedy in the family some two or three hundred years ago – that a peculiarly wicked owner of Mervyn, who flourished in the latter part of the sixteenth century, had been murdered by his wife who subsequently committed suicide. We knew that the mysterious curse had some connection with this crime, but what the curse exactly was we had never been able to discover. The history of the family since that time had indeed in one sense been full of misfortune. Not in every sense. A coal mine had been discovered in one part of the estate, and a populous city had grown over the corner of another part; and the Mervyns of to-day, in spite of the usual percentage of extravagant heirs and political mistakes, were three times as rich as their ancestors had been. But still their story was full of bloodshed and shame, of tales of duels and suicides, broken hearts and broken honor. Only these calamities seemed to have little or no relation to each other, and what the precise curse was that was supposed to connect or account for them we could not learn. When she first married, my aunt was told nothing about it. Later on in life, when my father asked her for the story, she begged him to talk upon a pleasanter subject; and being unluckily a man of much courtesy and little curiosity, he complied with her request. This, however, was the only part of the ghostly traditions of her husband's home upon which she was so reticent. The haunted chamber, for instance – which, of course, existed at the Grange – she treated with the greatest contempt. Various friends and relations had slept in it at different times, and no approach to any kind of authenticated ghost-story, even of the most trivial description, had they been able to supply. Its only claim to respect, indeed, was that it contained the famous Mervyn cabinet, a fascinating puzzle of which I will speak later, but which certainly had nothing haunting or horrible about its appearance.

My uncle's family consisted of three sons. The eldest, George, the present baronet, was now in his thirties, married, and with children of his own. The second, Jack, was the black-sheep of the family. He had been in the Guards, but, about five years back, had got into some very disgraceful scrape, and had been obliged to leave the country. The sorrow and the shame of this had killed his unhappy mother, and her husband had not long afterwards followed her to the grave. Alan, the youngest son, probably because he was the nearest to us in age, had been our special favorite in earlier years. George was grown up before I had well left the nursery, and his hot, quick temper had always kept us youngsters somewhat in awe of him. Jack was four years older than Alan, and, besides, his profession had, in a way, cut his boyhood short. When my uncle and aunt were abroad, as they frequently were for months together on account of her health, it was Alan, chiefly, who had to spend his holidays with us, both as school-boy and as undergraduate. And a brighter, sweeter-tempered comrade, or one possessed of more diversified talents for the invention of games or the telling of stories, it would have been difficult to find.

For five years together now our ancient custom of an annual visit to Mervyn had been broken. First there had been the seclusion of mourning for my aunt, and a year later for my uncle; then George and his wife, Lucy, – she was a connection of our own on our mother's side, and very intimate with us all, – had been away for nearly two years on a voyage round the world; and since then sickness in our own family had kept us in our turn a good deal abroad. So that I had not seen my cousins since all the calamities which had befallen them in the interval, and as I steamed northwards I wondered a good deal as to the changes I should find. I was to have come out that year in London, but ill-health had prevented me; and as a sort of consolation Lucy had kindly asked me to spend a fortnight at Mervyn, and be present at a shooting-party, which was to assemble there in the first week of October.

I had started early, and there was still an hour of the short autumn day left when I descended at the little wayside station, from which a six-mile drive brought me to the Grange. A dreary drive I found it – the round, gray, treeless outline of the fells stretching around me on every side beneath the leaden, changeless sky. The night had nearly fallen as we drove along the narrow valley in which the Grange stood: it was too dark to see the autumn tints of the woods which clothed and brightened its sides, almost too dark to distinguish the old tower, – Dame Alice's tower as it was called, – which stood some half a mile farther on at its head. But the light shone brightly from the Grange windows, and all feeling of dreariness departed as I drove up to the door. Leaving maid and boxes to their fate, I ran up the steps into the old, well-remembered hall, and was informed by the dignified man-servant that her ladyship and the tea were awaiting me in the morning-room.

I found that there was nobody staying in the house except Alan, who was finishing the long vacation there: he had been called to the Bar a couple of years before. The guests were not to arrive for another week, so that I had plenty of opportunity in the interval to make up for lost time with my cousins. I began my observations that evening as we sat down to dinner, a cozy party of four. Lucy was quite unchanged – pretty, foolish, and gentle as ever. George showed the full five years' increase of age, and seemed to have acquired a somewhat painful control of his temper. Instead of the old petulant outbursts, there was at times an air of nervous, irritable self-restraint, which I found the less pleasant of the two. But it was in Alan that the most striking alteration appeared. I felt it the moment I shook hands with him, and the impression deepened that evening with every hour. I told myself that it was only the natural difference between boy and man, between twenty and twenty-five, but I don't think that I believed it. Superficially the change was not great. The slight-built, graceful figure; the deep gray eyes, too small for beauty; the clear-cut features, the delicate, sensitive lips, close shaven now, as they had been hairless then, – all were as I remembered them. But the face was paler and thinner than it had been, and there were lines round the eyes and at the corners of the mouth which were no more natural to twenty-five than they would have been to twenty. The old charm indeed – the sweet friendliness of manner, which was his own peculiar possession – was still there. He talked and laughed almost as much as formerly, but the talk was manufactured for our entertainment, and the laughter came from his head and not from his heart. And it was when he was taking no part in the conversation that the change showed most. Then the face, on which in the old time every passing emotion had expressed itself in a constant, living current, became cold and impassive – without interest, and without desire. It was at such times that I knew most certainly that here was something which had been living and was dead. Was it only his boyhood? This question I was unable to answer.

Still, in spite of all, that week was one of the happiest in my life. The brothers were both men of enough ability and cultivation to be pleasant talkers, and Lucy could perform adequately the part of conversational accompanist, which, socially speaking, is all that is required of a woman. The meals and evenings passed quickly and agreeably; the mornings I spent in unending gossips with Lucy, or in games with the children, two bright boys of five and six years old. But the afternoons were the best part of the day. George was a thorough squire in all his tastes and habits, and every afternoon his wife dutifully accompanied him round farms and coverts, inspecting new buildings, trudging along half-made roads, or marking unoffending trees for destruction. Then Alan and I would ride by the hour together over moor and meadowland, often picking our way homewards down the glen-side long after the autumn evenings had closed in. During these rides I had glimpses many a time into depths in Alan's nature of which I doubt whether in the old days he had himself been aware. To me certainly they were as a revelation. A prevailing sadness, occasionally a painful tone of bitterness, characterized these more serious moods of his, but I do not think that, at the end of that week, I would, if I could, have changed the man, whom I was learning to revere and to pity, for the light-hearted playmate whom I felt was lost to me for ever.

II

The only feature of the family life which jarred on me was the attitude of the two brothers towards the children. I did not notice this much at first, and at all times it was a thing to be felt rather than to be seen. George himself never seemed quite at ease with them. The boys were strong and well grown, healthy in mind and body; and one would have thought that the existence of two such representatives to carry on his name and inherit his fortune would have been the very crown of pride and happiness to their father. But it was not so. Lucy indeed was devoted to them, and in all practical matters no one could have been kinder to them than was George. They were free of the whole house, and every indulgence that money could buy for them they had. I never heard him give them a harsh word. But there was something wrong. A constraint in their presence, a relief in their absence, an evident dislike of discussing them and their affairs, a total want of that enjoyment of love and possession which in such a case one might have expected to find. Alan's state of mind was even more marked. Never did I hear him willingly address his nephews, or in any way allude to their existence. I should have said that he simply ignored it, but for the heavy gloom which always overspread his spirits in their company, and for the glances which he would now and again cast in their direction – glances full of some hidden painful emotion, though of what nature it would have been hard to define. Indeed, Alan's attitude towards her children I soon found to be the only source of friction between Lucy and this otherwise much-loved member of her husband's family. I asked her one day why the boys never appeared at luncheon.

"Oh, they come when Alan is away," she answered; "but they seem to annoy him so much that George thinks it is better to keep them out of sight when he is here. It is very tiresome. I know that it is the fashion to say that George has got the temper of the family; but I assure you that Alan's nervous moods and fancies are much more difficult to live with."

That was on the morning – a Friday it was – of the last day which we were to spend alone. The guests were to arrive soon after tea; and I think that with the knowledge of their approach Alan and I prolonged our ride that afternoon beyond its usual limits. We were on our way home, and it was already dusk, when a turn of the path brought us face to face with the old ruined tower, of which I have already spoken as standing at the head of the valley. I had not been close up to it yet during this visit at Mervyn. It had been a very favorite haunt of ours as children, and partly on that account, partly perhaps in order to defer the dreaded close of our ride to the last possible moment, I proposed an inspection of it. The only portion of the old building left standing in any kind of entirety was two rooms, one above the other. The tower room, level with the bottom of the moat, was dark and damp, and it was the upper one, reached by a little outside staircase, which had been our rendezvous of old. Alan showed no disposition to enter, and said that he would stay outside and hold my horse, so I dismounted and ran up alone.

The room seemed in no way changed. A mere stone shell, littered with fragments of wood and mortar. There was the rough wooden block on which Alan used to sit while he first frightened us with bogey-stories, and then calmed our excited nerves by rapid sallies of wild nonsense. There was the plank from behind which, erected as a barrier across the doorway, he would defend the castle against our united assault, pelting us with fir-cones and sods of earth. This and many a bygone scene thronged on me as I stood there, and the room filled again with the memories of childish mirth. And following close came those of childish terrors. Horrors which had oppressed me then, wholly imagined or dimly apprehended from half- heard traditions, and never thought of since, flitted around me in the gathering dusk. And with them it seemed to me as if there came other memories too, – memories which had never been my own, of scenes whose actors had long been with the dead, but which, immortal as the spirit before whose eyes they had dwelt, still lingered in the spot where their victim had first learnt to shudder at their presence. Once the ghastly notion came to me, it seized on my imagination with irresistible force. It seemed as if from the darkened corners of the room vague, ill-defined shapes were actually peering out at me. When night came they would show themselves in that form, livid and terrible, in which they had been burnt into the brain and heart of the long ago dead.

I turned and glanced towards where I had left Alan. I could see his figure framed in by the window, a black shadow against the gray twilight of the sky behind. Erect and perfectly motionless he sat, so motionless as to look almost lifeless, gazing before him down the valley into the illimitable distance beyond. There was something in that stern immobility of look and attitude which struck me with a curious sense of congruity. It was right that he should be thus – right that he should be no longer the laughing boy who a moment before had been in my memory. The haunting horrors of that place seemed to demand it, and for the first time I felt that I understood the change. With an effort I shook myself free from these fancies, and turned to go. As I did so, my eye fell upon a queer-shaped painted board, leaning up against the wall, which I well recollected in old times. Many a discussion had we had about the legend inscribed upon it, which in our wisdom we had finally pronounced to be German, chiefly because it was illegible. Though I had loudly professed my faith in this theory at the time, I had always had uneasy doubts on the subject, and now half smiling I bent down to verify or remove them. The language was English, not German; but the badly painted, faded Gothic letters in which it was written made the mistake excusable. In the dim light I had difficulty even now in deciphering the words, and felt when I had done so that neither the information conveyed nor the style of the composition was sufficient reward for the trouble I had taken. This is what I read:

"Where the woman sinned the maid shall win;
But God help the maid that sleeps within."

What the lines could refer to I neither had any notion nor did I pause then even in my own mind to inquire. I only remember vaguely wondering whether they were intended for a tombstone or for a doorway. Then, continuing my way, I rapidly descended the steps and remounted my horse, glad to find myself once again in the open air and by my cousin's side.

The train of thought into which he had sunk during my absence was apparently an absorbing one, for to my first question as to the painted board he could hardly rouse himself to answer.

"A board with a legend written on it? Yes, he remembered something of the kind there. It had always been there, he thought. He knew nothing about it," – and so the subject was not continued.

The weird feelings which had haunted me in the tower still oppressed me, and I proceeded to ask Alan about that old Dame

Alice whom the traditions of my childhood represented as the last occupant of the ruined building. Alan roused himself now, but did not seem anxious to impart information on the subject. She had lived there, he admitted, and no one had lived there since. "Had she not," I inquired, "something to do with the mysterious cabinet at the house? I remember hearing it spoken of as 'Dame Alice's cabinet.'

"So they say," he assented; "she and an Italian artificer who was in her service, and who, chiefly I imagine on account of his skill, shared with her the honor of reputed witchcraft."

"She was the mother of Hugh Mervyn, the man who was murdered by his wife, was she not?" I asked.

"Yes," said Alan, briefly.

"And had she not something to do with the curse?" I inquired after a short pause, and nervously I remembered my father's experience on that subject, and I had never before dared to allude to it in the presence of any member of the family. My nervousness was fully warranted. The gloom on Alan's brow deepened, and after a very short "They say so" he turned full upon me, and inquired with some asperity why on earth I had developed this sudden curiosity about his ancestress.

I hesitated a moment, for I was a little ashamed of my fancies; but the darkness gave me courage, and besides I was not afraid of telling Alan – he would understand. I told him of the strange sensations I had had while in the tower – sensations which had struck me with all that force and clearness which we usually associate with a direct experience of fact. "Of course it was a trick of imagination," I commented; "but I could not get rid of the feeling that the person who had dwelt there last must have had terrible thoughts for the companions of her life."

Alan listened in silence, and the silence continued for some time after I had ceased speaking.

"It is strange," he said at last; "instincts which we do not understand form the motive-power of most of our life's actions, and yet we refuse to admit them as evidence of any external truth. I suppose it is because we MUST act somehow, rightly or wrongly; and there are a great many things which we need not believe unless we choose. As for this old lady, she lived long – long enough, like most of us, to do evil; unlike most of us, long enough to witness some of the results of that evil. To say that, is to say that the last years of her life must have been weighted heavily enough with tragic thought."

I gave a little shudder of repulsion.

"That is a depressing view of life, Alan," I said. "Does our peace of mind depend only upon death coming early enough to hide from us the truth? And, after all, can it? Our spirits do not die. From another world they may witness the fruits of our lives in this one."

"If they do," he answered with sudden violence, "it is absurd to doubt the existence of a purgatory. There must in such a case be a terrible one in store for the best among us."

I was silent. The shadow that lay on his soul did not penetrate to mine, but it hung round me nevertheless, a cloud which I felt powerless to disperse.

After a moment he went on, – "Provided that they are distant enough, how little, after all, do we think of the results of our actions! There are few men who would deliberately instill into a child a love of drink, or wilfully deprive him of his reason; and yet a man with drunkenness or madness in his blood thinks nothing of bringing children into the world tainted as deeply with the curse as if he had inoculated them with it directly. There is no responsibility so completely ignored as this one of marriage and fatherhood, and yet how heavy it is and far-reaching."

"Well," I said, smiling, "let us console ourselves with the thought that we are not all lunatics and drunkards."

"No," he answered; "but there are other evils besides these, moral taints as well as physical, curses which have their roots in worlds beyond our own, – sins of the fathers which are visited upon the children."

257

He had lost all violence and bitterness of tone now; but the weary dejection which had taken their place communicated itself to my spirit with more subtle power than his previous mood had owned.

"That is why," he went on, and his manner seemed to give more purpose to his speech than hitherto, – "that is why, so far as I am concerned, I mean to shirk the responsibility and remain unmarried."

I was hardly surprised at his words. I felt that I had expected them, but their utterance seemed to intensify the gloom which rested upon us. Alan was the first to arouse himself from its influence.

"After all," he said, turning round to me and speaking lightly, "without looking so far and so deep, I think my resolve is a prudent one. Above all things, let us take life easily, and you know what St. Paul says about 'trouble in the flesh,' – a remark which I am sure is specially applicable to briefless barristers, even though possessed of a modest competence of their own. Perhaps one of these days, when I am a fat old judge, I shall give my cook a chance if she is satisfactory in her clear soups; but till then I shall expect you, Evie, to work me one pair of carpet-slippers per annum, as tribute due to a bachelor cousin."

I don't quite know what I answered, – my heart was heavy and aching, – but I tried with true feminine docility to follow the lead he had set me. He continued for some time in the same vein; but as we approached the house the effort seemed to become too much for him, and we relapsed again into silence.

This time I was the first to break it. "I suppose," I said, drearily, "all those horrid people will have come by now."

"Horrid people," he repeated, with rather an uncertain laugh, and through the darkness I saw his figure bend forward as he stretched out his hand to caress my horse's neck. "Why, Evie, I thought you were pining for gayety, and that it was, in fact, for the purpose of meeting these 'horrid people' that you came here."

"Yes, I know," I said, wistfully; "but somehow the last week has been so pleasant that I cannot believe that anything will ever be quite so nice again."

We had arrived at the house as I spoke, and the groom was standing at our horses' heads. Alan got off and came round to help me to dismount; but instead of putting up his arm as usual as a support for me to spring from, he laid his hand on mine. "Yes, Evie," he said, "it has been indeed a pleasant time. God bless you for it." For an instant he stood there looking up at me, his face full in the light which streamed from the open door, his gray eyes shining with a radiance which was not wholly from thence. Then he straightened his arm, I sprang to the ground, and as if to preclude the possibility of any answer on my part, he turned sharply on his heel, and began giving some orders to the groom. I went on alone into the house, feeling, I knew not and cared not to know why, that the gloom had fled from my spirit, and that the last ride had not after all been such a melancholy failure as it had bid fair at one time to become.

III

In the hall I was met by the housekeeper, who informed me that, owing to a misunderstanding about dates, a gentleman had arrived whom Lucy had not expected at that time, and that in consequence my room had been changed. My things had been put into the East Room, – the haunted room, – the room of the Closed Cabinet, as I remembered with a certain sense of pleased importance, though without any surprise. It stood apart from the other guest-rooms, at the end of the passage from which opened George and Lucy's private apartment; and as it was consequently disagreeable to have a stranger there, it was always used when the house was full for a member of the family. My father and mother had often slept there: there was a little room next to it, though not communicating with it, which served for a dressing-room. Though I had never passed the night there myself, I knew it as well as any room in the house. I went there at once, and found Lucy superintending the last arrangements for my comfort.

She was full of apologies for the trouble she was giving me. I told her that the apologies were due to my maid and to her own servants rather than to me; "and besides," I added, glancing round, "I am distinctly a gainer by the change."

"You know, of course," she said, lightly, "that this is the haunted room of the house, and that you have no right to be here?"

"I know it is the haunted room," I answered; "but why have I no right to be here?"

"Oh, I don't know," she said. "There is one of those tiresome Mervyn traditions against allowing unmarried girls to sleep in this room. I believe two girls died in it a hundred and fifty years ago, or something of that sort."

"But I should think that people, married or unmarried, must have died in nearly every room in the house," I objected.

"Oh, yes, of course they have," said Lucy; "but once you come across a bit of superstition in this family, it is of no use to ask for reasons. However, this particular bit is too ridiculous even for George. Owing to Mr. Leslie having come to-day, we must use every room in the house: it is intolerable having a stranger here, and you are the only relation staying with us. I pointed all that out to George, and he agreed that, under the circumstances, it would be absurd not to put you here."

"I am quite agreeable," I answered; "and, indeed, I think I am rather favored in having a room where the last recorded death appears to have taken place a hundred and fifty years ago, particularly as I should think that there can be scarcely anything now left in it which was here then, except, of course, the cabinet."

The room had, in fact, been entirely done up and refurnished by my uncle, and was as bright and modern-looking an apartment as you could wish to see. It was large, and the walls were covered with one of those white and gold papers which were fashionable thirty years ago. Opposite us, as we stood warming our backs before the fire, was the bed – a large double one, hung with a pretty shade of pale blue. Material of the same color covered the comfortable modern furniture, and hung from gilded cornices before the two windows which pierced the side of the room on our left. Between them stood the toilet-table, all muslin, blue ribbons, and silver. The carpet was a gray and blue Brussels one. The whole effect was cheerful, though I fear inartistic, and sadly out of keeping with the character of the house. The exception to these remarks was, as I had observed, the famous closed cabinet, to which I have more than once alluded. It stood against the same wall of the room as that in which the fireplace was, and on our right – that is, on that side of the fireplace which was farthest from the windows. As I spoke, I turned to go and look at it, and Lucy followed me. Many an hour as a child had I passed in front of it, fingering the seven carved brass handles, or rather buttons, which were ranged down its center. They all slid, twisted, or screwed with the greatest ease, and apparently like many another ingeniously contrived lock; but neither I nor any one else had ever yet succeeded in sliding, twisting, or screwing them after such a fashion as to open the closed doors of the cabinet. No one yet had robbed them of their secret since first it was placed there three hundred years ago by the old lady and her faithful Italian. It was a beautiful piece of workmanship, was this tantalizing cabinet. Carved out of some dark foreign wood, the doors and panels were richly inlaid with lapis- lazuli, ivory, and mother-of-pearl, among which were twisted delicately chased threads of gold and silver. Above the doors, between them and the cornice, lay another mystery, fully as tormenting as was the first. In a smooth strip of wood about an inch wide, and extending along the whole breadth of the cabinet, was inlaid a fine pattern in gold wire. This at first sight seemed to consist of a legend or motto. On looking closer, however, though the pattern still looked as if it was formed out of characters of the alphabet curiously entwined together, you found yourself unable to fix upon any definite word, or even letter. You looked again and again, and the longer that you looked the more certain became your belief that you were on the verge of discovery. If you could approach the mysterious legend from a slightly different point of view, or look at it from another distance, the clew to the puzzle would be seized, and the words would stand forth clear and legible in your sight. But the clew never had been discovered, and the motto, if there was one, remained unread.

For a few minutes we stood looking at the cabinet in silence, and then Lucy gave a discontented little sigh. "There's another tiresome piece of superstition," she exclaimed; "by far the handsomest piece of furniture in the house stuck away here in a bedroom which is hardly ever used. Again and again have I asked George to let me have it moved downstairs, but he won't hear of it."

"Was it not placed here by Dame Alice herself?" I inquired a little reproachfully, for I felt that Lucy was not treating the cabinet with the respect which it really deserved.

"Yes, so they say," she answered; and the tone of light contempt in which she spoke was now pierced by a not unnatural pride in the romantic mysteries of her husband's family. "She placed it here, and it is said, you know, that when the closed cabinet is opened, and the mysterious motto is read, the curse will depart from the Mervyn family."

"But why don't they break it open?" I asked, impatiently. "I am sure that I would never have remained all my life in a house with a thing like that, and not found out in some way or another what was inside it."

"Oh, but that would be quite fatal," answered she. "The curse can only be removed when the cabinet is opened as Dame Alice intended it to be, in an orthodox fashion. If you were to force it open, that could never happen, and the curse would therefore remain for ever."

"And what is the curse?" I asked, with very different feelings to those with which I had timidly approached the same subject with Alan. Lucy was not a Mervyn, and not a person to inspire awe under any circumstances. My instincts were right again, for she turned away with a slight shrug of her shoulders.

"I have no idea," she said. "George and Alan always look portentously solemn and gloomy whenever one mentions the subject, so I don't. If you ask me for the truth, I believe it to be a pure invention, devised by the Mervyns for the purpose of delicately accounting for some of the disreputable actions of their ancestors. For you know, Evie," she added, with a little laugh, "the less said about the character of the family into which your aunt and I have married the better."

The remark made me angry, I don't know why, and I answered stiffly, that as far as I was acquainted with them, I at least saw nothing to complain of.

"Oh, as regards the present generation, no, – except for that poor, wretched Jack," acquiesced Lucy, with her usual imperturbable good- humor.

"And as regards the next?" I suggested, smiling, and already ashamed of my little temper.

"The next is perfect, of course, – poor dear boys." She sighed as she spoke, and I wondered whether she was really as unconscious as she generally appeared to be of the strange dissatisfaction with which her husband seemed to regard his children. Anyhow the mention of them had evidently changed her mood, and almost directly afterwards, with the remark that she must go and look after her guests, who had all arrived by now, she left me to myself.

For some minutes I sat by the bright fire, lost in aimless, wandering thought, which began with Dame Alice and her cabinet, and which ended somehow with Alan's face, as I had last seen it looking up at me in front of the hall-door. When I had reached that point, I roused myself to decide that I had dreamt long enough, and that it was quite time to go down to the guests and to tea. I accordingly donned my best teagown, arranged my hair, and proceeded towards the drawing-room. My way there lay through the great central hall. This apartment was approached from most of the bedrooms in the house through a large, arched doorway at one end of it, which communicated directly with the great staircase. My bedroom, however, which, as I have said, lay among the private apartments of the house, opened into a passage which led into a broad gallery, or upper chamber, stretching right across the end of the hall. From this you descended by means of a small staircase in oak, whose carved balustrade, bending round the corner of the hall, formed one of the prettiest features of the picturesque old room. The barrier which ran along the front of the gallery was in solid oak, and of such a height that, unless standing close up to it, you could neither see nor be seen by the occupants of the room below. On approaching this gallery I heard voices in the hall. They were George's and Alan's, evidently in hot discussion. As I issued from the passage, George was speaking, and his voice had that exasperated tone in which an angry man tries to bring to a close an argument in which he has lost his temper. "For heaven's sake leave it alone, Alan; I neither can nor will interfere. We have enough to bear from these cursed traditions as it is, without adding one which has no foundation whatever to justify it – a mere contemptible piece of superstition."

"No member of our family has a right to call any tradition contemptible which is connected with that place, and you know it," answered Alan; and though he spoke low, his voice trembled with some strong emotion. A first impulse of hesitation which I had had I checked, feeling that as I had heard so much it was fairer to go on, and I advanced to the top of the staircase. Alan stood by the fireplace facing me, but far too occupied to see me. His last speech had seemingly aroused George to fury, for the latter turned on him now with savage passion.

"Damn it all, Alan!" he cried, "can't you be quiet? I will be master in my own house. Take care, I tell you; the curse may not be quite fulfilled yet after all."

As George uttered these words, Alan lifted his eyes to him with a glance of awful horror: his face turned ghastly white; his lips trembled for a moment; and then he answered back with one half- whispered word of supreme appeal – "George!" There was a long- drawn, unutterable anguish in his tone, and his voice, though scarcely audible, penetrated to every corner of the room, and seemed to hang quivering in the air around one after the sound had ceased. Then there was a terrible stillness. Alan stood trembling in every limb, incapable apparently of speech or action, and George faced him, as silent and motionless as he was. For an instant they remained thus, while I looked breathlessly on. Then

George, with a muttered imprecation, turned on his heel and left the room. Alan followed him as he went with dull lifeless eyes; and as the door closed he breathed deeply, with a breath that was almost a groan.

Taking my courage in both hands, I now descended the stairs, and at the sound of my footfall he glanced up, started, and then came rapidly to meet me.

"Evie! you here," he said; "I did not notice you. How long have you been here?" He was still quite white, and I noticed that he panted for breath as he spoke.

"Not long," I answered, timidly, and rather spasmodically; "I only heard a sentence or two. You wanted George to do something about some tradition or other, – and he was angry, – and he said something about the curse."

While I spoke Alan kept his eyes fixed on mine, reading through them, as I knew, into my mind. When I had finished he turned his gaze away satisfied, and answered very quietly, "Yes, that was it." Then he went back to the fireplace, rested his arm against the high mantelpiece above it, and leaning his forehead on his arm, remained silently looking into the fire. I could see by his bent brow and compressed lips that he was engaged upon some earnest train of thought or reasoning, and I stood waiting – worried, puzzled, curious, but above all things, pitiful, and oh! longing so intensely to help him if I could. Presently he straightened himself a little, and addressed me more in his ordinary tone of voice, though without looking round. "So I hear they have changed your room."

"Yes," I answered. And then, flushing rather, "Is that what you and George have been quarreling about?" I received no reply, and taking this silence for assent, I went on deprecatingly, "Because you know, if it was, I think you are rather foolish, Alan. As I understand, two girls are said to have died in that room more than a hundred years ago, and for that reason there is a prejudice against putting a girl to sleep there. That is all. Merely a vague, unreasonable tradition."

Alan took a moment to answer.

"Yes," he said at length, speaking slowly, and as if replying to arguments in his own mind as much as to those which I had uttered. "Yes, it is nothing but a tradition after all, and that of the very vaguest and most unsupported kind."

"Is there even any proof that girls have not slept there since those two died?" I asked. I think that the suggestion conveyed in this question was a relief to him, for after a moment's pause, as if to search his memory, he turned round.

"No," he answered, "I don't think that there is any such proof; and I have no doubt that you are right, and that it is a mere prejudice that makes me dislike your sleeping there."

"Then," I said, with a little assumption of sisterly superiority, "I think George was right, and that you were wrong."

Alan smiled, – a smiled which sat oddly on the still pale face, and in the wearied, worn-looking eyes. "Very likely," he said; "I daresay that I am superstitious. I have had things to make me so." Then coming nearer to me, and laying his hands on my shoulders, he went on, smiling more brightly, "We are a queer-tempered, bad- nerved race, we Mervyns, and you must not take us too seriously, Evie. The best thing that you can do with our odd ways is to ignore them."

"Oh, I don't mind," I answered, laughing, too glad to have won him back to even temporary brightness, "as long as you and George don't come to blows over the question of where I am to sleep; which after all is chiefly my concern, – and Lucy's."

"Well, perhaps it is," he replied, in the same tone; "and now be off to the drawing-room, where Lucy is defending the tea-table single-handed all this time."

I obeyed, and should have gone more cheerfully had I not turned at the doorway to look back at him, and caught one glimpse of his face as he sank heavily down into the large arm-chair by the fireside.

However, by dinner-time he appeared to have dismissed all

painful reflections from his mind, or to have buried them too deep for discovery. The people staying in the house were, in spite of my sense of grievance at their arrival, individually pleasant, and after dinner I discovered them to be socially well assorted. For the first hour or two, indeed, after their arrival, each glared at the other across those triple lines of moral fortification behind which every well-bred Briton takes refuge on appearing at a friend's country-house. But flags of truce were interchanged over the soup, an armistice was agreed upon during the roast, and the terms of a treaty of peace and amity were finally ratified under the sympathetic influence of George's best champagne. For the achievement of this happy result Alan certainly worked hard, and received therefor many a grateful glance from his sister-in-law. He was more excited than I had ever seen him before, and talked brilliantly and well – though perhaps not as exclusively to his neighbors as they may have wished. His eyes and his attention seemed everywhere at once: one moment he was throwing remarks across to some despairing couple opposite, and the next he was breaking an embarrassing pause in the conversation by some rapid sally of nonsense addressed to the table in general. He formed a great contrast to his brother, who sat gloomy and dejected, making little or no response to the advances of the two dowagers between whom he was placed. After dinner the younger members of the party spent the evening by Alan's initiative, and chiefly under his direction, in a series of lively and rather riotous games such as my nursery days had delighted in, and my schoolroom ones had disdained. It was a great and happy surprise to discover that, grown up, I might again enjoy them. I did so, hugely, and when bedtime came all memories more serious than those of "musical chairs" or "follow my leader" had vanished from my mind. I think, from Alan's glance as he handed me my bed candle, that the pleasure and excitement must have improved my looks.

"I hope you have enjoyed your first evening of gayety, Evie," he said.

"I have," I answered, with happy conviction; "and really I believe that it is chiefly owing to you, Alan." He met my smile by another; but I think that there must have been something in his look which recalled other thoughts, for as I started up the stairs I threw a mischievous glance back at him and whispered, "Now for the horrors of the haunted chamber."

He laughed rather loudly, and saying "Good-night, and good-luck," turned to attend to the other ladies.

His wishes were certainly fulfilled. I got to bed quickly, and – as soon as my happy excitement was sufficiently calmed to admit of it – to sleep. The only thing which disturbed me was the wind, which blew fiercely and loudly all the earlier portion of the night, half arousing me more than once. I spoke of it at breakfast the next morning; but the rest of the world seemed to have slept too heavily to have been aware of it.

IV

The men went out shooting directly after breakfast, and we women passed the day in orthodox country-house fashion, – working and eating; walking and riding; driving and playing croquet; and above, beyond, and through all things, chattering. Beyond a passing sigh while I was washing my hands, or a moment of mournful remembrance while I changed my dress, I had scarcely time even to regret the quiet happiness of the week that was past. In the evening we danced in the great hall. I had two valses with Alan. During a pause for breath, I found that we were standing near the fireplace, on the very spot where he and George had stood on the previous afternoon. The recollection made me involuntarily glance up at his face. It looked sad and worried, and the thought suddenly struck me that his extravagant spirits of the night before, and even his quieter, careful cheerfulness of to-night, had been but artificial moods at best. He turned, and finding my eyes fixed on him, at once plunged into conversation, discussed the peculiarities of one of the guests, good-humoredly enough, but with so much fun as to make me laugh in spite of myself. Then we danced again. The plaintive music, the smooth floor, and the partner were all alike perfect, and I experienced that entire delight of physical enjoyment which I believe nothing

268

but a valse under such circumstances can give. When it was over I turned to Alan, and exclaimed with impulsive appeal, "Oh, I am so happy, – you must be happy too!" He smiled rather uncertainly, and answered, "Don't bother yourself about me, Evie, I am all right. I told you that we Mervyns had bad nerves; and I am rather tired. That's all." I was too passionately determined just then upon happiness, and his was too necessary to mine for me not to believe that he was speaking the truth.

We kept up the dancing till Lucy discovered with a shock that midnight had struck, and that Sunday had begun, and we were all sent off to bed. I was not long in making my nightly preparations, and had scarcely inserted myself between the sheets when, with a few long moans, the wind began again, more violently even than the night before. It had been a calm, fine day, and I made wise reflections as I listened upon the uncertainty of the north-country climate. What a tempest it was! How it moaned, and howled, and shrieked! Where had I heard the superstition which now came to my mind, that borne upon the wind come the spirits of the drowned, wailing and crying for the sepulture which had been denied them? But there were other sounds in that wind, too. Evil, murderous thoughts, perhaps, which had never taken body in deeds, but which, caught up in the air, now hurled themselves in impotent fury through the world. How I wished the wind would stop. It seemed full of horrible fancies, and it kept knocking them into my head, and it wouldn't leave off. Fancies, or memories – which? – and my mind reverted with a flash to the fearful thoughts which had haunted it the day before in Dame Alice's tower. It was dark now. Those ghastly intangible shapes must have taken full form and color, peopling the old ruin with their ageless hideousness. And the storm had found them there and borne them along with it as it blew through the creviced walls. That was why the wind's sound struck so strangely on my brain. Ah! I could hear them now, those still living memories of dead horror. Through the window crannies they came shrieking and wailing. They filled the chimney with spirit sobs, and now they were pressing on, crowding through the room, – eager, eager to reach their prey. Nearer they came; – nearer still! They were round my bed now! Through my closed eyelids I could almost see their dreadful shapes; in all my quivering flesh I felt their terrors as they bent over me, – lower, lower...

With a start I aroused myself and sat up. Was I asleep or awake? I was trembling all over still, and it required the greatest effort of courage I had ever made to enable me to spring from my bed and strike a light. What a state my nerves or my digestion must be in! From my childhood the wind had always affected me strangely, and I blamed myself now for allowing my imagination to run away with me at the first. I found a novel which I had brought up to my room with me, one of the modern, Chinese-American school, where human nature is analyzed with the patient, industrious indifference of the true Celestial. I took the book to bed with me, and soon under its soothing influences fell asleep. I dreamt a good deal, – nightmares, the definite recollection of which, as is so often the case, vanished from my mind as soon as I awoke, leaving only a vague impression of horror. They had been connected with the wind, of that alone I was conscious, and I went down to breakfast, maliciously hoping that others' rest had been as much disturbed as my own.

To my surprise, however, I found that I had again been the only sufferer. Indeed, so impressed were most of the party with the quiet in which their night had been passed, that they boldly declared my storm to have been the creature of my dreams. There is nothing more annoying when you feel yourself aggrieved by fate than to be told that your troubles have originated in your own fancy; so I dropped the subject. Though the discussion spread for a few minutes round the whole table, Alan took no part in it. Neither did George, except for what I thought a rather unnecessarily rough expression of his disbelief in the cause of my night's disturbance. As we rose from breakfast I saw Alan glance towards his brother, and make a movement, evidently with the purpose of speaking to him. Whether or not George was aware of the look or action, I cannot say; but at the same moment he made rapidly across the room to where one of his principal guests was standing, and at once engaged him in conversation. So earnestly and so volubly was he borne on, that they were still talking together when we ladies appeared again some minutes later, prepared for our walk to church. That was not the only occasion during the day on which I witnessed as I thought the same by-play going on. Again and again Alan appeared to be making efforts to engage George in private conversation, and again and again the latter successfully eluded him.

The church was about a mile away from the house, and as Lucy did not like having the carriages out on a Sunday, one service a week as a rule contented the household. In the afternoon we took the usual Sunday walk. On returning from it, I had just taken off my outdoor things, and was issuing from my bedroom, when I found myself face to face with Alan. He was coming out of George's study, and had succeeded apparently in obtaining that interview for which he had been all day seeking. One glance at his face told me what its nature had been. We paused opposite each other for a moment, and he looked at me earnestly.

"Are you going to church?" he inquired at last, abruptly.

"No," I answered, with some surprise. "I did not know that any one was going this evening."

"Will you come with me?"

"Yes, certainly; if you don't mind waiting a moment for me to put my things on."

"There's plenty of time," he answered; "meet me in the hall."

A few minutes later we started.

It was a calm, cloudless night, and although the moon was not yet half-full, and already past her meridian, she filled the clear air with gentle light. Not a word broke our silence. Alan walked hurriedly, looking straight before him, his head upright, his lips twitching nervously, while every now and then a half-uttered moan escaped unconsciously from between them. At last I could bear it no longer, and burst forth with the first remark which occurred to me. We were passing a big, black, queer-shaped stone standing in rather a lonely uncultivated spot at one end of the garden. It was an old acquaintance of my childhood;

but my thoughts had been turned towards it now from the fact that I could see it from my bedroom window, and had been struck afresh by its uncouth, incongruous appearance.

"Isn't there some story connected with that stone?" I asked. "I remember that we always called it the Dead Stone as children."

Alan cast a quick, sidelong glance in that direction, and his brows contracted in an irritable frown. "I don't know," he answered shortly; "they say that there is a woman buried beneath it, I believe."

"A woman buried there!" I exclaimed in surprise; "but who?"

"How should I know? They know nothing whatever about it. The place is full of stupid traditions of that kind." Then, looking suspiciously round at me, "Why do you ask?"

"I don't know; it was just something to say," I answered plaintively. His strange mood so worked upon my nerves, that it was all that I could do to restrain my tears. I think that my tone struck his conscience, for he made a few feverish attempts at conversation after that. But they were so entirely abortive that he soon abandoned the effort, and we finished our walk to church as speechlessly as we had begun it.

The service was bright, and the sermon perhaps a little commonplace, but sensible as it seemed to me in matter, and adequate in style. The peaceful evening hymn which followed, the short solemn pause of silent prayer at the end, soothed and refreshed my spirit. A hasty glance at my companion's face as he stood waiting for me in the porch, with the full light from the church streaming round him, assured me that the same influence had touched him too. Haggard and sad he still looked, it is true; but his features were composed, and the expression of actual pain had left his eyes.

Silent as we had come we started homeward through the waning moonlight, but this silence was of a very different nature to the other, and after a minute or two I did not hesitate to break it.

"It was a good sermon?" I observed, interrogatively.

"Yes," he assented, "I suppose you would call it so; but I confess that I should have found the text more impressive without its exposition."

"Poor man!"

"But don't you often find it so?" he asked. "Do you not often wish, to take this evening's instance, that clergymen would infuse themselves with something of St. Paul's own spirit? Then perhaps they would not water all the strength out of his words in their efforts to explain them."

"That is rather a large demand to make upon them, is it not?"

"Is it?" he questioned. "I don't ask them to be inspired saints. I don't expect St. Paul's breadth and depth of thought. But could they not have something of his vigorous completeness, something of the intensity of his feeling and belief? Look at the text of to-night. Did not the preacher's examples and applications take something from its awful unqualified strength?"

"Awful!" I exclaimed, in surprise; "that is hardly the expression I should have used in connection with those words."

"Why not?"

"Oh, I don't know. The text is very beautiful, of course, and at times, when people are tiresome and one ought to be nice to them, it is very difficult to act up to. But – "

"But you think that 'awful' is rather a big adjective to use for so small a duty," interposed Alan, and the moonlight showed the flicker of a smile upon his face. Then he continued, gravely, "I doubt whether you yourself realize the full import of the words. The precept of charity is not merely a code of rules by which to order our conduct to our neighbors; it is the picture of a spiritual condition, and such, where it exists in us, must by its very nature be roused into activity by anything that affects us. So with this particular injunction, every circumstance in our lives is a challenge to it, and in presence of all alike it admits of one attitude only: 'Beareth all things, endureth all things.' I hope it will be long before that 'all' sticks in your gizzard, Evie, – before you come face to face with things which nature cannot bear, and yet which must be borne."

He stopped, his voice quivering; and then after a pause went on again more calmly, "And throughout it is the same. Moral precepts everywhere, which will admit of no compromise, no limitation, and yet which are at war with our strongest passions. If one could only interpose some 'unless,' some 'except,' even an 'until,' which should be short of the grave. But we cannot. The law is infinite, universal, eternal; there is no escape, no repose. Resist, strive, endure, that is the recurring cry; that is existence."

"And peace," I exclaimed, appealingly. "Where is there room for peace, if that be true?"

He sighed for answer, and then in a changed and lower tone added, "However thickly the clouds mass, however vainly we search for a coming glimmer in their midst, we never doubt that the sky IS still beyond – beyond and around us, infinite and infinitely restful."

He raised his eyes as he spoke, and mine followed his. We had entered the wooded glen. Through the scanty autumn foliage we could see the stars shining faintly in the dim moonlight, and beyond them the deep illimitable blue. A dark world it looked, distant and mysterious, and my young spirit rebelled at the consolation offered me.

"Peace seems a long way off," I whispered.

"It is for me," he answered, gently; "not necessarily for you."

"Oh, but I am worse and weaker than you are. If life is to be all warfare, I must be beaten. I cannot always be fighting."

"Cannot you? Evie, what I have been saying is true of every moral law worth having, of every ideal of life worth striving after, that men have yet conceived. But it is only half the truth of Christianity. You know that. We must strive, for the promise is to him that overcometh; but though our aim be even higher than is that of others, we cannot in the end fail to reach it. The victory of the

Cross is ours. You know that? You believe that?"

"Yes" I answered, softly, too surprised to say more. In speaking of religion he, as a rule, showed to the full the reserve which is characteristic of his class and country, and this sudden outburst was in itself astonishing; but the eager anxiety with which he emphasized the last words of appeal impressed and bewildered me still further. We walked on for some minutes in silence. Then suddenly Alan stopped, and turning, took my hand in his. In what direction his mind had been working in the interval I could not divine; but the moment he began to speak I felt that he was now for the first time giving utterance to what had been really at the bottom of his thoughts the whole evening. Even in that dim light I could see the anxious look upon his face, and his voice shook with restrained emotion.

"Evie," he said, "have you ever thought of the world in which our spirits dwell, as our bodies do in this one of matter and sense, and of how it may be peopled? I know," he went on hurriedly, "that it is the fashion nowadays to laugh at such ideas. I envy those who have never had cause to be convinced of their reality, and I hope that you may long remain among the number. But should that not be so, should those unseen influences ever touch your life, I want you to remember then, that, as one of the race for whom Christ died, you have as high a citizenship in that spirit land as any creature there: that you are your own soul's warden, and that neither principalities nor powers can rob you of that your birthright."

I think my face must have shown my bewilderment, for he dropped my hand, and walked on with an impatient sigh.

"You don't understand me. Why should you? I dare-say that I am talking nonsense – only – only – "

His voice expressed such an agony of doubt and hesitation that I burst out –

"I think that I do understand you a little, Alan. You mean that even from unearthly enemies there is nothing that we need really fear – at least, that is, I suppose, nothing worse than death.

But that is surely enough!"

"Why should you fear death?" he said, abruptly; "your soul will live."

"Yes, I know that, but still – " I stopped with a shudder.

"What is life after all but one long death?" he went on, with sudden violence. "Our pleasures, our hopes, our youth are all dying; ambition dies, and even desire at last; our passions and tastes will die, or will live only to mourn their dead opportunity. The happiness of love dies with the loss of the loved, and, worst of all, love itself grows old in our hearts and dies. Why should we shrink only from the one death which can free us from all the others?"

"It is not true, Alan!" I cried, hotly. "What you say is not true. There are many things even here which are living and shall live; and if it were otherwise, in everything, life that ends in death is better than no life at all."

"You say that," he answered, "because for you these things are yet living. To leave life now, therefore, while it is full and sweet, untainted by death, surely that is not a fate to fear. Better, a thousand times better, to see the cord cut with one blow while it is still whole and strong, and to launch out straight into the great ocean, than to sit watching through the slow years, while strand after strand, thread by thread, loosens and unwinds itself, – each with its own separate pang breaking, bringing the bitterness of death without its release.

His manner, the despairing ring in his voice, alarmed me even more than his words. Clinging to his arm with both hands, while the tears sprang to my eyes –

"Alan," I cried, "don't say such things, – don't talk like that. You are making me miserable."

He stopped short at my words, with bent head, his features hidden in the shadow thus cast upon them, – nothing in his motionless form to show what was passing within him. Then he looked up, and turned his face to the moonlight and to me, laying his hand on one of mine.

"Don't be afraid," he said; "it is all right, my little David. You have driven the evil spirit away." And lifting my hand, he pressed it gently to his lips. Then drawing it within his arm, he went on, as he walked forward, "And even when it was on me at its worst, I was not meditating suicide, as I think you imagine. I am a very average specimen of humanity, – neither brave enough to defy the possibilities of eternity nor cowardly enough to shirk those of time. No, I was only trying idiotically to persuade a girl of eighteen that life was not worth living; and more futilely still, myself, that I did not wish her to live. I am afraid, that in my mind philosophy and fact have but small connection with each other; and though my theorizing for your welfare may be true enough, yet, – I cannot help it, Evie, – it would go terribly hard with me if anything were to happen to you."

His voice trembled as he finished. My fear had gone with his return to his natural manner, but my bewilderment remained.

"Why SHOULD there anything happen to me?" I asked.

"That is just it," he answered, after a pause, looking straight in front of him and drawing his hand wearily over his brow. "I know of no reason why there should." Then giving a sigh, as if finally to dismiss from his mind a worrying subject – "I have acted for the best," he said, "and may God forgive me if I have done wrong."

There was a little silence after that, and then he began to talk again, steadily and quietly. The subject was deep enough still, as deep as any that we had touched upon, but both voice and senti- ment were calm, bringing peace to my spirit, and soon making me forget the wonder and fear of a few moments before. Very openly did he talk as we passed on across the long trunk shadows and through the glades of silver light; and I saw farther then into the most sacred recesses of his soul than I have ever done before or since.

When we reached home the moon had already set; but some of her beams seemed to have been left behind within my heart, so pure and peaceful was the light which filled it.

The same feeling continued with me all through that evening. After dinner some of the party played and sang. As it was Sunday, and Lucy was rigid in her views, the music was of a sacred character. I sat in a low armchair in a dark corner of the room, my mind too dreamy to think, and too passive to dream. I hardly interchanged three words with Alan, who remained in a still darker spot, invisible and silent the whole time. Only as we left the room to go to bed, I heard Lucy ask him if he had a headache. I did not hear his answer, and before I could see his face he had turned back again into the drawing-room.

V

It was early, and when first I got to my room I felt little inclined for sleep. I wandered to the window, and drawing aside the curtains, looked out upon the still, starlit sky. At least I should rest quiet to-night. The air was very clear, and the sky seemed full of stars. As I stood there scraps of schoolroom learning came back to my mind. That the stars were all suns, surrounded perhaps in their turn by worlds as large or larger than our own. Worlds beyond worlds, and others farther still, which no man might number or even descry. And about the distance of those wonderful suns too, – that one, for instance, at which I was looking, – what was it that I had been told? That our world was not yet peopled, perhaps not yet formed, when the actual spot of light which now struck my sight first started from the star's surface! While it flashed along, itself the very symbol of speed, the whole of mankind had had time to be born, and live, and die!

My gaze dropped, and fell upon the dim, half-seen outline of the Dead Stone. That woman too. While that one ray speeded towards me her life had been lived and ended, and her body had rotted away into the ground. How close together we all were! Her life and mine; our joys, sufferings, deaths – all crowded together into the space of one flash of light! And yet there was nothing there but a horrible skeleton of dead bones, while I – !

I stopped with a shudder, and turned back into the room. I

wished that Alan had not told me what lay under the stone; I wished that I had never asked him. It was a ghastly thing to think about, and spoilt all the beauty of the night to me.

I got quickly into bed, and soon dropped asleep. I do not know how long I slept; but when I woke it was with the consciousness again of that haunting wind.

It was worse than ever. The world seemed filled with its din. Hurling itself passionately against the house, it gathered strength with every gust, till it seemed as if the old walls must soon crash in ruins round me. Gust upon gust; blow upon blow; swelling, lessening, never ceasing. The noise surrounded me; it penetrated my inmost being, as all-pervading as silence itself, and wrapping me in a solitude even more complete. There was nothing left in the world but the wind and I, and then a weird intangible doubt as to my own identity seized me. The wind was real, the wind with its echoes of passion and misery from the eternal abyss; but was there anything else? What was, and what had been, the world of sense and of knowledge, my own consciousness, my very self, – all seemed gathered up and swept away in that one sole-existent fury of sound.

I pulled myself together, and getting out of bed, groped my way to the table which stood between the bed and the fireplace. The matches were there, and my half-burnt candle, which I lit. The wind penetrating the rattling casement circled round the room, and the flame of my candle bent and flared and shrank before it, throwing strange moving lights and shadows in every corner. I stood there shivering in my thin nightdress, half stunned by the cataract of noise beating on the walls outside, and peered anxiously around me. The room was not the same. Something was changed. What was it? How the shadows leaped and fell, dancing in time to the wind's music. Everything seemed alive. I turned my head slowly to the left, and then to the right, and then round – and stopped with a sudden gasp of fear.

The cabinet was open!

I looked away, and back, and again. There was no room for doubt. The doors were thrown back, and were waving gently in the draught. One of the lower drawers was pulled out, and in a sudden flare of the candle-light I could see something glistening at its bottom. Then the light dwindled again, the candle was almost out, and the cabinet showed a dim black mass in the darkness. Up and down went the flame, and each returning brightness flashed back at me from the thing inside the drawer. I stood fascinated, my eyes fixed upon the spot, waiting for the fitful glitter as it came and went. What was there there? I knew that I must go and see, but I did not want to. If only the cabinet would close again before I looked, before I knew what was inside it. But it stood open, and the glittering thing lay there, dragging me towards itself.

Slowly at last, and with infinite reluctance, I went. The drawer was lined with soft white satin, and upon the satin lay a long, slender knife, hilted and sheathed in antique silver, richly set with jewels. I took it up and turned back to the table to examine it. It was Italian in workmanship, and I knew that the carving and chasing of the silver were more precious even than the jewels which studded it, and whose rough setting gave so firm a grasp to my hand. Was the blade as fair as the covering, I wondered? A little resistance at first, and then the long thin steel slid easily out. Sharp, and bright, and finely tempered it looked with its deadly, tapering point. Stains, dull and irregular, crossed the fine engraving on its surface and dimmed its polish. I bent to examine them more closely, and as I did so a sudden stronger gust of wind blew out the candle. I shuddered a little at the darkness and looked up. But it did not matter: the curtain was still drawn away from the window opposite my bedside, and through it a flood of moonlight was pouring in upon floor and bed.

Putting the sheath down upon the table, I walked to the window to examine the knife more closely by that pale light. How gloriously brilliant it was! darkened now and again by the quickly passing shadows of wind-driven clouds. At least so I thought, and I glanced up and out of the window to see them. A black world met my gaze. Neither moon was there nor moonlight: the broad silver beam in which I stood stretched no farther than the window. I caught my breath, and my limbs stiffened as I looked.

No moon, no cloud, no movement in the clear, calm, starlit sky; while still the ghastly light stretched round me, and the spectral shadows drifted across the room.

But it was not all dark outside: one spot caught my eye, bright with a livid unearthly brightness – the Dead Stone shining out into the night like an ember from hell's furnace! There was a horrid semblance of life in the light, – a palpitating, breathing glow, – and my pulses beat in time to it, till I seemed to be drawing it into my veins. It had no warmth, and as it entered my blood my heart grew colder, and my muscles more rigid. My fingers clutched the dagger-hilt till its jeweled roughness pressed painfully into my palm. All the strength of my strained powers seemed gathered in that grasp, and the more tightly I held the more vividly did the rock gleam and quiver with infernal life. The dead woman! The dead woman! What had I to do with her? Let her bones rest in the filth of their own decay, – out there under the accursed stone.

And now the noise of the wind lessens in my ears. Let it go on, – yes, louder and wilder, drowning my senses in its tumult. What is there with me in the room – the great empty room behind me? Nothing; only the cabinet with its waving doors. They are waving to and fro, to and fro – I know it. But there is no other life in the room but that – no, no; no other life in the room but that.

Oh! don't let the wind stop. I can't hear anything while it goes on; – but if it stops! Ah! the gusts grow weaker, struggling, forced into rest. Now – now – they have ceased.

Silence!

A fearful pause.

What is that that I hear? There, behind me in the room?

Do I hear it? Is there anything?

The throbbing of my own blood in my ears.

No, no! There is something as well, – something outside myself.

What is it?

Low; heavy; regular.

God! it is – it is the breath of a living creature! A living creature! here – close to me – alone with me!

The numbness of terror conquers me. I can neither stir nor speak. Only my whole soul strains at my ears to listen.

Where does the sound come from?

Close behind me – close.

Ah-h!

It is from there – from the bed where I was lying a moment ago!...

I try to shriek, but the sound gurgles unuttered in my throat. I clutch the stone mullions of the window, and press myself against the panes. If I could but throw myself out! – anywhere, anywhere – away from that dreadful sound – from that thing close behind me in the bed! But I can do nothing. The wind has broken forth again now; the storm crashes round me. And still through it all I hear the ghastly breathing – even, low, scarcely audible – but I hear it. I shall hear it as long as I live!...

Is the thing moving?

Is it coming nearer?

No, no; not that, – that was but a fancy to freeze me dead.

But to stand here, with that creature behind me, listening, waiting for the warm horror of its breath to touch my neck! Ah! I cannot. I will look. I will see it face to face. Better any agony than this one.

Slowly, with held breath, and eyes aching in their stretched fixity, I turn. There it is! Clear in the moonlight I see the monstrous form within the bed, – the dark coverlet rises and falls with its heaving breath... Ah! heaven have mercy! Is there none to help, none to save me from this awful presence?...

And the knife-hilt draws my fingers round it, while my flesh quivers, and my soul grows sick with loathing. The wind howls, the shadows chase through the room, hunting with fearful darkness more fearful light; and I stand looking,... listening...

*****

I must not stand here for ever; I must be up and doing. What a noise the wind makes, and the rattling of the windows and the doors. If he sleeps through this he will sleep through all. Noiselessly my bare feet tread the carpet as I approach the bed; noiselessly my left arm raises the heavy curtain. What does it hide? Do I not know? The bestial features, half-hidden in coarse, black growth; the muddy, blotched skin, oozing foulness at every pore. Oh, I know them too well! What a monster it is! How the rank breath gurgles through his throat in his drunken sleep. The eyes are closed now, but I know them too; their odious leer, and the venomous hatred with which they can glare at me from their bloodshot setting. But the time has come at last. Never again shall their passion insult me, or their fury degrade me in slavish terror. There he lies; there at my mercy, the man who for fifteen years has made God's light a shame to me, and His darkness a terror. The end has come at last, – the only end possible, the only end left me. On his head be the blood and the crime! God almighty, I am not guilty! The end has come; I can bear my burden no farther.

"Beareth all things, endureth all things."

Where have I heard those words? They are in the Bible; the precept of charity. What has that to do with me? Nothing. I heard the words in my dreams somewhere. A white-faced man said them, a white-faced man with pure eyes. To me? – no, no, not to me; to a girl it was – an ignorant, innocent girl, and she accepted them as an eternal, unqualified law. Let her bear but half that I have borne, let her endure but one-tenth of what I have endured, and then if she dare let her speak in judgment against me.

Softly now; I must draw the heavy coverings away, and bare his breast to the stroke, – the stroke that shall free me. I know well where to plant it; I have learned that from the old lady's Italian. Did he guess why I questioned him so closely of the surest, straightest road to a man's heart? No matter, he cannot hinder me now. Gently! Ah! I have disturbed him. He moves, mutters in his sleep, throws out his arm. Down; down; crouching behind the curtain. Heavens! if he wakes and sees me, he will kill me. No! alas! if only he would. I would kiss the hand that he struck me with; but he is too cruel for that. He will imagine some new and more hellish torture to punish me with. But the knife! I have got that; he shall never touch me living again... He is quieter now. I hear his breath, hoarse and heavy as a wild beast's panting. He draws it more evenly, more deeply. The danger is past. Thank God!

God! What have I to do with Him? A God of Judgment. Ha, ha! Hell cannot frighten me; it will not be worse than earth. Only he will be there too. Not with him, not with him, – send me to the lowest circle of torment, but not with him. There, his breast is bare now. Is the knife sharp? Yes; and the blade is strong enough. Now let me strike – myself afterwards if need be, but him first. Is it the devil that prompts me? Then the devil is my friend, and the friend of the world. No. God is a God of love. He cannot wish such a man to live. He made him, but the devil spoilt him; and let the devil have his handiwork back again. It has served him long enough here; and its last service shall be to make me a murderess.

How the moonlight gleams from the blade as my arm swings up and back: with how close a grasp the rough hilt draws my fingers round it. Now.

A murderess?

Wait a moment. A moment may make me free; a moment may make me – that!

Wait.

Hand and dagger droop again. His life has dragged its slime over my soul; shall his death poison it with a fouler corruption still?

"My own soul's warden."

What was that? Dream memories again.

"Resist, strive, endure."

Easy words. What do they mean for me? To creep back now to bed by his side, and to begin living again to-morrow the life which I have lived to-day? No, no; I cannot do it. Heaven cannot ask it of me. And there is no other way. That or this; this or that. Which shall it be? Ah! I have striven, God knows. I have endured so long that I hoped even to do so to the end. But to-day! Oh! the torment and the outrage: body and soul still bear the stain of it. I thought that my heart and my pride were dead together, but he has stung them again into aching, shameful life. Yesterday I might have spared him, to save my own cold soul from sin; but now it is cold no longer. It burns, it burns and the fire must be slaked.

Ay, I will kill him, and have done with it. Why should I pause any longer? The knife drags my hand back for the stroke. Only the dream surrounds me; the pure man's face is there, white, beseeching, and God's voice rings in my heart –

"To him that overcometh."

But I cannot overcome. Evil has governed my life, and evil is stronger than I am. What shall I do? what shall I do? God, if Thou art stronger than evil, fight for me.

"The victory of the Cross is ours."

Yes, I know it. It is true, it is true. But the knife? I cannot loose the knife if I would. How to wrench it from my own hold? Thou God of Victory be with me! Christ help me!

I seize the blade with my left hand; the two-edged steel slides through my grasp; a sharp pain in fingers and palm; and then – nothing...

*****

VI

When I again became conscious, I found myself half kneeling, half lying across the bed, my arms stretched out in front of me, my face buried in the clothes. Body and mind were alike numbed. A smarting pain in my left hand, a dreadful terror in my heart, were at first the only sensations of which I was aware. Slowly, very slowly, sense and memory returned to me, and with them a more vivid intensity of mental anguish, as detail by detail I recalled the weird horror of the night. Had it really happened, – was the thing still there, – or was it all a ghastly nightmare? It was some minutes before I dared either to move or look up, and then fearfully I raised my head. Before me stretched the smooth white coverlet, faintly bright with yellow sunshine. Weak and giddy, I struggled to my feet, and, steadying myself against the foot of the bed, with clenched teeth and bursting heart, forced my gaze round to the other end. The pillow lay there, bare and un-marked save for what might well have been the pressure of my own head. My breath came more freely, and I turned to the win-dow. The sun had just risen, the golden tree-tops were touched with light, faint threads of mist hung here and there across the sky, and the twittering of birds sounded clearly through the crisp autumn air.

It was nothing but a bad dream then, after all, this horror which still hung round me, leaving me incapable of effort, almost of thought. I remembered the cabinet, and looked swiftly in that direction. There it stood, closed as usual, closed as it had been the evening before, as it had been for the last three hundred years, except in my dreams.

Yes, that was it; nothing but a dream, – a gruesome, haunt-ing dream. With an instinct of wiping out the dreadful memory, I raised my hand wearily to my forehead. As I did so, I became conscious again of how it hurt me. I looked at it. It was covered with half-dried blood, and two straight clean cuts appeared, one across the palm and one across the inside of the fingers just below the knuckles. I looked again towards the bed, and, in the place where my hand had rested during my faint, a small patch of red blood was to be seen.

Then it was true! Then it had all happened! With a low shud-dering sob I threw myself down upon the couch at the foot of the bed, and lay there for some minutes, my limbs trembling, and my soul shrinking within me. A mist of evil, fearful and loathsome, had descended upon my girlhood's life, sullying its ignorant innocence, saddening its brightness, as I felt, for ever. I lay there till my teeth began to chatter, and I realized that I was bitterly cold. To return to that accursed bed was impossible, so I pulled a rug which hung at one end of the sofa over me, and, utterly worn out in mind and body, fell uneasily asleep.

I was roused by the entrance of my maid. I stopped her exclamations and questions by shortly stating that I had had a bad night, had been unable to rest in bed, and had had an accident with my hand, – without further specifying of what description.

"I didn't know that you had been feeling unwell when you went to bed last night, miss," she said.

"When I went to bed last night? Unwell? What do you mean?"

"Only Mr. Alan has just asked me to let him know how you find yourself this morning," she answered.

Then he expected something, dreaded something. Ah! why had he yielded and allowed me to sleep here, I asked myself bitterly, as the incidents of the day before flashed through my mind.

"Tell him," I said, "what I have told you; and say that I wish to speak to him directly after breakfast." I could not confide my story to any one else, but speak of it I must to some one or go mad.

Every moment passed in that place was an added misery. Much to my maid's surprise I said that I would dress in her room – the little one which, as I have said, was close to my own. I felt better there; but my utter fatigue and my wounded hand combined to make my toilet slow, and I found that most of the party had finished breakfast when I reached the dining-room. I was glad of this, for even as it was I found it difficult enough to give coherent answers to the questions which my white face and bandaged hand called forth. Alan helped me by giving a resolute turn to the conversation. Once only our eyes met across the table. He looked as haggard and worn as I did: I learned afterwards that he had passed most of that fearful night pacing the passage outside my door, though he listened in vain for any indication of what was going on within the room.

The moment I had finished breakfast he was by my side. "You wish to speak to me? now?" he asked in a low tone.

"Yes; now," I answered, breathlessly, and without raising my eyes from the ground.

"Where shall we go? Outside? It is a bright day, and we shall be freer there from interruption."

I assented; and then looking up at him appealingly, "Will you fetch my things for me? I CANNOT go up to that room again."

He seemed to understand me, nodded, and was gone. A few minutes later we left the house, and made our way in silence towards a grassy spot on the side of the ravine where we had already indulged in more than one friendly talk.

As we went, the Dead Stone came for a moment into view. I seized Alan's arm in an almost convulsive grip. "Tell me," I whispered, – "you refused to tell me yesterday, but you must now, – who is buried beneath that rock?"

There was now neither timidity nor embarrassment in my tone. The horrors of that house had become part of my life for ever, and their secrets were mine by right. Alan, after a moment's pause, a questioning glance at my face, tacitly accepted the position.

"I told you the truth," he replied, "when I said that I did not know; but I can tell you the popular tradition on the subject, if you like. They say that Margaret Mervyn, the woman who murdered her husband, is buried there, and that Dame Alice had the rock placed over her grave, – whether to save it from insult or to mark it out for opprobrium, I never heard. The poor people about here do not care to go near the place after dark, and among the older ones there are still some, I believe, who spit at the suicide's grave as they pass."

"Poor woman, poor woman!" I exclaimed, in a burst of uncontrollable compassion.

"Why should you pity her?" demanded he with sudden sternness; "she WAS a suicide and a murderess too. It would be better for the public conscience, I believe, if such were still hung in chains, or buried at the cross-roads with a stake through their bodies."

"Hush, Alan, hush!" I cried hysterically, as I clung to him; "don't speak harshly of her: you do not know, you cannot tell, how terribly she was tempted. How can you?"

He looked down at me in bewildered surprise. "How can I?" he repeated. "You speak as if YOU could. What do you mean?"

"Don't ask me," I answered, turning towards him my face, – white, quivering, tear-stained. "Don't ask me. Not now. You must answer my questions first, and after that I will tell you. But I cannot talk of it now. Not yet."

We had reached the place we were in search of as I spoke. There, where the spreading roots of a great beech-tree formed a natural resting place upon the steep side of the ravine, I took my seat, and Alan stretched himself upon the grass beside me. Then looking up at me – "I do not know what questions you would ask," he said, quietly; "but I will answer them, whatever they may be."

But I did not ask them yet. I sat instead with my hands clasping my knee, looking opposite at the glory of harmonious color, or down the glen at the vista of far-off, dream-like loveliness, on which it opened out. The yellow autumn sunshine made everything golden, the fresh autumn breezes filled the air with life; but to me a loathsome shadow seemed to rest upon all, and to stretch itself out far beyond where my eyes could reach, befouling the beauty of the whole wide world. At last I spoke. "You have known of it all, I suppose; of this curse that is in the world, – sin and suffering, and what such words mean."

"Yes," he said, looking at me with wondering pity, "I am afraid so."

"But have you known them as they are known to some, – agonized, hopeless suffering, and sin that is all but inevitable?

Some time in your life probably you have realized that such things are: it has come home to you, and to every one else, no doubt, except a few ignorant girls such as I was yesterday. But there are some, – yes, thousands and thousands, – who even now, at this moment, are feeling sorrow like that, are sinking deep, deeper into the bottomless pit of their soul's degradation. And yet men who know this, who have seen it, laugh, talk, are happy, amuse themselves – how can they, how can they?" I stopped with a catch in my voice, and then stretching out my arms in front of me – "And it is not only men. Look how beautiful the earth is, and God has made it, and lets the sun crown it every day with a new glory, while this horror of evil broods over and poisons it all. Oh, why is it so? I cannot understand it."

My arms drooped again as I finished, and my eyes sought Alan's. His were full of tears, but there was almost a smile quivering at the corners of his lips as he replied: "When you have found an answer to that question, Evie, come and tell me and mankind at large: it will be news to us all." Then he continued – "But, after all, the earth is beautiful, and the sun does shine: we have our own happiness to rejoice in, our own sorrows to bear, the suffering that is near to us to grapple with. For the rest, for this blackness of evil which surrounds us, and which we can do nothing to lighten, it will soon, thank God, become vague and far off to you as it is to others: your feeling of it will be dulled, and, except at moments, you too will forget."

"But that is horrible," I exclaimed, passionately; "the evil will be there all the same, whether I feel it or not. Men and women will be struggling in their misery and sin, only I shall be too selfish to care."

"We cannot go outside the limits of our own nature," he replied; "our knowledge is shallow and our spiritual insight dark, and God in His mercy has made our hearts shallow too, and our imagination dull. If, knowing and trusting only as men do, we were to feel as angels feel, earth would be hell indeed."

It was cold comfort, but at that moment anything warmer or brighter would have been unreal and utterly repellent to me. I hardly took in the meaning of his words, but it was as if a hand had been stretched out to me, struggling in the deep mire, by one who himself felt solid ground beneath him. Where he stood I also might some day stand, and that thought seemed to make patience possible.

It was he who first broke the silence which followed. "You were saying that you had questions to ask me. I am impatient to put mine in return, so please go on."

It had been a relief to me to turn even to generalizations of despair from the actual horror which had inspired them, and to which my mind was thus recalled. With an effort I replied, "Yes, I want to ask you about that room – the room in which I slept, and – and the murder which was committed there." In spite of all that I could do, my voice sank almost to a whisper as I concluded, and I was trembling from head to foot.

"Who told you that a murder was committed there?" Something in my face as he asked the question made him add quickly, "Never mind. You are right. That is the room in which Hugh Mervyn was murdered by his wife. I was surprised at your question, for I did not know that anyone but my brothers and myself were aware of the fact. The subject is never mentioned: it is closely connected with one intensely painful to our family, and besides, if spoken of, there would be inconveniences arising from the superstitious terrors of servants, and the natural dislike of guests to sleep in a room where such a thing had happened. Indeed it was largely with the view of wiping out the last memory of the crime's locality, that my father renewed the interior of the room some twenty years ago. The only tradition which has been adhered to in connection with it is the one which has now been violated in your person – the one which precludes any unmarried woman from sleeping there. Except for that, the room has, as you know, lost all sinister reputation, and its title of 'haunted' has become purely conventional. Nevertheless, as I said, you are right – that is undoubtedly the room in which the murder was committed."

He stopped and looked up at me, waiting for more.

"Go on; tell me about it, and what followed." My lips formed the words; my heart beat too faintly for my breath to utter them.

"About the murder itself there is not much to tell. The man, I believe, was an inhuman scoundrel, and the woman first killed him in desperation, and afterwards herself in despair. The only detail connected with the actual crime of which I have ever heard, was the gale that was blowing that night – the fiercest known to this countryside in that generation; and it has always been said since that any misfortune to the Mervyns – especially any misfortune connected with the curse – comes with a storm of wind. That was why I so disliked your story of the imaginary tempests which have disturbed your nights since you slept there. As to what followed," – he gave a sigh, – "that story is long enough and full of incident. On the morning after the murder, so runs the tale, Dame Alice came down to the Grange from the tower to which she had retired when her son's wickednesses had driven her from his house, and there in the presence of the two corpses she foretold the curse which should rest upon their descendants for generations to come. A clergyman who was present, horrified, it is said at her words, adjured her by the mercy of Heaven to place some term to the doom which she had pronounced. She replied that no mortal might reckon the fruit of a plant which drew its life from hell; that a term there should be, but as it passed the wisdom of man to fix it, so it should pass the wit of man to discover it. She then placed in the room this cabinet, constructed by herself and her Italian follower, and said that the curse should not depart from the family until the day when its doors were unlocked and its legend read.

"Such is the story. I tell it to you as it was told to me. One thing only is certain, that the doom thus traditionally foretold has been only too amply fulfilled."

"And what was the doom?"

Alan hesitated a little, and when he spoke his voice was almost awful in its passionless sternness, in its despairing finality; it seemed to echo the irrevocable judgment which his words pronounced: "That the crimes against God and each other which had destroyed the parents' life should enter into the children's blood, and that never thereafter should there fail a Mervyn to bring shame or death upon one generation of his father's house.

"There were two sons of that ill-fated marriage," he went on after a pause, "boys at the time of their parents' death. When they grew up they both fell in love with the same woman, and one killed the other in a duel. The story of the next generation was a peculiarly sad one. Two brothers took opposite sides during the civil troubles; but so fearful were they of the curse which lay upon the family, that they chiefly made use of their mutual position in order to protect and guard each other. After the wars were over, the younger brother, while traveling upon some parliamentary commission, stopped a night at the Grange. There, through a mistake, he exchanged the report which he was bringing to London for a packet of papers implicating his brother and several besides in a royalist plot. He only discovered his error as he handed the papers to his superior, and was but just able to warn his brother in time for him to save his life by flight. The other men involved were taken and executed, and as it was known by what means information had reached the Government, the elder Mervyn was universally charged with the vilest treachery. It is said that when after the Restoration his return home was rumored the neighboring gentry assembled, armed with riding whips, to flog him out of the country if he should dare to show his face there. He died abroad, shame-stricken and broken-hearted. It was his son, brought up by his uncle in the sternest tenets of Puritanism, who, coming home after a lengthened journey, found that during his absence his sister had been shamefully seduced. He turned her out of doors, then and there, in the midst of a bitter January night, and the next morning her dead body and that of her new-born infant were found half buried in the fresh-fallen snow on the top of the wolds. The 'white lady' is still supposed by the villagers to haunt that side of the glen. And so it went on. A beautiful, heartless Mervyn in Queen Anne's time enticed away the affections of her sister's betrothed, and on the day of her own wedding with him, her forsaken sister was found drowned by her own act in the pond at the bottom of the garden. Two brothers were soldiers together in some Continental war, and one was involuntarily the means of discovering and exposing the treason of the other. A girl was betrayed into a false marriage, and her life ruined by a man who came into the house as her brother's friend, and whose infamous designs were forwarded and finally accomplished by that same brother's active though unsuspecting assistance. Generation after generation, men or women, guilty or innocent, through the action of their own will or in spite of it, the curse has never yet failed of its victims."

"Never yet? But surely in our own time – your father?" I did not dare to put the question which was burning my lips.

"Have you never heard of the tragic end of my poor young uncles?" he replied. "They were several years older than my father. When boys of fourteen and fifteen they were sent out with the keeper for their first shooting lesson, and the elder shot his brother through the heart. He himself was delicate, and they say that he never entirely recovered from the shock. He died before he was twenty, and my father, then a child of seven years old, became the heir. It was partly, no doubt, owing to this calamity having thus occurred before he was old enough to feel it, that his comparative skepticism on the whole subject was due. To that I suppose, and to the fact that he grew up in an age of railways and liberal culture."

"He didn't believe, then, in the curse?"

"Well, rather, he thought nothing about it. Until, that is, the time came when it took effect, to break his heart and end his life."

"How do you mean?"

There was silence for a little. Alan had turned away his head, so that I could not see his face. Then –

"I suppose you have never been told the true story of why Jack left the country?"

"No. Was he – is he – ?"

"He is one victim of the curse in this generation, and I, God help me, am the other, and perhaps more wretched one."

His voice trembled and broke, and for the first time that day I almost forgot the mysterious horror of the night before, in my pity for the actual, tangible suffering before me. I stretched out my hand to his, and his fingers closed on mine with a sudden, painful grip. Then quietly –

"I will tell you the story," he said, "though since that miserable time I have spoken of it to no one."

There was a pause before he began. He lay there by my side, his gaze turned across me up the sunbright, autumn-tinted glen, but his eyes shadowed by the memories which he was striving to recall and arrange in due order in his mind. And when he did speak it was not directly to begin the promised recital.

"You never knew Jack," he said, abruptly.

"Hardly," I acquiesced. "I remember thinking him very handsome."

"There could not be two opinions as to that," he answered. "And a man who could have done anything he liked with life, had things gone differently. His abilities were fine, but his strength lay above all in his character: he was strong, – strong in his likes and in his dislikes, resolute, fearless, incapable of half measures – a man, every inch of him. He was not generally popular – stiff, hard, unsympathetic, people called him. From one point of view, and one only, he perhaps deserved the epithets. If a woman lost his respect she seemed to lose his pity too. Like a mediaeval monk, he looked upon such rather as the cause than the result of male depravity, and his contempt for them mingled with anger, almost, as I sometimes thought, with hatred. And this attitude was, I have no doubt, resented by the men of his own class and set, who shared neither his faults nor his virtues. But in other ways he was not hard. He could love; I, at least, have cause to know it. If you would hear his story rightly from my lips, Evie, you must try and see him with my eyes. The friend who loved me, and whom I loved with the passion which, if not the strongest, is certainly, I believe, the most enduring of which men are capable, – that perfect brother's love, which so grows into our being that when it is at peace we are scarcely conscious of its existence, and when it is wounded our very life-blood seems to flow at the stroke. Brothers do not always love like that: I can only wish that we had not done so.

VII

"Well, about five years ago, before I had taken my degree, I became acquainted with a woman whom I will call 'Delia,' – it is near enough to the name by which she went. She was a few years older than myself, very beautiful, and I believed her to be what she described herself – the innocent victim of circumstance and false appearance, a helpless prey to the vile calumnies of worldlings. In sober fact, I am afraid that, whatever her life may have been actually at the time that I knew her – a subject which I have never cared to investigate – her past had been not only bad enough irretrievably to fix her position in society, but bad enough to leave her without an ideal in the world, though still retaining within her heart the possibilities of a passion which, from the moment that it came to life, was strong enough to turn her whole existence into one desperate reckless straining after an object hopelessly beyond her reach. That was the woman with whom, at the age of twenty, I fancied myself in love. She wanted to get a husband, and she thought me – rightly – ass enough to accept the post. I was very young then even for my years, – a student, an idealist, with an imagination highly developed, and no knowledge whatever of the world as it actually is. Anyhow, before I had known her a month, I had determined to make her my wife. My parents were abroad at the time, George and Lucy here, so that it was to Jack that I imparted the news of my resolve. As you may imagine, he did all that he could to shake it. But I was immovable. I disbelieved his facts, and despised his contempt from the standpoint of my own superior morality. This state of things continued for several weeks, during the greater part of which time I was at Oxford. I only knew that while I was there, Jack had made Delia's acquaintance, and was apparently cultivating it assiduously.

"One day, during the Easter vacation, I got a note from her asking me to supper at her house. Jack was invited too: we lodged together while my people were away.

"There is no need to dwell upon that supper. There were two or three women there of her own sort, or worse, and a dozen men from among the most profligate in London. The conversation was, I should think, bad even for that class; and she, the goddess of my idolatry, outstripped them all by the foul, coarse shamelessness of her language and behavior. Before the entertainment was half over, I rose and took my leave, accompanied by Jack and another man, – Legard was his name, – who I presume was bored. Just as we had passed through into the anteroom, which lay beyond the one in which we had been eating, Delia followed us, and laying her hand on Jack's arm, said that she must speak with him. Legard and I went into the outer hall, and we had not been there more than a minute when the door from the anteroom opened, and we heard Delia's voice. I remember the words well, – that was not the only occasion on which I was to hear them. 'I will keep the ring as a record of my love,' she said, 'and understand, that though you may forget, I never shall.' Jack came through, the door closed, and as we went out I glanced towards his left hand, and saw, as I expected to see, the absence of the ring which he usually wore there. It contained a gem which my mother had picked up in the East, and I knew that he valued it quite peculiarly. We always called it Jack's talisman.

"A miserable time followed, a time for me of agonizing wonder and doubt, during which regret for my dead illusion was entirely swallowed up in the terrible dread of my brother's degradation. Then came the announcement of his engagement to Lady Sylvia Grey; and a week later, the very day after I had finally returned to London from Oxford, I received a summons from Delia to come and see her. Curiosity, and the haunting fear about Jack, which still hung round me, induced me to consent to what otherwise would have been intolerably repellent to me, and I went. I found her in a mad passion of fury. Jack had refused to see her or to answer her letters, and she had sent for me, that I might give him her message, – tell him that he belonged to her and her only, and that he never should marry another woman. Angry at my interference, Jack disdained even to repudiate her claims, only sending back a threat of appealing to the police if she ventured upon any further annoyance. I wrote as she told me, and she emphasized my silence on the subject by writing back to me a more definite and explicit assertion of her rights. Beyond that for some weeks she made no sign. I have no doubt that she had means of keeping watch upon both his movements and mine; and during that time, as she relinquished gradually all hopes of inducing him to abandon his purpose, she was being driven to her last despairing resolve.

"Later, when all was over, Jack told me the story of that spring and summer. He told me how, when he found me immovable on the subject, he had resolved to stop the marriage somehow through Delia herself. He had made her acquaintance, and sought her society frequently. She had taken a fancy to him, and he admitted that he had availed himself of this fact to increase his intimacy with her, and, as he hoped ultimately, his power over her. But he was not conscious of ever having varied in his manner towards her of contemptuous indifference. This contradictory behavior, – his being constantly near her, yet always beyond her reach, – was probably the very thing which excited her fancy into passion, the one strong passion of the poor woman's life. Then came his deliberate demand that she should by her own act unmask herself in my sight. The unfortunate woman tried to bargain for some proof of affection in return, and on this occasion had first openly declared her feelings towards him. He did not believe her; he refused her terms; but when as her payment she asked for the ring which was so especially associated with himself, he agreed to give it to her. Otherwise hoping, no doubt against hope, dreading above all things a quarrel and final separation, she submitted unconditionally. And from the time of that evening, when Legard and I had overheard her parting words, Jack never saw her again until the last and final catastrophe.

"It was in July. My parents had returned to England, but had come straight on here. Jack and I were dining together with Lady Sylvia at her father's house – her brother, young Grey, making the fourth at dinner. I had arranged to go to a party with your mother, and I told the servants that a lady would call for me early in the evening. The house stood in Park Lane, and after dinner we all went out on to the broad balcony which opened from the drawing- room. There was a strong wind blowing that night, and I remember well the vague, disquieted feeling of unreality that possessed me, – sweeping through me, as it were, with each gust of wind. Then, suddenly, a servant stood behind me, saying that the lady had come for me, and was in the drawing-room. Shocked that my aunt should have troubled herself to come so far, I turned quickly, stepped back into the room, and found myself face to face with Delia. She was fully dressed for the evening, with a long silk opera-cloak over her shoulders, her face as white as her gown, her splendid eyes strangely wide open and shining. I don't know what I said or did; I tried to get her away, but it was too late. The others had heard us, and appeared at the open window. Jack came forward at once, speaking rapidly, fiercely; telling her to leave the house at once; promising desperately that he would see her in his own rooms on the morrow. Well I remember how her answer rang out, –

"'Neither to-morrow nor another day: I will never leave you again while I live.'

"At the same instant she drew something swiftly from under her cloak, there was the sound of a pistol shot and she lay dead at our feet, her blood splashing upon Jack's shirt and hands as she fell."

Alan paused in his recital. He was trembling from head to foot; but he kept his eyes turned steadily downwards, and both face and voice were cold – almost expressionless.

"Of course there was an inquest," he resumed, "which, as usual, exercised its very ill-defined powers in inquiring into all possible motives for the suicide. Young Grey, who had stepped into the room just before the shot had been fired, swore to the last words Delia had uttered; Legard to those he had overheard the night of that dreadful supper: there were scores of men to bear witness to the intimate relations which had existed between her and Jack during the whole of the previous spring. I had to give evidence. A skillful lawyer had been retained by one of her sisters, and had been instructed by her on points which no doubt she had originally learnt from Delia herself. In his hands, I had not only to corroborate Grey and Legard, and to give full details of that last interview, but also to swear to the peculiar value which Jack attached to the talisman ring which he had given Delia; to the language she had held when I saw her after my return from Oxford; to her subsequent letter, and Jack's fatal silence on the occasion. The story by which Jack and I strove to account for the facts was laughed at as a clumsy invention, and my undisguised reluctance in giving evidence added greatly to its weight against my brother's character.

"The jury returned a verdict of suicide while of unsound mind, the result of desertion by her lover. You may imagine how that verdict was commented upon by every Radical newspaper in the kingdom, and for once society more than corroborated the opinions of the press. The larger public regarded the story as an extreme case of the innocent victim and the cowardly society villain. It was only among a comparatively small set that Delia's reputation was known, and there, in view of Jack's notorious and peculiar intimacy, his repudiation of all relations with her was received with contemptuous incredulity. That he should have first entered upon such relations at the very time when he was already courting Lady Sylvia was regarded even in those circles as a 'strong order,' and they looked upon his present attitude with great indignation, as a cowardly attempt to save his own character by casting upon the dead woman's memory all the odium of a false accusation. With an entire absence of logic, too, he was made responsible for the suicide having taken place in Lady Sylvia's presence. She had broken off the engagement the day after the catastrophe, and her family, a clan powerful in the London world, furious at the mud through which her name had been dragged, did all that they could to intensify the feeling already existing against Jack.

"Not a voice was raised in his defense. He was advised to leave the army; he was requested to withdraw from some of his clubs, turned out of others, avoided by his fast acquaintances, cut by his respectable ones. It was enough to kill a weaker man.

"He showed no resentment at the measure thus dealt out to him. Indeed, at the first, except for Sylvia's desertion of him, he seemed dully indifferent to it all. It was as if his soul had been stunned, from the moment that that wretched woman's blood had splashed upon his fingers, and her dead eyes had looked up into his own.

"But it was not long before he realized the full extent of the social damnation which had been inflicted upon him, and he then resolved to leave the country and go to America. The night before he started he came down here to take leave. I was here looking after my parents – George, whose mind was almost unhinged by the family disgrace, having gone abroad with his wife. My mother at the first news of what had happened had taken to her bed, never to leave it again; and thus it was in my presence alone, up there in my father's little study, that Jack gave him that night the whole story. He told it quietly enough; but when he had finished, with a sudden outburst of feeling he turned upon me. It was I who had been the cause of it all. My insensate folly had induced him to make the unhappy woman's acquaintance, to allow and even encourage her fatal love, to commit all the blunders and sins which had brought about her miserable ending and his final overthrow. It was by means of me that she had obtained access to him on that dreadful night; my evidence which most utterly damned him in public opinion; through me he had lost his reputation, his friends, his career, his country, the woman he loved, his hopes for the future; through me, above all, that the burden of that horrible death would lie for ever on his soul. He was lashing himself to fury with his own words as he spoke; and I stood leaning against the wall opposite to him, cold, dumb, unresisting, when suddenly my father interrupted. I think that both Jack and I had forgotten his presence; but at the sound of his voice, changed from what we had ever heard it, we turned to him, and I then for the first time saw in his face the death-look which never afterwards quitted it.

"'Stop, Jack,' he said; 'Alan is not to blame; and if it had not been in this way, it would have been in some other. I only am guilty, who brought you both into existence with my own hell-stained blood in your veins. If you wish to curse anyone, curse your family, your name, me if you will, and may God forgive me that you were ever born into the world!'"

Alan stopped with a shudder, and then continued, dully, "It was when I heard those words, the most terrible that a father could have uttered, that I first understood all that that old six-teenth- century tale might mean to me and mine, – I have realized it vividly enough since. Early the next morning, when the dawn was just breaking, Jack came to the door of my room to bid me good-by. All his passion was gone. His looks and tones seemed part and parcel of the dim gray morning light. He freely with-drew all the charges he had made against me the night before; forgave me all the share that I had had in his misfortunes; and then begged that I would never come near him, or let him hear from me again. 'The curse is heavy upon us both,' he said, 'and it is the only favor which you can do me.' I have never seen him since."

"But you have heard of him!" I exclaimed; "what has become of him?"

Alan raised himself to a sitting posture. "The last that I heard," he said, with a catch in his voice, "was that in his misery and hopelessness he was taking to drink. George writes to him, and does what he can; but I – I dare not say a word, for fear it should turn to poison on my lips, – I dare not lift a hand to help him, for fear it should have power to strike him to the ground. The worst may be yet to come; I am still living, still living: there are depths of shame to which he has not sunk. And oh, Evie, Evie, he is my own, my best-loved brother!"

All his composure was gone now. His voice rose to a kind of wail with the last words, and folding his arms on his raised knee, he let his head fall upon them, while his figure quivered with scarcely restrained emotion. There was a silence for some mo-ments while he sat thus, I looking on in wretched helplessness beside him. Then he raised his head, and, without looking round at me, went on in a low tone: "And what is in the future? I pray that death instead of shame may be the portion of the next gen-eration, and I look at George's boys only to wonder which of them is the happy one who shall some day lie dead at his brother's feet. Are you surprised at my resolution never to marry? The fatal prophecy is rich in its fulfillment; none of our name and blood are safe; and the day might come when I too should have to call upon my children to curse me for their birth, – should have to watch while the burden which I could no longer bear alone pressed the life from their mother's heart."

Through the tragedy of this speech I was conscious of a faint suggestion of comfort, a far-off glimmer, as of unseen home-lights on a midnight sky. I was in no mood then to understand, or to seek to understand, what it was; but I know now that his words had removed the weight of helpless banishment from my spirit – that his heart, speaking through them to my own, had made me for life the sharer of his grief.

VIII

Presently he drew his shoulders together with a slight de-termined jerk, threw himself back upon the grass, and turning to me, with that tremulous, haggard smile upon his lips which I knew so well, but which had never before struck me with such infinite pathos, "Luckily," he said, "there are other things to do in life besides being happy. Only perhaps you understand now what I meant last night when I spoke of things which flesh and blood cannot bear, and yet which must be borne."

Suddenly and sharply his words roused again into activity the loathsome memory which my interest in his story had par-tially deadened. He noticed the quick involuntary contraction of my muscles, and read it aright. "That reminds me," he went on; "I must claim your promise. I have told you my story. Now, tell me yours."

I told him; not as I have set it down here, though perhaps even in greater detail, but incoherently, bit by bit, while he helped me out with gentle questions, quickly comprehending gestures, and patient waiting during the pauses of exhaustion which per-force interposed themselves. As my story approached its climax, his agitation grew almost equal to my own, and he listened to the close, his teeth clenched, his brows bent, as if passing again with me through that awful conflict. When I had finished, it was some moments before either of us could speak; and then he burst forth into bitter self-reproach for having so far yielded to his brother's angry obstinacy as to allow me to sleep the third night in that fatal room.

"It was cowardice," he said, "sheer cowardice! After all that has happened, I dared not have a quarrel with one of my own blood. And yet if I had not hardened my heart, I had reason to know what I was risking."

"How do you mean?" I asked.

"Those other two girls who slept there," he said, breathlessly; "it was in each case after the third night there that they were found dead – dead, Evie, so runs the story, with a mark upon their necks similar in shape and position to the death-wound which Margaret Mervyn inflicted upon herself."

I could not speak, but I clutched his hand with an almost convulsive grip.

"And I knew the story, – I knew it!" he cried. "As boys we were not allowed to hear much of our family traditions, but this one I knew. When my father redid the interior of the east room, he removed at the same time a board from above the doorway outside, on which had been written – it is said by Dame Alice herself – a warning upon this very subject. I happened to be present when our old housekeeper, who had been his nurse, remonstrated with him warmly upon this act; and I asked her afterwards what the board was, and why she cared about it so much. In her excitement she told me the story of those unhappy girls, repeating again and again that, if the warning were taken away, evil would come of it."

"And she was right," I said, dully. "Oh, if only your father had left it there!"

"I suppose," he answered, speaking more quietly, "that he was impatient of traditions which, as I told you, he at that time more than half despised. Indeed he altered the shape of the doorway, raising it, and making it flat and square, so that the old inscription could not have been replaced, even had it been wished. I remember it was fitted round the low Tudor arch which was previously there."

My mind, too worn with many emotions for deliberate thought, wandered on languidly, and as it were mechanically, upon these last trivial words. The doorway presented itself to my view as it had originally stood, with the discarded warning above it; and then, by a spontaneous comparison of mental vision, I recalled the painted board which I had noticed three days before in Dame Alice's tower. I suggested to Alan that it might have been the identical one – its shape was as he described. "Very likely," he answered, absently. "Do you remember what the words were?"

"Yes, I think so," I replied. "Let me see." And I repeated them slowly, dragging them out as it were one by one from my memory:

"Where the woman sinned the maid shall win;
But God help the maid that sleeps within."

"You see," I said, turning towards him slowly, "the last line is a warning such as you spoke of."

But to my surprise Alan had sprung to his feet, and was looking down at me, his whole body quivering with excitement. "Yes, Evie," he cried, "and the first line is a prophecy; – where the woman sinned the maid HAS won." He seized the hand which I instinctively reached out to him. "We have not seen the end of this yet," he went on, speaking rapidly, and as if articulation had become difficult to him. "Come, Evie, we must go back to the house and look at the cabinet – now, at once."

I had risen to my feet by this time, but I shrank away at those words. "To that room? Oh, Alan – no, I cannot."

He had hold of my hand still, and he tightened his grasp upon it. "I shall be with you; you will not be afraid with me," he said. "Come." His eyes were burning, his face flushed and paled in rapid alternation, and his hand held mine like a vice of iron.

I turned with him, and we walked back to the Grange, Alan quickening his pace as he went, till I almost had to run by his side. As we approached the dreaded room my sense of repulsion became almost unbearable; but I was now infected by his excitement, though I but dimly comprehended its cause. We met no one on our way, and in a moment he had hurried me into the house, up the stairs, and along the narrow passage, and I was once more in the east room, and in the presence of all the memories of that accursed night. For an instant I stood strengthless, helpless, on the threshold, my gaze fixed panic-stricken on the spot where I had taken such awful part in that phantom tragedy of evil; then Alan threw his arm round me, and drew me hastily on in front of the cabinet. Without a pause, giving himself time neither to speak nor think, he stretched out his left hand and moved the buttons one after another. How or in what direction he moved them I know not; but as the last turned with a click, the doors, which no mortal hand had unclosed for three hundred years, flew back, and the cabinet stood open. I gave a little gasp of fear. Alan pressed his lips closely together, and turned to me with eager questioning in his eyes. I pointed in answer tremblingly at the drawer which I had seen open the night before. He drew it out, and there on its satin bed lay the dagger in its silver sheath. Still without a word he took it up, and reaching his right hand round me, for I could not now have stood had he withdrawn his support, with a swift strong jerk he unsheathed the blade. There in the clear autumn sunshine I could see the same dull stains I had marked in the flickering candle-light, and over them, still ruddy and moist, were the drops of my own half-dried blood. I grasped the lapel of his coat with both my hands, and clung to him like a child in terror, while the eyes of both of us remained fixed as if fascinated upon the knife-blade. Then, with a sudden start of memory, Alan raised his to the cornice of the cabinet, and mine followed. No change that I could detect had taken place in that twisted goldwork; but there, clear in the sight of us both, stood forth the words of the magic motto:

"Pure blood shed by the blood-stained knife
Ends Mervyn shame, heals Mervyn strife."

In low steady tones Alan read out the lines, and then there was silence – on my part of stunned bewilderment, the bewilderment of a spirit overwhelmed beyond the power of comprehension by rushing, conflicting emotions. Alan pressed me closer to him, while the silence seemed to throb with the beating of his heart and the panting of his breath. But except for that he remained motionless, gazing at the golden message before him. At length I felt a movement, and looking up saw his face turned down towards mine, the lips quivering, the cheeks flushed, the eyes soft with passionate feeling. "We are saved, my darling," he whispered; "saved, and through you." Then he bent his head lower, and there in that room of horror, I received the first long lover's kiss from my own dear husband's lips.

*****

My husband, yes; but not till some time after that. Alan's first act, when he had once fully realized that the curse was indeed removed, was – throwing his budding practice to the winds – to set sail for America. There he sought out Jack, and labored hard to impart to him some of his own newfound hope. It was slow work, but he succeeded at last; and only left him when, two years later, he had handed him over to the charge of a bright-eyed Western girl, to whom the whole story had been told, and who showed herself ready and anxious to help in building up again the broken life of her English lover. To judge from the letters that we have since received, she has shown herself well fitted for the task. Among other things she has money, and Jack's worldly affairs have so prospered that George declares that he can well afford now to waste some of his superfluous cash upon farming a few of his elder brother's acres. The idea seems to smile upon Jack, and I have every hope this winter of being able to institute an actual comparison between our small boy, his namesake, and his own three- year-old Alan. The comparison, by the way, will have to be conditional, for Jacket – the name by which my son and heir is familiarly known – is but a little more than two.

I turn my eyes for a moment, and they fall upon the northern corner of the East Room, which shows round the edge of the house. Then the skeleton leaps from the cupboard of my memory; the icy hand which lies ever near my soul grips it suddenly with a chill shudder. Not for nothing was that wretched woman's life interwoven with my own, if only for an hour; not for nothing did my spirit harbor a conflict and an agony, which, thank God, are far from its own story. Though Margaret Mervyn's dagger failed to pierce my flesh, the wound in my soul may never wholly be healed. I know that that is so; and yet as I turn to start through the sunshine to the cedar shade and its laughing occupants, I whisper to myself with fervent conviction, "It was worth it."